Clutching Dust and Stars

Clutching Dust and Stars

Laryn Kragt Bakker

*culture is not optional ✹
Three Rivers, MI

Copyright © 2009 by Laryn Kragt Bakker

All rights reserved. Printed in the United States by *culture is not optional

Extracts from Fyodor Dostoevsky's *Crime and Punishment* W.B.Yeats' *Second Coming* are used from versions in a public domain archive. Other cultural references may be copyrighted by their respective holders.

Bakker, Laryn Kragt.
Clutching Dust and Stars: a novel / Laryn Kragt Bakker
ISBN 978-0-9814839-2-4

Printed in the United States of America
*culture is not optional website address: www.cultureisnotoptional.com
Clutching Dust and Stars website address: www.clutchingdustandstars.com

Book design and cover illustration by Laryn Kragt Bakker

For Caritas

The Second Coming

Turning and turning in the widening gyre
The falcon cannot hear the falconer;
Things fall apart; the centre cannot hold;
Mere anarchy is loosed upon the world,
The blood-dimmed tide is loosed, and everywhere
The ceremony of innocence is drowned;
The best lack all conviction, while the worst
Are full of passionate intensity.

Surely some revelation is at hand;
Surely the Second Coming is at hand.
The Second Coming! Hardly are those words out
When a vast image out of Spiritus Mundi
Troubles my sight: somewhere in sands of the desert
A shape with lion body and the head of a man,
A gaze blank and pitiless as the sun,
Is moving its slow thighs, while all about it
Reel shadows of the indignant desert birds.
The darkness drops again; but now I know
That twenty centuries of stony sleep
Were vexed to nightmare by a rocking cradle,
And what rough beast, its hour come round at last,
Slouches toward Bethlehem to be born?

–W.B.Yeats

Contents

Part One

We hold in one hand a morsel of dust, and in the other a cluster of stars.

–The Kabbalah (paraphrase)

"The urge to destroy is also a creative urge."

– Michael Bakunin, Anarchist (1842)

"It is very difficult for me to explain that the more enchanted I become with the person and teaching of Christ, the farther away I feel from all institutional Christianity."

–Malcolm Muggeridge, *Jesus Rediscovered*

Food Not Bombs

She pushed the bag of groceries up against the wall to flip the light switch, holding the door open with her leg. The bulb flickered with a staccato burst of light and went dark again.

"Damn it."

Light bulbs in this house were dying. They had been swapping bulbs from room to room in an attempt to maintain an even distribution of light: where there were two bulbs one was taken. By now they were spread thin like twilight. She could forsee a time when she would be huddled in a room with her housemates, gathered at night around the last remaining light as though for warmth. She had forgotten to buy bulbs again.

She remembered this moment months later as she looked down at a mound of loose earth, freshly dug. Her fingernails were caked with mud, her hands dirty. How exactly had all of the events between here and there worked out as they did? The fact that a light bulb has burned out is generally considered insignificant in the grand scheme of an entire life. But it is the insignificant events of the past that nourish the present as they decompose beneath us and behind us. The genealogies of events, like those of people, are built on anonymous ancestors.

She set the paper bag on the table and wandered from room to room testing switches. There were no more pairs to separate, so she stole the last bulb from the bathroom. She stood on a chair in the entryway to remove the old light and tighten the new one into place.

Shawn and Tinker were probably already at the coffee house—they liked to be early for Philosophy Night. She was late today, but didn't care much. One of Tink's friends was leading tonight and she always wanted to talk about her latest attempt at profundity. Last time it was a short story about a Buddhist cockroach. It was awful.

If someone was late on the nights that this particular person was leading, and they happened to miss the first half of the evening...so be it.

She hoped that this was not what people felt like when she brought out her paintings, or talked about the thought process that went into them, but she feared that it was. She rarely showed them to anyone.

The light bulb reduced only slightly the gloom of an evening on the verge of dusk. Welcome to the Pacific Northwest in autumn. She left most of the food inside her canvas grocery bag, moving a few items into the fridge.

She set a saucepan on the stove and broke dry spaghetti noodles into the water, turning the burner to high, lacking the patience to wait for the water to boil first. She opened the door to her room and walked over towards the desk against the far wall. She needed a candle to light the bathroom.

Most of what was visible on her desk was wax, running down to the desktop in various colors. It was years in the making—she always took home the nubs and butt-ends of candles that came into the store and melted them down into this shrine. There were bronze candlesticks on either side of it like pillars, and a dozen other candles welded on top at various angles. Underneath and within the wax were items that held special meaning to her: photographs of important people in her life, a well-used paintbrush, part of a chicken's leg bone from the last piece of meat she had eaten, the key to the house she had grown up in, a page torn from a Bible. Everything was hidden, buried in wax. In Memoriam.

It was relatively enormous. Its basic shape and a good part of its bulk was given by a set of wooden boxes nested one inside the other, like Russian dolls. They had been sealed shut with wax as the other items were added and now formed the core of the shrine, deep inside, surrounded by wax and other artifacts. She didn't even remember everything that was in there. If this shrine were excavated, archaeologists would find layers of information from different time periods in her life.

She pulled the candlestick pillars from the wax that anchored them in place and carried them over to the bathroom. She set them on the tank of the toilet and lit them. They cast shadows on the walls around her which intensified when she closed the door. Sitting on the toilet, she could see her silhouette at different angles, overlapping on the wall beside her. Her hairbrush was on the counter beside her, and the bristles cast a long shadow, as though bowing down. The silent flickering of the flames from behind her reminded her of votive candles. It is not often that a bathroom feels like a holy place, or that urination becomes a sacred act; she tried to meditate for a moment.

Laryn Kragt Bakker

When she emerged, the smell of burning hung in the air. The water had boiled dry and the noodles had begun to scorch. She blew at the smoke and thrust the pot under the faucet. The water hissed on contact with the pan and she left it in the bottom of the sink with the water running so she could open the front door for circulation.

The pasta was charred and the pan discolored. It reminded her of what her mother had said more than once when Natalie was in high school and her father was working late: *burnt offerings for dinner.*

But she didn't eat burnt offerings anymore. Maybe she could get something at the coffee shop. She wished she hadn't decided to stay and work in the studio today. She left the pan in the sink to soak and walked out on the porch to unlock her bike. The ride was mostly downhill, so the way there would be easy. She coasted down to Holly Street and turned left on a yellow, making it through three sets of lights before she hit opposing traffic. On her right was a small Mexican restaurant and her stomach lurched. She debated for a moment, then pulled her bike onto the sidewalk and ran in, nearly slipping on the wet floor.

She needed to make time at work for lunch. In the last five months she'd been working through lunch more regularly. Dorrie had put her in charge of the day shift and was out of the store more often, and Natalie found herself working through lunch accidentally without another person to remind her. There was so much work to do— Dorrie was a disaster in terms of organization, especially after the stroke.

Natalie's friends were always amazed at how ordered she seemed for an artist. It wasn't really fair, and it bothered her. They had this idea that in order to be a true artist you had to first be a slob. She sometimes felt that she didn't fit into any of the standard categories, but rather lay sprawled out across them all. But part of the reason the comment bothered her was that she was scared it might have a grain of truth to it, that maybe all the clocks and bells and alarms that whip each day into a structured submission had shackled her thoughts as well.

Dorrie had cleared out a space in the back room at the store for Natalie to use as a studio, and there she painted and sketched, surrounded by Gut Busters and jigsaw puzzles. She felt as though she were working in a little nest that had been hollowed out of the debris and sometimes it felt like the one safe place in the world. Some days, though, spending so much time in and around items that had been used and discarded made her feel used up, too.

"It's okay, I got it."

The voice behind her reminded her vaguely of Rob, a guy she used to date—the longest relationship she'd had. She turned her head just enough to look toward the voice with her peripheral vision. It wasn't him—someone in a wheelchair was talking to a restaurant employee.

She still found herself thinking about him, despite the fact that it was almost two years since she'd seen him. They had broken up after they returned from a trip around the world—or rather, they had begun to break up during the trip and upon their return things fell apart completely. When he moved down to Seattle she had let the bitterness and anger fester. His photograph was still face down on her desk. An accidental wax spill had fastened it to the desk and the shrine had evolved on top of it. She hadn't even talked to him since he had left, but he still came to mind occasionally. Less often now than in the beginning. Some days she thought she hated him, some days she wondered if she still loved him. Mostly she just tried not to think about him.

The cashier handed her a small bag, warm and folded over on top.

"Thanks." She began to move away from the counter before she had turned around and she collided with an empty wheelchair.

"Sorry," she said, grabbing the chair so it didn't roll away.

"Natalie?"

It was as though she had birthed him from synapses and gray matter onto the slick tiles in front of the condiments and napkins counter. He was on his hands and knees, looking up at her from five feet away. A ground beef burrito lay spread out in front of him like a placenta, and he was paused in the act of gathering it up in handfuls of napkins. He pushed himself up and leaned forward to pull the wheelchair towards himself, the right wheel severing the tortilla into two parts. He was smiling a great, toothy smile and his eyes were fastened on her face. He lowered himself into the chair and wheeled it closer.

"It is you! Something about your voice clicked; it took a second to make sure, but damn! I guess you're still up here." He tapped his index finger against the side of his head and then lifted his arms, requesting a hug.

"Rob?" She bent over and gave back a half-hearted grip, asking his name as though it were a question.

He looked largely the same: short cropped black hair with a hint of a widow's peak (slightly more pronounced than she remembered), thick eyebrows and enormous brown eyes. His goatee was shorter and the mustache was gone. The major difference was that he was crammed into a wheelchair. She resisted the urge to ask him about it.

"Yeah, wow; don't get too excited, though. It's only been what, two years?" He was still smiling but she could tell he thought he deserved a warmer reception.

"Sorry, but you were about the last person I'd expect to see. You know? I'm still getting used to the idea. Rob's in front of me."

It was strange how nearly every time she'd thought of him over the past two years she had first remembered their last big fight, but now here he was in front of her smiling like they were the best of friends again.

He sat there, watching her with his earnest smile and letting the awkward silence continue. She looked down at him and sorted the most basic question out from the flurry of thoughts in her mind. "Why are you here?"

He looked behind him at the burrito which was being scraped up by one of the restaurant workers. "I'm thinking of moving back." He turned toward her. "To Bellingham. What do you think?"

She wasn't sure—her body was giving mixed signals. It was either fear or excitement.

"Really?" The word felt about as complete as shrapnel but she wasn't sure how the next part should go.

Extinction is forever

Years ago, one of his college friends had told him that he had the Midas touch, but in reverse: he touched gold and it turned to shit. Imagine just bumping into her like that. And then botching it up. He hadn't wanted her to see him with the wheelchair. Standing, even with a cane, would have been better. And he hadn't planned on seeing her from within a burrito. He should have just let that kid pick it up. So there he was with two strikes against him when she walked in. Not only was he an invalid, he was also a slob.

Why did he care? It's not like he wanted to get back together with her. He'd like to be friends again, of course, if he moved back up here. Certainly in the span of minutes that they had been in the restaurant together he had wondered whether he could get her in bed, and he had imagined being with her again, but that didn't necessarily mean much. He wasn't sure whether she was far enough in his past that these thoughts were the same ones that accompanied introduction to any new girl, or whether they were something residual, left over from the time before.

He was driving south on I-5 now, heading home, replaying the scene in his mind. All day as he had been looking at apartments he had been imagining different ways in which they might happen to cross paths. He'd be stopped at a red light, would randomly turn his head and see her in the car beside him and she'd jump out and smother him with kisses. Or he'd see her down the street as he was looking at an apartment and would call out to her. She'd recognize him and come running over. And smother him with kisses.

He hadn't really expected it to happen, and especially not as it had. He hadn't even been sure that she still lived in town. Then, seeing all the familiar places in Bellingham had resurrected thoughts. Today she had haunted him like a poltergeist, knocking memories from their shelves and thumping noisily up old staircases in his brain.

But when he heard her voice he had forgotten all the clever things he thought he would say and spent most of the conversation smiling like an idiot and saying nothing. Two years was a long time. Where do you start?

And her response was characteristically vague. How did she feel about the possibility of him moving back? He wished that she had been visibly excited to see him. He couldn't really blame her—he wasn't even sure how he felt about seeing her. It had been long enough that it was a kind of curiosity, seeing her in front of him, but there was a mixture of emotion that hadn't had time to separate into parts, some rising to the surface and some sinking down. The first thought, always, was that she had broken up with him, and that hurt. But he also remembered laughter, and something closer to love than anything he'd had since.

Maybe he should have asked her if he could come to the coffee house with her. That was the first place he remembered seeing her.

He had been on the staff of the student newspaper at the time. It was a Wednesday night and he had come there seeking a corner to work in alone as he tried to finish his story for the next issue, due the next day. He was on the second floor balcony, looking down on the performers in the main room. His article was spread out on the table in front of him and the table lamp cast a hard light on the papers, spotlighting the fact that he was getting nowhere.

Nat had just started working at the coffee house, and though she spent most of her time behind the counter, she occasionally made the rounds with a cloth to wipe tables or stepped outside for a cigarette on her break. Watching her soak up a spilled cappuccino from the table next to his, his first thought about her was that she looked easy. She was wearing a tight black V-neck T-shirt that accentuated her breasts—perky things and not large, but enough to captivate the imagination. No bra. Her hair was short on the sides and back with some length on top, dirty blond.

To his credit—at least he thought so—the impression that formed over the next weeks and months was that she didn't need to be easy. She had a magnetism about her, something that drew him in. He was always wanting more of her—in all manners of the phrase.

He remembered how he'd go for weeks without seeing that slight gap between her front teeth. It was always in hiding and came out in little glimpses as she talked. It was a special treat when she laughed hard and her whole rack of teeth opened up with this gaping void front and center, unabashedly imperfect. If she was laughing hard, her nostrils would flare and she would hold her nose inside her fist as though to control it while she snorted. He was often tempted to tear her hand away and stare at her with all of her defenses down.

He swerved back into his lane, coming up out of his thoughts like a whale for air, jolted by a flash of bright headlights. The rain was coming down heavily and the sun was obscured by clouds. Dark trees brooded on either side of the road, harboring secrets or conspiring against the highway which cut so flippantly through them. It seemed wilder than usual, with lush vegetation on both sides. It was nice to be reminded that the world was not completely concrete.

He found himself thinking of home and was surprised that a landscape thick with trees could remind him of home: a tire swing and a wide open space. Home was non-existent now, or rather, the space that was once home now existed underneath a strip mall, having been paved over three years ago. He didn't see how another fast food restaurant could be worth more than a tire swing, but he wasn't completely impartial. He remembered being outraged when his parents had told him about the sale of the land. His father was getting old, but Rob had never considered the possibility that he might leave the farm in any way other than stiff and in a pine box.

They still lived nearby, but in town in Bonney Lake, and he didn't think their farm habits translated to the new location. His father had remained active on the farm until the day he sold it. Now he wandered around the tiny house listlessly, his meaty fingers hanging by his sides half flexed, prepared to grab anything that might materialize in the hall: a tractor in need of repair, a cow heavy with milk.

And his mother, who had kept the same house for thirty-six years had to adjust not only to a new house, but to this old man wandering around inside of it. Last time Rob had been over, his father had walked back and forth to the store three times. The first trip was for carrots, and half an hour later he went to buy peppermints. A few minutes after returning he discovered that the cashier had given him an extra dime back, so he wanted to return it to her. His mother had confided in him while his father was fetching peppermints that having Dad around all day was difficult. This house was smaller, so the housework didn't take as long, and she felt like she was being lazy if she sat down with a crossword puzzle or talked on the telephone while he hovered behind her. And they had a dishwasher now, which took even the warm familiarity of soapy water from her. She had tried to do the dishes in the sink for the first few weeks after they had moved in and Dad would grumble behind her the whole time. After a week or so, he had finally reached over and pulled the plug out of the sink as she filled it.

"You don't need to do this. Use the dishwasher—we paid good money for it."

He wondered if Dad ever kicked himself for selling the old place. He remembered the conversation. He had been in school yet, just before graduation.

Once his father had determined that Rob wasn't going to be coming back to take over the farming, he had to decide whether to hire someone to help him or just sell it off, because it was getting to be too much for him. He had decided to sell.

"There's no sense working myself into the ground so some man I never knew can take the farm."

"You're really going to sell it?"

"Do you want to come take over?"

"I told you Dad, I'm going to be a journalist. I just don't feel farming the way you do."

"Then I'm really going to sell."

"No you're not. Farming's in your blood. You can't just quit like that."

"Well, I can't do it alone anymore. I'm getting older. I figure I might as well spend a little more time in my last days with Mom."

So now he had more time to spend with Mom.

Thinking about home and seeing Bellingham again made him wonder where all his energy had gone. He had been full of it while in high school, intent on getting away from there. And university had been a great petri dish for ideas and emotion—all his ambition was swabbed into the dish and cultivated at just the right temperature, with just the right amount of light.

And the energy began to grow, to build up inside. But somehow it had evaporated completely—or maybe it leaked out somehow. He pictured a handful of newly graduated students looking helpless in the middle of a city, leaking in their pants.

His thoughts had become more localized: they tended to be about what his next meal would be or how to pitch a certain boring story and make it seem exciting. Besides, TV commercials and soundbites don't raise the same issues as a political science class.

He knew this and still found himself absorbing candy culture regularly. It was so easy not to think. Animals aren't the only things endangered by modern life: genuine thoughts and ideas are poached by advertisements and the media, their tusks hacked off and their bodies left lying in the sun. It's difficult to think when your head is full of rotting flesh.

His first experience with journalism was an internship at a local Bellingham newspaper, exposing him to a little bit of everything but not enough of anything. He told himself that this was small town; the big city was bound to be more like he imagined: a renegade reporter tracking down secret stories, interviewing important people, causing a ruckus. This was what he had been following, if not in those words, when he packed up and moved down to Seattle. He still maintained that he had been following something, not running from someone.

So there was some shock when the realization came that it wasn't going to be as he had imagined. The stories and the people were not nearly as important as they thought. There was generally no ruckus—at least for him. It was just before the WTO protests last year that he ended up in the hospital with a shattered leg, excusing him from all the excitement. If he had believed in signs from above, he would have taken that as an indication that he was in the wrong field.

Either way, his career hadn't turned out as planned, and he was starting to think of himself as disillusioned. Now he had some decisions to make. He had been toying for a while with the idea of a career change. He was planning to use the money from the insurance settlement after the accident to finance life for a short time while he made up his mind about who he wanted to be and what he wanted to do.

He wasn't quite sure when the idea to return to Bellingham had entered his mind. The idea had come and gone a few times, but last week he had felt again a strong urge to leave Seattle behind him, and Bellingham was an attractive option.

Yesterday the shower head fell off and as he stood under the blunt stream of water holding his foot, he felt a growing revulsion of this apartment, this city, his life in general. If the farm had still been around, he might have even considered moving back there. Bellingham was the last place where he had been happy for any length of time, and even though he knew it was not logical, he decided he was going to drive up and look at apartments, just to see what was available. He spent the two-hour drive convincing himself that he really could do this, just pick up and move out. Start fresh.

Or not so fresh. As he approached Bellingham, Natalie had been flittering in his mind like a butterfly, floating around the edges all day, never quite landing until he saw her. The last thing he had heard her say before today was goodbye. Not that it was an odd thing to say when someone was leaving, but she had said it rather firmly.

She had been going through some rough times toward the end of the trip. Her parents had divorced, for one thing. That's hard to come home to. And she had gone through another crisis of faith—perhaps a crisis of non-faith—during their trip, or she had begun the journey at any rate. He didn't think she had gotten to the other side yet. During all the time he had known her, she had never once acted as though her upbringing held any significance to her. Just the opposite: she had always been searching for meaning in any direction but backwards. For some reason the trip dismantled her and she brought everything back to the table to sort through from the beginning.

She went through various crises and emergencies more often, and he stood back at a healthy distance, waiting for the thing that she was obsessed with to change or die. It had always been her passion that attracted him, generally not the things that she had been passionate about. Maybe in the back of his mind, he'd always assumed that eventually all of these phases would come to an end and she'd be in the same place as him: passionately resigned to the fact that we can't know anything but what we can see with our eyes and touch with our hands.

He was a little worried that he had spent nearly the whole ride back thinking about her. He should have been thinking about the apartments he had seen, or calculating rent payments or something. She shouldn't have this much power over him after two years.

His father would be disappointed. About a week after he had moved back to Seattle he had been very close to driving back up for a weekend. He had called his parents and in a rare moment of vulnerability, he had told his dad that he wanted to go back, to work it out, to at least talk to her. His father, in his gruff voice, had said, "Never buy back your old horse."

He rolled his window down and turned the key for the gate. When he had descended into the parking lot underneath the apartments, he cut the engine and opened his door, but didn't get out. The oil dripped methodically into the oil pan as he sat in his seat. During the first few weeks after he had moved here, he had sat down here occasionally and concentrated on all the physical sensations he experienced. It was always cool and dark, and during rain the pipes dripped puddles in the middle of the floor. There were not many distractions. No cars honking, no people yelling, not even any garbage being blown in the wind.

He could have done the same sitting in his living room, he supposed, but there was something about the air down here. It was cool on his skin and smelled moist; it made it easier to concentrate on sensation. He took a step away from his car and turned to the left, trying to count all of the things that had been affected by changing his location slightly: the direction of the sound of the oil dripping, the feel of the slight breeze on a new patch of skin, the perspective of the car on the other side of the lot. He imagined that this was something like how a baby must feel, all the senses feeding information to the brain and feeling new, unused.

The main lobby itself was always such a contrast from the parking garage: hot, stale air and bright lights. There was a large mirror inset into the ceiling and he was compelled to look up into it every time he wheeled himself underneath. It was like an antique mirror in a movie star's dressing room, surrounded by light bulbs on all sides. The bare lights seemed twice as bright because the mirror reflected it all back. People kept stealing them, and as soon as they were gone, someone kept refilling the empty sockets, never learning a lesson.

His mailbox was nearly empty, housing only junk mail for a correspondence school and a telephone bill. He wheeled over to the elevator. He had made a vow never to ride this elevator again after he had walked in one day and found the floor slick with urine. Unfortunately he couldn't get up the stairs in the chair so he had had to make a temporary concession.

The hallway always smelled of stale sweat; today it also had a hint of marijuana. Stains of various colors and intensities spotted the carpet, but the building seemed content in its real-world aesthetics, like a middle-aged woman who has stopped wearing make-up and has made peace with the size of her nose and the stubble in her armpits.

Apartment 201 was a little run-down, but mostly in that lived-in way which made it feel like home. The stink of the hallway stopped at the door, or by that time he had grown accustomed to it. He closed the door behind him and locked it out of habit. He had lived here nearly two years now, and it was frightening to think of all the crap he had accumulated. Inertia tempted him to just forget about moving anywhere and settle in for another year's lease.

Maybe his dad would give him his inheritance early and he could just be a bum for the rest of his life. He was pretty sure his dad had made bank when he sold off all the farmland, though he never talked much about it. How could he not have? Land values had skyrocketed here in the last thirty-five years. Maybe he had millions coming to him when his parents kicked off—if his dad hadn't written him out of the will when he didn't come back to farm.

He picked up his cane, cracked a beer and moved out to the balcony, drinking deeply. He had the corner apartment, and so his deck wrapped around. It wasn't much of a deck, and lichen had claimed the outer edge where the wood had been softened by moisture, but it was nice to be able to sit outside. There was always a slight smell of decay out here and he half expected the whole thing to come crashing down one of these days when he stepped out onto it. *More insurance money, please.* He slouched in a high-backed wicker chair that he had found beside the dumpster last month, listening to the cars go by and an occasional voice.

He wished he had thought to put on long sleeves, but to do so now would mean getting up and finding them. It was easier to endure the cold. A ceramic flowerpot lay on its side near his feet, its load of wet cigarette butts spilled. This grey time of year leading into winter always made him a little depressed. Everything was so dismal, as though the Fenris-wolf had finally caught up with the sun and devoured it. All these years of chasing it finally paid off. It must feel good.

If he didn't move to Bellingham, maybe he could find a better place here. Maybe closer to Dave and Tad. A little further from Cindy. He polished off the beer, toying momentarily with the idea of picking up completely and moving somewhere sunny. California. New Mexico. Some Caribbean island. Thoughts like this came often during the hibernation of winter, and he had to push through them, live off the fat he had stored up during the gorgeous summers.

He set the empty bottle beside the chair and rubbed his eyes. He felt like he should either go to bed or do something to make the fact that he was leaving this place official, even if he didn't know exactly where he was going. Something to thumb his nose at this apartment. Nyah nyah. Maybe write on the walls, or piss on the carpet, but he didn't have the motivation and he was going to have to live here for a few more days at the least.

He was beginning to feel like a nomad, not because he had moved often—he hadn't—but because he felt as if he was drifting through life. The feeling was strong lately, especially, since he had lost interest in writing and had no real goals anymore, leaving him without a place to plant his roots. Officially approaching his upper twenties, he had never imagined that he would be just as clueless about the future as he had been in high school.

He pulled himself up and limped into the living room. He dragged a box from beside the ancient television toward himself. It was labeled in black felt marker: Movies. He shuffled randomly through the cassettes, not really paying attention but wanting to feel like he was doing something.

Corrugated cardboard, bent where he had fallen on it, looking generally beat-up, labeled with black marker: people need boxes to organize their world. Back at Western, he had thought himself so smart for realizing that and he had plagiarized a theory from an introductory psychology class. Children learn to develop simple schemas into which they fit all their observations and make sense of everything around them. As they observe more and more, the schemas are refined, made more and more complex. So a schema built for a dog might start off as anything with four legs and a tail, but is gradually refined into smaller compartments to allow for other animals such as cats and ferrets.

His brilliant corollary was that people didn't turn off this instinct once it was finished with its task. So they keep refining these boxes in their heads, making them smaller and smaller, one inside the other. It explained everything: racism, sexism, nationalism— whatever you wanted. And the theory extended beyond larger stereotypes; it worked on many levels. It also applied to individual relationships: once you think you know someone, you will try to understand them based on the box you have created for them.

He remembered how excited he had been after writing a few pages to describe the theory. Natalie read it, unimpressed and showing it.

"So, people make stereotypes? This is your theory?"

Her response had left him deflated, a cake that had been rising nicely until she had yanked open the door and peeked into the oven quickly, unenthusiastically. But really, she was mostly right. You put someone in a box, you fit them to a stereotype mould, you stick a label on them. And the people you have labels for have their own labels for other people, who have their own labels about you and pretty soon everybody is just covered in sticky tape. But it's not really a horribly new discovery.

The trouble was, his mind had latched onto the thought and wouldn't let go of it. He often found himself wondering what other people were writing on the label of the box he was being made to live in in their minds, or another person's box. Who gives a shit? But he couldn't help it.

Eventually he had decided there was no harm in doing internal inventories: what boxes he had stored in his brain, who and what were in them. The label on his own personal box changed depending on his mood—or he could jump from box to box at any rate. Natalie's box had labels written and crossed-out all over it, replaced with a big question mark. He extrapolated what she might be like now based on past trends, as though she were a stock and he an investor. Her graph was sporadic, the kind that was always about to climb or plunge aggressively. The kind that required faith. He twisted open another beer as he entertained two possibilities based on projections from the last months before they broke up.

It was possible that she had continued the trend that she had been following the last time he had seen her—that she was still inching forward on the tips of her toes toward the faith she grew up with. Who knows, maybe she had dived in head first by now.

Another option: perhaps she had passed through that phase and maybe even a number of others in the meantime. Maybe she was an atheist or some shade of agnostic. That would be nice. He wished he wasn't so curious about her, but part of the intrigue was the knowledge that it could easily be a third option: none of the above. That thought both attracted and repelled him.

He wasn't getting very far with his packing. It had already been half an hour since he came in from the deck and all he had done was pull out a box of movies before sinking into the couch. He wanted to go to bed now, but he also wanted to complete some sort of groundbreaking, like digging a shovelful of dirt with a silver spade. He emptied his CD rack, packing them into the box on top of the VHS tapes. He found a marker in the kitchen and made an addendum to the label: + *Music*.

It was good enough to make it official: he was going to move out of this place, though he didn't know where. It didn't matter.

Poverty or violence

Tinker stood up and walked over to the cupboard. She pulled out a bag of potato chips and unrolled the top.

"Why did you break up with him in the first place?"

"Potato chips for breakfast?"

Tink nodded.

"Well?"

"I told you—we were drifting apart. Things weren't comfortable anymore."

"No, you said that's what you told him. I mean, what caused the drift?"

She exhaled slowly. She didn't like the feeling of being dug up and turned over like old compost, not even if it was by one of her best friends. "I don't know, I think maybe some of the things that happened on the trip affected me differently than him. We started to seem like different people than we were at the beginning."

"Like what? Why are you dodging it? All I'm saying is, if just seeing him for a second brings back all this emotion, maybe things weren't as finished as you thought. Something's bothering you—I could see it right away yesterday. I've never heard you so silent on a Thursday night." She opened her mouth to capture another small handful of crumbled chips and looked over with one eyebrow raised, chewing. "Or, I've never not heard you so much. You know what I mean."

Tink ran her tongue between her gums and lips to create enough suction to pull loose the remains of chips from the crevices of her teeth. Natalie watched her without saying anything. "Listen, I've got to run. I'm working Meghan's early shift today. We'll talk again later, okay?"

"Yeah."

Natalie was still formulating a response to the question. Was she dodging? Maybe. If you avoid an issue long enough it becomes a habit. Then, sometimes, your friends come along and pry up your comfortable defenses like planks in an old house and you've nowhere to stand.

After she had graduated, she and Rob had gone traveling; backpacking "around the world" was how they described it then, though it was only technically that. They had flights into a handful of cities from a handful of others and by the end they had completed a jagged loop around the globe in five months, ending up in Central America. They made their way back up to Bellingham by bus and train. That was the longest stretch of land travel on the trip. Most of the distance had been covered in the air, so they hadn't seen as much as they had expected to—although they had seen enough to discover that the world was more complex than the slogans they had spouted on campus. She had had this idea that somehow they'd change the world by traveling in it. It seemed instead that they had been changed themselves, or maybe revealed to each other more fully.

One night as they sprawled out in a muggy hotel room in Nicaragua near the end of the trip they had discussed what they could do in the face of so much need with so little to offer. The thing that pissed her off was how it all seemed to bounce off Rob. He saw the same poverty and pain as her but it didn't affect him. They had just been talking with a lady in the street outside the hotel and had managed to interpret bits and pieces of her story. Her husband was unemployed and they had seven children, but he was never around. He had other women and other children as well. She was asking for money, like most of the people they came in contact with.

Rob lay on the bed with his shirt off, rubbing his Coke bottle on his forehead and saying all the wrong things.

"You shouldn't have given her that much. We'll probably have a zoo waiting outside our door in the morning, each telling us about how they have nineteen children and they all have diarrhea, and could we please spare some money?"

She stopped digging in her backpack. "Enough! I told you already, stop being so rational. Just try to feel with your heart instead of your mind, just once."

"Oh, is money the universal love language now?" He laughed. "And from the excess of the heart floweth forth a river of cordobas."

She shook her head and muttered to herself. "Bastard. Sometimes you are really annoying."

And inconsistent. Not long after they had arrived in Managua, a filthy man had approached them and Rob tried to talk to him in Spanish while he replied in the little

English he knew, trading shards of one language for those of another. As they were leaving, he asked Rob for money, and Rob searched his pockets, coming up with only cigarettes because they hadn't had time to change money yet.

"If you're so opposed to giving them anything, why'd you give that creepy guy those smokes in Managua?"

"Come on. We had just talked for ten minutes—it wasn't like he just came up off the street and asked for money."

"So he's a little smoother than this lady. Is that a reason to punish her children?"

"Let's drop it already. I didn't think you were going to take a shit on me. All I'm saying is most of the personal interactions we'll have here are an act and money isn't going to solve it. People don't see us, they see dollar signs."

Rob stopped talking and she thought for a moment that the argument might be over. "Remember those two children and the gum?" he asked.

She pulled on a light shirt and a pair of shorts. She did remember. Yesterday just before they'd reached the beach, they had seen two children sitting in the dirt beside the path. They had the saddest looks on their grimy faces, like they'd been practicing for television commercials. They put out their hands timidly. She had given them each a stick of gum, and their faces had flickered briefly, but then returned to their sad state. About twenty feet down the road, Rob had turned back to look at them. He said they had huge smiles on their faces as they unwrapped their gum; as soon as they saw him looking, their smiles sagged and they looked close to tears again, hands out.

She didn't want to talk about it anymore, so she went out to the lobby of the hotel. They were at one of those points in the trip where they were completely on their own—they had parted ways with a gay German couple a few days before and they hadn't found anyone else to travel with yet, so the options seemed to be to talk to Rob or nobody.

She came up with an alternative, using her tattered Spanish to get directions to a phone and calling home for the first time in nearly two months, hoping for something to cheer her up. Her mother sounded like she had just woken up—her voice was thick and sounded unnatural at first.

"Hi, baby!"

"Hi, Mom. Me and Rob just had a fight and I needed to talk. How are you doing?"

"I'm okay..." Her voice betrayed her and Natalie sensed something trying to escape from underneath the words.

"Not very good, huh? What's the matter?"

Her mother started to cry in great sobbing gasps, punctuated by sharp breaths as though she were trying to suck it all back in, but each time it was too much and it couldn't be contained. Natalie was frozen with the receiver to her ear, completely off-guard and scared. She wasn't very close to either of her parents, but the thought that something had happened to her father or that her mother might have cancer sparked fear inside her, unexpectedly.

"What is it, Mom?"

She fished broken words and phrases from the rush of emotion and laid them out into a rough storyline, eventually determining that her father had moved out—moved in with another woman. Things weren't finalized yet, but he was physically gone and had been for a few days already. Her mother hadn't told anyone yet. All of her friends were from the church, and she was scared to admit, in her words, "what a perfect fuck-up" her life had become. That was testimony in itself to what she was going through: Natalie had never once heard a foul word come from her mother's mouth. She reminded herself that she was a major part of the problem, but she had been for so long that it felt like most of the burrs had worn off.

Her mother was still going to work and trying to pretend that everything was normal, coming home to an empty house which had been home to a son (now dead), a daughter (now reprobate), and a husband (soon to be ex). The only comfort Natalie could offer was the fact that she'd be home soon and would come to visit; she had the feeling that, reprobate or not, she would be welcome.

She brushed her teeth by the faint light of an old bulb and drank water from a dirty faucet despite the warnings in the guidebook. She didn't sleep well that night, wondering who the hell had lived with them all those years of growing up, who was deep inside the shell that she had called "dad."

She listened to Rob's deep breathing and imagined that there was some kind of beast or creature nested inside him, underneath this skin, waiting for an opportunity to escape. She tried to find some strain of logic or love in a mind that would give a full pack of cigarettes to a shiftless man and then in the next breath deny a mother and her starving children a little bit of money for food. She unlatched the door and stepped out into the inner courtyard of the hotel again.

The roofed rooms were connected in a square, leaving a space in the center that was open to the sky, surrounded by cinder block walls on all sides, like a primitive solarium without the glass. The middle of the courtyard was an area full of small palm trees, lush vegetation and a few small walking paths. She wandered among them slowly. If it weren't for a crate of empty Coke bottles beside the wall and the dark thoughts running through her mind, it could have been Eden before the Fall.

She had spent the first eleven years of her life faithfully growing up a Calvinist, and a handful more unfaithfully. At seventeen she and the church had decided—somewhat mutually, she thought—to stop seeing each other. She imagined her mom sitting there all alone next Sunday. What would she say? What would they say? It wasn't a good sign if she had been keeping it secret for days already; she had no one to turn to besides her church friends.

There was a length of time as a teen when Natalie had wavered, going to church to satisfy her parents some weeks and staying home to satisfy herself on the others. When she did go, she sat in the back and left immediately after the benediction while everyone else was sitting and waiting for the minister to walk back down the aisle, leading the way. The organ music leading into one of those hymns never failed to make her yawn, and she was conditioned to wake up and stand up at the words "the Lord bless you and keep you, the Lord make his face shine upon you, and give you peace."

Until now, she had thought that she had done pretty well at counteracting the conditioning in all these years since she'd gone to church. But she was beginning to realize—and hate—the fact that despite everything she had done, certain aspects of this past had never vanished completely. They were only dormant, shriveled down to tight, tiny seeds, waiting for water like desert flowers.

Over the course of this trip, there had been trickles running down to these waiting seeds. An uncomfortable silence, like the space of time between a question and an unwanted answer, while they drove in a taxi with a small, bloodied Jesus being crucified on the rearview mirror, staring down at her. Something flopping like a fish inside her during the first Catholic Mass she'd ever seen. And now this onslaught of poverty, betrayal, and conflict, like a flash flood she hadn't been prepared for. She wasn't sure what was happening. Something was opening inside of her like a wound.

So people were depraved after all. As a kid all the emphasis on depravity that had been pounded into her made her feel like she'd been created in the image of the devil rather than in the image of God. She had come to terms with herself but was still seeing devils in some of the people around her.

The next weeks were awful. She was miserable and it seemed a shroud had been cast over the trip by the fight and the phone call. She thought about her mother often, living alone in the house, or her father, living in another house, with another woman. She blamed her moods on her stomach, which hadn't been settled since the faucet in the hotel—although that was purely coincidental, she found out later. Rob had been no help at all, saying nothing about the divorce, as though ignoring it would be best for everyone involved. Luckily it had happened right near the tail-end, as they made their way up through Central America into Mexico and then back up the coast.

Once they had returned, she had begun the real process of sorting and processing the emotions and questions. Rob had come home with a bundle of flowers he had picked from neighbors' yards and a short note that said he was sorry without specifying why. He was standing with his back to the door when she answered his knock, and he dripped some saline solution into his eyes and turned around, presenting her with the flowers as saline ran down his face to simulate tears and repentance. She laughed despite herself and tried to let it go.

The laughter didn't last long. She remembered the day he came up to her with his big plan. She had started working part-time at the coffeehouse again and as she leaned over to pick up an empty mug, she felt hands around her waist and a face pressed up behind her ear.

"Let's go to Seattle."

She had misunderstood him at first, looking at her watch. "What, now? I'm not off for a few hours yet."

"Right now. Let's just go. Dave says he can get me in with an editor at the *Times* tomorrow."

She hadn't caught on yet. She turned her head so her mouth was directed toward him. "Listen, I can't go right now. Why don't you drive down, though, if you want to meet him." She pulled out of his grip and turned around.

"Nat, I want us to move to Seattle. To live there."

She looked at him, at the cup in her hands, at her apron.

He was smiling, searching her face like a man who thinks he has won the lotto and is waiting for the final ball to drop.

She was suddenly conscious of everything going on around her. They were standing between the guitarist and the audience, so it seemed that everyone was watching them. She felt flustered and pulled Rob, who was still grinning as though he were being dragged straight to Seattle even now, out of the main room, past the dog-eared posters and through the front door. It was dark out, lit only by dim streetlights and the cherries of cigarettes. Shadowy figures talking in low voices were clustered around the entrance and the piano could still be heard in the background, as though it had followed them like an aroma.

Rob's grin looked like it was beginning to take effort, and she let go of his hand. "What the hell was that?" she asked.

The grin slid from his face but he didn't respond.

"Rob, I can't go to Seattle. I've got enough on my plate trying to figure out my life as it is, and I don't need the rug pulled out from under me. I don't think I can deal with that right now."

"Hey...it was just an idea."

Every so often he had these impulse ideas which he pitched with such enthusiasm; she was trying to remember if she had ever shot one down so quickly and mercilessly before. Moving in together, getting a puppy, traveling the world. And none of them worked as well as he had promised they would.

He had gone to Seattle alone and met with the editor, but he came back. A few days after he returned, she found out for certain that she was pregnant. She hadn't been sure. That next week all she could remember was alternately being annoyed with him for moping and struggling to decide how or if to tell him. He hung around the house, obviously heartbroken about his plan, as though he expected her to look at his sacrifice and suddenly change her mind.

One night she sat on their porch with the light off, wrapped in blankets against the cold. She watched cars go by, unconsciously counting them as they passed, the way she found herself counting her steps, or counting telephone poles during a car ride. She had decided that she was going to tell Rob tonight, but she was nervous and couldn't concentrate on anything else, so she was waiting here for him to come home.

Finnegan, the one-time puppy, strained against his leash, which was tied around the trunk of the tree in the front yard. He had been named after a puppet on *Mr. Dress-up,* one of the only shows their television could pick up so close to the Canadian border.

She wondered if this child that was coming into existence here inside her would watch the same TV shows she had, if she would like the same things as her mother, or if her teeth would grow in with the same gap in front, if her mind would struggle with the same doubts and questions. She didn't even know for sure that it would be a girl.

She almost gave in and let Finn loose, putting him back into the house, but the sight of the little pile of shit nestled in the shag carpet beneath the living room window was still fresh in her mind. Now was not the time for mercy. Rob gave the dog no discipline so it felt like she was fighting two fronts: first disciplining the dog, then trying to fix what Rob's bad influence had undone.

It used to be that when she thought of something that annoyed her about Rob, two good things would also come to mind and overpower it. Lately that wasn't happening as much. She had the sense that their paths were diverging while they each denied it, or simply failed to acknowledge it, and so a piece of themselves was silently being torn from inside them while they pretended it didn't hurt. And now there was this little development down here, she thought, massaging her stomach gently.

She was sitting quietly, shrouded in blankets and shadows, when Rob staggered out of the taxi. He hadn't worked much since they'd been back, writing a few freelance articles about their travels and applying for a job every now and then if it appealed to him. School was closing for Christmas and Rob had been spending a lot of time partying away the final days before break with those friends who hadn't quite finished last year and were completing some extra classes.

Rob lurched toward the porch, then redirected himself as he noticed Finnegan by the tree. He dropped down beside the dog and took it in his arms, trying to be playful but landing on top of the dog. Finn took any amount of abuse from Rob without complaint. Natalie watched, wondering what he would do when he saw her there.

But Rob was oblivious to her presence. He scratched the dog's head roughly and exhaled. "What's a matter? What's a matter with us, Finny? Are you a sinner like me? Did you sin again? Did Finnegan sin again?" He paused and began to chuckle at his rhyme. "Sinnegan Finnegan, are we in the doghouse? Let's see if she'll let me in."

He fumbled with the leash until it was loosened and stepped cautiously toward the door, feeling out the pavement with his foot. Finnegan was up against the door already, but Rob was picking his steps more cautiously. She felt like crying. She couldn't tell him when he was like this.

She swallowed the secret again. Funny how she felt lonelier now that he was home.

She didn't speak until he was beside her, reaching for the doorknob.

"Finn shat on the carpet again."

Rob jumped back from the door and leaned against the railing with both arms. "Holy shit!" After a brief pause, he added, "You just about killed me. What're you doin'?"

She didn't respond to his question. "Finn shat on the carpet again. I don't want him in the house yet."

Rob looked at the dog, who looked back from his place at the door and whimpered as though he knew they were talking about him.

"It wasn't him, Nat. It was me. Don't punish him for it." He had his head hung in mock shame, a hopeful smile straining the edges of his frown.

She didn't move from her cocoon of blankets, turning her head back to the street to wait for the next car to come by so she could count it. Quietly he whispered, just loud enough that she could hear, "Change my diaper?"

After the door had closed behind him, she sat there until she was cold. He was asleep when she came to bed.

Nights like that were probably why she still had so much emotion pent up inside even now, years later. It felt strange to be in the house this late in the morning. She sat in her pajamas beside the kitchen table, rocking the loose joints of the chair.

She had had a dream last night, but she hadn't written it down immediately when she woke up. Now it eluded her—hanging in the void between her memory and her imagination. She tried to relax her mind but it didn't come. She looked down at the page in front of her and read the scrawled sentence from the night before last.

Sunk down to waist in ground. Could feel tendrils of me growing, pushing through soil.

Remembering the dreams wasn't the only problem. She also needed to find herself a Joseph or a Daniel to help her interpret them. And the faith to believe that they actually meant anything. The place she was trying to reach was always somewhere just beyond the wingspan of her faith.

The clock beeped once and she was startled to see that it was approaching 10 o'clock already and she was going to be late again. It didn't matter what time she was scheduled to start, she always got there five or ten minutes later. She tossed her bagged lunch into her knapsack on her way to her room. The jeans she had worn yesterday were hanging over the chair by her desk, so she slipped out of her pajama's and pulled them on. She scooped the pajamas into a pile on the bed and crawled into a white t-shirt and a sweater.

She unlocked her bike and wheeled it to the sidewalk before mounting it. She hadn't met Tyler, the new volunteer who was coming in to help Dorrie early this morning. She had talked with him on the phone and she hoped he was still there when she arrived so she could meet him in person.

The store was just over seven blocks away, near the coffeehouse where she used to work. It was set up in an old house, shabby on the outside, but perfect for a second-hand store on the inside. She locked her bike to the back railing and unbolted the door into the dim, musty space of the back room, her dimly lit studio.

She had a section of floor cleared on the side near the window where she had managed to fight back the encroachment of used goods. An easel stood in the middle of the open space and she had some supplies on a small table beside her stool. The door to the back room was the only interior door in the store. The rest had been removed in an attempt to tie the rooms together and counteract the oppressive weight of the walls on all sides.

She could see someone who must be Tyler in the front room, kneeling down to zip his backpack shut in the front room behind the counter. He looked young. She tried to remember what they had talked about on the phone: he was a sophomore majoring in computer science. That's about all.

She stopped a few feet in front of him.

"Hi, Tyler."

His head jerked up, eyebrows arched, and she was no longer certain that this was Tyler.

"The other one, the old lady, went somewhere. I've got to go to class. It starts in about five minutes."

"I'm sorry. I should have been here a little sooner. I hope you can still make it."

"Okay."

"What did you think of the place?"

He pursed his lips and nodded slightly, moving his face up and down as well as back and forth so that his head made tiny circles in the air. Was that a nod, or a shake?

"Great. There's a lot of stuff to organize." He glanced over his shoulder.

"Thanks for coming."

He hefted his pack and trudged toward the front door.

"Call me and let me know when you want to come again. If you want to come again."

"I'll call."

She watched him until he was out the door and then turned back to the front counter. Was he really going to just walk out and leave the store unattended? That was her fault. No wonder they didn't get many volunteers.

Tyler reminded her in some ways of Scott as he was just before he died. Talking in short phrases. Answering the question without volunteering anything or asking a question of his own.

She wandered into the room beside the front counter, which stored all the old electronic equipment people had donated. It was cleaner than she remembered: Tyler must have started in here this morning. She had always neglected that room purposely. Old technology made her sad. In the not-too-distant future, all the greatest technology of today would be in a room like this, too. By then probably even people would be machines.

She heard the front door open and slam shut again. She poked her head out and saw Dorrie standing there, her arms draped with clothes.

"We hit a jackpot this morning," she said between short breaths. "A family over on Texas is moving and had a bunch of stuff ready for a garage sale—the forecast is rain, so they decided to just get rid of it and save the hassle. I've got most of it in the truck."

"Dorrie! You could have waited until I got here."

Dorrie was not the kind of person to go gently into that good night. She was going on 80 but had barely slowed down, even after the stroke. In fact, it might have been the opposite—she had given Natalie more of the organizational and paperwork responsibilities without saying much about it, while she continued her routine of physically gathering and moving things to and from the store, with a wide old pick-up truck that bore a hand-painted advertisement for the store on each door:

2nd Chances

Quality Used Goods

After they had unloaded the truck, Natalie spent most of the day upstairs with the books. There were so many of them that it was taking a small eternity to get them organized. She got frustrated after working with them for a few hours because it was so hard to feel as if she had accomplished anything.

Most of the upstairs was books. There were two small rooms which held miscellaneous items that didn't fit into any of the main categories, and everything else was wall-to-wall shelves. She even had rows of bookcases in the middle of each room.

When she had started, the books had been completely random. She tried to sort them but it felt like a make-work project and she always ended up distracted by the books, flipping through the art books or skimming a novel.

"You awake up there?" Dorrie was still breathing harder than usual as she worked her way up the stairs.

"Yeah." Natalie straightened her slouch and wiped away the beginnings of a drool from her mouth. She grabbed a few books, grateful for the bookshelf between them. "How's it going down there?"

Dorrie shuffled through the doorway, holding an old book in her hands.

"Found this down in an old box from that garage sale." She handed it to Natalie and leaned against the shelf. It was a paperback copy of *Crime and Punishment* from the days when they printed the price directly on the front cover: fifty cents. It had a woodcut illustration of a man on his knees, arms open, before a young girl who was sitting on the edge of a table. A lighted candle was beside her, casting sharp spikes of light in all directions.

Some of the pages were loose and the glue on the spine was yellow and brittle. The edge of the book was uneven where chunks of pages had come out and been pushed back in. The paper was orange at the outside, as though over time the pigment had been leaking toward the sides, settling toward the bottom of the page.

Dorrie ran her bony fingers through her hair and scratched the back of her skull. "Have you read it?"

"No, I never did."

"It's a classic."

Natalie looked up after a moment of silence. Dorrie was staring at the book in Natalie's hands, but it looked like she wasn't seeing it.

"Dostoevsky was epileptic. And he gambled away most of his money and cheated on his wife repeatedly."

Natalie looked back at the cover, at the man on his knees, maybe apologizing, or about to have a seizure.

"You can have it if you want, or put it on the 'free' shelf. It's falling apart," Dorrie said. "And I think I'll head home a little early today."

"No problem." Natalie gave her a sideways grin as she leaned forward, slipping the book into her back pocket. "I'll be here. I can lock up at the end of the day. Make sure you get your rest."

"I'm not that old."

She turned around and started back for the stairs.

"Have a good weekend, Dorrie."

She didn't turn, but raised a hand to show that she had heard.

Natalie was grateful for Dorrie. When she had first started here, she had been confused and unsure of what to do. She didn't feel like she could trust anything around her, let alone herself, and the more she thought about it, the more depressed she became. She added up the negatives: her brother dead, her parents divorced, Rob gone. Depressing to say the least.

Dorrie didn't know any of the details, and she didn't try to fix anything with a cliché or a little punch on the shoulder. She just shared herself and her life with Natalie, in little bits and phrases, the bad and the good combined.

She was one of those people who is genuinely interested in your life, but who respect you enough to allow you your distance. There was never an agreement in which they traded bits of themselves ounce for ounce with the other. Dorrie just talked. Natalie just took, drinking it in, and rarely giving back. She found that as she learned more of Dorrie's past, it was easier to dwell less on her own.

When she looked at the way Dorrie was now, she wondered how she had come through it all with the ability to smile. Her life had a higher body count and more collateral damage than a summer blockbuster. She was born not long after the first world war, lived through the Depression and married a few years before the US got involved in the next war, which promptly killed her husband. She gave birth to a daughter while the fighting continued and then married again several years after it ended. She had another daughter and a son. So things were looking up for a while, until the sixties, when her oldest daughter overdosed on LSD. Her son committed suicide in the early seventies, and her last remaining daughter married and moved to Kansas. About ten years ago, her husband had a stroke and died. When Dorrie had the stroke, it must have been hard not to just give up, but she was still flailing, refusing to go down and somehow still smiling.

It was overwhelming when it was all in one place, all in a row like that. Dorrie hadn't told it that way, of course. She'd told one piece at a time, with weeks in between sometimes. But every time Natalie heard that girlish laughter spilling out of Dorrie's throat, she knew that there was hope, somewhere.

It was Dorrie who had suggested the painting space in the back room first. Without that space, Natalie probably wouldn't have been as quick to start again—just having a separate area that was meant for painting full-time allowed her to keep her art turned on in her mind. When she felt compelled to lay down newspaper before she started and then clean it up again when she was done, it really seemed that she packed it away in her mind as well. Somehow just knowing that the canvas was sitting there wide open and waiting for paint helped.

She enjoyed talking to Dorrie. During the first weeks here she had accidentally revealed more about the pregnancy than she had intended. Dorrie listened without seeming surprised at an awkward half-confession that she had shared with her mother alone. She remembered sitting over coffee with her mom a few weeks after it happened and quietly telling her about it, first revealing the fact that she had been pregnant and then the fact that she was no longer. It was strange, but the fact that her mom hadn't gotten emotional made her feel more alone with it than before she had told her. She didn't know what she wanted, but it wasn't someone just telling her that she was okay and not to worry too much about it.

So it was still more or less a secret, and she had been prepared to pull back into her shell, expecting Dorrie to try to extract more information with blunt and unwieldy words. Instead, when Natalie's mouth ran aground in the middle of her sentence, Dorrie didn't say anything. She gave her just two seconds of silence, in case she was going to finish after all, and then hugged her. The wordless embrace lasted only a moment, and then she loosened her soft arms and Natalie hurried into another room, pretending to organize a rack of shirts.

She found it funny that they had grown so close. If she had been told when she started working there that one of her best friends in the world would be this 76-year old lady who drank a cup of warm milk every night and wore a diaper to bed, she would have laughed at the outrageousness of it.

But it seemed that outrageousness was the norm. Who would have guessed that Rob would blip back into existence on the floor of *Casa Grande*? Not her. But she also hadn't guessed that her father would come back to Lynden with his new wife, or that he'd run off in the first place. Who would have guessed that Scott, not yet old enough to drive, would be out with friends and wind up dead later that night, washed up on shore with seaweed and sand, his lungs filled up with salted water?

She locked the doors and turned the sign to "Closed" a few minutes early and settled into the back room, slipping out of the jeans and sweater that she was wearing and into the paint-spattered sweatpants and t-shirt that were draped on the stool in front of the easel. The book in the back pocket of her jeans was hanging out, about to fall, so she pulled it out and set it on top, and the pages almost slipped out of the binding. Dostoevsky had cheated on his wife. Maybe he moved back to town with his new wife a few years later, too. She shuffled some old newsprint and squares of carpet samples with her foot to fill in the cracks and give the floor complete coverage. She wished that she had taken the time before Dorrie left to talk to her about her meeting with Rob.

She sat staring at the canvas for some time before picking up her brush. Something about one of Francis Bacon's early popes, trapped in a wireframe box and silently, perpetually screaming, had sprouted a hybrid concept in her mind, and so she decided to run with it and see where it took her. It was hard to explain how or why the image held her, and she often remembered the Bacon quote that one of her professors had up above the door to the studio: "Painting is its own language and is not translatable into words."

She was mimicking his technique and echoing some of his symbols, trying for a piece that spoke her words with Bacon's accent. This one had been underway for a few weeks now. Whenever she could squeeze an hour or two from her schedule, she'd sit back here with it. She had started out painting on the back of a primed canvas with a piece of cloth torn from an old shirt that didn't look saleable, crumpling it and dabbing it in the paint, then smearing and balling that on the canvas, adding dust and sand from the floor to her paint for added texture. She used anything that struck her at the moment as workable: fingers, cloth, cotton swabs, and sometimes even paint brushes.

Working impulsively, without sketching ideas or concepts first was new to her. To be so completely dependent on spontaneous inspiration was a leap of faith she had never had the courage to take before and it was exciting. She found that throughout the process, her original idea was evolving like a living organism. The other thing was that she had to use acrylics in this room and racing against fast-drying paint forced her to make spur of the moment decisions that she normally might have squelched.

It was much more abstract than the initial concept she had half-formed in her brain. The beginnings of the self-portrait which was seated off to one side in the barren scene was turning to look over her shoulder—a reference to looking back, to childhood and the past. The loose strokes that made up the face looked much too sad, almost tormented. She had started off exploring the way that a person was raised and the way she interacted with the world when she was grown.

The more she thought about it, the more intriguing was the idea that a person's upbringing formed structures and patterns of thought into their mind, which can never be fully broken down. Somehow the attempt she was making to play with this idea in paint wasn't coming to life. Part of it was the scream. She hadn't intended to have such a pervasive mood of despair.

The only visual clue that this was bred from a Bacon image was the wire frame box around the self-portrait, which seemed to glow in the darkness like a neon sign. She wasn't really happy with the cynical direction she was headed, but the theme seemed apt given the choice she needed to make for this piece: scrap it or work with it. Granted, choosing whether to add more paint to a botched painting was a little easier than choosing how to deal with the consequences of a botched life.

She silenced the scream with a smear of flesh-colored paint on the end of her index finger.

"Shhh," she whispered.

Her mind and her heart disagreed often. It was a peaceful struggle, or a violent agreement that went on inside of her. She often felt caught wrestling with her past, locked in battle like Jacob with God, refusing to let it go until it blessed her. But in the midst of that struggle, when things are evenly matched and unmoving, it can be hard to believe, and afterwards, there is still a limp.

I'm not as think
as you drunk I am

He had already said the requisite curses, standing in the damp darkness of the parking garage beside a small pile of shattered safety glass next to his car. The small window behind the rear driver's side door had been smashed and the front door hung open. He examined the interior, making a preliminary list of what had been plundered: all of his CD's, a small day-pack, and his point-and-shoot camera. The dashboard was torn up but the stereo was still intact.

He said the curses again, feeling strangely hollow in his stomach but full in his head and chest—as though he had been drinking on an empty stomach. Top heavy. He decided that he was going to move to Bellingham.

He turned around and slowly climbed the stairs back to his apartment. He had packed a bunch of boxes with the stuff he didn't use every day, and had stacked them in the middle of his living room. He sat on the couch and propped his gammy leg on a low box. He was such a lazy ass. The thought of moving was exciting and dreadful. There were so many details to take care of—the most important of which was the question of where he was going to live.

He opened his backpack and roughed up the papers that were crumpled inside it. He had taken notes on a few of the places he'd visited. He shuffled them around until he found the one he was looking for. Gordon Nerburn, single occupancy room with shared kitchen.

"Six months at minimum, and once you've been here that long, you might never leave," Gordon had told him, bug-eyed and frantic, wagging his knobby fingers in the empty space between their heads. "Some of my tenants've been around here for ten times that long. Twenty times. If I don't kick you out, you'll stay."

He doubted it, but it was cheap. He dialed the number that he had scrawled on the paper. The phone rang twice and there was a violent sound, like someone had dropped the receiver on the other end.

He heard someone breathing into the phone, and then "Hello?"

"Good morning. Is this Gordon?"

"This is."

"Hi, Mr. Nerburn. I talked with you yesterday about the room you're renting."

"Yeah?"

"Well, I'm interested in signing the lease."

"Can you come tonight?"

"No. I'm in Seattle right now, but I'm planning to move before the end of the month."

"You mean tomorrow?"

"Is that the end of the month already? Yeah, I guess so. Damn."

"Well, okay. I can hold the room on the first floor for you until tomorrow, but I might not be around when you come. I'll leave the front door unlocked. If it's not unlocked, knock. If no one answers, call me. Leave your check in the drawer beside the sink, in that kitchen area. First month, deposit and last month, two-fifty each. I'll collect it from there. The key to the room will be in closet number four, beside the water heater. Call me when you're moved in to confirm. Okay?"

He grabbed a credit card offer from the pile of junk mail on top of the fridge and started writing the instructions down on the back of it. "I...think that's great. Thank you."

"Okay," said Gordon Nerburn, and hung up.

Rob continued scribbling notes with the phone beside his ear. This was crazy. Tomorrow? It was already mid-morning, so he didn't have much time to get this thing planned. The phone dangled from his fingers by the antenna. He needed to call some people. He left messages for a few of his friends to break the news and invite them out drinking. They'd been planning to get together, anyway. Now they had a reason to drink.

He spent some time separating belongings into boxes, digging out everything that had settled to the bottom of the drawers and the closets. These were mostly the things that he had been hanging onto for years, walking around them, tripping over them, until they found their way into the unobtrusive corners and niches of the place. Now he had to ask himself why he kept them all this time just to throw them out now. Papers. Lots of notebook papers, printed pages and old newspapers. Stories he thought might sell but didn't. Scrawled notes. Junk mail from two years ago. Here was a thin paperback book that Natalie had given him years ago: *Norse Legends and Heroes*. She told him that he must have had some Viking background because his last name was Erickson.

It was interesting how information sticks in your brain. He had forgotten about the book, but certain details from it still surfaced in his brain every now and then, unbidden. How much of our belongings or our friends become imprinted on us?

He sank onto the couch and flipped through the book again. Dave had found it lying around the apartment when Rob had first moved here and had called him Thor for a while. When they were mock fighting, he would sometimes cry out, "Thor's going to bring the hammer down," and shrink back from him.

He tossed the book into the open box in front of him and, finding himself already sitting near the entertainment center decided it was time to take a break. He bent down to pick up the gamepad, pushing in the power button on the console with his big toe.

"Piece of shit!" His voice re-oriented him to the room around him: the open boxes, the diffused light double-filtered, first by clouds and then by half open curtains. He gave the television the finger. Computers were a waste of time. Like most things. The more you do the less you feel like you've done anything important. Welcome to Viking hell—a banquet table full of food sitting right there in front of you, but the more you eat, the hungrier you get.

It had taken his dad more than sixty-five years to get to the point where he wandered the house aimlessly with nothing productive to do. Rob bettered that score by more than half. Here he was still years away from thirty and in the same spot.

He killed the game and walked out onto the balcony to feel the chill of the air. Two red-nosed children played down below in the parking lot, a girl and her little brother by the looks of it. He leaned against the railing and watched the boy drag a broom through fallen leaves as his sister grabbed handfuls and threw them in the air. The leaves fell down around them, not so much fluttering as simply dropping.

He wandered into the kitchen. The bread was dry and the lettuce was brown-edged and droopy. He toasted the bread and slathered mayonnaise on the lettuce. With a good tomato and a stack of meat, it still worked.

He leaned with his elbows on the counter, holding the sandwich over the sink so that the mayo splashed into the basin when it squeezed out. He brushed the crumbs into the sink and grabbed his keys from on top of the fridge.

It felt good to take the stairs again, even if he was slow. When he got to the car, he kicked the broken glass against the wall and crawled into the back seat to work out a solution to the hole. He slammed a plastic grocery bag in the door and pulled it over the place where the window had been. He reached over to the glove compartment and pulled out his emergency stash — a disposable ballpoint pen wrapped tightly with duct tape. He peeled it off in short sections and used it to fasten the plastic in place.

The air was moist, and everything felt grey. Colors seemed dull, brightness layered with dirt like hypocrisy in reverse. It was a good day to think of leaving. The bag flapped noisily and he wasn't quite sure where he was. He backtracked around several blocks before he found the small U-Haul lot he had been searching for. He took the only truck they had left and had the agent install a tow dolly for the car.

He drove slowly back to the apartment, his car following submissively behind him. The textured rubber grip of the truck's steering wheel and the woven fabric of the seat began to drag the abstract concept of moving out of the air and lock it down, transforming it into tangible fact. When ideas were in the process of becoming reality, it felt like a drug; he got high on potential.

When he returned, the boxes were still as he had left them. It shouldn't have been surprising. He sank down on the couch and looked across the room at the fireplace. It contained a charred remainder of a processed log which he had purchased at a gas station early last spring. He had seen them stacked and wrapped individually by the entrance when he went in to pay for his gas, and on an impulse he had bought a few of them, thinking a fire inside with the cold and wet outside would be cozy. There had been a few people over to play drinking games and cards, and they had lit two of the logs only to find that the chimney was blocked up.

With all the smoke coming in, someone decided that they might as well smoke their cigarettes inside, too, and somehow he had agreed. They had added a few burn marks to the carpet that night, and had reinforced the smell that still haunted the furniture and the carpet.

He stretched out on the couch. According to his lease, he was probably supposed to take the ashes out of the fireplace before he left and give the whole apartment a thorough cleaning, but he was pretty sure that he wasn't going to. He relaxed his body and pulled the fleece throw blanket over himself.

In the periphery of his vision as he lay there he saw the light on the answering machine flashing and his heart sank; its blinking urgency seemed a silent protest against sloth. He pushed himself up and leaned on an elbow, reaching over to hit the button.

"Robbie, this is Dave, returning your call, you dirty rotten bastard. I guess I'll have to kick your ass when I see you, and break your leg again. Uh, give me a call back when you get this and I'll head over to help you move the big stuff. Oh, and know this: we're going to party tonight!"

Dave was a graphic designer who divided his time between freelance work and a part-time job with a new media company in town. He was one of Rob's closest friends in Seattle—they had gone through high school together and remained friends through most of it. Dave had moved to Seattle after high school and had been here ever since. When Rob had come down from Bellingham, he had stayed with Dave and his roommate, Tad, for two months before getting his balance in the city. He would have stayed longer if there had been another room in the apartment.

He dialed Dave's number.

"Hey, whore." Dave said before Rob had a chance to talk.

"Hi, bitch. I hate caller ID. You can't surprise anyone anymore."

"Yeah, you can. Just tell them you're moving in less than 24 hours. That'll surprise them."

"Fair enough," Rob said. "Are you going to cry about it, or come over and help me move?"

"Maybe both."

It wasn't packed as well as he had thought—there seemed to be no end to the hidden treasures in various cupboards and drawers. Dave ended up hauling a lot while Rob threw things into boxes. The truck was way too big, so he didn't feel the need to pack it efficiently. They threw the couch over the balcony near the dumpster. It hit with a crack and then slowly fell backwards, slouched in the middle like it had given up, pillows scattered on the asphalt nearby.

When the truck was loaded and the rest of the junk from the apartment had been pitched over the edge, they locked the door and went downstairs. Rob dropped the key off at the manager's apartment with a short note.

"I put your address on there, so they might send my security deposit to you."

"Great, but don't get your hopes up."

"What?"

"You think they're going to give you anything back after you check out the day before the end of the month? You didn't tell them a month in advance, did you?"

"The lease is up."

Dave shrugged. "Let's go."

They left the truck parked sideways across a row of parking spots with his car up on the hitch. "Let's go to my place and I'll call Tad and Cindy. We'll take a cab tonight, yeah?"

The pub was dingy and the four of them were seated in a booth, two on each side. Dave had a pint of Guinness and Tad had already commented on its dark thickness; he kept one hand cupped around it protectively.

It wasn't uncommon for the comments to turn to the beer, a universal experience to rally around. Once every few months it became the topic of an extended conversation— Dave would order his Guinness or some kind of beer you couldn't see through and then Tad and Cindy would proceed to talk for twenty minutes about how disgusting it was. He wouldn't be surprised if Dave enjoyed that more than the beer itself.

They always argued for way too long about whose beer was more pissy or shitty. Dave was holding his glass out in front of him, sniffing it, rotating it and looking into its color as though it were a fine wine. Cindy was quiet tonight, hands clasping opposite elbows which rested on the table to prop her torso up.

Rob looked across the table to Cindy. "Have you given up on the debate, Cin?"

She smiled thinly and straightened up. "No, I guess not. I'm just not in the mood to argue right now."

"No one's arguing," said Dave. "We're just sharing our opinions with each other."

Rob nudged her with his foot. "What's up? Did you have a bad day at work today? Was there 'an incident'?"

It was another well-worn joke. Cindy worked at a retirement home as a recreation director, planning and organizing events. The stories she had shared from the collective pool of her coworkers were too vivid to forget: images of old people and walls both covered in diarrhea, of dirty old men groping the staff and wheezing, "Come to bed with me."

She wasn't in the mood for that conversation either.

"I don't know what it is. Sorry to be a downer."

"Come on—this is supposed to be a party." Rob reached over and used his thumb and forefinger to lift the corners of her mouth into a half-hearted smile. She turned her head to the side and took the skin between his fingers in her lips and kissed it gently. She gave him a sad little smile as he flinched and pulled away.

"There you go! Keep smiling."

He felt some guilt for a number of the things he had said to her over the last six months, for pulling her strings the way it seemed she wanted them to be pulled. The words had seemed appropriate to the moment, the way that they would have been written in an early rough draft if his life were a script.

He realized that he hadn't really given her any warning about the fact that he was going to move. But he hadn't really given anyone any warning, including himself. And he didn't really feel like they had an official relationship in that sense—just potential. Enough to get high on, once upon a time.

Tad and Dave had turned their attention to the TV in the corner and were watching the Mariners without much hope. Rob slid out of the bench, bracing himself on it as he stood. "I'll be right back."

He walked with his cane, staring down anyone bold enough to look at it for any length of time. He stopped at the far end of the bar first and ordered a double round of shots for the table and then continued to the restroom.

There were two urinals, but one was taped off and bore an "Out of Order" sign. He leaned the cane against the wall and positioned himself in front of the functioning one. Two guys walked in, talking loudly and laughing. One of them was about Rob's size, and the other was a few inches shorter. They stopped short when they saw that the only urinal was in use. One of the men went into the stall and started pissing noisily into the water in the toilet bowl.

Rob looked straight ahead. They had a bulletin board with the sports page tacked up at eye level in front of the urinals so that people could pretend they were reading it.

He tried to think of something to say to Cindy to cheer her up, but he couldn't. This was the night that the shit came home to roost, so to speak. She had to find out at some point. Maybe she wasn't as attached to him as he thought—but he doubted it. He had had a premonition that he was brewing trouble when he started sleeping with her and it seemed he was right. At least he was right about something.

The waitress was just setting down the shots when he returned.

"What is it?" Dave asked, grabbing one to sniff and then wrinkling his nose immediately.

"No smelling!" Rob slid a shot to each of the other two and then lifted his own. "To Bellingham!"

The shot burned all the way down, lighting up his esophagus and stomach.

"To us!" Dave passed a second shot glass to everyone while they were still breathing fire, as though chasing the last shot down with another would help. They all dutifully picked their shots up and tipped them back.

Cindy had a sick look on her face. "I think I'm going to vomit."

Dave offered her an empty shot glass to use as a pail and she finally broke a real smile. They both started sputtering. Tad was watching them impassively, a slight smile playing itself on his lips every few seconds until he could control it.

Rob put an arm around Tad. "I love you guys," he said.

Dave raised an eyebrow. "Then why are you leaving us?"

"Shut up." Rob smiled.

"All I can say is she must be quite a piece."

Cindy's smile had shriveled up, so he was careful to keep his at full size. "Where do you come up with this shit?"

He waved his hand beside his head. "It just comes to me. Divine inspiration, and all that."

Cindy pushed her way out of the bench and started toward the restroom.

"You okay? No vomit yet, that I've seen."

"I think I'll be okay. I'll be back in a second."

There was silence in her wake until Tad spoke up. "Leaving tomorrow, huh? That was a quick decision."

"Yeah, I know. I guess that's my style."

Dave pinched his face up apologetically. "Sorry 'bout that. I forgot about her."

"What's this about a girl?" Tad asked.

"I've told you about Natalie before."

"You guys are getting back together?"

"No! That was Dave's ass talking."

"But she's still up there? She hasn't moved out of town?"

"No, she's there."

"And you saw her when you drove up the other day?"

"We bumped into each other."

"So you see her again once and suddenly you're moving back to Bellingham. Did you get some?"

"I saw her for about one and a half minutes." Rob looked over and found Tad still looking at him, waiting. "No, I didn't 'get some.' I haven't even talked to her or heard from her in almost two years."

"Not once since you left? You never even talked on the phone?"

"Nope. Well, about a week or two after I left, I called her place and got her answering machine. I didn't leave a message." He looked up in the direction that Cindy had gone. "Let's talk about something else. I don't think she's the reason I'm moving."

"That's an interesting way to put it. She get hitched in the meantime or something?" Rob paused and looked at Tad. "Huh. I guess I don't know."

They each picked up their beer, one after the other, and drank. Tad dropped his glass like a gavel. "Well if tonight's the night, we're going to have to do something other than sit on our asses and drink beer. Pub crawl?"

By the time Cindy had returned, they had paid the tab and were all standing with their coats on.

"That's it?" She looked incredulous.

"Oh no, no, my dear. Follow me," said Dave, putting his arm around her waist.

Rob sat alone by the table, drowning in sound waves as the beat pulsed through him. The air was cool on the walk over, and the cane clicking on the sidewalk was like the cold persistent tap-tap-tapping of a conscience. It wasn't far from here that he had been struck while walking across the street last year—something he tried not to think about whenever possible. His other option at the moment, thanks to Tad, was to contemplate deeply who Natalie might be with. That was enough to change his mood about this whole move.

Tad came back knuckling four bottles, and he grounded two of them in front of Rob. "Now we don't have to get up right away for another one," he yelled.

"I don't know if I'll last for two."

"Bullshit—it's your night! You're not going to get away that easily. I think Dave's getting something for you, too."

Rob was already buzzing from the shots and the beer he had taken at the pub. Tad reached over the table with both hands and shook Rob's shoulders.

"Yee-haw," he said firmly.

"I guess I better get started then," Rob sighed, gripping the first bottle and taking a deep breath.

If his count was right it was one and a half more beers and another shot before Tad and Dave's energy began to infect him. They waded into the grinding mass of dancers, churning hot and dripping sweat and somehow loving it. He vaguely remembered spinning in time with the music, holding his arms out, laughter; he had sprawled back on one of the speakers and stayed there, waiting for the room to slow down while the beat thumped beneath him like an animal thrashing in its cage.

"Hey! Sober up or you're out of here!" The bouncer had looked angry, but Rob remembered laughing at him and then feigning fear for the rest of the night, crouching behind other dancers any time he caught the bouncer watching him, putting on an expression of terror until he couldn't hold the laughter in. He heard Cindy's laughter sparkle and that encouraged him.

As they were absorbed into the crowd, people pressed in around them. Rob was being elbowed and jostled from all sides and somebody splashed him with sweat. He turned to look for a path out and caught the eye of the bouncer. He stopped moving and crouched slightly to make himself smaller. Tad's elbow caught his jaw and sent him further off balance. He fell backwards.

Dancers pushed against the rest of the crowd to make room for his body as he fell, closing in again when he was on the ground. He thought for a moment that he would be trampled. He was fighting for breath amid the force of the crowd, thrashing against them; hands yanked him up.

He saw Dave's and Tad's concern on their faces, and the crowd parting as the bouncer waded in, his face set.

"Get the hell out of here," he said, gripping Rob's shirt and propelling him toward the fringes of the crowd. The music was still going but most of the people had stopped dancing and the lights played over unmoving bodies. They emerged on the other side and the rift healed itself, trapping the other three inside as the organism began to pump again.

The bouncer deposited him outside the door, meeting his drunken resistance easily. A small crowd of guys who would perhaps become paparazzi or lawyers followed them out, hoping for a bigger struggle, for some blood or shouting. They dispersed soon, and Rob leaned against a telephone pole, groggily watching the bouncer at the front door as he flirted with the women who came and went, gently holding their hands to check for their stamp, or stamping the cute ones who hadn't paid the cover charge, winking.

A hotdog vendor was set up beside the entrance, waiting for the club to close and for all the people, hungry from a night of dancing, to walk near him. He smiled at Rob, but Rob didn't say anything. The hotdog man took the plastic clip from a bag of buns and cracked it in half, fitting a half on one of his fingers and cocking it. He was biting his lower lip in concentration and let it fly as a car drove by.

He turned to Rob. "I got it right into an open window more than a block away one time." Rob raised an eyebrow.

"How much for a hotdog?"

"I'm serious. I couldn't believe it when it happened," he said. "They're four dollars."

"Four? How do you sleep at night?" he muttered, reaching into his pocket for the money.

It was hot, at least, and he took extra cheese sauce on it. He wandered a few telephone poles down so he could enjoy it in peace, and began to watch the ecosystem of the city block at night. Taxis and police cars were already circling the block like vultures, their eyes fixed on the people emerging from the club. People were leaving in pairs and small groups and occasionally fed at the hotdog stand. And inside, of course, was the big mating ritual.

A smattering of unconnected words and phrases floated free of the general noise that the building was churning out. His leg had begun to throb.

Tad came bouncing out of the entrance, wearing an enormous grin. "Good show in there. Sorry about the elbow, though." He rubbed his arm as if to console him with the fact that he had been hurt as well.

"Don't worry about it."

Dave and Cindy came out immediately behind him, and Dave was carrying Rob's coat over one arm and pretending to be an old man with Rob's cane. They were only half an hour from closing time, so they called it a night. Tad and Dave punched Rob's fist in farewell, and then Dave jumped on him, pretending to cry. His leg nearly buckled and he clenched his jaw.

Dave and Tad caught a southbound cab, while Rob and Cindy headed north in another. He set the cane against the door of the cab and leaned forward. It always seemed to happen this way: he stopped moving and it felt like a truck hit him. Cindy didn't say much to him, talking only to give the driver directions to her place, about five blocks from Rob's. She hadn't said much all night, though, so she was still in character.

When the cab pulled to stop in front of her building, she nudged him. "You gonna get out and say goodbye to me, or what?"

He got out as Cindy was paying the driver, and felt his head drain empty of blood. He crouched down and pinched the bridge of his nose as though to stop a nosebleed, but it didn't seem to help. He heard a door close and then the taxi started to pull away. He looked up. "Shit," he muttered. "Didn't you tell him to wait a second?"

Cindy shrugged. "He said he had another call, so I told him he could go. Sorry." She came over to him and gave him a little hug, setting his cane on the sidewalk. "You're really going, huh?"

He put his arms around her lightly and felt her grip tighten. He grunted affirmatively through her hair, smelling old cigarettes on her. She pulled her head back and looked up at him.

"Why?" she asked quietly. He had known it was coming but hadn't invented a good response yet.

"I don't know," he said finally, tightening his arms slightly.

They stood without talking for a handful of breaths. He leaned on her, stealing structural support in the guise of an embrace while she inhaled him, her nose buried in his chest again.

"Okay babe. I should go," he said, loosening his arms.

"Come in and let's talk for a few minutes. We never had any chance to talk tonight."

He knew he shouldn't, but he also knew he should. He hadn't really been fair to her with the words he had given her; he felt like he owed her a few more, real ones.

She jangled her keys in the lock at the door to the building, struggling with it for a moment before it came open. She held it open for him and followed him in. He walked slowly down the hall in the path he had moved so many times before and she passed him, moving quickly—more alert than he had expected. She fumbled with the keys again at her door, then put her finger to her lips and slowly opened it. She slipped inside and was gone for just a moment before she opened the door the rest of the way.

"It's okay—she's not here."

Good. He had knocked heads with Cindy's roommate, Michelle, too many times and was in no mood to get lectured or to listen to her rant tonight. Tad and Dave thought that was that she was a lesbian, but they thought that any girl who didn't like them must be gay.

He dropped his body into the couch and felt that it would take an earthquake to move him. Cindy had disappeared into the kitchen, and then rematerialized with a glass of water and a bottle of multivitamins.

"First things first," she said as she straddled him. She shook a few of the pills out. "This'll help you in the morning."

He swallowed the vitamins and drank the water while she tilted the glass for him and watched.

"Cindy, I can't stay long," he began. She kissed his nose; the interior of her mouth was warm, or his nose was cold. "I don't—" Her lips were kissing him; he did what he had been trained to do, feeling like a drunken robot, performing sloppily and without emotion.

It took him a moment to remember where he was and whose blankets these were when he came awake. As it came back to him, he let his head fall back on the pillow and his breath go out in a rush. He was sprawled across the whole bed, alone, as though during a nocturnal battle for space and blankets Cindy had been knocked to the floor. The multivitamins hadn't worked completely, but instead of the splitting headache he was expecting, he had a lesser throbbing in his skull, so maybe it had helped.

She wasn't on the floor. He heard the shower running and painfully got to his feet. It didn't feel like much of a day for driving; it didn't feel like much of a day for anything except bed. He gathered his clothes as he limped toward the bathroom, putting them on one by one and trying to ignore the stench of the club. His leg was sore today.

He opened the bathroom door and took one step inside. Steam had already condensed on the mirror and was swirling around the air from behind the shower curtain. "Morning," he croaked. "Listen, I'm sorry about last night. We need to talk."

"Good morning, pig. And don't come in here."

"Sorry."

"What are you sorry about? The fact that you snore like a chainsaw, or the fact that you continually treat Cindy like a piece of meat?"

"Sorry," he said again. "Where is she?"

"Probably working. Most people do."

He tried not to imagine Michelle's naked body behind the floral print of the shower curtain, standing there, glistening and dripping water with steam swirling around her. He reached down and adjusted his penis.

"Can I give you a note for her?"

"I'm not going to do your dirty work for you. You used her up and now it's time to skip town, huh?"

"It's not like that." He started to leave, but couldn't help hearing her response.

"No, I'm sure it wasn't. I'm sure it was beautiful, pure, unadulterated love that went on last night. She thought so."

He left the bathroom door open slightly, so he could still hear the water. He leaned over an empty note page by the telephone, knowing what he wanted to write, but wondering how to phrase it. The shower stopped and he heard the curtain open. He paused for a moment, then left the page blank and left the apartment quickly.

The pain in his leg was sharp, and as he walked home he began to question the decision to return the wheelchair. As he waited for the light at the first crosswalk, he hunched his shoulders and thrust his hands into his pockets, cradling his cane under his left armpit. He felt something that might be money and pulled it out.

It was a note from Cindy, on a folded piece of note paper that had a picture of a disheveled cartoon blonde behind a desk stacked high with papers.

I was going to wake you to say goodbye, but you looked too comfortable and I am late for work. Thanks for staying last night. Call me when you get settled up there. I miss you already. Love Cindy XOXO.

His heart sank when he read the hugs and kisses. If only he had just said what he had to say on the sidewalk and not gone upstairs. This was bad news. He would have to call her later. He shoved the note back into his pocket and limped across the street.

As he pulled the truck into traffic slowly, it reminded him of the trucks and tractors of home, even though it was relatively small and had an automatic transmission. He hadn't driven anything but his car for a long time. But he couldn't go back home if he wanted to. He had to satisfy himself with memories of tractors and of the smell of grass and diesel while cutting.

Returning to Bellingham was something of a homecoming in itself—he had lived there for five years. He waved his hand at the concrete and grime of Seattle by way of farewell. This was an empty valediction to accent a lonely departure; it seemed to contrast sharply with the energy of the club the night before.

But it didn't take long to put those thoughts away. To be actually on the road, with all his earthly possessions in the back of the truck and heading toward something not completely known made him feel alive again. Besides, he was leaving Cindy and that whole mess behind him in the tangled sheets in her apartment.

Before these last few days, he hadn't felt free for a long time. It was hard to explain, but it had to do with the unknown, the feeling that he was flirting with something uncontrollable, that he was choosing something that could get away from him. It was like the feeling he'd had in high school when he drove the truck around the corner without braking and felt for a moment like he was going to overturn. Or a night he remembered only vaguely: headlights and adrenaline and him trying to hustle his inebriated carcass off the road...except this time he didn't intend to end up with a shattered leg.

He nestled his ass cheeks against the seat as though settling into a nest and stretched his leg. That's all life is—moving our bodies back and forth to try and make things around us more comfortable. Our friends, our apartments, our jobs. Wiggle around a bit and settle in. Everybody settled in in his own unique way, and nobody would do it in exactly the same way. Go through a fresh cycle of friends every few years or stick with the old ones until you drop. Keep the kitchen appliances polished and bright or use the dishwasher as a storage compartment for plastic grocery bags. Wait for the perfect job and go hungry or take the one that's really unfulfilling but pays the bills. So here he went, making a new nest again.

Maybe it was the parasites driving him back home to Bellingham. Last Tuesday when he was on the toilet he had read an article in *Discover* magazine about how parasites can actually influence actions that the host makes. Lancet flukes live in cows and lay their eggs in the intenstines, so the cows shit them out. Snails eat the eggs from the shitpile, the flukes hatch in the snail's intestines and have more babies which are eventually coughed up by the snail in a slime ball, which is devoured by a passing ant. The flukes find their way to the ant's head, which they use like a steering wheel, driving the ant like a Cadillac and parking it in the evenings on the tips of grasses, hoping for a grazing cow to munch them during the night and bring them back home.

There is also a barnacle that injects itself into a crab at the elbow, sneaking through a chink in the armor. It sends out roots, stealing nutrients from the crab's bloodstream, eventually getting far enough to wrap around the crab's eyestalks. The crab acts as though it's pregnant while the invader sits there and makes eggs, which the crab gives birth to as if they were its own.

He imagined enormous fingers snaking through his veins and wrapping around behind his eyeballs, and then for a moment he did feel something tickling inside his torso. Was the fluke in his brain driving him to Bellingham for its own sinister purposes? He gripped the wheel and tensed his arms.

"Why are you doing this to me?" he yelled into the empty cab, then burst out laughing.

He turned on the radio and watched the steady stream of dismal traffic heading down into Seattle. The parasites must like that city. There were people who drove all the way from Bellingham and back every day. He felt validated because he was going against the flow, and not in some small way, trying to sneak out of the city in a Geo Metro or something. He was going big, U-Haul-style, taking everything he could take with him and leaving no apologies.

It was good that it was cloudy and wet. For one thing it was easier to look at things that weren't bright this morning, but it also made him feel better because he felt like he was leaving a dismal chapter of life behind him and heading for something new. Of course, it might be nice to pull into Bellingham in the sun, but that didn't seem likely.

He was always amazed at how he could zone out while driving, taking corners, braking and accelerating without consciously thinking about it, as though he had an autopilot setting for his brain. He always snapped to attention when something abnormal started to happen—like now. He approached a stopped car that was halfway in his lane and halfway on the shoulder, lights flashing. He performed an emergency shoulder check, pulling halfway into the other lane largely on faith.

He was driving directly over the middle line on the road, half on the left and half on the right; the short painted lines ran underneath him like he was being slowly bisected, running himself very carefully on the serrated edge of a knife, or the blade of a band saw. In the cartoons, the truck would separate into two parts whose paths would slowly pull apart from each other, starting off almost invisibly and then veering apart and back together repeatedly.

He pulled back into the slow lane because the tow dolly that was holding his car had been designed for a maximum speed of 45 miles per hour. Whenever cars passed him he was tempted to speed up but he didn't want to lose the car on the highway.

Bellingham looked the same as two days ago, but it felt different, maybe because this was not just a visit anymore. He exited the freeway and traced his way around corners and past stores that were familiar, others that were new. This was near the university, in what was known to students as "the ghetto."

He pulled into the narrow parking lot beside two old houses and a small apartment complex, trying to stay toward the far side, just past the dumpster and the recycling bins so as not to double park the row of cars. He unfolded the torn envelope from his back pocket and re-read the instructions he had jotted while on the phone yesterday.

-First floor: if door unlocked OK; if not knock; if no one home call
-key in closet #4

-beside water heater
-call to confirm when moved in
-leave check in bottom drawer ($750 = first+last+deposit)
-to: Gordon Nerburn

He folded the note again and pocketed it, then looked around and felt distinctly that this was not home. The house was two stories high, built on the slope of a small hill that ran down from 26th Street. The two carports, already occupied, were off the side of the building nearest the parking lot and opposite the hill. Tiny covered balconies from each room looked like the entrances to caves.

His balcony would be on the other side, on the corner of the first floor. He decided to walk in and take a look around. He mounted the concrete staircase which led up to a set of wooden steps. The front door was unlocked and he opened it cautiously, peeking in so he didn't surprise anyone, but there was no one home.

It was more dingy and run-down than it had seemed a few days ago. Each of the four numbered doors that came off this room had a small accordion-style closet door beside it. He pulled his open and found an upright vacuum cleaner and a small hot-water tank. There were two small shelves beside it, and one of them had a sheet of white paper on it. He lifted it and found three keys lying underneath, labeled with shaky handwriting on masking tape: *Laundry; Front door; Apt. #4.*

He smiled. This would be an interesting landlord. It was all clandestine and secretive. Here he had taken the keys from their hiding spot in a closet and was moving in, with directions to leave the money in one of the drawers in the kitchen. Next month, maybe he would be instructed to put it in an unmarked paper bag, drop it into the dumpster outside and walk away; Gordon Nerburn would be watching, and he would come disguised as a garbage man to collect.

The deadbolt snapped back and Rob pushed the door open. It was dark. Dim light filtered through the hanging blinds on the sliding door directly across the room, illuminating it enough to see that it was completely bare except for the refrigerator immediately to the right of the entrance. He searched for the light switch and found it on the wall halfway behind the fridge.

He pulled the cord to open the blinds and looked out to the balcony. It was more of a deck than a balcony because of the slope of the hill. His view consisted of a lot of dead grass which peaked at the road in a cluster of trees and bushes. They looked as though they had been planted up there to hide the road from the people on the deck, or maybe to hide the deck from the cars.

He propped the door open by wedging his cane underneath the doorknob and walked back out to the truck. He started hauling the smaller boxes while he worked on a plan to get the big items in without wrecking himself. He stacked the manageable ones in the middle of the room, slowly building the base outwards as the partially filled boxes crushed each other and the pile began to lean. It was going to be a bear to unpack this.

When he stepped back into the kitchen, he saw a lanky guy with shaggy hair, probably a student, turning a key in the lock to number two.

"Excuse me."

"What's up."

"I'm Rob. Moving in to number four."

"Chad. Number two." He pointed at the plastic number that was screwed to his door as evidence.

"Nice to meet you. Could I ask you a favor? I busted up my leg a while ago, and I'm not supposed to strain it. Would you help me move a few of the bigger things in? I'll pay you."

Chad's eyes had reflexively dropped to study Rob's legs as soon as he had mentioned them and bobbed back to his face in the time it took to process the childhood command, *Don't stare.*

There wasn't much that was very large: the fold-out sofa, an easy chair, the entertainment stand and the television. Chad had gone next door and recruited Kenton to be the double. They moved a bunch of the smaller items as well, and they had it in the apartment in under twenty minutes. It wasn't organized, but it was inside, placed around the perimeter of the boxes that Rob had stacked.

Rob gave them twenty dollars, which they refused to accept initially, until he told them to go buy some beer. He was relieved that it had worked itself out so well. He closed up the apartment and got back in the truck. He was out of practice—it took three tries to back the trailer out of the parking lot before he headed out toward the nearest U-Haul drop point.

After he had gotten rid of the truck, he drove back in the direction of the apartment, taking a detour to drive by the university, and a handful of houses where he had lived before. One of them, the one he had lived in as a junior, had been torn down and rebuilt, but the others were all there. He sat outside of the one he had lived in most recently and for the shortest amount of time, feeling like a stalker sitting there in the car and watching, but wanting to see. It would have been better to have parked a few doors down, but this was where the open spot was. He hoped nobody noticed him and made a show of checking his watch every so often, as though he had agreed to meet someone in front of this house.

The flower garden was still there, though it was bare dirt at the moment. The house was still white, and the same ugly pea green trim lined the windows and the deck. Someone had taken down Natalie's hand-painted street number, replacing the free-spirited "312" and the brightly colored stylized flowers with generic silver decals from a hardware store. The tree out front had been pruned a little too enthusiastically; it reminded him of a newly clipped dog or a sheep after shearing. Mostly it was the same. If he made a list of what was different and what was the same, mostly it was the same.

Somehow it felt good to see things relatively unchanged—he wasn't sure why—but it also resurrected all the emotions that he had carefully buried, all the unanswered questions, the hurt. This house was where she had ended it. She was the only girl who had ever broken up with him; all the other times he had been the one to initiate it. Sitting here and examining the house's every detail was like slowly peeling the scab off of an old wound. If he had stayed in Seattle, all this would have stayed dead.

He was an idiot. What next: knock on the door and ask if he could just take a peek inside? "Ah, excuse me, I just need to check if the rim on the toilet seat is still loose, if you don't mind. And while I'm here anyway, can I push your couch back and see if that hammer hole in the drywall remains? I used to live here, it's okay."

He missed Natalie. He should not have come back to Bellingham—what was he going to tell her? There really was no reason for him to be here. She was going to assume that it was her. Maybe it was.

A boy of about fifteen walked by, his skateboard under one arm, and turned his head to look at Rob as he walked by. Rob jerked his arm up and reflexively checked his watch. He shook his head, trying to act perturbed, carrying on the act even though the boy had already passed by.

He pulled out and started back up the hill. He turned the volume of the stereo up, tuning in to a Vancouver station. It wasn't enough to drown out the flapping plastic; he wasn't sure if it was even an improvement. He had had enough of unpacking and didn't feel like sitting home alone on the first night in town, especially considering it was a Saturday night. He might as well call her.

He turned into a gas station and parked beside the payphone. It was funny, in a way, to have to look up Natalie's phone number; it was a powerful reminder of the fact that no matter how tempting it was to look at the familiarity of Bellingham and the old houses, things were not the way they once were.

He found her number easily—the last name was still Williams, as he had hoped. He hadn't seen a ring on her finger in the restaurant, but there were two years to account for and who could say for sure if that meant anything? He imagined calling her and getting a burly man's voice, enjoying and hating the tension he was building up within himself.

He pulled the telephone book as far as the chain would allow and held it against the glass with his body. He was patting his pockets in search of a pen to write her number down when his cell phone rang. He had a momentary, irrational conviction that it was Natalie. It was an unlisted number.

"Rob?" she asked brightly.

"Yeah?" he said cautiously, knowing she did not have his cell number. He felt tangled up inside, like he had swallowed his stomach.

"It's Cindy! How was the ride?"

"It was...fine," he said, leaning his head back against the glass and closing his eyes. "I think I should've been a trucker."

She laughed. "There's still time." He could hear a crowd in the background. "I can't talk long. We're taking everyone to a show tonight—high school theater. I just wanted to say hi and see how the trip was."

"Well, ah appree-shiate that." The telephone book was slipping out from behind him. He pulled a pen from his jacket, shifting his weight to check the other pocket for paper. "I just dropped the truck off. I got two of my neighbors to move the heavy stuff. Nothing's organized yet."

"You know you're crazy, right?"

"Yeah."

They both listened to the people in the background for a moment, and Rob started to jot down Natalie's phone number on a scrap of paper from his pocket.

"What are you going to do tonight?"

"I'm not sure yet. Haven't made any plans," he said.

"Rob—have you talked to her yet?" Her voice was quieter than it had been a moment ago.

"Who?" He stopped his pen for a moment, adjusted the cell phone between his shoulder and ear. He quickly finished taking the number down and let the phone book drop.

"You know. That girl."

"What, Natalie?" He paused as though waiting for an answer. The phone book was swinging on the end of the chain. "No, I haven't. I'm not even unpacked yet."

"I was just wondering." She said. "Do you think you will?"

"Oh, I guess I'll probably get around to it sometime," he said. "We used to be good friends."

"Yeah. Did you get my note?"

"I got it."

He turned the scrap of paper over in his hand. The cartoon woman still looked harried, her hair springing out all over. He re-read what she had written that morning. Natalie's phone number was embossed in reverse in the middle of Cindy's loose script.

"I should run, I think the show's starting."

"Hey, let's talk some night when you've got more time, okay?"

"That would be good," she said. "Bye, Rob."

"Talk to you later. Thanks for calling."

He turned the phone off and stepped out of the booth. Two boys were standing next to the door of the booth, a pudgy one and a smaller one with a bad case of acne. The thin one was holding a quarter between two fingers, ready to be inserted. They looked like high school students—the ones that all the other kids made fun of.

"Maybe next time you can talk outside on your phone so we can use this one," he muttered as Rob walked by.

He could have let it pass, but it struck him the wrong way. Smart-ass kids these days. What was he, fifteen? He didn't turn but muttered back as he opened the car door. "Maybe next time you can stick it up your ass."

Rob swung the car around and gave them the finger as he drove by, then held the phone number against the steering wheel and dialed as he waited at the exit for a break in traffic. It would have felt better to be able to squeal out right away after giving someone the finger like that instead of having to sit there. It was starting to feel kind of silly.

"Hello?" It was a man's voice. He couldn't think what to say. He missed an opening in traffic.

"I, uh, is this the Natalie residence?"

The man made a sound like a rush of air leaving nostrils. "Well, I guess it is. It's also the Shawn residence and the Tinker residence. Would you like to talk with Natalie?"

"Please." He pulled into traffic, turning in the direction of his apartment.

He could hear the phone clatter against something hard, as though it had been set down roughly on a countertop. He tried to make out the voices he could hear indistinctly in the background. What was he doing? She was probably living with this guy. Maybe Tinker was their child. She was the sort of person who would name a child Tinker. Maybe he should just hang up—he hadn't given his name yet.

"Hello?" Too late.

"Natalie! It's Rob."

"Oh!" He gave her a moment to digest the information. "Wow, that's twice in one week. Twice in three days, even."

He was having trouble hearing her, so he pulled to the side of the road to silence the flapping of the bag in the back window.

"That you heard from me, you mean."

"Well, yeah. I mean, two years of silence, and then twice in one week. I think a little bit of surprise is understandable."

"I guess. But there are special circumstances. I was just calling because I'm here."

"You're in Bellingham again?"

"I moved in today."

"Moved in? Wow." She stopped talking, then continued, leaving a gap of silence like an irregular heartbeat. "You thought about that one for a really long time, didn't you. Not that it's bad! I mean, it might be good, well, it is good."

"Thanks so much. I feel all warm and fuzzy inside."

"Come on." There was another awkward pause. This wasn't going well. "Well, we're having a few friends over tonight, so if you want to stop by, feel free. We're just going to be hanging out."

"Maybe I will. Where do you live?"

"Oh yeah. We're on the corner of Chestnut and Garden. There's a few bikes locked up on the porch beside a beat-up old recliner, and the house is white with brown trim."

"Not pea green?" he asked, regretting it instantly.

"No, it's...no, definitely not pea green."

He dug around in his bags and boxes until he found his toiletries and a towel. As he shook the shaving cream, he noticed that the basin of the sink had a chip out of it. He hadn't filled out a damage report yet. He hadn't called Gordon Nerburn yet either, or put the money in the drawer.

He set the bottle down and stepped back into the main room to do that before he forgot. He dialed the number, holding the phone with one hand while he searched for his checkbook with the other.

"Hello..."

"Hi, Gordon—" He was cut off.

"...please leave me a message. I will contact you."

"Hello Gordon, this is Rob Erickson. We talked on the phone the other day and I'm calling to let you know I've arrived and have my stuff inside the room. I'll put the check in the agreed upon location."

He wrote the check and tore it off, then stepped out into the main room. Chad was stirring macaroni in a pot on the stove.

"Hey, Chad. What's up."

"Oh, hey...Rick?" He looked apologetic.

"Rob." The drawer was on the other side of Chad, so he walked around the island. "Do you see the landlord much?"

"Nope. He's not around too much."

"I'm supposed to put the money in this drawer."

"Oh, yeah. If you're late paying, he sometimes does that so he can pick it up right away. Money must be tight. Usually he wants it in the mail, but if you forget, he wants to get it right away. He lives out of town or something."

Rob dropped it in and slid the drawer closed again. Chad made no move to let him through the short-cut back to his room, so he started back around the island.

"What do you do again?" Chad asked, as though Rob had told him before. "School? Work?"

Rob paused. "Nope. Nothing, really," he said, and wondered what the hell he was doing here.

He scraped two days of stubble into the sink and rubbed his hands on his smooth cheeks to search for patches that felt like Velcro. He slung his towel over the bathroom door, realizing for the first time that he had no shower curtain. He stripped down, folding his clothes onto the floor to act as sponges, and angled the water toward the inside wall of the shower.

It wasn't easy to shower while trying to keep his body between the water and the lack of a curtain; eventually he just gave up and tried to go as quickly as possible. He could smell cigarettes as the water ran through his hair and down his face.

When he was done the mirror was completely fogged, so he picked his boxers up and wiped it as best as he could. He analyzed his face in the mirror, trying to remember what he had looked like two years ago. When you see yourself every day the changes are gradual—hair slowly disappears here, sneaks in there. He was probably a little less bulky than he used to be, but not much. Even his hairstyle, if it was a style, was the same: cropped short all around with the front slightly longer and spiked, like a counterpoint to the goatee.

Like she cared. He wrapped the towel around his waist and stepped over the pile of mushy clothes into his room. He didn't feel like organizing or unpacking anything else, but he didn't want to arrive at Natalie's house too early, either. He was starting to wonder whether he should even go. He pulled on a fresh pair of boxers and wrapped his blanket around himself, collapsing in the chair.

He felt like he had just failed a test. Bellingham already seemed as dingy and filthy as Seattle. Now here he was with no job, no plan, and one possible friend who had a family. Maybe they'd ask him to babysit, or let him watch *The Little Mermaid* with them.

He hadn't unpacked the boxes yet, so there was still the possibility that he could grab Gordon Nerburn's check out of the drawer and run. The only problem was that he'd have to reload a truck, and he had no place to go.

He should have at least talked to Natalie for more than two minutes before casting his life back at her feet. But he told everyone that she had no part in the decision to move back. If you tell a lie to enough people you begin to believe it, but that doesn't mean that it begins to come true.

He yawned. What were his parasites going to do about this?

The car seemed to be driving itself, and all the controls responded sluggishly, as though there was a delay built in. He wanted to get to Natalie's house, but the streets all seemed to be rearranged; Chestnut and Garden weren't where they were supposed to be. The car was enormous. His feet barely reached the pedals.

Cindy and Dave were asleep in the back seat, wrapped up in cocoons, oblivious to everything. A car in front of him slowed down, and he slid ahead on the seat to jam the brake pedal down. The car decelerated casually, stopping only inches from the rear bumper in front of him. The pedal was soft and kept sinking. When he had it completely down to the floor and he was standing off the seat completely, straining with his leg to reach and still be able to see over the dash, the car began to crawl forward again.

He saw a house with pea green trim to his left, but the brakes were gone and the car was slowly picking up speed again. He opened the door and jumped out, leaving the two sleeping in the back seat as the car pulled away.

The door to the house was open, but it opened into his apartment in Seattle, somehow. He walked through the kitchen, observing stacks of dishes on the counter with a sinking feeling. Someone had put his couch back in the living room, and the television. He tried to remember why that seemed wrong.

He pushed the door to the bedroom open, and his bed was there, strewn with clothes. He recognized a blouse of Cindy's on the floor in front of him; he picked it up and sat on the bed. Natalie walked out of the closet, in the same jeans and sweater that she had been wearing in the Mexican restaurant. He smiled at her, relieved because now he remembered that he had been trying to find her.

She smiled back, but it was emotionless. He got up to give her a hug. A small fleshy worm slid out of her mouth, bright pink, as though her uvula had elongated and was out exploring. It moved slowly in a circular motion, tasting the air. Natalie's stomach swelled and he reached out reflexively. A baby fell into his hands, wide-eyed and quiet.

He felt sick. His eyes felt tight, dry. He rubbed the snot from the corners of his eyes and looked around, blinking rapidly to try and budge his contacts, to moisten them. Sleeping before bedtime always disoriented him, and he always seemed to dream more than usual. It felt like the beginning of a new day after he had slept for days. Slowly things fell into place. Bellingham. Moving in. Natalie. It was completely dark outside and he had no clock set up in the room yet; he was sure he had just slept through the evening.

Whomever had lived here last had made a little star system on the ceiling with glow-in-the-dark stickers. He searched for constellations for a moment and smiled, surprised at how the surprise of worthless bits of plastic and phosphors could feel like a gift. Sure, the room is small, but look—there are little stickers on the ceiling.

It reminded him of the ceiling of one of mad King Ludwig's rooms in Bavaria. He and Nat had visited it when they went through Germany. After Ludwig's father had died, he had a night sky painted on the royal bedroom ceiling, then had the stars gouged out. They wedged fragments of crystal in the holes and lit oil lamps in the room above so

Clutching Dust and Stars 71

the stars flickered below. Glow-in-the-dark was the modern equivalent: easier and even more artificial, more removed from reality.

The room was cold. He pulled some clothes out of his suitcase and put them on before locating and adjusting the thermostat. He stuck his head under the tap and sucked up some water to try and dilute the feeling in his stomach.

He limped out to the car—his leg wasn't hurting as much as before—and turned the key backwards in the ignition to light up the clock. 9:17. Earlier than it felt and he could still stop in.

The house lights were on when he drove by, but the blinds were closed and he couldn't see in. He felt nervous about the fact that he was moments away from finding out for sure that he had just moved to Bellingham for no reason at all. It might be better to drive away and pretend this never happened—at least he could try to fool himself into believing that there had been the possibility of something if he had stayed. The remote potential for something seemed better than the absolute certainty of nothing.

He stopped the car anyway. He parked a half block away so that he could walk for a moment before arriving and wake completely. Light from inside an old Presbyterian church pushed its way through a handful of stained glass windows near the front doors, the colors rich and deep in contrast to the stark street lamps. They were like the backlit signs at a strip mall, but instead of U-bake pizza, the offer was salvation. Everything was an advertisement.

He walked up the sidewalk toward the corner and looked at the house. Two old bicycles were chained on the front deck underneath the mailbox. He hugged his arms around himself, wanting not to go in. He hoped no one would open the door or peek through the blinds and see him standing there. He was feeling self-conscious, and he hadn't even met anyone yet—but he was generally good at swallowing his discomfort and pretending he fit in. He prepared himself.

The button for the doorbell was cracked and unlit. A small, weathered piece of paper was tacked above it; a loose sketch of a hand with the fingers bunched into a fist and block letters above it directed him to "do it the old-fashioned way," as though doorbells were a new fad that the residents of this particular house refused to give in to. He knocked.

A belly dancer opened the door, her skirt fluid as though her torso was floating on air. She was beautiful, but seemed very tired and too thin.

"You must be Rob," she said, taking his hand and leading him in. "We were wondering if you were going to show up or not. I'm Tinker. Natalie's told us all about you." She emphasized the word all.

He felt numb; he could have kissed her if he weren't frozen. She was Tinker! He felt like running, but allowed Tinker to lead him into the living room. The place smelled like dope.

He saw Natalie right away, sitting on the couch with her knees up, watching him come around the corner with a curious smile.

"Well, hey, you decided to grace us with your presence after all." She got to her feet and gave him a light hug. He hugged back with force.

"You didn't think I'd come?"

She broke his hold, turning around. "Hey everyone, this is Rob—Rob, this is everyone. I'll let them introduce themselves. Here, have a seat. We're kind of low key tonight."

He heard the names but didn't pay attention to remembering them. He was still thinking about the fact that Tinker was not a child, and especially the fact that she was not Natalie's child. He nodded at each person and said the required words after they had introduced themselves. When it came to Shawn, he snapped out of it, remembering him from the phone and remembering that he lived with Natalie.

"Hey, Rob. We already met, kind of."

"Kind of," Rob agreed.

He was short and stocky, with close-cut hair and a direct look about him. He was massaging another girl's shoulders, and Rob felt himself relaxing.

"This is Dara." He clapped his hands twice on her shoulders and let them rest there.

She passed a something to him over her shoulder, then leaned her head back to look up at him. He inhaled and then leaned forward and kissed her. They coughed and giggled.

Rob sat next to Shawn and Wade, a greasy-haired guy with slouched posture. He hadn't said anything but his name when introducing himself. He seemed strange, not completely safe.

Tinker came back from the kitchen with a glass of water and paused for just a moment when she found Rob in her seat.

"So anyway, now Rob's here, so we'll have to talk about someone else." She sat herself in Wade's lap, draping an arm around his neck.

"You just got in today?" Natalie asked.

"Yeah. Thursday I looked at a few places and I signed up over the phone yesterday. I'm not sure how it'll be, but I didn't have much time." He was formulating his reasons in his mind and hoping no one would ask him why he moved.

"You're not sure how what will be?"

"The place I'm in, I guess. The landlord seems a little eccentric, and it's pretty small."

Natalie got up. "Anybody want a cup of coffee?"

She counted and went into the kitchen. She looked older, but not old. He remembered other times that she had stood up, other times she had walked away.

"Natalie, Rob was looking at your bum!" Tinker shrieked. "He was staring at it the whole way to the kitchen."

"Come on," he murmured, unsure how to respond in this group. Everyone was laughing at him.

"Why'd you come back here, anyway?"

There it was. He thought it was a bit aggressive but he had worked out his defense.

"Well, it's kind of a long story." He saw half of Natalie beyond the door to the kitchen as she moved into a position to see him. "I got hit by a car last year and had to roll in a wheelchair for a while. So I've been walking and riding the wheelchair off and on for a while, and I decided it might be better here, you know, with all the hiking trails around. So I can walk it around on something other than concrete."

They seemed to be digesting that.

"Bullshit," Tink said and snuggled into Wade. Natalie disappeared again.

"What are you going to do here besides hike around?" Shawn asked through a mouthful of a cookie.

Rob raised his shoulders and left them up. "I've got to figure that out yet."

"Must be nice."

Natalie set a tray of coffee cups on the table.

Shawn scratched his stubble and wiped his mouth with his fingers. "Hey, if we go camping next weekend, we'll do a little hiking. Rob can come."

"Shawn wants to go camping next weekend," Natalie said.

Rob felt awkward sitting there and talking about plans and everyday life. He and Natalie had two years of the past in between them like a giant void that he wanted to rush and fill, but not with all these others around. He didn't want to ask her if she wanted to go for a walk, either—she might say no. So he sat, and laughed, and joked as if there was nothing strange about being in Natalie's house.

Tinker offered Rob a drag, turning the cigarette she had just lit toward him.

"Nah. I get paranoid. Last time this dog started barking outside and I went psycho, throwing myself against doors and walls, trying to get away."

"Give it another chance," she said.

"No thanks. Can you give me a light, though?" He pulled out his smokes and shook one out.

Tinker shrugged and threw a matchbook at him. "Whatever, but even Natalie's partaking tonight."

"Can I smoke in here?" he asked with the cigarette dangling from his lips, inches from a lit match.

"You can do anything you want," Tinker said. "We're going to have to air this place out anyway."

Rob leaned towards Natalie, pulling his cap off and scratching his head, his cigarette held between two fingers, the filter toward his head.

"You know, it was weird, I accidentally fell asleep just before I came here and I had this crazy dream."

"Oh yeah?"

"Well, first of all, I guess, was when Shawn answered the phone, he said it was the Natalie and Shawn and Tinker residence, and it sounded like a little family. So I was thinking Tinker was, well, you and Shawn's baby," he said, addressing Natalie.

Tinker screamed, clapping her hand over her mouth, and Natalie laughed. Shawn was smiling faintly, as though he were enduring the topic, but not especially enjoying it.

"Sometimes it feels that way," Natalie said, grinning at Tinker.

Rob took a drag. "All evening I had this idea that maybe I'd come over here and there'd be a little kid running around, and stuffed animals on the floor." He stopped talking and there was silence, as though they were waiting for more. "That's my story."

"Isn't it past Tink's bedtime?" someone asked.

"It's always past Tink's bedtime."

Natalie was looking intently at him. "What about the dream?"

"Oh!" He shrugged. "It was stupid. I don't even remember too much of it, just one image sticks out. It's not as good as I made it sound."

"Well, you have to tell us now," she said.

"Okay. From what I remember, it went like this: I was coming into my apartment in Seattle, but it was mixed up...no, I was coming in an old house, you know the one we had on Alabama?"

Natalie nodded, her eyebrows pinched in the middle as she listened.

"Well, I was walking in there, but as soon as I got through the door, it was actually my apartment in Seattle. You were in there and I gave you a hug, and a little worm poked out of your mouth."

Everyone was smiling politely, except Natalie, who was still at rapt attention. She nodded for him to continue as he put the cigarette to his lips again.

"This part's kind of bizarre," he said, the words escaping in explosions of smoke from his mouth, fading away into the haze that was developing above them. "But your stomach started to expand, kind of like a balloon, and I reached over and this baby fell out from under your sweater."

Tink started laughing and said how beautiful it was to hear her birth story, but Natalie was scowling. She picked up her mug and took a long drink, hiding behind it. When she put it back down, her face was expressionless.

Mommy, what were trees like?

It was still strange to see him—probably because they hadn't filled in all the blanks yet and the questions still rubbed uncomfortably, like shoes that haven't been broken in, and that was fine with her.

He had stopped by briefly on Sunday afternoon during a break from organizing his place, and again on Monday evening, after she was finished at the store. Tuesday he had come by the store and picked up a few things—a lamp, some dishes, and a lifeless print in a garish frame which Natalie had initially thrown away and Dorrie had then rescued.

He seemed to have no problem with the idea of just jumping back into her life, but she was a little more cautious—always one toe to test the waters first. She was trying to be intentional about forcing things to roll out slowly. Instead of spending a full day with him and going over everything that had happened in the interim, she preferred short visits here and there. Otherwise, once the past was ironed out, they'd be sitting there all caught up on each other, with the question hanging between them: what now? And she wasn't sure how to answer that yet.

So she was coming up with excuses, finding reasons to be gone, to keep the visits short or at least in the presence of a group of friends. They were both different people than they had been two years ago, and it would do them well to acknowledge it. She hadn't told him about this studio space in the back room yet—she liked having the ability to disappear back here and paint.

On Monday morning, she had spent some time talking with Dorrie about the situation—or talking at Dorrie about it. Dorrie usually made sure she had all the information before she gave away comments.

"You don't sound completely thrilled about him coming back, you know. If you asked me, I'd say that you seem a little bit scared about it, to be honest. You've never told him about what happened, have you."

She said the last part so that it wasn't a question and brought the unspoken worry that lurked beneath Nat's words closer to the surface.

"I don't know if I'd say 'scared,' but 'apprehensive,' maybe, yes."

Dorrie was right. It wasn't just the fact that Rob had come back that was bothering her. Having someone from the past come back was one thing—having them come back from an unresolved past was another.

She had stayed late and painted for a few hours that day, too, knowing that she was not likely to be disturbed and could organize her thoughts, or maybe even figure them out. When she got home, she found two notes that Rob had called, and he showed up at the door halfway through supper. He was "just in the neighborhood," of course, so he'd stopped by to say hello.

When he had come in the store yesterday, she had talked with him for a few minutes and directed him to the rooms that contained what he was looking for. She had to smile when she remembered Dorrie zoning in on him, walking up and playing the old lady with her innocent questions, as though she didn't know who he was. It reminded her of the way Finn used to run up and sniff the legs of visitors, making sure they were safe.

She squeezed out some blue paint and began to mix other colors into it absently. She felt a little bit dishonest, working back here and knowing he couldn't find her, but she wasn't sure how to tell him directly that she wasn't sure how she felt about him. So she spent the time hiding back here and talking to herself with paint and hoping that she could figure it out.

Rob seemed almost shy at times when they were alone. It was kind of cute; it made it seem like there was no history between them, like he was just a boy and she was just a girl, which was what she would have chosen if it were an option.

You can't change the past—she had prayed for that upon occasion. What is the past but memories? Memories that leak into the present and color the future, seeping out like tea from a bag, darkening the water nearest it first and then dispersing.

When she got home, she went to her room without turning on any lights and lit the candles on her desk. It was already getting dark outside. She used a loose candle from beside the shrine and dripped wax into the cracks where the two side candles had been peeled out, welding them back onto the structure to make it whole again. She loved candlelight. It was not controlled by any switch. It was something real, flickering inconsistently like faith.

She had a worn out Catholic missal that someone had donated in a box full of religious books. It had Latin on the left hand side of the page and English on the right. She read the Latin by candlelight once in a while—a quick way to cash in on a sense of holiness and history.

Sanctus, Sanctus, Sanctus, Dominus Deus Sabaoth.
Pleni sunt coeli et terra gloria tua.

She was sure that she mangled the Latin, but she trusted God to figure out what she was saying. She pressed her thumb into the soft wax, leaving a fingerprint as a seal. Some days she went through entire candles just sitting here and tipping them, spilling their wax onto the shrine so the drips built up and solidified.

There were no notes or messages from Rob today. Was he giving up on her? The bastard. Her mother had left a long message on the machine. Sometimes she thought that her mother must be so lonely up there. Often when she had a day off, she would call Natalie's place just to talk to the answering machine or to hear Natalie's voice on it. She hadn't sounded too bad today, just chatty. They talked once or twice every few weeks—usually not long, but they talked.

She sat with the candles for a few moments longer before blowing them out. Tink was still working, so Natalie decided to run down to the store and get a few things. She picked up her shopping bags from the closet and set out.

It was getting cool out, but earlier it had actually been sunny, a holdout day from the summer. Maybe the weather would allow for camping after all. As of yesterday when she had talked with Shawn, the weekend was still a go. She tried to make a list of what to get for the weekend, and what they could take from home.

Tink was ringing somebody up when she entered the store and didn't see her walk in. She grabbed a handbasket and speed-walked toward the fruit.

She stroked the items from the list as she found them: apples, bananas, bread, buns, instant oatmeal, pancake mix, vegetarian hotdogs. She always ended up packing the basket to overflowing and then carrying a few things in her other hand. It was kind of a check on how much she bought—once she couldn't carry any more she had to go home.

She waited behind an extra person so she could go through Tink's line.

"Did you get everything?"

"I've got most of it, and we've got some back home. Maybe you could pick up a few snacks, though."

"We're going to need some snacks."

"I leave it in your hands."

Tink grinned as she weighed the bananas. "Oh, hey, Rob called earlier. I forgot to leave a message."

"I was beginning to wonder if he was losing interest."

"Not yet, but if you don't smarten up, he might. He was wondering if camping was still on."

"And what did you tell him?"

"I told him it is. And I invited him to the coffeehouse tomorrow."

That was okay; the coffeehouse was safe.

It was Thursday after her shift and she was in the studio. It had been some time since she had heard the sound of the front door slamming or of Dorrie talking with a customer, which meant that it was probably closed already. Dorrie was very strict about not disturbing Natalie while she was working, not even to say goodbye.

She intentionally didn't wear a watch, or even put up a clock in the studio. It was probably almost time to head home if she wanted to eat anything before going to the coffeehouse. She had given up on the Bacon piece a few days ago, and it was faced against the wall beside her until she received further inspiration. Bad painting. Sit in the corner until you behave.

She had started a new piece using the same approach—take a loose idea and let it grow itself. She had begun with simple thoughts on communication: how what she was trying to say through the paint could be so different from what the painting actually said to the people who looked at it.

She had started with two heads, one in three quarter view and the other looking straight on. She painted the faces roughly and then began to paint connectors between them: pipes, bridges, telephone cords, bare wires and electrodes. The heads had the brain area cut out, like an old medical diagram from before they knew anything, revealing the thoughts of each.

The first head was thinking hot, sharp-edged flames in a blaze of oranges and reds, while the second was more subdued, thinking leaves and sky in cool blues and greens. One of the connecting pipes was made of glass, and the fire and the leaves came through from each end and met in the middle, where they muddied up against each other into

Laryn Kragt Bakker

a mass of brown and purple as though the thoughts had mixed together and ended up impure, the pipes and bridges clogged with sludge.

She pulled off her paint-spattered clothes and draped them over the chair. She was just buttoning up her jeans when someone knocked on the back door, startling her. She found her t-shirt and pulled it on quickly. Sometimes people knocked as they left their load, even if it was after hours.

She opened the door and found Rob.

"Hi," he said. "Tinker said to check if you were here."

"Oh. Well...why?" Now she had nowhere to hide.

"Tonight is Coffee House Night, remember?"

"I know that. What time is it, then?"

"Nearly seven. I stopped by your place and Tink said you hadn't been home yet, so I should come here in case you lost track of time."

"Thanks." She turned and looked at the room, trying to remember if she had taken anything else this morning.

Rob saw the easel and started through the doorway; her arm snapped like a mousetrap, holding him outside.

"There's no time to look. I've got to lock up. Nothing's ready to be looked at besides."

"Okay." He backed out, bumping into a small recliner that somebody had left on top of the steps without her noticing. She started to drag the chair through the door and Rob pushed from the back. She sent Rob on ahead, to let people know she was coming, and would be there shortly.

She unlocked the bike, formulating in her mind places where she could remain hidden from Rob. Maybe she could keep using the back area while wearing earphones.

Other people were still showing up when she got there. She ordered a drink and a bagel. They had the chairs pulled out into a circle, with a few tables in the middle, and some wrinkled computer print-outs claiming the empty chairs: RESERVED FOR PHILOSOPHY NIGHT.

She chose a chair not opposite him and not next to him, either. Wade and Tink were in between them. That way they wouldn't be looking at each other the whole time, but they wouldn't be close enough to touch. Everybody settled into chairs and conversations, and she took a bite of her bagel.

"You found her," Tink observed to Rob. Natalie chewed and looked straight ahead, as though she were zoned out, while she listened. Rob talked quietly.

"Yeah, she was in the back. I think she was just leaving. I'm not sure I should have gone there." She took another bite and kept staring ahead, chewing.

"Why do you say that?"

"I don't know. It seemed like she was pissed off at me or something." She tried to look at him with her peripheral vision. Was he looking at her? A faint smile pulled on the corner of her mouth. She turned her eyes slowly in her head without moving her neck. Tink's back was facing her but Rob was looking right at her. He winked.

Her cover was blown so she looked anyway, and he was smiling. She laughed, and held up her hand to make sure the mouthful of bagel stayed in.

Tink looked over and gave her a look that asked why she wasn't in on the joke, but Natalie just smiled. She popped the last of the bagel in and Tink started to call the meeting to order.

"Okay, everybody, Natalie's going to start us off tonight."

Natalie wiped her mouth. "Actually, what I'm going to do is throw out a couple of possible leads that I've been mulling this past week and we'll follow whichever one gets picked up first."

"Aren't you going to introduce the new guy?" Marie asked.

"Oh yeah. Rob is his name. This is Marie." She motioned with her hands. "I think everybody else has met him already."

There were nods all around. "So, one after the other, here's the possibilities. One: What is time? Can we change the past? Can we change the future? Do you believe in fate? Two: Is true communication even possible in this world? Or does the attempt to communicate thoughts necessarily lose something?"

Nobody spoke. If you spoke too soon you often ended up defending something you didn't actually believe and wished you hadn't said. Rob was looking around, looking a little unsure of himself.

"I think people communicate at times, and not at others," he said.

"No." Natalie jumped on his comment, cutting him off before he could clarify himself so that she could try to back him into a corner he didn't necessarily intend to get into. "Never perfectly. It always loses something, like a law of Physics. There's always waste heat."

"Choose your sides," Wade said.

Everyone except Natalie and Rob stood up, like musical chairs.

"Waste heat, this side," Wade called, moving toward Natalie.

"The rest of us, over by Rob," called Tink.

Wade slouched back in his new chair.

"Okay, Rob. We start these discussions off like they used to fight wars—each side takes a turn shooting while the other side just stands there, no interrupting. Then after we've each given our main points, we open the floor up completely. You don't confer with your team, which makes it possible for a few threads of argument to open up. You don't even have to agree with anything anyone on your team says if you don't want to."

"And try to sound intellectual, even if you're talking out of your ass. It's in the unwritten rules," Natalie added. "I'll go first. Here's what I think: each person has a unique background, and therefore a unique perspective on life. Everything they do and think is shaped to some extent by their past, and when they communicate, anyone who interprets what they are saying interprets it from the perspective of their own unique past, at best combined with an incomplete idea of the other person's past. So while they may get an accurate idea of what is being communicated, it can never be perfect."

Tink started off for the other side. "Okay. What you are saying may be true for big chunks of communication. But there are small moments of insight, of connection between two people, which are pure. Kind of like distillations of pure communication."

They began to go one after the other, each delivering their argument in a single sentence.

"Feelings can't be put into words—communicating feelings involves reliance on abstractions, which are interpreted based on each individual's own experience of that abstraction."

Marie set down her mug. "Some things are easier to communicate than others. Feelings, as you say, can't be communicated easily. But concrete details can be given without waste heat being produced. For example: the man went to the store. There's a kernel in there that comes through."

Wade shook his head. "What man? Which store? How did he go? Translating thoughts into words loses something, and then translating those words back to thought loses again. It's like exchanging currencies—you lose every time you do it."

"The kernel! I've communicated, even if it's surrounded by questions."

"The question was not whether you've communicated at all, but whether you've communicated perfectly."

"This is good," Natalie said. "I was thinking specifically in terms of art, not necessarily just words. There can't really be any perfectly pure communication, if by that you mean something being transferred exactly from one person's head to another person's head. And that's critical to art, because art is meant to involve the viewer in the piece, not necessarily beat them over the head with something that came out of the artist's head. But that's a whole other topic. I don't know if we'll have time to start into that one tonight."

It was Rob's turn. "Well, then, here's a question. What about the method? If the mode of communication changes form and maybe even goes through a number of people or channels, but the idea still comes through on the other end, that's still communication, right? Even though the message has been put through the ringer, the idea can still come through if it's pure enough."

"I'd still like to pick up on what Wade said," Tink broke in. "I think there can be pure communication beyond the factual approach of a man going to the store. There are universal experiences that we all share, despite the differences in our past. Eventually, we all experience love, hate, loss, joy, and I think these are the channels that real communicators know how to tap into."

"You sound like an advertiser," Rob said. "Talking about the channels you want to tap into. But maybe that's why it feels like we can't communicate anymore. Our channels are all worn out and stretched, because we're bombarded all day by these people who are trying to shove their products up and down them—shoes, and cars, and lowest prices."

"Wrong team," Wade said.

"Oh, yeah. All I'm saying is that it's no wonder we feel a little beat up."

"I feel a little violated. Who's sticking what where?"

"Well, maybe we should feel more violated than we do," he said. "When we see the advertisements everywhere, never giving us a break, trying to sell us this car, trying to make us want that drink...It seems to me that they're sticking Coke bottles where they don't belong, and we just yawn and turn over and wait for the next one."

She laughed. No matter how different some things were, some things were still the same. Rob still got worked up about things. She was a little uncomfortable at the surge of affection that fact brought.

She crammed her sleeping bag into its tiny stuff sack and pulled the top shut. It was going to be wet, she knew. Everyone was talking positively, religiously refusing to say the word "rain," but they were bringing enough canvas to build a tarp city up there.

They had gone up last year over the Labor Day weekend and every one of the regular places was packed full with two or three vehicles, so they had just kept driving down the logging road, bouncing through potholes in the darkness, eventually stopping at what might have been a good spot.

And they had made it into a good spot. It had been less than a handful that time—Shawn, Dara, Tink, and herself. They had stumbled over the piles of broken boulders to an area that seemed flat in comparison, and pitched the tent by electric lamplight. The river was fifty feet away, though it sounded closer. It felt like they had been plucked and set down in the middle of the wilderness.

They curled up inside only to discover that they were on a steeper slope than they had thought. They spent a few minutes laughing and rolling down on top of Shawn, who was at the base until someone, probably Shawn, convinced them that it was healthier to sleep head down, so the blood circulated in the brain easier. They all did the ninety degree rotation and it worked, though it took getting used to.

She wondered if the extra blood up there changed the content of a person's dreams, making them richer, more vivid. Or the environmental effects like the sound of the river, the wind on the tent, the birds. Unfortunately she had slept too deeply to remember anything she had dreamt that night.

The next day when they had woken up they had discovered that the site had looked better in the darkness—there was the small open section where the tent was, the broken rock piles, and the rest was overgrown with brambles. They had spent hours pulling up brambles and flattening out the sand beneath, and once they were done, everyone was covered in nicks and scrapes. The challenge this year was going to be remembering exactly where that spot was so they didn't have to do that again.

She put a rubber band around *Crime and Punishment* to keep the pages from falling out and packed it into one of the side pockets of her bag. She threw a deck of cards in at the last minute and zipped it all shut. The two cars were parked out front—they were taking Rob's Jetta and Wade's beat-up Taurus. Most of them were outside playing catch with a frisbee on the sidewalk and lawn, all of their stuff packed in the trunk already.

She squeezed her pack into Wade's trunk and slammed it, then turned and smiled at everyone.

"Ready when you are."

The trip started out like all road-trips do, with high energy and plenty of fooling around. Shawn had a walkie-talkie set, so the two cars traded comments as they barreled up the interstate. Natalie was in Wade's car with him and Tink, while Shawn and Dara rode with Rob. For a moment there it had looked like it was going to be Rob and her all alone in the car, with the other four in Wade's car, but she had spoken up in time.

"Let's see, we might as well go three and three to keep things even. Shawn and Dara, you guys can ride together with Rob and I'll ride in the back of Wade's car."

The Canadian border was not even an hour away. As they neared it, they ironed the story out.

"All we need to say is we'll be gone for two days camping," Shawn's voice insisted over the radio.

"But what if they ask us other questions? We should go over all our information again," said Tink.

"They won't."

"What if they do?"

"All we need to say is who we are and what we're doing. Camping for two days."

"But—"

"TWO DAYS!" he yelled.

There was silence until they reached the border. Wade pulled into his gate and was waved through. Shawn was still talking with the guard, and after a moment the guard directed Shawn to the side.

"Oh, shit," said Wade.

Shawn walked into the building and a few minutes later came out with a different guard, who made everyone get out of the car.

"They'll find something. They'll plant something there if they need to. We're screwed," Wade muttered as the guard began to paw through the trunk.

Wade pinched his eyes and leaned forward, refusing to look back.

"They're letting them go," Natalie said, and his head snapped around.

"Lucky as hell," he whispered.

They took turns trying to sound like truckers with the radios. "Breaker Breaker One Nine, this is the Big Dog calling Little Bo Peep, do you have yer ears on?"

"Ten Four, good buddy, and be advised there's a Smokey on your tail."

Shawn had forgotten to fill up before the border, so they stopped at a Petro-Canada and Rob ran in to buy a pack of cigarettes while the rest of them got out to stretch. They pulled out a map to verify their route before climbing back into the cars.

Once the darkness arrived, Natalie found the sleeping bags and pillows which were stacked around her in the back very inviting. She woke up again on the logging road as they pitched and heaved through the potholes.

The campsite was still there, and the piles of sharp boulders were as bad or worse than she remembered. They took their time, stumbling and picking the way down with lamp light, testing rocks for stability and avoiding sharp edges, using hands and feet to probe ahead.

They had one large tent to set up and they each carried an armload of tent poles except for Shawn and Wade, who teamed up to carry the tent itself. Rob had volunteered but had been shot down because, as Shawn said while motioning to Rob's leg, he was "4-F." There was no rain falling from the sky, but it was pooled on the ground in places. They spread out the biggest tarp they had and Shawn began to erect the tent.

Everyone else grabbed a tent pole and pretended to be doing something with it for a moment, but it was clear he was the only one who really knew how the tent worked. It was a big old army tent. Rob put down his tent pole and began climbing back over the rocks.

Shawn was trying to direct Wade on which loop to feed which pole through when they heard the car start. The conversation stopped and everybody looked up as Rob backed away from the side of the road and then ahead again so that the headlights were pointed toward them.

It was strange to be in the glare of headlights—her first thought was that she was about to be run over. It was no wonder the deer froze up.

Rob opened the door and the car's interior light blinked on. It was such complete blackness out here without the street lamps and city lights that the car stood like a beacon, a lighthouse to warn against the broken rocks along the side of the road.

"Is that going to help?" he called.

"Yeah, I think so. Better than my headlamp alone," said Shawn.

Everyone began to trek back and forth from the tent to the cars to transport the goods, and Wade turned on the lights of the other car, positioning it at another angle to cut out some of the hard-edged shadow.

If it hadn't been quite so late, they would have probably set up a campfire and fooled around for a few hours, but everyone knew that once the tent was up, they would all be in it. In fact the tent was only half up, still sagging, when they began to crawl inside to unroll sleeping bags and claim their spots.

Rob took the lantern and headed back to the road to turn the headlights off. Tinker was peeking out from her mummy-bag, one arm awkwardly stuck out the top to hold her lighter aloft as people crawled in. Shawn was the only one with a light besides the lantern.

Natalie began to feel a tinge of claustrophobia with all these bodies packing themselves into this thing. She closed her eyes, but the noises surrounded her: breathing, shuffling, muttering, giggling. Personal space was always at a premium in a tent.

A dim glow from outside the tent grew brighter, foretelling the coming of Rob, or maybe a Canadian park ranger. It was Rob. He poked his head in with his eyes squinted, as though trying to make out the people, to determine whether this was the correct tent.

"Over beside Natalie," Tinker called out from within her bag.

He was still squinting—the lamp was right beside his face and it was the only thing easily visible. She didn't want to call out "Come here, Rob," because that sounded a little more inviting then she wanted it to, so she was quiet.

"Where, now..." he muttered.

"Say something, Nat!" came Tink's voice again.

"He'll figure it out," she said casually, quietly, glad for a chance to say something without saying it directly to him.

Rob fell into place by his sleeping bag. "He'll figure it out," he muttered. "Thanks."

She turned her face sluggishly toward him and made a noise to acknowledge him which implied that she was too far into sleep to actually open her mouth and respond with words. She smiled with her eyes closed. The nice thing about camping, and tents in particular, was that you could pretend you were sleeping and get away with it.

She watched him settle into his spot through half-open eyes. The lantern cast a hard shadow across his face; he looked at once familiar and unknown as he wriggled in place, trying to make a nest by forming the sand to his body.

When the lantern was off, she lay with her eyes open and watched the darkness. Whispered voices slowly died, the words becoming fewer and spaced further apart before finally disappearing and settling into breaths. It wasn't long before Rob began to snore; she was caught off-guard at the memory of that sound, and of other times, years ago, when she and Rob were lying beside each other, she awake with her thoughts and worries floating in the air around her, and he next to her, snoring.

The past didn't want to stay there. It was a flammable cocktail that was brewing inside of her. She visualized all her emotions boiling around inside her, squeezing out of her throat. She imagined vomiting them into her hands and offering it all to God.

That was how she prayed. Two or three years ago, when she had started trying to pray again, or maybe it was for the first time, she kept running stuck. She tried to gather all her thoughts and questions together and when they were all there for one brief instant, churning and massing and pushing at the edges, she would try to turn to God. The thin membrane that was holding everything ready in a pretty package would burst and she would be sitting alone on her bed like a popped balloon.

It was a learning process. Prayer isn't a time for holy thoughts, or purity, or carefully crafted phrases, she was discovering. It's a time for rage, for pain, for despair and hope. A time to sit in the dirt and joy of everyday life, to purge herself of the questions that plagued her by flinging them at God. Sometimes when she prayed, all she could do was sit there with her torso ripped apart and her guts in her hands. When you pray you sweat blood.

Turning emotion into words loses in the translation; instead of mouthing words that never represented what was circulating inside her, she tried to speak in emotion, which seemed closer to God's native tongue. It was easier to pray without ceasing that way—emotions keep coming where words fail, and then you just spit them up and let God deal with them.

They woke up early, or rather, Shawn woke up early and made such a noise getting out of the tent that everybody else had no choice. Natalie stayed curled up in her sleeping bag, not as warm as she liked to be in the morning and feeling a little stiff. Rob tried to talk to her once in his morning voice but she just curled deeper. He yawned and crawled out.

There were three of them inside yet—Tink, Wade, and herself. The others had left their sleeping bags hollow like spent cocoons. She was relieved that Rob was not next to her anymore. Shawn was muttering about rain which made it feel better inside. It felt like they had divided into two parties which were camping independently of each other. She lay there, half-awake, vaguely translating the sounds that were coming from outside until she couldn't justify remaining in her bag any longer.

The others had constructed a canopy with rope, branches, and canvas; each square of canvas was stretched taut into a relatively flat plane and overlapped with the next, held there with ropes that were tied to trees or long branches acting as pillars.

They agreed that the three who had slept late would find firewood and cook breakfast since the others had already built the shelter from the coming rain. Shawn volunteered to get the stove going while the sleepers gathered wood.

Natalie walked out into the bushes behind the campsite, gathering anything that looked like it would burn and throwing it back towards the tents. Some of it was dry, but a lot of it was damp from a previous day's rain and from dew.

Rob was sitting in a lawn chair, watching them as they picked up logs. "You know," he said, "hunting and gathering isn't so bad."

Natalie turned around with three logs cradled in her arms. "Says the guy who's neither hunting nor gathering."

They cooked their breakfast on the stove—bacon and eggs in one pan and water in the other. The meat-eaters had taken the burner on the right side, which gave the most heat, so the water took a small eternity to boil. Wade was put in charge of the cooking, cracking eggs and putting raw bacon in beside it. He muttered "We're camping, dammitt," if anyone complained about the greasy eggs.

Once the water was hot enough, Natalie added some of it to her bowl of instant oatmeal and put a piece of bread on the flame toaster. She went to sit on a rock overlooking the river. It was cool out, there was no denying that. But there was something about camping near a river, or near any body of water for that matter, which compelled a person to go into it. Last year the water had been higher and faster; they had gone in one by one with a rope tied around their waist and fought the current with the other three holding the other end of the rope for safe measure.

"Who's going to go swimming in the river with me after breakfast?" She looked back at the campsite; a pack of greasy-mouthed carnivores stared back, hunched over their plates.

"In the river?"

"No way," Tinker called from behind the tent, where she was huddled with her oatmeal as though still recovering from the year before.

"I'm in," said Shawn.

"I'll do it," Rob followed.

Natalie was going to rinse her bowl out when she noticed something in the water. Tiny fish, bright orange, were floating in suspension near the shallows, their heads facing the current. Once she saw the first few, she could see them everywhere.

She called the others and they all stood on the edge, watching. Shawn flipped little pebbles at the fish—some darted out of the shallows into the current; others didn't seem to notice. Natalie threw crumbs of bread out and they gobbled them up.

They were smaller than she would have imagined, but they were still pointed against the flow. Tough little things. They didn't seem to be moving ahead, just holding their ground, barely. She knew the feeling.

They each had their own way of getting in the water. Rob thrashed out to the middle and plunged under, then jumped up and thrashed back out, hyperventilating. Shawn waded right in as though it didn't phase him, until he was in halfway between his knees and waist. He gasped quietly as the water soaked through his shorts and then he folded his knees, opening his arms and collapsing into the water. She stood on the shore, bare feet on stone, growing colder and colder.

Slowly she moved ahead. Rain was beginning to spit on them. The rocks were like knives pressed against her feet, which were growing numb and losing their feeling. The water licked up her leg, biting each time it rose higher than the last. It came just past her knees when she began to lower herself in slowly, horizontally, like she was on the downstroke of a push-up in slow motion.

"She's crazy," said Rob, who was already wrapped shivering in a towel.

She tuned out the voices and concentrated on the water as she went almost to eye level, watching the droplets of rain hit from point blank, and then she went under completely, her face into the current. She floated like that for a moment, clasping rocks to hold herself in place, trying to think like a salmon, holding her own against the flow of water. She could feel her core temperature dropping, and when she went up for air she couldn't make herself go back down.

"Get out of there! Your lips are blue," Tink said.

She tottered to her feet, holding her clinging t-shirt out with one hand, and staggering towards shore, unable to feel the ground or control her legs. Tink draped her in a towel and rubbed her down as though she had just won a fight.

"You look like a corpse."

"Thanks," she said through her teeth.

"Well, I think we were outdone," Shawn said to Rob. "Wanna go again?"

"No, but I will if you do."

Rob seemed to be pretty comfortable with her friends already. They splashed back in and out, whooping and screaming. In another crowd, she might have made a joke about them being 'double-dippers,' people who had been baptized twice. But not this crowd. She sometimes felt incredibly lonely, even in the middle of a group of friends. There was a piece of her that none of them could relate to, and she felt like she wasn't allowed to talk about it. Sometimes she wondered if anybody could understand her. Anybody who wasn't invisible and silent and almighty.

She felt like she was straddling a creek, one foot and all its doubts and questions planted over there with the pagans, and the other foot in all its audacity having fallen firmly in love with Jesus, planted on the other side with the Christians, so in the final count she didn't fit in completely on either side. Maybe there was no crowd where she would feel completely comfortable.

Everyone made their way back toward the tent, clustering near the campstove, where the water for dishes was boiling. She scooped up some water in a mug and dropped a teabag in it, setting it on the woodpile to steep. Rob sat down in a lawnchair, looking down at his chest and pinching one of his nipples. "These guys'll cut glass right now," he said, sticking his chest out like a weapon.

"Thanks for the warning," she said. "I claim the tent for a few minutes."

The rain was becoming a little more insistent, and Wade began to construct a teepee of branches in the firepit. He took the axe and began to split kindling from a dry log.

She zipped the tent shut behind her, dropped the wet towel, and started to peel off her clothes, listening to the outside conversation

"We've got a bunch of paper in a bag beside the tent," Tink said.

"I don't want any paper. I'm making this fire the real way."

It felt strange to be naked and separated from everyone by this thin piece of canvas alone. She felt exposed, as though the tent weren't thick enough.

"Whatever. You know where it is when you need it."

Natalie found her sports bra and got into it, then felt around in her pack. Rain was pattering on the canvas roof they had stretched above the tent. She pulled on big wool socks, sweatpants and a sweatshirt, then wrapped herself in her sleeping bag and unzipped the tent.

Rob smiled when he saw her. "Someone's not planning to go too far for a while."

She smiled. "I just need to sit down inside this for a while to get the blood flowing again."

"Your lips are still blue."

She sucked her lips into her mouth to hide them.

"That looks like a good idea," Tink said, eyeing the sleeping bag.

Tink went into the tent to get her bag and Nat curled up on one of the chairs in hers, holding her tea in two hands. It felt heavenly. Rob was still sitting there with his shirt off, which made her feel warmer and colder at the same time. He leaned forward to find a stick, preparing to poke in the ashes, and she saw the spray of moles across his back like ink spots on a page from her past. She saw herself lying in bed beside him, where was it—Berlin? Amsterdam? He was on his stomach reading to her from a guidebook and she was parallel to him, playing connect-the-dots with these small brown growths scattered between his shoulder blades, inventing constellations with them or running her fingertips across them, reading him like Braille.

Wade pulled some newspaper out of the grocery bag, glancing guiltily at the tent where Tink had gone in and silently holding a finger to his lips, motioning to the others not to reveal to her his secret.

Rob shook a cigarette from the box.

"Did you see these warnings?" he asked, handing the box to Wade, who passed it around.

There was a photograph of a pregnant woman holding a cigarette, emblazoned with the words *Cigarettes Hurt Babies*.

"I got these because I'm not pregnant. The other brand gives you nasty teeth or makes you impotent."

"That was wise," Wade said.

Once the fire was going, they all sat around it for a short time and made comments about it.

"That heat is just what we needed."

"Will it melt through the tarp?"

"I doubt it."

"I hope so; we definitely need a chimney here."

"Hey! You used paper!"

It took some time for them to devise a system to allow the smoke to float out. They took a long branch that had been broken off of a tree and propped it up under one side of the roof, so that it was a slant roof and the smoke could float up and out while the rain rolled down and off. At least that was the theory. There was still a lot of smoke under the tarp.

They decided to go for a little hike while it aired out. The rain had tapered off, though the sky was still overcast. Upstream in the river, they could see a huge boulder which they had hiked onto last year and which overlooked both the river and the campsite. Slightly downstream, a little bridge spanned the river, built of huge logs and tied down with cables. Driftwood and branches were crammed into the crevices, much higher up than the river went, evidence that the water was low.

They followed the gravel logging road up past a little wooden hut and then ducked into the trees on the left side, picking their way back down towards the sound of the water. Dara slipped on a fallen tree that had been stripped of its bark and slid part of the way down the slope, nearly taking Shawn down with her.

The rock they were headed toward jutted out from the side bank, forcing the river around it, but they had to scale down a rock wall to a section that had been eroded out between the rock and the bank. Water eddied in front of it, some being forced around the rock, but a portion of it pooling off to the side. It continued building up and periodically overflowed so that water surrounded both sides of the rock, making it into an island temporarily, and then subsiding.

Shawn was down first, walking a rib of stone that was elevated above the shallow pools of water that remained on either side of it. It was slick and he balanced with his arms out like he was walking a tightrope. When he was at the other side, he turned and reached out his hand.

He could reach just far enough that they could grab his hand and steady themselves. One by one they made their way across. The water came up on Tink when she was right in the middle of the crossing and soaked her feet, but everyone else made it across dry.

They climbed on the rock, exploring it again. It was split in two, like the hemispheres of a brain, and a large piece of driftwood that had been stuck in the crack last year was still there. It was perhaps a little whiter, and now with a small graffito on the surface. JD '00.

"Aw. We should have carved our names last year," Shawn said, pulling out his jackknife.

Natalie watched him scratch his name out like a sculptor, or a cave man. She smiled—the rest of them were watching him, too, waiting patiently for their chance to mark their territory.

She took the knife when her turn came and carved out her name in block letters: NAT. She gave Rob the knife and scampered over to the other side of the rock, climbing over the edge near the river and down onto a wide ledge that formed a natural seat. She dangled her feet over the edge so that they hung out above the water.

Last year she had sat here for hours, just watching the river go by, always the same, always new. Maybe the reason that she loved nature was that she could see herself in different parts of it. The rock: passively being eroded, sculpted without much say in the matter. The river: sculpting the landscape, carving a path for itself. The salmon: pushing against the current, knowing that they're going in the right direction because of the effort it takes to stay where you are. The trees: stretching upwards, shaping themselves, being shaped.

Tink came and sat down next to her. She looked over and smiled.

"What's on your mind, girl?"

"Oh, art...life. I'm kind of just breathing this all in. It's amazing."

Shawn and Dara were having a contest to see who could hit a stump on the opposite bank with rocks, and Rob and Wade were trying to scale a part of the rock from another angle about ten feet down from where they had all climbed up.

"I wouldn't mind a little more sun, though." She hugged her arms around herself.

"I guess this is what we get for trying this in mid-October, huh?"

"Yeah. But there's always that hope." She looked down at her wet feet. "I'm actually thinking of heading back. My feet are making me really cold."

Lunch was a fend-for-yourself event; she went into the cooler and pulled out the bagels and cream cheese. They disbanded in pairs: Tink and Rob ate and then went into the tent to nap, Shawn and Dara took some sandwiches and apples and wandered off into the woods for a picnic. This left Wade and her by the fire. He was quietly poking it with a stick until the end was charred, then writing on stones with it, scratching out hieroglyphics.

When she was finished the bagels, she went over to her backpack and pulled out her book. She sat in the lawn chair with her sleeping bag wrapped around her again. The sun was behind a thin cloud now and the rain had stopped again, so it was not as gloomy as it might have been.

After he had poked the fire enough, Wade started to play with the axe, taking a few pieces of wood out of the pile they had made that morning. He was about twenty feet from her, facing away, hacking at the stumps. She tried to ignore the grunts and the sound of the axe head striking the wood, but the sounds began to mesh too well with the story.

Raskolnikov was standing in front of the pawnbroker.

"But what has he tied it up like this for?" the old woman cried with vexation and moved toward him.

He had not a minute more to lose. He pulled the axe quite out, swung it with both arms, scarcely conscious of himself, and almost without effort, almost mechanically, brought the blunt side down on her head. THWACK! Grunt.

She stared blankly at the page for a moment, watching Wade through her peripheral vision.

She cried out, but very faintly, and suddenly sank all of a heap on the floor, raising her hands to her head...Then he dealt her another Grunt! *and another blow* THWACK!

with the blunt side and on the same spot. The blood gushed as from an overturned glass, the body fell back.

She kept reading as Raskolnikov ransacked the pawn shop, and Wade kept at the piece of wood, persistent as a regret.

He suddenly heard steps in the room where the old woman lay...In the middle of the room stood Lizaveta with a big bundle in her arms...Seeing him run out of the bedroom, she began faintly quivering all over, like a leaf, a shudder ran down her face; she lifted her hand, opened her mouth, but still did not scream...He rushed at her with the axe; her mouth twitched piteously...And this hapless Lizaveta was so simple and had been so thoroughly crushed and scared that Grunt! *she did not even raise a hand to guard her face...*THWACK! *The axe fell with the sharp edge just on the skull and split at one blow all the top of the head. She fell heavily at once.*

She closed the book and then her eyes so she didn't have to see Wade holding Lizaveta's head down with his foot, rocking the axe back and forth to loosen it. She felt like an accomplice.

A gentle snore came at more or less regular intervals from the tent. Putting the book down, she made a show of yawning widely. "I think I'm going to catch the last part of that nap," she said.

Wade wedged the axe into one of the stumps and turned around.

"Oh, okay."

She carried her sleeping bag from the chair and crawled into the tent. Rob was lying on his side, taking up space in his and her spot. She dropped her bag in the middle, on top of Shawn's, and got in. It felt great—not only did she have Shawn's sleeping bag as padding, but his mattress as well. She would have slept a lot better last night if she had a mattress like this.

Tink's voice startled her. "Maybe you'll have better luck than me. I can't sleep."

"I think I will. But either way, it sure feels good just laying here right now."

"Yeah, and it sounds like Wade finally put that stupid axe down."

They were each quiet, waiting for sleep to come. Natalie was slowly finding it when Tink's voice came again.

"What's going on with you and Rob?" she asked.

It was strange to be asked a question like that at the moment before going under, and when he was lying right there.

"I don't know," she said quietly, worried that the answer would wake Rob. "It's all too sudden yet. Maybe nothing."

They didn't get to sleep for long. Shawn and Dara were waking everyone up to see if they wanted to go on a walk. She rubbed her hands over her face, exploring the perimeter of her eyeballs with her fingers while the others performed their own private rituals for waking up.

Wade was sleeping in the car with his seat tilted back and the stereo on. They made Tink go wake him up, because Shawn was making everyone go on a walk with him—for Rob, he said, reminding them of Rob's leg. That was the reason they had come, after all.

It wasn't really a hike, which would imply a trail through the forest. It was more of a walk up the logging road with trees and shrubs on either side. The gravel followed the river for almost half a mile, and then slowly veered off so that there were more and more trees between them and the water. At one point the road was up against a rock wall which had lichens and moss growing on it, and a miniature waterfall running down the side, and they all began to wish that they had thought to bring a water bottle. Rob began to lag behind, not complaining, but favoring his leg. The rain started soon after, and they all turned back. It started slowly and built up in intensity. By the time they reached camp again, it was a downpour.

Shawn lit a fire while the rest of them shook out their jackets and some of them pulled out dry clothes. The smoke hung under the tarps as though it were hiding from the rain as well.

They played cards for a while and then sat around the fire, talking while they each did their own thing: absently poking the fire, tossing things in and watching them burn, or blowing on the embers as darkness slowly surrounded their camp. Natalie watched the fire play on the faces of everyone around the circle. They said that firelight was the most complimentary light for people's faces.

Wade stood up. "Anybody want a beer?"

He had taken an old mesh laundry bag along and had loaded it up with beer bottles, tied it closed and hung it in the river. Last year they had tried to make a little storage compartment on the edge of the river, using rocks to shape a wall and keep the beers in, but while they were sitting by the fire, the current had knocked some rocks loose and taken half of their beer.

He thrust one into her hands. It was colder than she expected and the cap didn't twist off as easily as it was supposed to. It cut through the top layers of skin on the inside of her thumb when she tightened her fingers around it and the bottle still gave its little hiss of pleasure as the cap came off.

She had very few memories of alcohol from her childhood. In general, the only time she had anything to do with it was when it was passed in front of her in church or when she scavenged for empties in the ditches around her house.

A year or two before her brother Scott had died, She was at church with Jenny Vandermeulen after the Lord's Supper. All of the adults had vacated the sanctuary to talk outside after the service and they had gone from pew to pew, gathering up all the little plastic cups from the specially bored holes in the rack that held the bibles and hymnals in the back of the benches.

They poured the remnants of each cup into one: a drop here, two drops there until she had three quarters of a thimble-full of the blood of Christ. Jenny had balked, leaving Natalie to gulp it down and worry about it alone. She had wanted to see what was so mystical about it, to test whether some kind of change would take effect inside her. She hadn't noticed one.

Hunting for discarded beer bottles seemed to be on another end of a spectrum— trudging through ditches, digging bottles out of the mud and carrying them in a soiled garbage bag, slung over her shoulder as though she were elf to a pauper Santa. Every so often she'd come across a bottle partly full of beer or cheap whiskey that she'd open and pour out, watching it soak into the earth.

But those were just her earliest memories of alcohol. She had other later memories, most of them more like the current scenario. Friends and beer, beer and friends, and pretty soon it's hard to distinguish between the two.

But she had to be careful not to sink too far down inside herself here or now. Whenever she did that she came out depressed. Enjoy the now. Let the past bury its own dead. The dead will come back to haunt you later, just like they always do.

Shawn got up off the cooler he was sitting on and pulled out some hotdogs and buns. He skewered two hotdogs on one of the sticks and held it out over the fire.

"Isn't this the life? Out in the woods, sitting around a fire with beers for everyone, getting ready to eat."

"Yeah, alcohol and smokies are about all you need and life is good." Rob leaned over and grabbed the package.

Natalie suddenly craved something to go with her beer. She wasn't enjoying it much on its own. "Something about camping increases my metabolism, I think. I eat a lot more, but I don't think I do too much more."

Shawn looked skeptical. "You're always a bit of a pig, just admit it."

She tore open the package for the veggie dogs.

"Those are disgusting. Unnatural," he said.

"Have you ever tried them?"

"Never have, never will."

"This from the guy who's eating hotdogs. You do know what they make those out of, right?"

"Lies. Old wives' tales. Rumors put out by the people who make those kind of things," he said, motioning toward the end of her stick with his chin.

Rob was rotating his stick as though it were a spit. "Have you guys read anything by Douglas Coupland?" He looked up, but nobody raised their hand. "A few years ago I went through a Coupland phase and read everything of his that I could get my hands on. There was a section in one of them where they're debating veggie dogs—which lend support to meat culture by trying to mimic it."

"But the whole point is that they're not meat," Tink said.

"I'll say they're not; look at that!" Shawn always made a big deal about them. They were somewhat rubbery, and when they went in the fire, they blistered and mutated.

"Yeah, but, why make them look like meat then? It's like hot dogs are the true thing in Plato's cave and veggie dogs are the shadows."

"You have to wean yourself off of meat with things like this," Tink said.

"No way—you've been weaned off of meat for years and you're still eating that, still trying to fit into the meat culture, which undermines your whole argument."

Natalie set the dog down inside a bun and reached for the ketchup as Tink turned to her. "Come on, give me some help here!"

"I'm thinking, I'm thinking."

"Well, if you guys would watch my video, you'd be happy to eat veggie dogs and never touch red meat again. If you saw the look on those cow's faces just before their eyes exploded..."

"You and your video. You're preaching about it every chance you get."

"I am not! I'm just saying—"

"Yeah, yeah. Who wants to watch a slaughterhouse?"

"You should see where your food comes from."

Wade spoke up for the first time in a while. "Did you know that Indians ate buffalo eyeballs like gum? They're pretty chewy, I guess."

"Yeah. I turned green and just about puked in grade eight when we dissected cow eyes," Rob said.

"Do you know that they hang calves with these big straps, in the darkness, so they don't ever use their muscles, and beat them with sticks to tenderize them? And then they butcher them."

"And, let me guess, then their eyeballs explode."

"Well, if they butcher them that same way. But the point of it is that the meat is so soft you can cut it with a fork on the plate. Don't you think that's wrong? To do that to an animal?"

"Maybe it feels like a massage with the sticks," Wade said, chopping with the edges of his hands in the air.

"I can cut my hot dog with a fork," Rob said.

"Shut up."

Natalie swallowed the last part of her bun. "Well?" Shawn asked. "What did you come up with in all that thinking?"

"You know, I don't think there'll be veggie dogs in the perfect world."

"Oh, great. Now Nat's not even going to eat veggie dogs." Shawn laughed. "What have we done?"

"I didn't say that; I've got to think about it a little more. In the meantime, I guess I might as well have another, just in case."

Rob went down to the river and harvested more beer.

Tink was sulking about the argument, but she started cooking another one as well. Rob brought back the entire net of beer, like a catch of fish, and passed bottles around. He asked Shawn to slide over and put the extras in the cooler, then filled up the net with warmer beer. The bottles clinked as he slung it over his shoulder and turned back to the river.

Natalie hadn't meant to drink much, but it had happened anyway. Everyone had stopped eating except Rob, who was on his sixth or seventh hotdog, claiming that he didn't get very good mileage. It was dark all around, except for the fire, which tied them all together like a band of thieves gathered in the night. They were taking turns telling ghost stories. She watched the light flicker on Tink's face. Everyone's gaze seemed to be drawn to the fire as they told their stories, rising every now and then to double check that everyone else was still there, that they hadn't silently been taken, or risen and left the storyteller alone, talking to the flames and embers.

Natalie was just starting to tell a story she had read as a child from a collection of supposedly true, unexplained events.

"Okay, the story is set in the Depression. This man was working at a sort of a corner store, and it was a stormy night."

"Not unlike tonight," Shawn said in a slow, drawn-out voice.

"Right," she said. "But for about four days, this thin lady who was dressed in rags had come in—"

"Not unlike Tinker," Shawn broke in.

"—and she wouldn't say anything—she'd just stand by the milk bottles. He had noticed she was carrying a baby's bottle and had decided to give her the milk for free. She had disappeared into the darkness on foot each day. Today, she seemed especially agitated, and he was starting to worry because every day she looked worse, as though she were getting sicker and sicker.

"He tried to talk with her, but she wouldn't, or couldn't, reply. He told her to wait for a moment and rang the doctor. She began to get very nervous, and looked like she might leave without the milk, but he wanted to keep her there until the doctor came, so he wouldn't give her the milk. Just before the doctor came, she turned and ran out into the storm. The shopkeeper watched her disappear into the darkness. He stood facing the rain for a few moments and then got his wife from the back."

"His wife worked at the corner store, too?" Tinker asked.

"Well, the store was attached to their house, I think, so she was just in the house. But he had told her about the lady, and when the doctor came, they all set off in the direction that he had seen her go before she disappeared into the darkness.

"They had lanterns to light the way, and they could follow the footprints in the mud, because she seemed to avoid well-traveled paths. The prints were perfectly clear and led straight to the local cemetery, until they stopped sharply at the edge of this mound of dirt.

"The doctor had turned white. They took a few moments debating what to do, and the shopkeeper told them all again about her child, and how sick the lady herself had looked that night. He decided to uncover whatever was buried here and started scraping the loose dirt away."

"With what?"

"Maybe he ran back and got a shovel, I don't know. But it wasn't long before he hit the top of the wooden coffin. It was a cheaply made coffin, and for a moment he wasn't sure what to do. He started filling it back in when he thought he heard a sound.

"The doctor was still pale, and explained that he had been at the burial ceremony of a young mother and her child late last week. He moved stiffly, but helped him pull the coffin out and they opened it up. The shopkeeper recognized the dead lady inside as the mysterious visitor of the last five nights; in her arms was a small child who was crying weakly, and beside her in the casket, four empty milk bottles."

"Oooh." Tinker said.

"Come on, that's not scary," said Shawn.

"Who said anything about scary? It's just supposed to be mysterious." Natalie said.

"Oooh." Shawn said.

"I'm not sure that the guy would have enough motivation to actually start digging there. That's not quite believable," Wade said.

Natalie rolled her eyes at him and shrugged her shoulders.

Rob poked the fire with his hot dog stick. "I have a story, but it probably won't be scary as a story—it was actually a dream I had, and at the time was quite spooky. It might not work as a story though."

"Shoot," said Wade.

"Well, it was a kind of a camp-out, and it was a younger version of me and my father together with a friend and his father. We were around a small fire, with the kids here and the dads here," he said, motioning around the fire with his hands. "His father was telling all these stories, I don't even remember what about. Escaped criminals, or ghosts, or creatures, or some unknown evil. Anyway, after the story, we all got ready for bed, and we camped a little ways away from the grown-ups so we could feel kind of courageous.

"We were lying there and came up with this plan to scream and see if we could freak our parents out. So we yelled, but then we started laughing. And this is where the perspective of the dream changed. Instead of me looking from my perspective, it swings around like a movie camera, and I'm looking over my dad's shoulder like I'm hovering there." He indicated a sweeping motion with his hands and twisted slightly in his seat to show the perspective change.

"I can hear us laughing a little ways up, and the lamp my dad is holding gets blown out. I hear this thump, and the other dad lights his lamp and comes over. He sees my dad's body on the ground and checks his pulse, then lifts the lamp up and tries to crane his neck to where we are still giggling. I can see us both, like I'm having an out of body experience, looking back down on myself. We look up at his dad, smiling, but then our expressions turn to terror as we look behind him, and it seems like they're looking at me, at my floating, out-of-body presence. And at that moment, I am hit with the certainty that I'm the one that blew out the light, killed my own dad, I'm some kind of evil presence floating in the shadows, and I'm moving in on them." His eyes flickered up and he looked past Tinker into the darkness.

There was silence for a moment and everyone stared at Rob, whose gaze had dropped again so that he was staring into the fire introspectively as though lost in thought and wishing not to be disturbed.

"BWAAH!" Rob said, jerking his head and bringing his hands up like claws. Natalie had flinched back slightly but she didn't think it had been visible to the others in the darkness.

"Not bad, but not too good," Wade concluded.

"What can you do," Rob said. "I tried."

"Let's tell happy stories," Tink suggested.

"Start us off, then, Tink."

"Well, I don't know. Maybe we could tell funny childhood stories."

"Go for it."

"I've got to think about it."

"Okay, anybody then," Wade said. "Somebody's got to have a story. We're just looking for some plain old stories to get us started here. Did anybody eat their goldfish or shave the cat?"

"It's not a story, but I have a question about goldfish," Rob said. "Is it really true that they can only remember the past thirty seconds of life? Someone told me that if a goldfish is out of water for a short time, it'll forget it ever lived in water."

"I don't know about that."

"Yeah, that sounds a little fishy," Shawn said and Wade hit him.

"I don't know how they could measure that. It would be a neat thing if it were true though."

There was silence, and Rob spoke up again. "I have another question about goldfish, and this one relates to something in my childhood. Is it true that the size of the goldfish is determined by the size of the tank—that they stop growing if they're getting too big for their bowl?"

"I think that that one's true," Shawn said.

"Well, either way, I took that theory as a young boy and applied it to underpants." He faltered, as though he was unsure about whether to tell the rest of the story. Natalie shook her head. She knew where this was going.

"You put goldfish in your underwear?" Wade looked confused.

"No! I just had a parallel theory. Call it the 'goldfish theory of underpants.'"

"I don't understand," Wade said.

Rob looked up from the fire apologetically, scratching his goatee. "This was maybe not a good story."

"So that's it?" Wade asked.

"He thought that his penis would get bigger if he wore bigger underwear," Natalie said, louder than she intended. She set her bottle down to slow her pace.

Rob pinched his eyes shut with a grimace and she burst out laughing. She felt her nostrils flaring and put a hand up to block her nose from view.

Rob's face lit up. "Man, I haven't seen that in a *long* time. That's awesome."

"What?" she asked, feeling apprehensive suddenly. How was it that he was laughing at her?

"That thing, the way you cup your nose in your hand when you laugh. I love it."

"Hey, hey, hey," Tink broke in. "No changing the subject. We were in the middle of talking about your theory about penises. Penii."

"No, come on. That was about all. It was just that my mom would always buy me these tighty-whiteys, so I started asking for boxers to test the theory."

"Did you get them?"

"Yeah, eventually."

Tink was laughing. "Did it work?"

Rob glanced down, then back up, his eyebrows asking whether he was really supposed to answer that.

Someone started passing more beers around.

Wade gave a little snort. "Anybody else want to tell a story about their genitalia?"

Rob shook his head.

There was a pause again. She was subconsciously counting the pauses in the conversation and tried to stop.

Shawn yawned and arched his back. "The license plates are right. This is super. Natural."

Natalie was starting to feel light-headed. She took one last mouthful and set her half-empty beer on the ground beside her again. Or was it half-full? She was at the point where the happy buzz she had going was getting ready cross over to the other side. If she drank any more, she knew she'd feel sick shortly.

But maybe she had already had too much. She started to turn inwards again, watching the rest of them but slowly disappearing into her own head. The conversation moved and shifted like smoke, and she silently watched. Here they were, a bunch of people growing old but pretending not to, sitting around the fire. She felt a chill and pulled her jacket on.

She skewered a plastic grocery bag with her stick and turned it over the fire. The plastic shrunk and pulled; holes appeared. She held it in the flames and watched it melt, then catch fire. The bag began to drip from the stick in tiny blobs that trailed tails of fire like meteors or falling stars, and she was tempted for a moment to drop one on her skin like she sometimes did with hot wax.

She was catching only snippets of the conversation. Shawn tried to give her another beer, so she picked up the one she already had. She had planned to hold it just long enough for him to go away, but she took a swig of it like a reflex.

"I'm out of it right now," she said, and they smiled.

She poked the fire again. They were talking about their families now. Dara spoke for only about the third time tonight, to say that Wade was still living at home, and everyone laughed. Tink complained that talking to her dad was like talking to the radio.

Natalie didn't feel like contributing to this one. Her family was not as much a group chat topic. Your little brother is trying to decide which schools to apply to? My brother drowned when he was fifteen. Your mom still treats you like a child? My mom suffers from severe depression and blames everything on herself. Your dad talks like a radio? My dad ran off with a lady from our church, and then came back a few years later because she wanted to be near her family. Hello ex-family, we're going to be neighbors now, isn't that swell? And here she was, going to be solidly in her late twenties in a few weeks, still acting like a child, sitting around a campfire and getting wasted. Not sure what her life was for. She worked in a second-hand store. The product of a model Christian home. She tried not to think about her family unless she was alone, because it made her no fun to be around.

Rob was staring at her. "You okay, Nat?"

"Yeah. Well, no. I don't feel too good."

She had the impression that she was about to vomit. "Thanks. I think I'm going to go for a walk in the trees for a bit."

She stood up and made her way out from under the tarp, trying to discreetly hold back whatever was trying to escape from her throat.

She had to go all the way out to the road to get to the trees, unless she wanted to squeeze through the brambles. She began to pick her footsteps carefully on the rocks. Everything was black except for the glow of the fire behind her. The air was cool. She was halfway to the cars when she heard a burst of laughter from behind her.

Wade called out, "Choose your spot wisely!"

She leaned a hand against a rock to balance herself. She wasn't going to have much choice about it. She bent down to minimize the splash and vomited onto the rocks. She felt better and she felt worse. She spit and wiped her mouth, then continued toward the road.

Her eyes had begun to adjust to the night, and she could pick out faint shapes now—the bridge, the road, the trees. She crossed the bridge and entered the trees on the other side, tripping on the roots, the uneven ground. She went far enough that the road was no longer visible.

Not that anything was fully visible. It was the idea of it. She sat down on a seat of moss that was growing on an old log and the water soaked through her pants immediately. It was a connecting point and it brought her to attention. She imagined that she was becoming a part of the area, drawing water up from below. She curled her hands around the bottom of the log she sat on, gripping it as though her fingers were roots, searching for something.

She became like the trees, and the trees became almost human. Her fingers were roots, their branches were arms. She stretched upwards, they stretched upwards, bent down, twisted and laid flat. If trees had thoughts, she wondered whether the saplings ever wondered what to do with their lives, or wished to fill a space in the sky that right now they could only look up at. Or if they ever felt like they were growing in the wrong place.

Did fish ever question whether or not this was really the right river to be in? Did they ever just want to give up and let the current take them? Did unsprouted seeds sometimes think that maybe it would be more comfortable to just sleep down in the little bed they were in instead of pushing up to the surface? Were there ever any bees who decided a life wasn't worth sacrificing for a fraction of a tablespoon of honey?

But they all seemed to keep going, for the most part. She tried to trace the outline of a tree with her eye. The saplings kept growing, pushing against the sky like salmon against the current, slowly making headway. And in the process, each young tree grew and was shaped, becoming stronger, filling a hole in the sky. It was all slow, and much of it behind the scenes, not dramatic enough to make the news, but it happened, and it kept happening.

The branches dug into the sky like roots, tasting it, drawing energy from it, while under the soil, roots stretched into the ground like branches, and worms made nests in them. Perhaps young trees sometimes felt like they were growing with the upside down, or maybe they eventually realized that they were really downside up. This thought helped; sometimes she felt that way.

She didn't know what time it was. She started back toward the road. It was cold. Time spent in this way was like a conversation spoken in hints and nudges, an unseen force molding her thoughts, shaping her impressions as they grew.

A gentle rain began again, and she crouched in the middle of the bridge, looking up at the sky, at the stars which she knew were behind the dark of the clouds. She felt her equilibrium going and sat down, leaning back on her arms. A raindrop landed on her forehead and she closed both eyes, but kept her face upturned as more drops found her. For a moment, the rain felt like a blessing and then it ran into her eyes.

Laryn kragt Bakker

kill your t.v.

He had decided to get a part-time job. There was a job fair going on today and he wasn't sure he wanted to go, but he knew he probably should. His bank account had taken a hit moving up here, and besides, having no job wasn't quite the Shangri-la that he had hoped it might be. Everybody else was busy during the day, and he was left to himself. As soon as they got home, he was itching to do something, so he would call, or stop by. He knew that he was probably getting annoying, but he couldn't help himself. He needed people around him and things to do during the day.

The few days of camping had been great; hanging out with people during the day, and no one was worried about what time it was, or whether they had to go somewhere, or do something. He had been spending a lot of time in the library these past few days, reading magazines, drifting off into daydreams, thinking. There was a time when that would have sounded like the ideal life, but there was something missing—he needed some sort of goal to aim toward. He wasn't researching for a newspaper article or writing a paper for school, and at first that hadn't bothered him.

He pulled a grey polo shirt from the ball of warm clothes in the middle of his bed and spread it out. He brushed his hand over the shirt. It was still covered in little black streaks, and this was the second time he had washed it. The pants too, probably. He pulled them out. Shit.

You pay a dollar to wash the clothes, and you expect them to come out a little cleaner than they went in, or at least not dirtier. He'd have to have words with Gordon Nerburn about that.

He turned on the old computer and waited for it to boot up. Did he need to put an objective on the resume? He wasn't sure exactly what he wanted, yet—he was hoping that he'd find it staring him in the face. Maybe something part-time with limited responsibilities. That didn't get too boring. And had human interaction. He opened a blank resume template and deleted the objective. He typed: To obtain part-time employment.

He spent time staring at the computer screen, then the empty wall behind it or the rest of the apartment. He could use a few more pictures, or even posters for the mostly naked walls. He had a single piece hanging, a still life with fruit. He had picked it up last week at the second hand store where Natalie worked. The colors were very bright and the frame was quite ornate, but it wasn't really his style at all.

It had been kind of an impulse thing. He had really just gone there to find a lamp to light the room better, but as he was passing the shelf with the pictures and frames on it, he had remembered that Natalie was painting again. She hadn't been painting much when he had left town, but it sounded like she had sunk herself into it again.

When they had first known each other, she had often told him that he needed to do something with his walls. She didn't like the combination of posters and bare walls. The framed print was a start. She hadn't said anything about it at the time, but sometimes it was better to be subtle about things like this. He was sure that she had noticed it.

Other than the wall décor, he had things more or less set up in the new apartment—he had the hide-a-bed across from the sliding door and the balcony so that when it was a couch, it faced the only source of natural light. There was enough space to pull that out at night, leaving just enough room between the two for his recliner to sit and swivel freely. He used the fridge as a divider; it was the first thing visible upon walking into the room and it made it feel like there was a tiny space carved out of the room for an entryway. His television was immediately behind the fridge, facing the recliner. To the left, beside the closet, was his little desk and the computer. It was still tight, there was no doubt about that, but there was something about that which appealed to him.

When he went to Western, he went through a big downsizing kick, where he sold a lot of his belongings. Living in voluntary squalor appealed to him. He had slipped a little over the last years, slowly accumulating things. Giving Dave his bed and pitching the couch over the edge of the balcony had felt good. He was making a list of other items that could possibly be thrown overboard: the video games for one, and potentially the television, the computer? There was a freedom in it, a cutting away of ropes and responsibilities. If he didn't have anything tying him down, he could pick up and go anytime, anywhere. And part of it was simply the knowledge that he still had the thinking capacity of his brain—the advertisements hadn't yet stewed his mind completely.

The thing about working on this resume was that while he wanted to do something productive, at least part-time, he didn't really want to do any of the jobs that were available. Then again, he could always quit if it sucked too much. The money from the accident could support an extremely spartan lifestyle for up to a few years, if necessary. But he had done some figuring, and by working part-time, and covering some of the basic costs of living that way, he could easily stretch the money out.

He printed a handful of copies of the resume and turned off the computer. They had little streaks across them, too, but he wasn't going to worry about it. Sometimes the print head got little hairs or wisps of something on it, and they dragged across the wet ink and smeared little thin black lines out of the letters. Maybe that could be his trademark—streaks on the paper, streaks on his clothes. He looked at the calendar to get the address from where he had jotted it. It was Wednesday already.

Tomorrow was Philosophy Night. Had it been nearly two weeks that he'd been here already? He had finally gotten the balls to call and talk with Cindy last Wednesday—a week ago. And he had meant to just cut it off, let her know that there was nothing between them, to tell her that there never was, if necessary. They had talked at first about the details of the move, how it was going and all of that, which was what he had expected. Then she had gone and pulled out her revelation before he could pull out his—she said that she had made plans to come for a visit.

So he had eased off on his trigger finger. Instead of blowing her out of the water, he convinced her to give him some more time to settle in before coming on any kind of a trip. He put off the confrontation, was how he was trying not to think of it. But maybe it wouldn't be so bad if she came for a weekend, if he could convince her to take Dave and Tad along. Natalie hadn't nibbled very aggressively at his hook and he might as well not burn all of his bridges down.

They had their tables all set up, lining the walls of the room with their banners and poster boards set up to suck every job-seeker in. It was like walking into a room full of advertisements and subjecting himself to them all, except they weren't just televisions that could be turned off. They were real people, walking up and shaking hands and introducing themselves, and it felt like a personal insult not to smile, feign interest and take whatever pamphlet or print-out they were trying to pawn off.

They were passing out trinkets and other useless items with their logos printed on them: cheap pencils, pens, buttons, or keychains. One group had their information printed on a plastic bag, and it began to fill up with papers that he didn't want.

He wondered that these companies didn't seem to notice or care that associating a company with all these disposable items cheapened the image, in a way.

He had never been to one of these before. It was different than any other time he had looked for a job—most of the freelancing that he'd done involved submitting queries and stories by mail. Instead of him competing with all the other job seekers, it was a combination: he was still competing with anyone else who might be interested in the same kind of job as he was, but these employers were set right up against each other, trying to draw prospects away from other tables, other possibilities. So they were smiling, working hard to be positive and upbeat in the middle of what must be an awful day for them.

He skimmed a few of the papers in his hand. Well let's see. He could be a wireless telephone salesman, or be telephone support. Dental assistant. Warehouse worker. Clerical. All these opportunities. Janitor, part-time. Nine dollars an hour to start. Proofreader. That could have had potential, but it was a grocery store, not a newspaper.

Why did it feel like a personal insult every time that he wasn't interested in a job? It was like walking through a yard sale and finding nothing. How do you politely say: sorry, I think your belongings are garbage.

He wandered from booth to booth for a while, but wasn't drawn to anything. His leg was starting to throb and he decided to just can the whole idea. He dropped the bag with all the papers in it into a trash can on the way out, keeping his resumes in a folder in his hand.

What would a job fair be like if the booths were being manned by employees who had actually worked in the positions that were being advertised? People who would tell you all the bad points along with the good—all the stuff that the recruiters won't mention and you'll end up finding out for yourself later, after you're on the hook.

He drove slowly around town, giving his leg a rest. He found himself near Natalie's place, and forced himself to drive past without looking at it. He turned slowly down the next street and started to circle back around the block, not wanting to turn around but doing it anyway. She probably wasn't home. This was stupid. He pulled into a parking lot to turn around again, and a Help Wanted sign caught his attention.

It was in the window of a dingy looking shop but the sign looked new. It was the only high contrast sign there; the others were sun bleached so all the magenta was faded out, leaving pale greens, blues and yellows. Pictures of waterfalls and palm trees and people, all washed out and sickly looking. It was a copy shop. He imagined working here and smiled. It was a funny picture.

He pulled into an empty spot and turned the car off. He went inside and filled in an application form at the little table, looking up now and then at the fluorescent lighting and the dirty self-serve area. He passed his resume and application to the guy behind the counter, without saying anything.

There. That was done.

He drove home and sat in his room. Chad was outside in the main room, cooking something that stunk like rotten fish. Rob opened the sliding door to the outside so that the fresh air would come in. He picked up the bag with his Playstation in it from beside his door, plugged it into the TV again and played hockey.

It wasn't long after he turned the videogame off that a sense of isolation set in. What was with the mood swings? He probably had Seasonal Affected Disorder. It seemed a good excuse as any.

He wanted to go over to Natalie's, and he almost did. He hadn't talked with her or even left a message for her for days now. But she hadn't called him, or stopped by, or left a message for him either. Which could be a very bad sign.

Maybe he had offended her this weekend. On Sunday he kept mentioning the fact that she had puked on the rocks, over and over. Everything had seemed to relate to vomit and alcohol. By the end, he knew he should stop, but the words kept coming out of his mouth. He thought she had started avoiding him more, but that might have been his imagination. Maybe he should call and apologize. But it had been three days already, and maybe she'd forgotten about it. Then she'd wonder why he let it eat away at him for three days before calling.

The telephone rang.

"Hello?"

"Hi, sir, my name is Jagwad, and I was wondering if you would mind answering a few questions for me this evening."

"Uh, no, it's not really a good time for me to talk."

"Why not—are you on the toilet?"

"What?"

"Rob, I can't believe that you've forgotten my voice already."

"Dave. I just wasn't expecting you to call, and the accent through me off."

"Hey, I forgive you. Quit gushing. How have you been?"

"Pretty good. I've met a handful of people through Natalie and we seem to get along. We hang out now and then."

"And Natalie?"

"Well, I don't know. We're getting along fine, but I can feel some kind of hesitation. I think she's scared of me or something. Which is too bad for me."

"So you admit it! You did go back hoping for more of her."

"I don't know. Depends on when you ask me."

"Is it that time of the month for you?"

"I guess so."

"Hey, this ties in a bit—last weekend Cindy was talking about making a little trip up to Bellingham to visit our little Ham-ster. Did you know about that?"

"Yeah, kind of. She was talking about coming up last weekend, but that didn't work out for me, so I told her to put it off."

"Well, she wants to come this weekend. Is that okay?"

Rob looked around. There wasn't much space, but he wouldn't mind the company.

"Are you and Tad coming also?"

"If we're invited."

"By all means—I'm not sure I'd want to be left alone with Cindy in this little apartment. Bring sleeping bags. There's not a lot of room in my place; well, actually, there's no room, but if you don't mind being cozy, we can sleep on the floor in a few spots, and I've got a small futon from a certain someone who shall remain nameless."

"I think Cindy's working Friday night, and I've got some work I'll need to finish up before Monday, so we'll probably come up Saturday morning and leave Sunday morning."

"That sounds good."

The next morning, he woke to the sound of the telephone ringing. It was worse than his alarm clock; a bad way to wake up from a good sleep.

"Hello?" His voice sounded thick, even to him.

"Hello, is Rob home?"

"I am," he croaked.

"Hi, Rob. This is Randall, calling from Copies On Demand. I hope I didn't wake you."

"No, no. I just haven't talked yet today."

"Right. Listen, would you be available for an interview later this afternoon? Say around two o'clock?"

"Of course. That sounds great."

"Alright, then. I'm looking forward to meeting you."

"Okay."

He spent the morning going through his computer files, re-reading old stories he had written. Here was the legacy he was creating with his life: stories about traffic on I-5, construction, the concert that had been coming up and was now ancient history. Was being a scribe to the mundane details of daily life really worth a lifetime? His work didn't really make any difference in people's lives: all it really did was use up trees, fill up recycling bins and line the bottoms of birds' cages.

So why was he going to go to an interview at a copy shop? Yes, he wanted to leave his mark on the world. People would remember him as the guy who made the best photocopies ever.

But in another way, the thought did appeal to him. Instead of running around and clawing over everyone else's back to get to the top, why not sink slowly to the bottom? Forget about it all. Why let your work be your life? Be a failure, but actually have a life. It seemed somewhere on the path towards enlightenment, or it should be.

He didn't have much interview experience. During high school, he had always worked on one of the farms near his place, and the only thing that might be considered an interview was really just a question from a man that he had known for years: do you want to work for me this summer?

The freelancing he'd done since then hadn't involved personal interviews as much as impersonal ones. They might look over your portfolio of previous stories, perhaps discuss it with each other, and if they're interested, they give you a new story. But that was always a temporary deal—you weren't guaranteed anything past today. So you market yourself and hope that they continue to like your style.

This was going to be a sit-down interview with people he'd never met, seeing whether they would match to settle into some kind of a symbiotic relationship. It was just a copy shop—why all the formality? It seemed like it should be more of a quick handshake and get to work. But it was how things worked. He found his resumes from the day before and pulled one out.

He was sitting just inside the front door in an upholstered office chair which was stained with coffee. People lined the counters, picking up bundles of papers and dropping orders off. He read the bleached-out signs in the windows from behind, advertising desktop publishing and six-cent black and white copies. The carpets were grimy, unless it was just the light. A warbly radio played from somewhere behind the counter, a sound track for the workers to work by. If anything was voluntary squalor, a job here would qualify. It was perfect—it would be something to do, and it wouldn't involve a whole lot of responsibility. And it wasn't far from his place; though it was closer to Natalie's—only three blocks from there.

He sat cradling his resume in his lap. It was almost two thirty already. Fifteen minutes was when he had began to think about just walking out of here. He was actually going to do it at half an hour.

The short, stocky woman he had introduced himself to at the front counter walked toward him. "Thanks for waiting, Rob. Sorry about that—all of a sudden we had this rush of people." She held out her hand and he transferred his resume to his other hand so they could shake. "I'm Bobbi," she said. "I'm the General Manager here. The gentleman on the other end of the counter is Randall, the Assistant Manager."

She took him back into the office and showed him a chair along the far wall. "I'll be right back. I just want to make sure we'll be covered while we're in here. Would you like a cup of coffee?"

"Sure." He was surprised to find that he really wanted to be offered a job here. Maybe part of it was that he was thinking of this as the lowest job on the totem pole, and if they turned him down here it would be quite a blow.

The desk beside him looked like an old military issue—big and metal. The desktop was mostly bare, except for a computer and a shallow wooden box that was nearly overflowing with papers, a container for a mess. The yellowed computer monitor was shooting stars at him, perpetually in warp drive but going nowhere. There was another empty chair beside him, and one behind the desk.

Bobbi came back with coffee in one hand and a little container of cream and a packet of sugar in the other. She set them on the side of the desk nearest to him. "Here you go. We'll be right in."

He set the resume down and stirred the cream and sugar in with the brown plastic stir-stick. It seemed to catch on the bottom of the styrofoam cup as he stirred. Did they still make styrofoam cups? He remembered big anti-styrofoam rallies at school. Or, they had seemed big at the time. Obviously they hadn't done much good. Hey! If you use styrofoam you're killing the planet! And the world shrugged. But he had to admit that it was cool that you could turn these cups inside out without breaking them. He tapped the stir-stick on the lip of the cup to knock coffee drips off.

When he was younger, he had rescued one of these plastic sticks from the floorboards of the pickup truck, where his father had tossed it after grabbing a coffee on the way home from town. He remembered trying to suck juice through it. The edges were curled over and created openings which looked like straws but were so narrow that just about all he could do was create a vacuum in his mouth, and no matter how much pressure built up, the juice wouldn't flow through it. He lifted his coffee cup up to his mouth with his right hand and held the stir-stick between the thumb and forefinger of his left. He began to suck on the end of it.

He heard the door and tried to drop the stick from his mouth, but it was stuck to his upper lip. He pulled it free and set the cup down, sloshing coffee over the edge. The ink smeared across the page as he tried to wipe it off with his palm.

"Whoops!" said Bobbi, as she walked behind him and sat down in the chair by the desk.

"You guys already have my resume, right?" He held it up with two fingers above the garbage can so the drips wouldn't get on the carpet.

She reached into the stack of papers and flipped the corners of the top few pages. "I think so. But before we get into that, why don't you tell us a little about yourself?"

He let the resume drop and sat there, unsure of when or where to start, how little or how much to give.

"Oh! I'm sorry." She turned to Randall. "Randall, this is Rob. Rob, Randall."

He wiped his hands on his pants and they shook hands, and then Rob found himself sitting there again, with both pairs of eyes on him.

He cleared his throat. "What do you want to know?"

"Whatever you want to tell us. Here, I'll start, to give you an idea. My name is Bobbi, and I've been working here for about five years now. I grew up in Seattle and actually lived there until I moved here. I never continued with my education after high school—I married the guy I dated all through high school and kept working at a local restaurant, moving my way up the ladder until I was an assistant manager there. When my husband and I divorced, I moved up here and took over the store. I have two boys, nine and eleven. I really like this town. And that's my life, in a nutshell. Randall?"

"Well, I've been here for almost three years already. I went to Western and this was actually my part-time job while I went to school. As I was graduating, things fell into place for an assistant-manager position, so I stayed. Before here, I lived in and grew up by Nugent's Corner, on the way up to the mountain, so Bellingham's kind of like a big city compared to where I come from."

He nodded. Great that we know each other so well now.

"I'm Rob, and I grew up just south of Seattle, near Bonney Lake. I came up to Bellingham to go to school at Western," he nodded at Randall, "where I took journalism. Since then I've been a freelance writer, mostly in Seattle. I've just moved back up here."

"Why do you want to work here? Why not continue freelancing?"

"Oh, well I might. I'm really just looking for a part-time job at the moment—you know, something guaranteed, so I can pay the rent whether I sell a story or not. And since I won't be working full-time, I'll still have the time to write, if I want to."

"So, you're just looking at us as a necessary evil."

"Kind of. I don't think I'd phrase it quite that way. And it's not really necessary—I've actually got some money in the bank, so I could actually live without the job. For a while, anyway. I guess I'm looking at it more in terms of the structure it will give my life, maybe. I really like the idea of part-time work, because I'll still put some time in, but I'll still have most of my life to myself."

They were both sitting there, still processing what he had said.

"And I don't think the freelancing opportunities are quite as abundant in Bellingham, either. So I'll probably be trying to figure out what I want to do with my life here. In the meantime, it'll be good not to have too much time all to myself. You know when you're sitting there with nothing to do, and it just feels like wasted time? I think working part-time will help to limit that."

"I see. Well, that's unique. Randall, do you have any questions for him?"

"What brings you back to Bellingham, Rob?"

There it was: the question everybody wanted an answer for. Well, he had a story, he might as well stick to it. "Health reasons, actually. I needed somewhere that wasn't in a big city, a place near the wilderness, for hiking and so on. And, having lived in Bellingham before, I knew it was a pretty good option."

"What would you say are your biggest strengths and your greatest weaknesses?"

"I'm very personable, I would say. I think that would be a strength. As far as weakness, I don't really know. I probably wouldn't be very good at repetitive, boring stuff."

"Well, this position will also include some desktop publishing, and will involve a great variety of jobs. But, I'll be honest, there will probably be some jobs that will be a little more tedious than others."

"The desktop publishing sounds fun. I didn't realize that."

"That's actually one of the reasons we called you. You list on your resume that you've done some work with Quark XPress."

"Oh, yeah. We had a class at school in setting up newspapers in Quark, and I worked on staff at the school paper for some time."

"That's important. We've got some basic templates that we try to use as much as possible for customer orders, but we want someone who knows their way around in the program." Randall looked down at his paper again. "If you were to work here, where do you see yourself going in relation to the store?"

He sounded like he was trying to appear efficient and professional, as though he had polished his questions up like daggers the night before and would get to the heart of the matter in just a few quick cuts and thrusts.

"I guess I'm not sure what you're asking."

"What goals do you see yourself having?"

"Well, honestly, most of my personal goals would probably be set outside the store."

Bobbi broke in. "So, you're hoping to just come to work, do your thing, and go home every day."

He nodded slowly. "I think so. I think that sounds good."

He noticed Randall glance over at Bobbi, but she was looking at Rob. "You know, in our environment, it's not really a job that you just come and do independently. There's different customers to deal with every day. How do you feel about that?"

"That would probably be good. Part of the reason I want this is to get some forced interaction with people—instead of sitting home alone and writing, I think I need time away from what I'm working on, time to be watching people, listening to them, and talking to them before I can be alone again."

Bobbi was looking down at the papers in her hand and she shuffled a page from the front to the back, then leaned on the desk and looked up at him. "Tell me something that has happened in your life that you thought was funny."

That was an unexpected question. He sat there and stared into space with a half-smile on his face. Thoughts tend to disappear in harsh light.

"You're smiling—what are you thinking of right now?"

"Well, I was just thinking that most of life is funny if you look at it right. But it's not really the kind of funny that you can tell in words—you have to experience it, find the humor in everyday life, in common things. The fact that you walked in while I was trying to suck coffee up a stir-stick, and that I spilled coffee on my resume, and that the ink smeared. The fact that I am saying this in a job interview. The fact that I might work in a photocopy shop. These are funny things that have happened recently."

Randall looked down and scratched the back of his neck. Bobbi was smiling.

They asked him a few more questions, and thanked him for coming in again.

"Thank you, we'll give you a call tomorrow or Monday and let you know the decision we've reached." Randall sounded like a man who wished he was a robot.

Bobbi seemed more human, at least. "Hey, it's been good to talk, Rob. I hope we'll be able to figure something out that will work for both of us."

"Sounds good. You have the phone number, so I'll wait to hear from you."

He walked outside and down the street with a little smile still on his face. It would be kind of fun to send resumes around to all these different positions in town and then be a complete idiot in the interviews. Say things that put them on the spot, instead of getting put on the spot himself. What was he looking for? Well, maybe a job that he didn't really have to do much, and there wasn't much responsibility or expectation, but which paid well. A job where performance couldn't easily be measured or assessed.

He could pretend to be homeless, and ask them if, hypothetically speaking, he were hired, he could sleep in the break room at night, or if he could use the telephone for personal calls and the address for personal mail delivery. Or he could pretend that he was illiterate. He could pretend to have an accent—a horrible and obviously fake accent. He could wear clothes that were too small or too big, or were from the 70's, and then he could starch and iron them and make it look like he was really trying to look professional.

It was a cool day, but it wasn't raining. He walked back to his car and pulled out his cane. He had left it there so that he wouldn't have to take it in to the interview. It was funny how it had become a familiar appendage—it felt as though he were missing something if he didn't have the head of the cane inside his fist, if he couldn't rub his thumb against the knobby wood of the handle.

He was only a few blocks from the *Herald* building. It was strange to see it again—he hadn't been near the building since just after they had come back from their travels. He had been living with Natalie then, and writing stories only occasionally; that was just before he went to Seattle. Before that, he had interned there for a year, while Natalie finished her last year at Western.

He kicked a stone into the street in the direction of the building. He didn't want to write for the *Herald*. The ratio of menial stories to interesting stories was too large.

He was near Natalie's house, and not far from the store where she worked. A week earlier, he would have stopped in at one or both places. Even now, he was tempted to. But he forced himself not to. He made his way down toward the waterfront instead.

He walked along the sidewalk down toward the harbor, past the pulp and paper mill. The posts of an old pier stuck out of the ground, set back from the water. They were eroded at the base as though a colony of beavers had come through years ago and started work on the pier, nibbling the posts all around and then abandoning the project to the barnacles and the sea. He could see the marina in the distance; the boat masts were congregated there like a floating orchard.

They were building a new fancy hotel down on the water. Just what the world needs—another ritzy hotel to help with the most pressing problems of the day. How did he slip into this pessimism again? Blame it on the rain—again.

He decided not to walk all the way around to the Maritime Park—it was misty out over the water and the telescope wouldn't be much help through that, anyway. He walked over to the education center near the marina.

The pond in the middle of the room was home to a variety of species of marine life, all housed in a shallow pool so that they couldn't hide. Maybe rockfish couldn't remember anything from more than 30 seconds ago, either, like goldfish. Maybe they think that this is all there is to life. Or maybe there was something built in, something deeper than experience, that calls out to them, that they feel in their guts, so that even a rockfish that had been hatched in captivity would know deep down that he's meant for something bigger.

He had that feeling sometimes. Quite often, lately. His life felt like an indoor pool, and he was just floating there. Every so often, he could swim from one side to the other, but he didn't really go anywhere. Maybe if he could just think hard enough, long enough, he could remember something from before he was put in this shallow pool. There was something out there, an ocean that he was meant to be in. He just had no idea where it was, or how to avoid the sharks.

He was late to the coffeehouse and he sat on the fringes with a cup of coffee. The group conversation seemed not to have caught on tonight and people were clustered in pairs. The conversations were mundane, about coffee drinks and work. Rob thumbed through an old magazine until his coffee was half gone. He stood up abruptly, stiffly.

"Next time I get a comfy chair." He slid the wooden chair under the table behind him. "I'm going to head out. See you guys later."

Natalie glanced up from a conversation she was having with Dara, so he waved at her as he walked away.

There was a mumbled goodbye from everyone. These nights were a little like the evenings he'd had with Dave and Tad and Cindy, except the discussions weren't about whose beer was thicker or darker or the worst. And they didn't end up getting more and more drunk as the debates went on.

Natalie caught his arm as he stepped through the front door.

"Hey Rob! I haven't heard from you for a while!"

"Oh, hey Nat. Yeah, I know. There's been a bunch of stuff happening. I've been looking for part-time work; something to keep me busy."

"Really? What are you going to do? Did you go back to the *Herald*?"

"No, it's not really much of a draw for me. I'm not really sure what I want to do. All I know is I want to do something. The most promising option right now is to work at Copies On Demand."

"What, just down the street here, doing photocopies?"

"Yeah. And taking orders. That sort of thing."

She looked skeptical. "What about writing?"

"Well, if I do this, it'll only be part-time, and I'll still have quite a bit of time to do my own thing. For some reason, writing doesn't really interest me the way that it used to."

"Why's that?"

"I don't know. I guess I'm not that interested in writing about whatever little stories they assign me. I want to write about things I want to write about, and they don't really give much of a selection to people like me. The choice they give me is to take it or leave it."

"So it's not really the writing then, it's the stories, the newspaper."

"Yeah, I guess, but it's really kind of the same thing. I can't write stories for your store, can I?"

"No, I guess not, but you could write them for magazines or something, couldn't you?"

"Maybe. I guess I could look into that."

"Or you could write them just for yourself."

"Yeah, I guess."

"Well, seriously, if you enjoy writing, you should write. Just for its own sake. I don't know—like my painting, I guess. I do it because I like it. I pour myself into it. If you found a topic you were interested enough in, you could write it out. I was thinking that you could probably write something about culture or advertising or the media quite easily—you say some great stuff in here." She motioned backwards into the coffeehouse with her thumb.

"Yeah, but you show it to people, don't you? Do you sell them? You don't just paint them and put them in storage, do you?"

"Sometimes." She laughed. "If they don't turn out well. But I never really start with the idea of showing them to people. Not that I don't think about it, but that's not the reason I do it. I do show people the ones that come out well. I'll have to take you through and show you some of them."

"I think so."

It was a good walk home. Natalie had come after him and touched his shoulder.

Maybe she had a point. Maybe he should just do some writing, without worrying about whether anybody would buy it. She was right about one thing—the thought of writing still appealed to him when he changed the terms. He could write whatever he wanted and not have to worry about an editor.

He would need to find a way to get the writing distributed, though. To write something and then pack it away, never showing it to anyone didn't seem right. Personal journals and diaries had their place, but writing was meant for communication. Maybe he would try sending something out to magazines.

Or, maybe he could publish them himself. He could start up his own little media company, publishing bits and pieces of stories and ideas and designs, and then distributing them across town. Or, better yet, an anti-media company. How ironic.

Laryn kragt Bakker

Ant raven liver

She and Dorrie had a game that they played during the day once in a while, when there were enough people browsing through the store. It was based on a kids' game that somebody had donated—it had tiles picturing a variety of different heads, torsos and legs. The idea was to mix and match them and create bizarre hybrids of people and animals, like Egyptian gods or cross-breeding experiments gone horribly wrong. They had taken the idea and transferred it into real life—they would have huddled discussions and see just how hideous an outfit, or how ugly a person they could make by mixing and matching various components from customers who were wandering the store.

Natalie was leaning on the counter and Dorrie was sitting in a chair beside her.

"Take his nose," she said, nodding discreetly toward a short man with a beak of a nose, "that guy's ears...her hair."

Dorrie's eyes twinkled and she sat there, shaking with silent laughter. "We're awful," she whispered, "and we're going to get in trouble one day, but it's so fun."

Natalie had the cash register and Dorrie was on a break for a moment. Tyler was out there, alternating between cleaning up after people and sorting books upstairs. It was so much help to have another body there during the busy times. He'd been coming in two or three times a week, usually after classes. It was too bad that they couldn't schedule the busy days, or accurately predict when the people would be there.

He was still helpful to have when there weren't many customers—he seemed to have a knack for organization, and he didn't seem to tire of it as quickly as her. Some days, when she needed a break from the drudgery of organizing, it seemed that her paints were calling to her from the back room. Once she had gone back there and looked at the painting she was working on and had been tempted to start working on it, but she knew she'd lose all track of time.

So she contented herself with thinking about the painting during the slow times, jotting thoughts or ideas if they came, imagining directions to take a piece in her brain. It wasn't quite the same as actually exploring the options with paint, but it was helpful. And so the next time she sat down to paint, she'd pull out all these scraps of paper and reread them to try and attempt the difficult process of recapturing the thought that she'd had.

"I should really get up and start doing something," Dorrie said.

"I disagree," Natalie said.

"You're right."

So they remained. Natalie rang somebody out, and leaned on the counter again.

Dorrie nudged her. "Have you talked to Rob lately?"

"Yeah...near the end of last week. Thursday after we had the coffeehouse, I talked with him for a bit. He seems to be distancing himself for some reason. Maybe I haven't shown enough interest, so he's giving up on me. He had some friends from Seattle up this weekend, but he never brought them over, or invited me over. I called him on Saturday but he couldn't talk long because they were just about to go out to eat."

"How long has he been in Bellingham now?"

"Almost three weeks."

"Not even a month, and he's giving up?"

"I don't know if he's giving up, but it feels that way lately."

"Does that bother you?"

"Well, yeah, I guess so."

"So why haven't you shown any interest, then?"

"I guess I'm not sure how I feel about him. I don't want to jump in again until I'm ready. If I ever get ready."

"And in the meantime, you want him to just keep coming around, keep calling on you?"

Someone came up to pay for a puzzle. She was glad for the delay.

"Do you know if all the pieces are in here?"

"No. But I'll tell you what—if you take that home and put it together and there's a piece missing, you can bring it back and trade it in for another puzzle."

That seemed to satisfy the lady. When she was gone from the counter, Natalie turned back to Dorrie.

"I guess it's just that I don't want to miss the window. What if he loses interest completely right when I figure out that I am interested after all?"

"You can't think that way. 'What if's' can kill a person. Just live. Don't jump into anything because you're scared it's going to get away. You'll get your arms pulled off if you grab a moving train. But don't be unfair to him, either. Don't drag him along, hinting at things to keep him on the hook, when you're miles away from what he's after."

Natalie sighed.

"Can't you just talk to him about it? Let him know where you are right now, and find out where he is. Deepen your friendship again before anything." If people lived by Dorrie's advice, everyone would be completely transparent. It would be wonderful.

"That's easy to say, but..."

"I know. I'm just flapping my gums again. You know I do that. You'll figure it out for yourself."

It was nearing five o'clock when Rob walked through the door. Natalie saw him and Dorrie bump in the entrance, and politely say a few words to each other. When Rob was walking toward Natalie, Dorrie gave her a quick wink and a wave from behind him and walked out the door.

"I made it," he said with a smile, checking his watch. "Do I have time to pick out a few shirts?"

"I'm fine, thanks for asking, and how are you?"

"Oh. Hi, how are you? I'm fine. Sorry."

"You've been keeping over on your side of the hill lately. What's happening over there that's so interesting?"

"Oh, little things to keep a guy busy. This last weekend, I had some friends from Seattle come up and we hung out."

"That's right—you mentioned that on Saturday night. You should have brought them over," she said.

"Well, I was thinking about it, and I almost did, but they were just here for a day, and Cindy," he paused for a fraction of a second before continuing, "had never been here before, so I thought I'd show them around. Dave and Tad have both been here before, but not for a long time."

"Cindy?"

"Yeah, she's one of my friends from Seattle. And Dave and Tad, too." He glanced at the shelf beside them and reached over, moving a salt and pepper shaker slightly.

"Hey, I got a job—yesterday was my first day."

"At that copying place?"

"Yep. Yesterday they took me on a walk-through of my position. It should be pretty funny for a while. I don't think I'll be there too long, but it's okay for now. I don't think the Assistant Manager likes me too much."

"Oh? Why's that?"

"I think he thinks I'm a slacker. Actually, that's why I need to get a few more shirts. I only have one button-up shirt, and apparently I'm supposed to wear them every day. Collars and buttons." He held up a shirt with a Hawaiian print on it. "This looks pretty good."

Natalie locked the front door and turned the sign over while he sorted through the shirts. As she walked back toward the men's clothing, she heard someone coming down the stairs and remembered Tyler. He came around the corner with his head down, reading the back cover of a book he was holding.

"Tyler! I forgot about you."

"Thanks," he said. "It's nice to know I'm appreciated."

"Aw." She made a kiss in his direction. "Are you the last one up there?"

"Yeah."

Rob was walking up to her with a number of brightly colored shirts slung over his arm. "Can I still get these?" he asked.

"Of course." She motioned toward him with her hand. "Tyler, this is Rob. Rob this is Tyler. He volunteers here a few times a week."

They shook hands, and Rob cocked his head to see the front cover of the book. *Moving from Print to the World Wide Web.*

"You do internet design?" Rob asked.

"Some. On the side. I'm studying computer science right now, but I develop some stuff on my own. I'm trying to get a portfolio together."

"I might have something you could help me with, if you're interested."

"I'm willing to talk about it."

"Well, that's about all I can ask, right? Here's my number." He pulled a receipt from his wallet and tore the bottom off. He flattened it out on the front counter, balancing his shirts on his arm as he jotted it down.

"What do you need to put on the internet?" Natalie asked, but Rob seemed not to hear.

"Give me a call sometime—it won't pay a lot, but it should be interesting. And it'll help with your portfolio."

Tyler shrugged. "All right."

Natalie followed him and thanked him at the door. She locked it behind him again. "What do you want his help with?"

"It wouldn't be a surprise if I told you now, would it?"

"No. But that's okay."

"Nope. I'm going to see if it works out first." He held up his shirts. "And now for these."

She rang him up for the shirts and counted out his change from a ten dollar bill. "Are they really going to let you wear those?"

"Let me? I'm just going to wear them."

He was still as pig-headed as she remembered and that carried a sort of fondness with it. She folded the shirts up, tossing the hangers into a cardboard box by her feet.

"Hey Rob, do you want to see some of my paintings?"

Why did it sound so abrupt when she said it out loud? She stood there with her arms crossed, trying to look casual.

"Yeah, of course."

She led him to the back entrance. "I've only got a little of it back here and they're not even all finished, but if you want to, we can walk down to the Casa Grande and look at what's on the walls there. Unless you saw that the other day."

"You've got stuff up there? No, I don't remember seeing it. All I remember is hearing you up at the counter, and looking up, and there you were."

"Okay, I'm not going to say too much about any of them, because that's too easy. You've got to look at them and process them before you get any direction from me. In fact, I'm not going to explain them at all. I'll just tell you the titles."

"You're making me worried."

"Why?"

"I don't know. Are they bizarre? You never used to have so many rules when I saw your work. You won't be offended if I don't understand them, will you?"

"Not as long as you try to. Sometimes people look at them and say 'What does it mean?' before they've even thought about it. That's not what it's about." She leaned a few canvases away from the wall and peeked at them to remind herself which ones were there.

"This one's called *Babel: aftershock*," she said, turning around the one with the two heads connected by pipes and bridges and telephone cords.

"I like the colors." His eyes were darting around as he followed the connections from head to head and back.

"Are they trying to build these things on themselves that wasn't meant to be there? Is it about genetic engineering?"

"I'm not going to say anything about them except the titles." It seemed appropriate that he didn't understand the point she had been trying to make on this one—communication never seemed to come through perfectly.

"Well, I will say that this one is based on something we talked about at Philosophy Night. I do that sometimes—either I'm already painting something that I bring up there, or I start painting something based on what we talk about."

"Communication," Rob said, and she gave a non-committal shrug.

"Here's another. *The past bleeds into the future.* This one's not really complete. I'm not sure it ever will be." She held up the one with the person who was sitting in the box, looking over her shoulder.

"Wow. That's different." He paused. "She's living in the past. It's like, when you're plowing, you've got to keep focussed on what's ahead of you. If you keep looking back, and then ahead, and then back, you get screwed up, and your plow lines are all crooked." He kept looking at it while she pulled another painting from behind an old desk. "Or, is something chasing her? Why does she look so scared? And why doesn't she have a mouth?"

It was like a strip show, unveiling these paintings before Rob. Or something more intimate. To hang a collection of pictures on a wall and have complete strangers come in and look at them was hard enough; to have a friend come into your private space and look at these parts of you one by one was something far more frightening. She was thankful that she had made the rule about giving no explanations.

There were only a few more paintings in the studio. The top one was a picture of a tree, or a woman, the face almost hidden in a tangle of branches that were raised like arms. The focus was on the base of the tree, the beginnings of roots that were visible above the soil. She turned the canvas toward him.

"*Self-portrait, rooted in earth.*"

He looked at the painting without saying anything and she began to wonder what he was thinking. He probably didn't like her paintings. They were stylized but not nearly as abstract as what she was doing before they traveled, which he had liked.

"You feel stuck somewhere? I don't know. I like the texture of the bark, but you're not really that gnarled."

"I think I am, in a lot of ways."

Rob was holding the painting up, rotating it so the light hit it differently. "The lighting's not too great in here, is it?"

"Not great. Not great at all." She turned the switch on the lamp beside the easel. "That's a little better."

"I like how you've woven your body into the trunk of the tree," Rob said, still examining. "At first glance it looks like a tree with a head, but the more you look at it, the more it seems like an entire body that's been transmogrified into a tree. Once you see the legs, the suggestion of breasts, you can't miss them. It's like you're right underneath the bark, like you have a rough shell over your skin."

She took the painting from him and turned it against the wall.

"Is it about hiding things from other people? Keeping our true selves hidden?"

"No," she said. "It's about people being part of the physical world, not something separate from it."

"Oh. That makes sense, too. Hey, what happened to no explanations?"

"Oops."

She turned around the final canvas.

"This is the last one I've got in here."

"Huh. What's this one called?"

"*The Christ at the ninth hour.*"

The painting had a dark palette and a lot of black around the edges. The central figure was viewed from above. He was lit up as though by fire from below him, though no fire was visible. She had used all the stereotypical symbols for a devil: horns on the head, reddish skin and cloven hoofs. His bearded face was twisted in agony as he looked up at the viewer. His arms were nailed to a weathered piece of driftwood that had been fashioned into a cross, and his shoulders were covered in cuts which oozed dark blood. Shadowy figures around the cross faded to black.

"It looks like a demon on a cross."

"You got it."

"I thought it was Jesus."

"Exactly."

"Jesus is a demon?"

"Or he looked like one at the time."

"I don't know. That's over my head." He looked at the stack of paintings that they had already seen. "I think it's cool, but I don't really get it."

"Okay, I guess I've as much as said it already anyway. It's the idea that Jesus was, you know, kind of a sin eater."

"Oh." He was looking around, as though he needed to look at something, anything except the painting she was still holding.

She set it face down against the wall. Damn. That was why there should have been no explanations. Nobody liked that picture. Nobody but her, and her only sometimes.

"Well, do you want to head over to the Casa Grande and look at a few more paintings, or have you had enough?"

"That would be great."

"It's just a few blocks, so we might as well walk."

"I don't think they check the meters after five, so I'm okay."

She pulled the back door shut behind them and turned the key.

"So, tell me more about your weekend! You had friends up from Seattle."

"Oh, yeah. We toured Bellingham during the day and sang karaoke at night. They just stayed one night."

"Karaoke! I wish I could have been there."

"You're better off not having seen it." He shook his head. "We're stupid."

"If they come up again, you'll have to let me know."

"Sure."

"Did they all fit in your apartment?"

"Yeah. That was funny. We all slept on the floor because we couldn't agree on who should get the futon. In the middle of the night I woke up and was going to crawl into the bed, but Dave was already in there, snoring away. They're pretty much the group I hung around with most of the last year, so it was a bit of a sad goodbye when I came up here."

"It's not so far away."

"No, but it was far enough that you and I never made the trip."

She didn't say anything. The fact that they hadn't made the trip was for another reason, not the distance. Not the physical distance.

They walked, both looking ahead. After they had walked over eight sidewalk squares, Rob spoke again.

"Nat, how have you changed the most since we were together?"

"Oh, man. That's a big question. A lot of things have changed."

"Like what? I was thinking about this for me, and in some ways it's like, yeah, tons of things have changed—so why am I in the same spot?"

"Which spot?"

"Maybe part of it is just coming back to town, but it kind of feels like I've been in a holding pattern for the last few years."

"In what way?"

"A lot of them. Wanting to come up with a way to do something important. Being disgusted with a lot about our culture. Having you on my mind."

She quickened her pace to make it across the street before the light changed, and to give herself time to think. She didn't know if she was ready for this conversation.

"Plus que change, plus que c'est la meme chose," she said when he caught up on the other side.

"I know," he said. "Do you think anything could ever work out between us again?"

She forced herself to look at him. He looked so sincere.

"You don't have to answer that," he said.

"No, it's just...I have changed a lot. I'm sure you have, too."

"I know. That's why I was asking. How have you changed?"

She was cornered, now. "I guess the biggest thing is I have a lot more questions than I used to."

"Wasn't that the official reason that we ended?"

"Yeah, I guess so."

He cracked his lips, but no words came out.

She didn't have that problem anymore. She felt like she was starting to burst—things had been dammed up inside her for so long that she couldn't just leak out a few sentences and patch it up again.

"I am intrigued by Jesus. It's like he's built into me. Everything else has a question mark. And I don't know if that's just because of the way I was raised. I don't think so. And there's a lot of stuff that I grew up believing that I don't believe anymore, but there's some stuff that I am finding out I do believe, in a different way. And some of the stuff I don't believe still seems to be inside me sometimes."

He was still watching her and not saying anything.

"I guess what I'm saying is that Jesus is one of the few things in the world that feels true, that makes sense."

She glanced over at him again.

"I'm sorry," she said.

"No! It's good," he said. "I like to know, to hear."

"I don't think God's some old man in the sky waiting for a chance to get pissed off, or sitting up there oblivious to us. I think he's working around us, in us, through us. We've just got to know it and find him."

"I can kind of respect that if you have come up with a good answer to the eternal question: What about all the shit?"

"Not really. I don't think God does it. I think he's sometimes active and sometimes, for a variety of reasons, he doesn't interfere."

"So he gets credit for the good stuff and he gets a pass for the bad stuff?"

"Kind of. It really makes me search for good in everything, you know? If God did this, what is he trying to accomplish by it?"

"And if he didn't?"

"How's he going to use it? How's he going to heal it?"

"Natalie's got FAITH," he said in a voice that was dangerously close to his mock-Southern preacher accent.

"Don't start the jokes again. And I don't know that it's any more faith than anyone else has. What are the chances that something's going to happen just randomly, exactly the way that it happened, out of all those possibilities? Probably one in a billion. One in a gazillion. I don't know. But things keep happening, exactly like they happen. Do you believe everything is random? That takes faith, too."

They were at the restaurant already. Natalie stopped talking and stood in front of the door, but Rob didn't say anything. She opened the door and ushered Rob in, taking him around the side to where the paintings were.

"Here they are—take a look, but I'm not going to explain anything. I mean it this time."

"Okay," he said.

She wandered to the side and stared up at the pictures on the wall. It would be easier not to be right next to him as he looked at them. She could watch him from a distance and the space between them was like a buffer zone.

She had a series of three pictures here in front of her—the "suspension" series. They were some of her favorites in the show. The first one, *I saw the light*, was of a figure, floating in the middle of the canvas with bright lights on every edge, illuminating her from all sides. Her arms and legs were curled in a fetal position, as though she were trying to block the light out. Behind the shadows cast by her arms, her eyes were visible, pinched shut in a grimace.

The place where I will stand was next in the series. A rock cliff emerged from the left side of the canvas and dropped straight down. The background was a gentle gradient of blue sky. Halfway between the edge of the cliff and the far side of the canvas, a naked woman stood with her feet firmly planted in the air, her arms crossed and legs shoulder-width apart. Her head was turned three-quarter view toward the left side of the canvas, and she was staring at the cliff.

The third in the trilogy was called *Gravity*. She had painted it from a random idea after she had done the two other pieces. She had consciously tried to make it unconscious by allowing her mind to come up with a random image. A girl was floating upwards, like a helium balloon, with a string tied to her ankle. A small boy who was standing on the ground clutched it in one hand. He was indifferent to the girl—he was licking an ice cream cone. The girl was limp but floating upwards into a sky of soft clouds, lit from behind by the sun. Natalie liked to hear what people read into it, because there was no intentional idea behind it.

Rob had walked through pretty quickly, and was nearing the last painting. She walked over and watched his eyes from the side. *Prayers of the saints*. A pious looking man in a black suit coat was in the foreground, a gentle smile on his face and a soft light illuminating him. His hands were folded, his eyes closed, and a mansion materialized in the thoughts above his head. It wasn't until a closer look that you noticed the ghosts that haunted the shadows around him—the twisted bodies, the starving children, distended bellies, the smoke, the death and pain.

Rob turned and saw her.

"Do you know what you remind me of?" he asked.

"What?"

"You're like the flip side of those televangelists, who go on TV railing against adultery, and then wind up caught in bed with a whore the next week. You're the opposite. Ever since I first met you, you were preaching against Christianity, like this, but somehow you ended up in bed with Jesus."

He lifted a hand almost immediately. "I'm sorry. That didn't come out in words like it seemed in my thoughts. I just meant, well, I don't know what I meant anymore."

She didn't say anything.

"Shit." He scratched his chin. "I like the paintings," he offered.

"Don't worry about it."

"Natalie—"

"I said don't worry about it. It's okay. Really."

They walked back to the store underneath clouds that felt heavy with the potential for rain. It was cool out and she hugged her thin jacket a little tighter.

"Do you want a ride home?" Rob asked. "I can put your bike in the trunk—it'll hang out a bit, but it'll be okay."

"Oh." She thought for a second. It was probably more trouble than it was worth. "No, I'll be fine. Thanks, though."

He stood beside her while she unlocked her bike.

"I was wondering if you feel like doing something tonight. I'd like to show you a different kind of art that I've been studying."

"Really? I didn't realize you did art now—what have you been up to?"

"I can't explain it right now," Rob said with a half-smile, "but I'll take you there tonight."

"Where are we going?"

"Just wait. I don't want to spoil the surprise."

It was already completely dark except for headlights, lampposts and neon signs. Tinker and Shawn had been full of questions when they learned that she and Rob were going somewhere this late on a weekday night, but Natalie kept her lips sealed. She had enough questions of her own. She wondered what he was being so secretive about. She could see Tink peeping from behind the curtain in her room as she sat down and pulled the car door shut.

"Buckle up," Rob said.

"Okay, but it better not be something dumb. Remember, I should be in bed by now."

"Yeah, yeah. You've turned into an old lady, you know?"

"I know."

Rob turned toward the waterfront.

"Let me guess: we're going to see the marina by night," she said.

"Nope. This is going to be a little more interactive than just looking at a nice picture. But no more questions. I'm not going to give it away."

He pulled into the parking lot at the harbor and drove around as he examined it. "Let's see, let's see. This should work." He pulled into the spot that was furthest from the streetlight.

"Are you parking in the shadows for a reason?" Interactive, indeed. That was a good line. Despite some misgivings, she decided she would kiss him back.

"Well, the shadows, and those shrubs. The car won't be as conspicuous to police cars that are driving by."

"Police cars? Rob, why am I getting nervous?"

He grinned and got out of the car without saying anything. He popped the trunk and reached inside, pulling out a few small items, which he cradled in one arm. He opened her door and looked in to where she was still sitting. "Come on," he whispered.

She got out of the car slowly, and the air felt cold on her skin. She tried to identify what Rob was holding, but he had it covered up with a sweatshirt.

"Are we going to be long? I'm getting a little cold."

"Long enough that a sweatshirt would be a good idea."

She reached back in the car for the sweatshirt he had given to her and pulled it on.

"Put the hood up so your face is harder to see," he said.

"What are we doing, Rob?"

"Remember, in art there is no asking questions." He pulled her hood on further with his free hand. "Okay. Are you ready?"

"I don't know. You tell me."

"You are. Here we go." He opened the bundle and pulled out something cylindrical and cold. "This is yours."

She took it, thinking it was a bomb for a moment. Spray paint. Rob was pulling a balaclava over his head.

"Let's go!"

She was scared. A car drove by and Rob crouched near the shrubs. He motioned with his arm urgently, like a soldier waving troops through an opening on the battlefield, and started to run across the road. He looked like Quasimodo, favoring his left leg in a lurching gallop, heading over the empty tracks toward the hulking bodies of unmoving trains. She felt helpless—she couldn't very well stand here waiting for him. Maybe she could hide under the shrubs. Oh, what the hell. She ran across the road.

Rob was waiting for her behind the first train. "Okay," he whispered, "choose the canvas."

"I don't think I can do this," she whispered back.

"You can."

A car passed by on the road and her muscles stiffened. She peeked around the side of the train and watched the headlights move away from them.

"Here, let's go further back."

She followed him because she had a mental picture of herself getting caught out there alone. Explain that one, ma'am. A paint can in her hand, a dark, hooded sweatshirt on, crouching in the shadows by the trains. Nothing suspicious?

Behind the second row of trains was a grassy hill that sloped up, peaking in a row of houses along the top. Lights were on in a handful of them.

"Rob!" She whispered, motioning to the houses in a convulsive stab with her thumb.

He moved back toward her. "It's okay—just make sure to keep whispering. If they've got their lights on, it means they can't see us. Same as the road. There's no way the cars on the road can see way back here, even with their headlights. They can see the road, and that's about all."

He turned to the train car beside them. "Good choice," he said.

"I didn't choose it!"

It was a huge mass of darkness in front of them, blacker than the sky. She touched it. It was rough, cold.

"Let's go." Rob uncapped his can of paint and started shaking it. The sound of the mixing ball rattling sounded like someone was banging on pots.

"Shhh!"

"I guess we should have done that back in the car, huh?" He smiled; his teeth showed through the mouth of his balaclava faintly in the dark, the only features she could make out.

"I don't know about this," she said, looking back at the houses on the hill.

"Here." He gave her the can he had just shaken and took the one she held to mix it. "You've got the lighter color, so I'll come behind and add some shadows or outlines or something."

"What colors are they?" she asked, knowing immediately it was the wrong question; instead of objecting, now she was already collaborating.

"You've got yellow, and this one is a dark green," he said, pulling the cap off. "I've got a few others if you want to get creative. Let's do it this way: you start something over here, and I'll start something over there. Then we switch and I'll add the dark to yours, and you can add the light to mine."

She didn't say anything. He was already moving down to the other end of the train car. She stood there staring at the side of the train for a moment, and it did feel like she was standing in front of an empty canvas, not knowing what to paint. That surprised her.

Rob was already started, his paint can hissing in the darkness.

"Boy, this is tough to see. I should have kept the yellow," he muttered.

She held the can with the tip under her index finger to get a feel for it. She tried to think of it as an airbrush—though she'd never used one of them before, either. It was heavy, compared to a paintbrush. She couldn't believe she was standing here, contemplating this.

"Are you just about done?"

"No! I haven't started!"

"What? Hurry up! We don't want to be here any longer than we have to!"

"Come on!" Rob was beside her now. "My side's all ready for you to highlight it."

"Give me a second to think. And don't look over my shoulder like that. I'll do it— alright? Just go away."

"Okay, I'll stand away, but I'm coming back in two minutes."

Two minutes to make art. Let's see: yellow and green. A dandelion, or sunflowers. She lifted the can and started to draw a petal. The yellow was visible not as yellow, but just as a dim stroke on the dark. There was no time to worry on details with a paint can—you had to move quick or you put too much paint in the same spot. That last one was dripping already. She started to swipe with the can, spraying the sunflower's rays in a cirle.

In the morning, this would probably look awful, but at the moment, it was amazing to see a sunflower appearing in the darkness. Rob was back at his end, doing touch-up work.

She had the ring of petals drawn. It wasn't bad for a first try. She brought the can up to touch up one of the petals.

"Pssst!"

She jerked her head to the right and was blinded by a flash of light. She was frozen there, her heart racing, as though she were gunning an engine in neutral. She couldn't see him, but she could hear Rob trying to keep his laughter in.

"You are evil!" She was shaking. "And I'm done. I can't do this anymore. Let's go."

"Wait a second, we're not finished!"

"I am."

She heard something rustling in the grass, partway down the hill.

"Did you hear that?" Rob asked, turning his head.

"Let's go," she whispered, and she started walking, or half-running, not looking to see if Rob was behind her. She jumped the connection between the train cars and was in between trains again. It felt good to have something between her and the road on the one side, and between her and the houses on the other.

She turned to see where he was. A light flashed from the other side of the train, escaping above and below it, silhouetting it. That idiot! Was he still back there, taking pictures? Someone was sure to see that from the houses and call the cops. She crouched close to the body of a train, breathing quickly. Even being this far from the scene of the crime felt better. She set the paint can down beside her and breathed a little easier.

Another flash. She saw a shadow dart through where she had just been and move toward her. The gravel crunched under his feet; he was walking quickly. The opportunity was too good to pass up. She jumped up at him with her fingers out like claws and grabbed his arm, hissing. He tensed up and wheeled toward her, bringing his other hand around like he was preparing for a fight.

"Rob!" She was startled, but laughed.

"Wow." He pulled his face mask off.

A number of things struck Natalie as odd all at once. Firstly, they were only about fifty feet from the graffiti, but they had stopped running. Secondly, there was a lot of adrenaline running in her bloodstream. She could see why people got addicted to the rush and the excitement.

The third thing was that she and Rob were standing very close. After she had loosened her grip on Rob's arm, and after he had put down his fist, they were in very close proximity to each other.

She could barely make out Rob's face: a light smudge in the darkness. He spoke, and she couldn't even see his mouth move. "That was fun! I've never done that before." He gave her a rough hug.

In a way, it felt like a continuation of the night so far—something was happening, but she wasn't sure exactly where it would go, or how she felt about it. She leaned forward and her mouth found his nose, then slid awkwardly down his face. It wasn't a long kiss, or even a big one, but it was a surprise to her that she had done it.

It did feel natural, or maybe just distantly familiar. Rob relaxed his grip around her and raised his hands to hold her face. She heard something moving in the grass on the other side of the train again, shuffling or thrashing.

She broke away from Rob, jumpy and nervous again, looking all around even though she couldn't see a thing. The noise had stopped.

"It was nothing," Rob said, his hands having dropped again and now lightly holding her elbows.

"I don't know," she whispered. "Let's go."

She peered around the train and watched a set of taillights disappear down the road. "We should go one at a time, so that we're not as conspicuous. You go first, so you can start the car."

He laughed out loud. "The get-away car! You're really worried, aren't you?"

"Shhh!" She was still sure there was something in the grass, or nearer at this point, and she couldn't see anything in the dark. "Are you going, or should I?"

"Okay already."

He was gone from beside her. She could see him jogging toward the road, a dark figure against the light of the streetlamp. He was about twenty feet from the road when he threw himself on the ground. A car was coming from the left.

It was moving slowly, and as it came under the glow of the streetlight, she could make out the lights on top. Oh, crap. Here were the police. Her heart quickened its pace once again. At least the lights weren't flashing.

The car drove by the parking lot, and turned into the next entrance. It backed out again and made its way back in the direction it had come from until it was out of sight. Rob stayed down while she imagined something sneaking up behind her in the dark. Maybe it was already there, sniffing her, preparing to attack.

She was crouched down, leaning with most of her weight on her arm, which was resting on one of her legs, and as she rose to start toward the car, she realized that she could not feel her leg. She stumbled along in the dark, unable to see or feel the ground, worried that she would sprain her ankle. She saw Rob get up and sprint across the road and behind the bushes to where the car was.

Her leg began to throb as the blood began to flow again, and she had to stop. She rolled onto her back and started massaging her leg. Her foot felt like it was burning up or being electrocuted. She set her leg down again and just lay there, breathing and tapping her foot on the ground every few seconds. With the streetlight positioned just right, she could see her breath in the air. If she blocked out the light from the streetlights, she could see the clouds passing in front of the stars.

She could have stayed there for a while longer. It was comfortable. But she heard a car's horn and saw lights projected out toward the trains. She rolled over, holding her head up. Rob's car was sitting in the entrance to the parking lot with its lights on high beam.

She took a look at the street to make sure no cars were in sight and made a rush for the road. Thanks, Rob. Now she was running with spotlights on her and she still couldn't see anything because they were aimed directly into her eyes.

She jumped into the passenger seat and slammed the door.

They looked at each other and Rob laughed as she let out an enormous breath. It felt good to pull out of the parking lot, safely in the car.

"I forgot my mask over there somewhere."

"I left my paint."

They drove to the coffeehouse and sat with a cup of tea, the excitement fading into memory as they joked about it. It felt good. She was surprised that they weren't the only people there—it was almost midnight on a Tuesday. But they must get customers or they wouldn't stay open this late. They never used to.

Natalie's pull-over sweatshirt had a green splotch on it and the working theory was that Rob had shot her with his paint can when she surprised him.

"You should have seen your face when I took your picture," he laughed. "I thought you were going to have a heart attack!"

"I probably did—you gave me no warning."

"You can't warn somebody before you surprise them. I really hope that picture turns out."

"I wish I had a picture of you when I jumped you—except you probably would have punched me."

"No," he said. "Well, maybe."

They both fell silent. She was thinking about that kiss. Rob was drinking his chai. The whole night seemed so surreal, looking back on it.

"What's on your mind?" he asked, setting his mug down.

"I'm still thinking about tonight—it was not something I expected to do tonight. What are you going to do with those pictures you were taking anyway?"

"Probably blackmail you some day." He pulled his camera from his pocket and opened the lens cover, pointing it at her.

"Don't," she said, giving him what was meant to be the look of death.

The flash went and she fought back a smile. "Put that—" the flash went off again. "Rob!" People were starting to look.

Flash. She was starting to get flustered. She put her hand out and partially blocked another flash. His camera started to hum and he set it down on the table.

"There. I just had to finish the roll."

She looked into the bottom of her cup for the third time to verify again that it was still empty.

"Do you want another one?" Rob asked.

"Oh no. Just a bad habit." She pushed the cup away from her. "In my subconscious, I'm always thinking, 'Hey, maybe there's just a little more in the bottom of this thing.'"

"And sometimes there is."

"Sometimes."

She wanted to say something to him—she wasn't even sure what—something about them, about the questions in her mind, the possibilities or the fear. Maybe there's still a little more in the bottom of this thing.

"So is graffiti art?" Rob asked.

"Not usually. I guess it could be, in some cases. But when somebody marks an anarchy sign on a garage door, it doesn't seem to me to be artistic. It seems more base than that, you know? Like marking territory, or some animal warning."

He rubbed one of his cheeks. "But it could be, don't you think? Isn't art kind of a base thing? What about the petroglyphs, or cave paintings?"

She didn't respond right away, so he continued. "I was reading an article in the library the other day, and it was an interview with this graffiti artist—if you'll let me call him that. He paints on trains, and he was talking about how he was having a national art show all the time, because his work goes from city to city, all across the country."

"That's where you got the idea for tonight, huh."

"Yeah."

Rob pointed at one of the paintings hanging on the wall beside them—an amateurish attempt at a sultry woman, scantily clad. "This is art, right?"

She responded carefully. "I would say yes. That doesn't mean it's good art, but I think bad art is still art."

"If I nailed a dirty sock to the wall, would that be art?"

"Maybe. I guess it would depend why you nailed it to the wall."

"How could you know why I nailed it to the wall?"

"You could tell me."

"Well, what if I nailed it to the wall for one reason, but told you I did it for another reason? Then you'd think it was art, but it really wouldn't be."

"I guess that's possible."

"So, what you're saying is that something might be art, but it might not be, depending on who did it. So two different people could produce exactly the same thing, and one would be art and one wouldn't."

"I don't think anyone can do things that are exactly the same, but in theory I guess that's true."

"So you can never know whether anything is art, then."

"It's not just a matter of the artist—the viewer has a role, too. If you interact with a piece, it becomes art. Maybe art isn't the physical piece of matter at all; maybe it's the connection that occurs between the artist and the piece, and between the viewer and the piece. So, you're doing art when you make something you connect with, and you're appreciating art when you connect with something you see. So you have to go through life looking for connections, finding art in everything—I mean, sometimes, I look at the ocean, or a bird, or a tree, and I feel this connection, like I'm seeing a masterpiece, and I think that it's art. I feel connected to something true, in the same way that I connect with an artist through a good sculpture."

"Then why all the special treatment for paintings, and sculptures?"

"Well, maybe they've been elevated because they've been produced specifically with those connections in mind. The artist presents something in the belief that there is a connection there, that it is worth someone's time to just look at it and think about it. It's really the responses that are critical, not the piece of art itself; the processes of creation and interaction are more important than the physical object we end up with."

"The way you're talking, art and life are almost interchangeable words."

"I know. But maybe everything is some kind of art. You have people who do visual arts, linguistic arts, performance arts, culinary arts, utilitarian arts. Maybe all of life is art, and then people have categories to keep the divisions separate from each other. It makes you really think about living creatively—consciously looking for connections in everyday life, finding things that keep on weaving together. Like our lives are one big knot of artistic potential, and the way we live them is art."

"I miss you, Natalie." He was sitting across from her, with his arms folded on the table in front of him, and staring at her, or through her. Her train of thought was derailed, and she stared back at him for a moment, then tipped her mug over and looked into the bottom of it.

"It's empty," he said with a little smile.

They didn't say much in the car. She lived just down the street and there was no time to talk about anything substantial, but there was nothing unsubstantial on her mind so she couldn't even make small talk properly. He dropped her off at her house and she stood there with the car door open, looking in.

"Thanks, Rob. That was fun." She hesitated, looked over her shoulder at the house. "Listen, about tonight...well, I guess...it scares me."

He didn't say anything, as though he expected her to keep talking.

"We'll talk later. I'm not sure yet." She ran out of words, but he was still silent. "Good night."

She swung the door shut and ran to the front door, fumbling with the key before she realized it was not locked. Rob hadn't pulled away from the curb yet, so she turned and gave a little wave before closing the door behind her.

Laryn kragt Bakker

Legalize happiness

It was good to be writing again. He had delusions of future grandeur—and he was fully aware that they were delusions. Probably. If he could find a way to get it out there, anything could happen.

Working at the copy shop had given him one idea—pragmatic and less than glamorous, but workable. The obvious starting point was to produce a sheet of writing and run a bunch of photocopies.

His first plan was to open up a few of the *Herald* newspaper boxes and insert his pages into the stack of papers by hand one morning. That plan had evolved. Now he was planning to design a page that looked exactly like the front page of the *Herald*, but with fake headlines and photographs, and affix it to the inside of the display glass on the boxes.

He just had to decide what to write about, and what pictures to put on the front. This one wouldn't even need much in the way of text—the headlines were the most important, and then a few lines of text, but there would be no complete story, since it was just a front page.

He had a handful of magazines spread out in front of him. Libraries were wonderful places. He had control of one table, his books and papers and magazines organized in an arc around him like the walls of a child's fort, so no one else tried to sit beside him. Personal space was important to him when he was doing research, though today might not qualify as that: the books and magazines all had to do with writing, but he hadn't read any of them. He had spent most of the time skimming, and then arranging them to maximize the intimidation factor of his spread, and then he sat staring out at about 45 degrees for the last hour, pen in hand but rarely moving. He had a few recent editions of the paper for inspiration.

He looked at his handwritten scrawls, attempts at headlines.

NOTHING HAPPENED TODAY
POLL SHOWS 4 OF 5 READ ONLY HEADLINES
LIFE AS WE KNOW IT TO END AT 3:30

He wasn't at his most creative. There was no sense forcing it. It was always tough to come up with anything when there was no direction. It shouldn't be hard to fill a single page with text, he just needed to get started.

He pulled the cap off of his pen with his mouth and chewed it, drawing a small series of scribbles in the corner to make sure the ink was still running. The paper had a front page article about the transient homeless population that came in summer and largely disappeared from sight in the winter.

MAYOR PRESENTS A MODEST PROPOSAL:
EAT THE HOMELESS
The mayor of Bellingham unveiled a modest proposal yesterday to help solve the issue of homelessness in the city. He outlined a solution which involves the systematic slaughter and packaging of anyone who lives in the streets. Opponents of the idea say that it lacks the brilliance of Swift's original concept, proposed in Ireland in the eighteenth century, which limited the age of potential candidates. Meat taken from an old man who has lived in the streets most of his life would undoubtedly be stringy and tough. "Obviously, we'll need to come up with a system for grading the meat," says the mayor, "and not all of the meat would be prepared for consumption—there are other options: dog food, glue factories."

He reminded himself that first drafts should not be judged too harshly. He did a quick sketch of the front page to get a sense of the number of stories and photos he would need. A few more lead-ins and a photo. He skimmed the paper again, flipping through until an article caught his eye. It was about a new theater that was opening north of town—the kind of non-story that he would have had to write about in another life.

BELLINGHAM RESIDENT COMPLAINS ABOUT LACK OF
SOMA

He crossed it out.

LOCAL RESIDENT COMPLAINS ABOUT STRENGTH OF SOMA
AVAILABLE

Laryn Kragt Bakker

"It's awful," says Bellingham resident Bridget Matthews. "I am constantly watching television, or going to the feelies, taking my prescription drugs, or hearing about things that have no bearing on my life, and yet, once in a while, I find that my real life keeps seeping in. It's, like, so annoying! Can't they make this stuff powerful enough to just knock me out completely?" Scientists developing Soma say that it is just a matter of time before it disintegrates a person's mind completely. 'We're in such an instant gratification society these days,' says Mitchell Plummer, a leading Hollywood scientist, "everyone just wants the Soma to render them comatose in two seconds flat. The truth is that it works better if it's a slower process—they need to take the time and subject themselves to the television for hours each day, or go to every new feely that we produce. Nothing good comes without a little hard work and plenty of time!'"

Good enough. If he wrote another story or two, and fleshed these out a bit, he could get this printed at work that afternoon. It would be a little tight—but he already had the layout template ready, so he just needed to do the typing and tweak it.

Last weekend, Dave had come up again, without Cindy or Tad this time. He had taken a disk with a bunch of software on it and installed it on Rob's computer. He had been excited about the idea and had taken a copy of the *Herald* to mimic, creating a template for Rob to use.

They had gone on a hike that afternoon. They drove up Alger Hill to the lower overlook, where the hang gliders took off from. Dave was funny when he went hiking, because he liked to go barefoot. This time he convinced Rob to try it as well, so they rolled up their pants and walked across the gravel of the parking lot in their sandals. Once they got to the trailhead, they strapped the sandals to Dave's daypack and started out.

"Be prepared to endure the stares and comments of 'the shod,' because they will come," he said.

It was amazing what a different experience walking in bare feet was—he usually didn't have to think much about the texture of the path, the temperature, the moisture. Feet are remarkably sensitive for being walked on all day. He loved the moss.

"Why'd you kiss Cindy last weekend?" Dave asked the question out of nowhere, on the tail end of a conversation about how well Rob's leg was doing.

"I didn't kiss her, she kissed me."

"Right. That's not what she said. What did you say to her before we left, anyway?"

"What did she say I said?"

"All I know is that the whole ride back to Seattle, I don't think she said one word. She was just sitting there in a bad mood."

"Shut up. You're making that up."

"No, not really. I talked with her on Tuesday and she said you had told her not to come up anymore."

"Well, not quite in those words. I just didn't want her to think that there was something between us, so I told her that it might be better for both of us to keep some distance between us for a while."

"This is what you said after you kissed her."

"She kissed me."

"Right. She kissed you."

He closed his notebook. His mind was not on headlines anymore. That situation probably did look bad from the outside—one of those "it's not what you think" moments. He couldn't really explain how some of the things had happened with Cindy. They just seemed to happen. He had actually been proud of finally saying something to her about it until Dave had mentioned it like it was something to be ashamed of.

And what about Natalie? What was going on there? Dave had asked him, but he honestly couldn't answer. That night with the train had been very strange. They had spent most of the evening together, walking, looking at art, painting grafitti on trains, sitting at the coffee house. It had felt like a date, one hundred percent. And there was that little matter of the kiss that his mind kept coming back to. He wondered if he should have walked her to the door that night. But that had been a week and a half ago and they hadn't communicated much in the interim, partly due to schedule conflicts and partly because he was testing her to some degree. She failed. She never called or came over.

He pulled out a package of photographs. The first shots were all pictures from moving, and a few of the group of them the night before he left. Cindy, smiling. Here was Natalie, wearing a look of terror beside the train. The picture was dark and her face was almost washed out completely by the flash. Behind her, the painting was barely visible in the shadows. She had made a sun, or a flaming star with the yellow. He was impressed. He hadn't expected her to go along with it. He flipped through the next few pictures. You couldn't even make out his artwork in the darkness, even if you knew what you were looking for—an anarchy symbol and an exclamation point. He was glad you couldn't see it. It felt clumsy, as though he had been trying to speak a new language with a working knowledge of the curses and swearwords alone.

Here she was at the end of the roll in a series of coffeehouse shots, each one with a new expression. Don't take that picture. I can't believe you took that picture. What the...! And the last one, with her hand out, fingers splayed and out of focus, an eye partly visible between her index and middle finger. There was the gap between her teeth, revealed as her mouth pulled open in a wide smile of surprise. She was beautiful because she was real, and here he sat, surrounded by a world that felt fake, wanting something real.

He shuffled the pictures back together and then tapped them on the table like playing cards to flush the edges. He looked at his calendar. It was almost the end of the month—almost Halloween, as the advertisements had informed him for the last month. The commercial media was now a sort of calendar for people, the way the leaves on trees used to be. Skulls and pumpkins meant it was October. Next came turkey and then the fat man.

He surprised himself by remembering that the proximity of Halloween meant it was even closer to Natalie's birthday. And tomorrow was the pre-Halloween costume party, which he still needed to get a costume for.

If he was going to get this typed up before work, it was going to have to be done now. He slid the stack of photos back into their envelope and put them with his notebook into his shoulder bag, leaving the books and magazines in a pile on the tabletop.

He hadn't quite finished the typesetting at home, but he had saved it on a disk anyway and brought it in to work. It usually worked out that the evenings were slow, and Randall tended to hole up in the office a few hours after Bobbi left. The first week he hadn't had much time to himself because Randall was training him when there was stuff to do and watching him when there wasn't, as though he feared that Rob might suddenly go on a rampage and destroy the place. That was the first week. This second week they had begun to let him settle in and work on projects alone, and these last few days, to be alone in the store.

So, if he had a good handle on the jobs for the evening, he had access to the computer behind the counter, and he could finish his own project. It was better than just standing around with nothing to do—though if Bobbi or Randall were around, they might suggest he do something else, like pull fallen staples out of the carpet or wash the handprints and grease from the glass door.

"There's always something to do here," Randall had said. "You just need to find out what it is."

He had created a folder for his files, camouflaging it by giving it a technical sounding name in an out-of-the-way directory and then storing his files in it. The last few days he had made a point of copying anything he had been working on onto a disk and erasing it from the computer, just to be safe. Randall had made it clear enough that he didn't like him and he didn't want to give him any dirt to bring before Bobbi, because he probably would. Rob didn't see a problem with it: if there was spare time, why not use it? It's not like he was neglecting his job. It's not like he was holing up in the office and looking at internet porn.

Actually he wasn't completely sure what Randall did in there, but two nights ago when Rob had needed to find out where the six millimeter coils were stored for a small bind, he had opened the office door, stuck his head in and asked him. And Randall had jumped high enough to knock one of his knees on the bottom of the desktop, flushing red and hitting keys in what seemed like desperation. Rob couldn't see the monitor, but he saw the light from the screen disappear from Randall's face and heard the beep which meant Ctrl-Alt -Delete: reboot.

Randall acted like Rob had violated some kind of protocol and threatened to write him up, but didn't. Feeling guilty, maybe. Tonight, though, when Randall retired to the office, Rob heard an extra little click. Whatever he was doing in there, he didn't want to be surprised again. Which worked out well, because now it took him longer to get out of the office—the sound of the lock being turned gave Rob plenty of warning. He had time to shut down what he was doing and pull up the store's e-mail, which he kept open underneath everything so he could bring it up in seconds. It was like the "boss mode" that they used to include in computer games, a fake screen that could be pulled up by a simple keystroke and made it look like you were checking your files or doing some kind of work while the game was paused and hidden in the background.

He had the whole page set up and was just tweaking it now, preparing it for print. He had forgotten about the front page photo and had come up with a solution on the spur of the moment—he went online and downloaded a shot of a fluke from some university's website. It wasn't a lancet fluke, but it was a fluke of some kind. It looked like abstract art, with these hairs out the sides and little circular blobs and stringy paint strokes on the body, and what looked like a partially developed rib-cage.

What did people mean when they said of a lucky thing, 'It was a fluke?' He plunked the graphic in the middle of the page and typed a small caption underneath it.

Scientists fear that flukes like this one may control peoples' inner workings, decision-making, that they can drive us like Cadillacs.

Finished. He just had to decide how many of these to print now, and whether to do it in color or black and white. He glanced up at the door of the office, then back at the screen. The lancet fluke had a nice fleshy colored background; it would be a shame to lose it. He sent it over to the Fiery to see how it looked on paper.

The color prints were technically more expensive, but he seemed to remember Bobbi telling him during those first few days that he should feel free to experiment a bit and get familiar with the equipment, the store's capability. He liked the ambiguity of the phrase "a bit" and decided that this project fit into it. The machine started to warm up, preparing to print.

He saved the project to his disk and erased the files from the computer, pocketing the disk. The page slid out of the side tray just as Randall began to fumble with the lock. Rob grabbed the print, glancing at it briefly before turning it upside down and sliding it into the recycle bin, underneath some other pages from previous jobs he had screwed up. He moved the file from the copier's list of recent jobs and into an archive folder, just in case.

Randall came right up to him and took a look at the display monitor of the copier. "What have you got going out here?"

"Not much. It's really slow, so I'm just familiarizing myself with the equipment again."

Randall opened the top file on the copier's list, squinting to see the tiny preview. It was a job Rob had run two hours ago, and Randall had already quality checked it by the front counter. He closed it and turned to Rob.

"What exactly have you been doing out here? It looked like you were working on that computer for a while."

So the bastard was spying on him. He nodded easily. "Yeah, Bobbi suggested that I get familiar with some of the software that you've got here."

Randall looked over at the computer, the e-mail box open on the screen. He paused for a second as though he were deciding whether he approved, then glanced at the clock.

"I think I'm going to send you home a little early today. It's so dead that it doesn't make much sense to keep us both here, especially on a Friday night."

"What time does that mean, exactly?" It was an hour and a half before he was supposed to be done his shift.

"Oh, any time now. Maybe just empty the trash and the recycling and then count down your till."

Rob didn't say anything, but gave a slight nod down his nose at Randall, his face expressionless, and walked away to begin gathering the trash. Randall stood there in his way, as though daring Rob to question his authority, and so they brushed shoulders, neither willing to move. Randall was staring at his back, he could feel it.

He was tempted to flip him off over his shoulder, but decided not to—the hostility between them was still underneath the surface; it hadn't broken through yet. Besides, he wasn't really angry, and he was just about ready to go home anyway now that his little project was almost done. He just didn't like Randall and wanted him to know it.

Randall settled back into the office, though Rob didn't hear the lock turn. He dragged a large plastic garbage can beside the 5090 and started shoving the waste from that machine in: papers which were wrinkled, or smudged, or which had been copied crookedly. When he reached the Fiery, he made sure he wasn't being too obvious and pulled up the list of files in the archive. He highlighted his and punched in a "20" and then "Print."

While it was silently spewing them out, page after page in a rhythm, he erased the file from the archive. Every so often, he'd glance up to make sure Randall was still in his kennel. This was the point that was the most dangerous, because if Randall came out now, he couldn't easily make the prints stop coming out. He went to the front counter and pulled a plastic bag from underneath it, stuffing it into the garbage bag to store his prints in. When the printer finished, he placed them, still warm, on top of the pile and continued on his cleanup route.

When he was at the cutter, he was out of view of the office, back near the break room. He pulled out his stack of prints and set the blade back. He had set these up for tabloid size paper, which wasn't exactly the size of the newspaper window, but he figured it didn't have to be exact. He jogged the paper so the edges were flush and positioned the stack roughly so that the extra white space on the one edge would be trimmed to make the margins all closer to being equal.

The blade came down from the top like a guillotine, but not straight down as he had expected the first time he had used it—it cut with a diagonal stroke, moving down and to the left. He waited for the blade to rise and then pulled the whole stack of papers off the counter and into the trash bag, slinging it over his shoulder.

The break room and office were connected by doors to the storage room, which had a garage-style loading door out back and a smaller door that Rob thought of as the "escape hatch" because he could duck out of it for a smoke now and then if he told Randall beforehand. He popped open the escape hatch now, pushing the rock on the steps between the door and the frame so it didn't lock shut on him and then carried the bag of recycling to the dumpster. It wasn't raining, but the ground was wet. He pulled out the stack of prints he had made, shuffling them back into a pile and inserted them into the plastic bag. He set them underneath the dumpster with a board from an old pallet on top as a paperweight.

Last year, Bobbi said, winds had torn the lid of the bin open and papered the neighborhood with overs from a confidential job that someone had been too lazy to shred before dumping. They had spent two days out walking with bags and picking up papers after that one, and she had an iron bar put on the top of the dumpster to hold the lid down until someone disengaged it. It was down right now—Ann from the day shift told him that only the rookies used it; after about a month they stopped.

He emptied the bag into the bin and swung the lid shut, engaging the bar to lock it in place. The last thing he needed was to have Randall find some good reason to get on him. He looked down the alley, which was dark already but for a few small lights on the backs of buildings, and wondered if he should have a smoke quick while he was still on the clock. If he was going to go home early anyway, he might as well take his smoke break before he did. Maybe the cost of the cigarette would be covered by the hourly wage.

There were only two left in the pack, and they were a little beat-up from the ride in his back pocket. This always happened once the packs were nearly empty because he'd move them from his coat pocket to his pants as they shrunk in size. He extracted the least battered one and then stuck a finger down into the pack, fishing around for the lighter. It was cool out. He wished he had thought to pull on his jacket quickly.

He bent down and pulled the top sheet off of his stack, holding it underneath the small light above the door. It looked good. Not bad for a first attempt, anyway. He started to skim the stories and had already found three typos when Randall stuck his head out the escape hatch.

"There you are. What's taking so long? We've got a customer out here."

"Oh, shit. Sorry. I was dumping the recycling and thought I'd take a quick drag while I was out here." He flicked his filter and the remaining half of the cigarette to the pavement and stepped on it, crumpling the paper in his hands.

Idiot. First he sends me home and then he gets mad at me for leaving.

"You've got to let me know before you do something like that," Randall said, as though Rob's negligence had nearly destroyed the store. "What have you got there?"

Rob had flipped down the iron bar and let the ball of paper drop into the bin. "Oh, that?" he asked. "Some piece of trash from earlier in the day, I think. The Doc 40 was leaving a stripe across the page," he adlibbed, glad that he had skimmed the daily log of machine problems.

He popped a piece of gum in his mouth as he walked out into the work area. An old man was beside one of the black and white copiers, fumbling with an envelope of old photos.

"Did you need a hand there?"

He looked up from his hands with an expression of surprise and then held the package out to Rob, who accepted it in reflex.

"I need to make copies of these," he said, turning to the copier.

"Did you want these copied on a black and white copier, or on a color copier?" Rob asked.

"They're all black and white," he snapped, glaring at Rob.

Rob clenched his jaw. One of these types.

"You can do them on the black and white machine, or you can use the color machine in black and white mode. It's more expensive, but the pictures come out better."

"How much better?"

"Quite a bit."

"How much are they?"

"Seventy four cents."

"For each one?"

Rob nodded once, slowly and deliberately.

"How much is this one?" the man asked, jabbing a crooked finger toward the black and white copier.

"Six cents."

"Do it on this one," he said, scratching the back of his left hand. "Let's do it on this one."

Rob popped the top of the copier up and positioned two of the pictures face down on the glass. "Okay, when you put them down, put them within this area," he said, indicating the markings on the sides.

The man was looking out the window, or at his own reflection in the window. He turned slightly as though surprised that Rob was still talking. "You just do it," he said, brushing his hand toward Rob dismissively before turning back to the window.

"I'm not going to do it for you," Rob said tightly, dropping the envelope on top of the copier. "If you want to place an order at the front counter, we'll have it ready for you in the morning." He turned around and walked away, part of him wishing to see the expression on the old man's face, or to turn and say something else, and the other part of him beginning to wonder if he was overreacting.

He had reached the front counter when he felt a tug on his arm, surprisingly firm. The old man's eyes were squinted, his nostrils flared. "What's your name?" he asked. "So I can complain about you, your attitude, to your manager."

If he meant to intimidate Rob, it didn't work—when Rob felt threatened, he dug in. "My name is Rob, and what's your name?" He paused. "So I can post a warning about you in the break room. And never touch me again."

Randall emerged from the office, walking slowly and looking from one to the other. "Is there a problem?"

"Are you the manager?"

"I'm the assistant manager; the manager is not in at the moment. What can I do for you?"

Rob rolled his eyes as he pulled his cash drawer out of the register. "I'm going to count down my till," he muttered as he walked past Randall, who looked like he wanted to say something to Rob but had given his attention to the customer and didn't want to tear it away.

"This young man," the voice came from behind Rob's back as he pushed open the office door, "has a definite attitude problem." Rob swung the door shut with his foot and it closed with a satisfying thump.

He set his tray on the counter beside the desk and sat down. He could see them through the office window; the old man was motioning toward the copiers, flapping his lips, and Randall's head was bobbing up and down like his neck was made of rubber and someone had just smacked his head with a bat.

He pulled out the cheques and credit card receipts from the bottom of the tray and began punching the numbers into the adding machine on the desk. There weren't that many tonight. He noticed he was chewing his gum quickly, tensely. He pulled out the twenties and began to count them. He was just finishing the pennies when Randall walked in.

"What was that all about?"

Rob didn't look up, pretending to be absorbed in his counting. He spit his gum into the trash can. "He was being a dick." He opened the log book and copied the numbers from the adding machine's tape into it.

"That's it? He was being a dick? He was a customer, and hopefully still is. I think I calmed him down this time, but he was a little steamed."

"Yeah, well, I would have told him to take his business and...get the hell out, for all I care. If he wants any respect from me he's going to have to treat me like a person. I didn't sign up to kiss anyone's wrinkly old ass; you don't pay me enough to do that."

Randall was standing there with his arms crossed, looking down at Rob where he was sitting. "That's where you're wrong. It's called customer service and it's what your job is all about, if you'll recall the interview we went through a few weeks ago. You can consider yourself on probation. I'm going to have to talk to Bobbi about this."

"Go right ahead. In fact, I'll tell her all about it myself tomorrow." Rob slid the cash into an envelope. Randall didn't work on Saturdays, so Rob would see Bobbi first. "Here's my drop. It's $152.46 and there's a hundred in the till."

He didn't care if they did fire him, but he felt bad for Bobbi's sake, because she seemed to like him, and she was trying to be nice. It was just a matter of time before something like this happened. He had expected Randall to come up with something sooner than this. He hadn't really done anything to win Randall's friendship. Randall had tried to get Bobbi to make Rob wear solid blue shirts like everyone else, but had actually lost ground to Rob in that discussion. Rob claimed that he matched the theme of the tropical posters hanging in the windows—which he thought needed to be reprinted because they had been bleached by sun. Not only had she had allowed him to continue wearing the Hawaiian prints, but she had asked Randall to help him reprint the posters as part of his training.

She also asked Rob to make notes of any ideas that came across his mind for the store, because she said she and Randall had lived in it so long that they didn't notice sometimes where things were starting to look "lived in." He was supposed to submit these notes into her mailbox. He had counted that as a major victory against Randall.

Randall finished counting the cash in the envelope and he sealed it, his mouth turned down into a slight frown. He turned it over and scrawled his name over the flap and passed it back to Rob, who did the same and pushed it back onto the counter.

"So, I'm out of here," he said stepping through the door. The old man was still standing out there, clutching his envelope of photographs in both hands and waiting to be waited on.

Rob pushed the door open into the break room and punched out, then grabbed his coat and his cane. He was standing in the door that linked the break room to the store, pulling on his coat, when Randall walked out of the office and toward the old man, wearing a huge smile.

"Okay! What are we working on tonight?"

Rob shook his head. He turned around, deciding to leave the back way so he didn't have to tempt his mouth by walking near them. He pushed open the escape hatch and the sight of the recycling dumpster reminded him of his prints. He let the door close behind him and click shut, then walked down the concrete steps and pulled his bag of papers from under the dumpster.

What a way to spend a Friday night. But it stood to reason that the new guy got the worst shifts. He walked around to the front of the store, feeling like he was in a scene from a movie—a solitary figure walking with a cane, the reflections of the store signs and street lights on the wet street, the darkness crouching behind everything.

He had been walking almost everywhere lately. The leg seemed to be strengthening, but he had learned from experience and wasn't about to push it. Walking for another month or two might even firm it up again enough for him to trust it with a gentle run every now and then.

He walked past a small clothing shop and stared at the jack o'lantern staring back at him from behind a smashed window. The window had been badly damaged but not shattered and a web-like pattern radiated out from a central point; someone clever had glued a big rubber spider in the middle of it. He had heard somewhere that Halloween had become the biggest holiday for expenditures. Or maybe it was still behind Christmas; it must be. But still, that it was second biggest was amazing. That's a lot of costumes and candy.

He was walking toward Natalie's house, not his own, his left hand gripping the cane and tapping it down in time with his steps. The bag of prints hung limply from his other hand as he swung it gently back and forth, accidentally knocking it against his knee every now and then.

The lights were off at Natalie's place; it was Friday night. He stopped on the sidewalk, looking into the shadows.

"Hey," the shadows said.

"Nat?"

She was sitting in the old recliner on the porch, staring into the street, her knees pulled up to her chest. He remembered another time that she had done the same thing—just before they had gone their separate ways, or he had gone his, anyway. If he remembered correctly, the world had been a lot less stable that night as he staggered toward the house and found her draped in blankets on the porch of their house. She seemed to retreat to the shadows when there was something on her mind, hiding, watching.

"Is something wrong?" he asked, walking slowly toward the porch. The streetlight barely penetrated this far; everything on the porch was lit dimly.

"I don't know, I think so," she said.

She stopped talking, and he stood there in front of her, in front of the deck, dangling his plastic bag. "What is it?"

"I'm not sure, exactly," she said slowly. "I think Wade just dumped Tink. Unexpected. On the phone. And I'm not sure where Tink went."

"Do you want to go inside?"

"No, not yet. What I want is a smoke," she said.

"Here." He set down the plastic bag so he could pull out his pack. The last cigarette was a bent white stick in the darkness, the shaft broken in the middle, but he held it out to her. "Sorry it's a little beat-up."

"That's okay," she said, breaking off the top and dropping it on the ground beside her. "Half a cigarette is about all I can handle these days. I don't smoke much anymore."

He cupped his hands around the lighter and she leaned her face into the light, breathing deeply. "Whoa," she said after a moment, laughing a little laugh. "Do you remember when you could still get drunk on cigarettes? Bzzzzz!" She fluttered her hands beside her head; he could see, faintly, her glittering wide eyes and crooked grin.

He sat down on the arm of the chair and it tilted slightly to his side. "When did she go?"

"Half an hour ago? An hour? We were getting ready to go to a movie, waiting for Wade to show up. He called on the phone, sounded nervous. I'm not sure what he said to her after I gave her the phone, but she was crying, she said he wasn't coming tonight." The cherry on the end of her cigarette ignited as she took a drag, an orange ember on her lips.

"I asked her if she wanted to stay home and talk, but she shook her head and ran out. I don't know where she went."

"Shitty night," Rob said, and she nodded.

The silence expanded and he felt that he had to either say something or leave. "Mine wasn't so good, either. I'll probably get fired tomorrow or Monday."

"What happened?"

"Well, for one thing, standing for hours at a time is a little rough on the leg. And would you believe that tonight I had words with an old man?"

"Yes. I would believe it. You didn't punch him or anything did you?"

"No, but I would have liked to. He was acting like I was his personal slave or something, telling me what to do and expecting me to jump at a wave of his hand."

"And so you told him off."

"Yeah. Unfortunately the assistant manager was right there."

"Well you lasted two weeks. That'll look good on the resume."

"Somehow I don't think I'll put it on there." He bent down and picked up the plastic bag at his feet. "But, there is a bright side. I got a few things printed before he sent me home tonight." He pulled out one of the sheets but it was too dark to read.

"Here, let's go inside," Natalie said, pulling herself out of the chair.

She put water on for tea and they read over his front page news. The whole thing was starting to seem a little silly to him, definitely not as great as it had seemed at first. The stories had seemed funny in the library but now they just seemed juvenile. Natalie sat down by the table and set the page down in front of her. He watched her profile as she read. She smiled a few times, and he peered over her shoulder to see which part had made her smile. She was reading the article about soma.

"You spelled 'there' wrong," she said, running her finger back and forth across the lines of text as she read.

"I know, I saw that later. I think the spell checker substituted the wrong one."

"What's this about a lancet fluke?"

"Oh, that was just kind of random. A last minute thing because I forgot about the front page photo. I read an article a while back about parasites and it has kind of stuck with me."

He watched her read until she pushed the paper away from her.

"What do you think?" he asked.

"Yeah, good. Funny. What are you going to do with it?" she asked, flipping through the stack.

"They're all the same," he said. "I'm going to stick them in the front of newspaper boxes so that people think they're real for a second." Why did it sound so stupid now?

"Funny," she said again. "How much did it cost to print all these?"

"It was a...perk. Part of my training at work was learning how to print things. I figure it's appropriate to practice my skills every now and then."

"You are going to get fired." She poured hot water over a peppermint tea bag for him. "It's good to see you writing again, though, even if it's so short."

"I don't care if I do get fired. That job's worthless anyway—standing in front of a cash register and pushing "Go" on the copier. And every now and then the excitement of binding a stack of papers together with a coil. Oh, and smiling and groveling to every old fart who wants you to do it all for him: pull down his pants and lift him onto the glass and push the button so he can have a perfect little copy of his ass. And informing him of the costs and quality differences so he can decide whether to spring for the color copy or just pay the six cents for a standard black and white."

"Wow," she said.

"It's kind of depressing, you know, to try to imagine a job that'll bring satisfaction, a feasible job I mean, one that will actually make enough money to live on. Because I can't think of one right now."

"Nothing at all? There's got to be something."

"I don't know of it. I was just thinking, okay, so I get fired from this meaningless job and then what? I get another one?"

"Meaningless is a little strong, don't you think? There's got to be something good about it."

"Well, I got to print all these for free. That was nice, but I guess that's not really the job."

"Look at my job—it's the same thing. I do the till, I organize things. Where's the glamour in that?"

"I'm not talking about glamour," he said, trying to backpedal a little bit. "And they aren't the same thing. My job's all machines and production. People become frustrated more easily, more demanding."

"I think you're still feeling the wounds of the old man incident. You think we don't get dicks in the store? We get all kinds. People who want the table twenty bucks cheaper than it is because of a little scratch they think we haven't noticed before, or who get upset that you have a certain shirt only in a size that's too small for them. You just have to learn to laugh at them." She narrowed her eyes and looked at him with a smile creeping in. "When they're gone from the store."

"I guess so." It sounded so easy when you were sitting at home, but when you were in the store and the old man was standing there saying, "You do it…"

Natalie lifted the corner of the page. "Are you going to do these more often? Or what's next?"

"I'm not sure. I'll see how these work tomorrow morning. Maybe I'll do something new."

She nodded. "I have a feeling that if you kept doing these, for one thing you'd get sick of them, and for another, the *Herald* would probably try to track you down."

"Yeah. Actually I was feeling the twinge of an idea forming just a moment ago. Maybe the next thing I'll do is make a bunch of photocopies of my own ass to distribute to the annoying customers. I could give it to them sealed in an envelope and give it to them with a smile as they pay, and then when they open it at home there I'll be, all life-sized and with a magic marker headline that says 'Kiss me, you fool.'"

He was leaning over, slapping his ass repeatedly when the front door opened. He turned to find Tink staring at him, red-eyed. She looked from him to Natalie with a confused expression that melted into tears and she flung herself through the door to her room and slammed it behind her.

Natalie's laughter had been cut off as though the door had slammed on it. She got up from the table, pushing her chair back as she stood.

"That didn't look good. I think I was supposed to be waiting here all alone when she came back. You should probably go—I've got to talk to her." She was talking quietly, as though loud noises might shatter Tinker's constitution at this fragile time.

"Yeah, of course," he said, grabbing the plastic bag from the table. They walked toward the front door silently and Nat stopped in front of Tink's door, just before the carpet sample that they had thrown down for people to wipe their shoes on.

"Thanks for stopping by, hey? See you at the party tomorrow." she was pressed up against Tink's door and was pushing it open slowly, like she was trying to sneak in.

"I'll be a little late, because I work…" Rob found himself standing alone in the entryway. He picked up his cane from where it was leaning against the wall and did a mental check. Shoes on. Cane in hand. Bag of prints. There was a copy of it still on the table, the one that Nat had been reading. He began to walk back but stopped in mid-step and decided to leave it in case she wanted to read it again.

Walking in the night air was always too invigorating, especially if you were feeling lousy. It left you wide awake, energized. As he made his way up the hill beside the university, he could see that the night was just getting underway: cars streaming in and out of the parking lots, people moving between buildings and vehicles, lights on everywhere. It looked like something was going on in the Viking Union but he wasn't sure what.

The thing was that he had to get up early tomorrow to distribute these things. It wasn't going to happen if he didn't go to bed early. He wasn't sure what time the newspapers got distributed in the morning but six o'clock seemed safe, and it was before most people got up. He wanted the papers to be in place first thing, so everyone who bought a paper would see it, not just the stragglers.

He rounded a corner and the hill began to descend again, down toward the ghetto, his home and his bed.

Six o'clock was early these days. He found it funny that he didn't remember having any trouble getting up early when he was still living at home on the farm. His dad would say that it was evidence that he had sunk to a certain level of depravity; his father got up religiously at five every morning, even after moving off the farm.

He was warm and it seemed that it would probably be very cold outside of these blankets. Come to think of it, why would it matter if he put these things in the newspaper boxes early or a little later? Most of the people would still see it, just not the early birds. Besides, he hadn't been able to get to sleep for what must have been hours last night and had lain there staring at the glow-in-the-dark stars.

When he woke again, he had been lying in a stupor somewhere between his dream world and reality for a long time, the thought that he should get up floating by on occasion but never really settling down in his brain now that he'd already made an exception. Besides, what were Saturdays for? The bad thing was that it was quarter after nine.

He threw his feet over the edge of the futon and sat there, wrapping his blanket around his body while his brain turned on. Sometimes his brain in the morning was like a car's engine in winter—it just needed to idle for a little while before it was ready to go. The bag with his prints in it was on the floor by his feet, so he picked it up and set it on the bed beside him.

The trick now was to find all those newspaper boxes. There was one just down the street from his apartment, and probably a bunch downtown. He pulled the top sheet out and skimmed it again. He wasn't sure why that instinct was there, but there was something about the written word, your written word, that made you want to review and review it, as though you expect to teach yourself something, or as though to ensure that no one has changed it since you last read it. He had had the same thing with his newspaper stories—he'd read them when the paper came out and then he'd read them again in the afternoon, and again at night, and they always said the same thing as they did in the morning, but he always found himself doing it.

The bathroom was twenty feet away. He stood up, keeping the blanket wrapped around him. There was a heat lamp right above the toilet, which must have been meant for standing under after a shower. It illuminated the toilet bowl like a spotlight, directly from above, and he was noticing things he'd never noticed before. His urine in the morning was a brilliant yellow, but it seemed there was sediment in it, or particles, and it swirled around in the tank like oil in water. Maybe his piss had always been like that but he just hadn't noticed it because of the bad lighting in most bathrooms. He shook his penis off, trying to keep the infamous "last drop" from ending up in his pants. He hunched forward slightly so the blankets didn't fall from his shoulders.

He wondered how Tink was doing this morning. Wade had never struck him as the faithful type. It would just take her a little while to adjust to him being gone, like anything else. When he had gotten contacts he had kept putting his hand up to adjust the phantom glasses that his subconscious kept expecting to be there, pushing empty air and being surprised at the absence. She'd feel an unexpected empty spot where Wade had been for a few days. But we all adjust to change, given time.

He pulled on the pants and shirt he had draped over the back of his chair the night before. He had to work in the afternoon today, so he had almost four hours to do this yet. His coat had fallen off of the door handle and was lying on the ground beside the fridge. What did he need besides tape, the prints and some quarters? That should be enough. He'd need to get change somewhere along the way, but he had enough for a few boxes.

He stuffed the bag with the papers in his jacket, trying not to bend them, and stepped into the kitchen. One of the doors on the opposite side of the room was open and he could see the guy in there, walking around in his bathrobe with the sound of the television coming from somewhere out of view. He had shelves on every wall and they were all packed full. He must have lived here for a while to get so settled. People actually lived in this house for a long time.

He hadn't really thought much past the concept of moving in, but he wondered how long he'd last here. He kept noticing how small it was, but maybe he'd grow into it, adapt. Given time. It had been a month already but he still thought of himself as having just moved in.

He had run into the landlord last weekend, just before Dave had arrived, the first time since he had moved in. The elusive Gordon Nerburn.

Now he knew why everything was the way it was around here: old, run-down, lived-in. That was how Gordon was, too. He was wearing an old sweater with elongated cuffs that went halfway to his elbows and a huge knit collar, turned up part way like a neck guard. He had oil stains on his old brown pants and scuffed work boots, but the best part was his face. It was mostly normal, if a little wrinkly, but the wrinkles seemed to be carved from stone. The wrinkles on his mother's face were soft, flaccid, but the knots and wrinkles in Gordon Nerburn's face were like vulcanized rubber. It seemed wrong that the salt-and-pepper stubble could be growing out of that substance.

He seemed like a good guy, though. He was of the old school, the pioneers, making things work instead of buying new ones, or if he couldn't make it work, just living with the old one. Rob had shown him a puddle of water behind the toilet in his room and Gordon had stuffed a wad of toilet paper where the water pipe came in from the wall, asking Rob to check it now and then, and reassuring him that sometimes "toilets heal themselves."

He hoped nothing major went wrong in the apartment.

The first newspaperbox was on this street, just up ahead. He unzipped his jacket with his cane hand and slipped one of the papers out, holding it in the other hand with the tape. When he got to the box he leaned the cane up against it and rummaged two quarters from his pants. He looked around quickly before pulling it open, and set the print on the inside of the glass window, tearing off four small pieces of tape, sticking them on the fingers of his left hand one at a time until he could put the rest of the roll back in his pocket.

He fastened one piece in each corner, holding the paper against the glass with the back of his wrist so he could peel the tape off his fingers, and then let the door snap shut. It looked good in the window. It was a little small and the paper was too bright to pass for newsprint, but it was okay.

He took the bus downtown and found a handful more boxes—not nearly twenty, but by the time he had stuck a page on the fifth one, he had had enough. He had spent his remaining two quarters on bus fare, and instead of getting change at a store, he had begun to stick the pages to the outside of the window. The last one went on crooked but someone was watching him and he left it. They'd probably get torn down within hours anyway.

He had enough nickels and dimes to get a bus ride home again, feeling less like the conqueror than he had thought he would. Probably no one would even stop to read them. He wasn't going to try this one again—he wanted something better. This one felt like a warm-up, not the main event.

Laryn kragt Bakker

Wear your own skin

Wearing sweatpants and a sweatshirt seemed to increase her level of laziness. She yawned, lifting her head from her arms. The silk shirt she had worn to the costume party on Saturday pressed against her hair—she had cast the shirt onto the desk that night and hadn't moved it since. It was partly draped over the melted mass of candles that made up her shrine, hanging down and covering the wax lumps like a coroner's shroud.

It had been a mediocre party at best. She and Tink were supposed to have spent Saturday piecing together their costumes with items that Natalie had been collecting all month from the store, but Tink couldn't concentrate, and Natalie had ended up doing both of them. She should have traded costumes with Tink, but she hadn't thought about it in time. Tink walked around the party all night with baggy patched pants, a tight striped shirt, and a painted clown face that was not masking the little frown that kept creeping into place. They had tried to use some spray-in hair coloring to turn her hair fluorescent red but it just ended up looking like somebody had tagged her head.

Rob had shown up with a huge translucent red garbage bag upside-down over top of him, with holes for his head and arms, and paper tassels glued up and down the seams. He had drawn some lines and circles on it with permanent marker, and it was only because she had seen the fake newspaper faceplate he had printed that she knew he was trying to be a blood fluke. Shawn, ever creative, was a spook, wearing the white sheet off his bed on top of himself, with two small holes cut out for his eyes, though he had gotten sick of it after a short time and draped it around himself, transforming it into a toga. Dara had painted her face and hands all white, with fake blood trickling from her mouth and darkened eye sockets—an undead corpse.

Nat had been a pirate, with a bright red silk shirt and black pants, and a homemade eyepatch that kept flipping up. She had spent an hour sewing the patches onto Tink's pants before she had started to rush things. It wasn't as fun when you were doing it all by yourself. She had pulled her hair back and tied it in a rough ponytail, and blacked out one of her teeth, but unfortunately it didn't look real next to the genuine gap between her front teeth.

Dara pulled out a cake early on in the evening and they gave Natalie a few birthday cards and sang. Rob had included a little coupon in his, good for "one free hour of time," which was kind of cute—daylight savings time ended that night. After the birthday portion was over, it almost seemed that nobody wanted to be too happy, for Tink's sake, and so they all sat around and drank beer in the living room, subdued. At one point she almost laughed just looking at the couch full of characters: the depressed clown, the listless corpse, the Greek philosopher downing his fourth beer. It's not that they were like that they whole night—they did laugh a fair amount—but there was an overall mood of sadness in the air and the laughs seemed disconnected from each other, separate. It was too bad. Dressing up was supposed to be fun.

As children, she and Scott had never been allowed to go out on Halloween night to collect candy. They heard the urban legends every year—the razor blades in the apples, the kidnappings and sacrifices. But most of her friends went every year and nothing happened to them. The church began to have a program one Halloween—Reformation Day—evening so that parents could offer an alternative to sitting at home with the lights out and trying to ignore the doorbells and knocks at the door.

Of course, the only thing that accomplished was to make the kids resentful. They ended up sneaking out when their parents were talking downstairs and the rest of the kids were all chasing each other around, hitting as many of the houses near the church as they could. They learned something about mercy on those nights, coming with no costume and asking for candy apologetically at a stranger's door.

"What are you supposed to be?"

"A girl?"

The last time they had done that, her parents had found out afterwards when she spilled her candy out across the table at night and her mother, who had put the church's goody bags together that year, didn't recognize most of the candy that she displayed.

She wondered why it was that people enjoyed the costumes and masks so much every year. It was something that everybody did every day, in a way. The disguises were just a bit more elaborate. Sometimes at the store she imagined all the people that came in as costumed actors, playing a role. Wasn't it J. Alfred Prufrock who said, "We prepare a face for the faces that we meet?"

When she tried to think of herself in that scenario, she felt like she was always always straining for her lines and her delivery, hoping she got the words right and wishing she could control the moods.

She wasn't much of an actor. Her own thoughts and emotions were like tiny shards of glass under the skin, or stones in a farmer's field—they always worked their way to the surface. She thought of the secret she had kept from Rob all these years, thinking he'd never be back and didn't need to know. She had almost forgotten it until he came back. Now it was burrowing its way out, inching toward the surface of her skin.

She knew she had to tell him, but she was waiting for the perfect moment, which she knew would never come. It was like peeling a Band-aid off slowly.

She picked the pirate shirt up and threw it onto the bed so that she could light the candles. Maybe a handful of times during a year she was tempted to break all this wax away and take the wooden boxes out from inside. She tested one of the candles on top, pulling it toward herself. It bent slightly and cracked away from the wax that held it in place. She didn't go further. This was cosmetic damage and easily repaired. She could never bring herself to break the whole shrine apart. It had taken so many years to grow.

She held the candle upside-down over the shrine, building up the rivulets and drip patterns with liquid wax. How many candles had dripped themselves out onto this thing over the years, spread themselves flat, running down to the fake wood grain laminate of the desktop? One of the rivulets overflowed its banks and landed on her left hand and she flinched back. But it lost its heat so quickly. The splash of red wax was already hardening on her hand.

She held the candle over her hand, dripping wax onto her fingers and knuckles, one firey little drop at a time. The pain was intense for a fraction of a moment and then faded. Each drop fused onto the other drops, but still kept its own shape, the soft shadowed outlines of circles overlapping within a solid field of red. Drip. Drip.

When the back of her hand was covered, she held it up in front of her. It was like a glove, a second skin. She jammed the candle back into its socket and touched the wax on her hand with a gentle finger. The coating of wax, already hardening, spread the pressure from the touch across the entire hand. She clenched her fingers into a claw. The wax whitened at the edges of the cracks, peeling up at the knuckles like scales. The underside of each scale held the pattern of her skin, a miniature landscape of parched earth, cracked and dry.

If she dripped wax over her entire body and then peeled it off in little fragments like this, she would have a copy of herself scattered around her feet. A self portrait. A broken woman. She peeled the skin off of the back of her hand and fed the pieces one by one back into the flame, watching them melt.

She wondered how Tink was doing, whether she had found Wade. She had left at least two hours ago—it was almost ten o'clock already. Wade hadn't called on Saturday even though Tink had tried to call him a few times during the day. He lived with his parents, but he had his own line. Once, Tink had called his parents on their line to ask where he was, and his mother answered. She said she'd get him, but when she came back to the phone, she said he must have stepped out. Tink thought he was there, but didn't want to take the call.

Natalie tried to make some sense of what she knew. She had answered when he had called Friday night.

"Hello?"

"Hey, Nat, is Tink there?"

"Yeah—we're waiting for you to get here!"

"Oh, uh, okay, can I talk to her?"

"You're not going to bail on us, are you? You're the one who wanted to see this thing in the first place."

"Well, I might, I'm sorry, but I've gotta talk to Tink."

She growled into the phone and called Tink, who bounded down the stairs two at a time, her braids lifting and falling each time.

"Hello-o-o," she sang into the phone. "Hey. We're waiting for you!" Her forehead tightened slightly. "What's wrong?...What?...Hey! Wade—"

Tinker was silent for some moments, listening, and then she held the phone out and stared at it.

"Fucker!"

"He's not coming tonight?" Nat asked.

"No," Tink said.

Nat leaned down to tie her shoes. "It doesn't matter. We can see whatever we want now." She looked up and Tink hadn't moved.

"He just dumped me. Two lines, and on the telephone."

Tink was holding back tears. "I'll kick his ass!"

Nat straightened up. "Oh, Tink."

Tink didn't say anything as Natalie moved toward her to hug her. "What did he say?"

Tink shook her head, biting her lip, then pushed past Natalie, slamming the door behind her.

If Rob hadn't shown up in the meantime, things might be a little smoother between her and Tink now. Every so often she'd go off about how Nat and Rob were together and she was all alone, and Nat would have to emphasize that they weren't together, and she was right here with Tink. It was a quick turn-around: one day she was pressuring Nat to do something so Rob didn't slip through her hands, and then the next she was pleading with her not to.

When Tink had returned that night Natalie had gotten the other side of the conversation, and Tink knew only slightly more than Natalie. All Wade had said was that he needed some time away from Tink and wouldn't be around this weekend. No explanations.

He hadn't returned any of Tink's phone calls for a few days. She thought he was screening his calls, but then she caught him yesterday when he answered the phone. She had started off with small talk—she'd missed him at the party Saturday night, what had he been up to these past few days—and then, phrased delicately, the question: What the hell is going on here?

He responded no less cryptically than the night before. He said he was confused about things and needed to think, and he'd give her a call later in the week. Tink was unsure of the status of anything, what had caused the problem in the first place, and whether it was something that would pass.

It was completely unfair of him, cutting things off but leaving threads attached, so she had told Tink to go over to Wade's place and get the details. She deserved to know what was going on. At first Tink had refused, claiming that she didn't want to throw a wrench into anything, but after a day she was starting to cave. Tonight she went.

Natalie blew the candle out, resting her chin on her hands. The smoke rose, thinning into a narrow thread as it wove its way up to the ceiling. She was already a full day past twenty-six years old. That was more than halfway to fifty-two.

She woke up cold when the front door opened and closed. Her face felt bent where she had been laying on it, and her mouth was dry. Good thing she had blown that candle out before she had fallen asleep. Her bedroom door opened and Tink slipped in, closing it behind her and flipping on the light switch.

"You awake, Nat?"

"Just about," she said with her eyes closed against the sudden light, which blazed through her eyelids and into her head.

Tink sat on a corner of the bed.

"What time is it?" Natalie asked.

"It's late."

"Did you find him?"

"Yeah. We're back together."

"Just like that? What was the problem?"

"Oh, he was just a little confused, but we worked it out."

Even as groggy as she was, she knew that Tink was holding back. "You sound like he did on Friday. What does that mean?"

Tink breathed and exhaled before she spoke. "I told him I wouldn't spread it all around," she said, "so you have to promise not to tell anyone."

"That sounds serious."

"Do you?"

"Okay already, you know you don't have to ask like that."

Tink looked down at the comforter she was sitting on. "Well, he was out with his buddies and they got a little hammered..."

"And?"

"And he somehow wound up in bed with someone." Her voice was barely audible.

"What?"

"You heard me," she said.

"When did this happen?"

"I don't know, Friday night I guess."

Natalie didn't want to press it too hard—she could tell Tink was still processing it herself. But she still had questions. "So, did he call here before or after this happened that night."

Tink stared at her without saying anything.

"I don't know," she said finally.

"If he called before he went out, then it was premeditated," she said slowly, "and I think he called too early to have finished an accidental round-trip to someone's bed."

"Listen, just drop it. We worked it out."

"What does that mean, exactly? You 'worked it out.'" But an idea occurred to her as she said this. "You didn't sleep with him tonight did you?"

Tink got up and walked toward the door, and Nat began to follow her.

"Did you?"

Tink whirled around, her face pinched. "Drop it, okay? Just because I am not a nun—"

But she broke off without finishing it. They faced each other for two breaths, not speaking. Light glinted off of Tink's wet cheeks as she turned back around.

Natalie stood looking at the inside of the door for a few moments after Tink had closed it behind her. Somehow that had gotten out of hand. Is that what Tink thought of her? Is that how she described Nat to her other friends?

She peeled back the comforter and inserted her body into the opening. Nat hadn't slept with anyone since Rob moved away. She found herself even thinking in euphemisms about it, as though she were keeping the details from herself. The intimacy of sex carried with it a sense of danger. She couldn't believe Tink had slept with him again so soon. It was like rewarding him for infidelity.

When she woke it was still early. It was one of those rare awakenings which are instantaneous and complete—she opened her eyes and was not groggy, with the final frame of her dream fresh in her mind. She swung her legs over the edge of the bed and picked up the notebook that was on the nightstand beside it, opening it to the bulge that was a pen closed inside it.

Her dream journal was filled with fragments, residual images and short scenes that remained in her head during the moments after waking. She uncapped the pen and started to write.

There are two "teams," one of men and one of women. We each have rolled up newspapers and have to whack a certain amount of the other team's players on the legs. They are trying to get up the stairs into the rooms of books at the store and we are trying to keep them down. Each time they get whacked they have to start again outside the store. It's a lot like the childhood game of "lava" because you have to hang on counters, tables, chairs, and can't touch the floor. When you whack someone the floor underneath them opens up and they fall through and eventually come in through the door again. They were near winning—it was just me and Tink and Dorrie, hanging from the banisters leading upstairs and all these guys were crowding around, and Wade hit Tink so she fell through the stairs. I yelled and jumped at him off the banister and everyone stopped, like they were shocked, and I hit the ground in front of him but didn't fall through, and everyone just stared at me.

She stared at the page but no interpretation formed in her mind. She had the dreaming part down, but she had no idea what to do with them once she had them, how to find out what they meant. As soon as she came up with a possibility (did she feel threatened by Wade?) another possibility presented itself (was she being too protective of Tink?) and so she was left guessing. Maybe she was trying too hard.

She flipped back a few pages in the notebook. She recorded her dreams in spurts: there were entries for a number of days in a row, and then nothing for weeks or months. This was from last week:

> *I'm in an empty room on a chair, tied, bare light above (like those gangster interrogations). My head is tilted back far and I can't move it. I think I'm naked—I feel the texture of the ropes on my skin. I see Rob standing beside me, he's wearing a balaclava so I can only see his eyes and his mouth. He's looking down at me, or at his hands. His arms are moving but I can't see what he's doing. I feel cold wet stripes across my body, like peroxide on bare skin, and he backs up to look at me from a distance, and if I strain my eyes as low as they can go, I can see he's got two cans of spray paint in his hands.*

She couldn't remember anything before or after this scene. She didn't know how she got in the chair, or if she got out. It intrigued her, the way dreams sometimes had moods that didn't match the content. As she read what she had written, she realized that it didn't come across quite right just to list the details. In the dream she had a detached interest, as if it wasn't her own body that she were looking out of, that was tied up naked to a chair.

Here was one from last month.

> *We were playing a game where you see who can get to the top of the mountain first—no holds barred. I was playing with a large lady (never seen her before) and I ambushed her, knocking her legs out. She rolled down a hill and over the cliff (which was accidental) and I stood on the edge and watched her float down—it was like watching spit fall off a bridge—she floated and took forever to land. In mid-air her head separated from her body and when she hit, there was blood all around. I thought for sure she was dead and I felt horrible. She got up and stuck her head back on and started climbing the mountain and when she caught me she picked me up by my feet and starting whacking me back and forth on the ground.*

It was disconcerting to have a book of dreams and not know what they meant, what the messages were. Here was a book of what might be words from God, in a language that she knew how to read but didn't understand.

She went into the kitchen and pulled out the milk and cereal. Was Tink still going to be mad today? She could hear the sound of the cereal crunching in her mouth and tried to chew quietly. She swallowed and made a loud gulping sound. The silence amplified her noises, these small reminders of her physicality: water in the throat and a digestive gurgle.

It was still almost half an hour before she usually left for work. Most days she got up about twenty minutes before eight, dashed through the shower, ate quickly, and hopped on her bike. So it was still about ten minutes before she usually woke up.

She stood in the shower longer than usual, letting the water hit her body and trickle down like warm rain. The sensation of water on skin was so elemental, so real. She closed her eyes and let it run down her face, over and between her breasts. She heard something in the background, a noise behind the sound of falling water that was out of sync, mechanical. She turned the water off and recognized the sound of her alarm clock.

She burst out of the bathroom wrapped only partially in her towel and fumbled with the alarm clock, looking for the right button. The sound cut short. She was clutching her towel to her front and her exposed skin, still wet, was cold. She noticed her hands were shaking as she set the clock down, moist fingerprints visible on smooth plastic.

She closed her door and finished drying herself. Her whole mood was changed. A peaceful early rise had somehow become an attack. That was how she felt: under attack, worried that something else was going to happen.

"Have a little trouble waking up this morning?" asked a bleary-eyed Tink when Nat came into the kitchen again.

"No, I woke up too early and forgot to turn the alarm off before getting in the shower. Sorry."

Tink started to peel a blackened banana without responding.

Nat wanted to make some kind of a connection before leaving for work. "I was in the middle of my shower when it went off." She smiled. "So I was tearing from the shower to my room just about naked. We haven't done that since Shawn moved in." Before Shawn had answered their newspaper advertisement another girl, Amy, had lived with them for almost a year. They used to run around the house in their bras and underwear, acting like school girls, snapping each other's straps and pulling underwear up from behind.

"Yeah. I think I stepped in some of your water outside my room."

"Oh...I'm sorry, I haven't had a chance to dry that yet." She felt like the whole morning was apologies—not the way she had hoped the first conversation after last night would go.

She had fifteen minutes before eight o'clock, so she decided to walk. She took an umbrella, but it wasn't raining when she left so she used it like a cane, imagining how Rob must feel.

Today was Halloween day. Last night was what her friends used to call "Gate Night" when they were young, the night when the gates of hell were opened, or something like that. Mostly it was the night when they'd take a few eggs from the refrigerator to throw on cars—one year she tried to buy a dozen of them from the store but they refused to sell them to her. Lynden, the town she had grown up in, was a town that decided what was good for its citizens and what wasn't: it was still hard to find a place that would sell alcohol on a Sunday. You had to go outside the city limits.

She hadn't gone back to live there after she'd come down to Bellingham for school, but she still went to visit her mother once in a while. Lately she hadn't been going up at all—she had her mom come down and they met in a restaurant and talked over a meal or a cup of coffee. It wasn't just that she didn't have a car, because she could borrow one quite easily. She was always scared that if she went up there, she was going to run into her father somewhere on a street or in a store.

Her mother had seen him a few times, but couldn't bring herself to go up and talk to him. She thought they lived south of town and that they went to the church that was directly across from the church that her mom went to. Luckily the morning service across the street finished an hour before hers, so she didn't have to worry about walking outside after church and accidentally seeing him on the other side. She had mostly gotten over the whole situation, but still tried to avoid reminders.

Natalie moved aside to let a guy struggle up the hill on his bike, breathing hard. Everybody's got problems. That guy on the bike was probably wrestling with something in his head. All these people in their cars, waiting for the light to change, they probably wonder how they'll make it through this day, or why they're spending their lives like they are, or if there really is such a thing as hope in the midst of brokenness.

The lady in the car on the street beside her was looking straight ahead when her face cracked open in a huge yawn. She's safe in her car, in her own little world. Natalie got one look before the lady accelerated off into oblivion, one glimpse to extrapolate her whole life story from. Did she have the answers? Either way, she's gone now.

All we've got to do is pretend to be just fine and the world will keep on spinning and the people will keep dying and fucking and lying and being born. She was in one of those moods. The day had started off so well.

She didn't know how long this was going to last with Tink. Maybe they'd be able to talk again tonight, now that the initial confrontation was past. If it came down to it, she'd probably even apologize and let it go. Tink was a big girl now, too. It was just that when you see someone making the same mistakes you've made many times, it seems like useless pain, unnecessary.

She and Tink had been living together for over two years now, and it seemed they had to have a good fight about twice a year in order to stay friends the rest of the time. They were about due.

They were close, but not intimate. There were still some fairly major things that Tink didn't know about her. She was still trying to learn how to open herself up like Dorrie did. She'd been programmed from birth to appear good and if possible, to be good, but if you weren't, at least pretend you were. So this idea of just living, and not worrying about people who are watching your mistakes more than your successes still felt foreign and she still felt lonely.

It didn't help matters that whenever she talked to her mother, her mom would tell her about how the people in church had looked at her last week, or what she thought they said behind her back. Some of the people Natalie disliked the most were Christians, who could love everything in abstractions but when a real person was in front of them, she was anathema.

There were a few bags outside the back door, underneath her handwriting: DROP-OFFS HERE. PLEASE NO SCAVENGING UNLESS YOU REALLY NEED TO. She pulled the door open with her key and tossed the bags inside.

Dorrie wasn't coming in until the afternoon today. Some days they both came early and stayed late, and some days it was just one of them in the morning. Dorrie ran this place but in a lot of ways, she didn't act like she was the boss—she had asked Natalie if it would be all right if she came in later today, as though Natalie needed to give permission.

Tyler was going to come in this morning, too. He had the whole electronics section done, and had thrown out much of it. She was glad, because that stuff never sold anyway, and she didn't know what was good and what wasn't. She had started him on the books. She organized for an hour or so a day and then needed a break from it, so it was taking a long time. Already she could see a great improvement when she walked up there, and she thought they were selling more books lately.

She unlocked the front door and went to the back room to open the bags. She didn't like arguing with Tink. She wished she weren't alone in the store right now.

It was about half an hour before noon when Rob showed up. Tyler was upstairs with the books, and Natalie was ringing out a customer.

"Hey, Nat," he said. "Is Tyler around?"

She tore off a receipt and dropped it in the bag. "Thanks," she said to the woman before turning to Rob. "Tyler? Yeah, he's upstairs. Why?"

"I want to ask him a question. I'll be back."

He gripped the banister and pulled himself out of sight. What was he up to? He had come over on Sunday afternoon for a piece of birthday cake that was left over from the night before and was still brainstorming for what he referred to it as his "next project." At the party on Saturday night, he had been disappointed with the way the newspaper thing had gone in the morning, but he had shown her a list that he had in his pocket of what he hoped would become the seeds of future projects.

A woman who looked to be about Natalie's age was browsing through the racks of children's clothing near the counter.

"What are you looking for today?" she asked, stepping out from behind the counter.

The lady grimaced good-naturedly. "Halloween costumes. I guess I left it until the last minute again, huh?"

"Well, you've got a few hours yet," Natalie said, looking at the clock on the wall. "What have you got so far?"

She held up a long, blue skirt that looked like it would fit her. "This is for my oldest son. I'll have to cut it open up the front here and try and make some kind of a cloak or a cape out of it quickly when I get home. Now I just need something for my younger son."

"Most of the obvious stuff is long gone," Natalie said, "so you're going to need to keep being creative."

"I was afraid of that."

"How big is he?"

"He's six, but he's small for his age." She looked up at the clock. "I'd better go and get this cloak figured out. I want to have it ready when he gets home from school. I think I'll just wrap Nelson up in toilet paper and masking tape again. He liked it last year."

Natalie laughed at the image. "That thing's been around here for a long time. Give me a buck for it and we'll call it even."

"Really? Oh, that's great."

Natalie stuffed the bill into the drawer.

"Have fun tonight."

"We always do," she said, rolling her eyes. "Bye!"

"See you next time."

Rob came down the stairs with a huge grin on his face.

"What are you so happy about?"

"Tyler's going to help me make a web page."

"What for?"

"For everything! So I can put all my projects on it."

"Great, I guess."

"Anyway, I should go soon, I've got to go to work."

"So you're not fired after all?"

"No! Didn't I tell you? I talked to Bobbi on Saturday and she had already heard a short message from Randall, but I explained it and she put me on probation, and said if I did it again I'd get fired."

"So you've got a few more days of work, then."

He smiled. "We'll see. Randall still hates me. We worked yesterday and I don't think he said more than five words in a row to me. I think it's because of the shirts." He pulled his jacket aside and she recognized the wild print of one of the shirts he had bought from the store.

"When I started wearing these he right away told me to stop, to wear white ones, or blue ones, but I pulled out the dress code he had given me and it only said 'a buttoned, collared shirt,' so I said I was going to keep wearing them. He took me to Bobbi for that, too."

"And she said it was okay?"

"Well, not at first. I showed her the dress code, too, and she said she was sorry that it hadn't been clear enough, but it was supposed to be white or blue, and so I told her I didn't think they were out of place because we've got these tropical prints in the window, palm trees and beaches, and she bought it. She was even thinking of making these kind of shirts standard for everyone, like a makeover for the store's image, but then she decided not to. That would have been great, seeing Randall having to wear them. Anyway, I should go."

"Nice listening to you," Natalie said.

Rob smiled over his shoulder as he walked away, then stopped and turned around. "What happened with Tink and Wade, anyway?"

"I guess they...worked it out," she said.

"Oh, good."

He was a few steps from the door and she was almost alone again.

She called out, "Why don't you stop by my place after work?"

Dorrie came in at noon, just after Tyler had gone. Natalie talked and worked for a few hours with Dorrie but there weren't many people, so Dorrie told her she didn't have to stay if she didn't want to. She went in the back and tried to paint but she couldn't get herself into it, so she walked home. Tink wasn't around, and Shawn said he and Dara were going out to eat and then to Dara's place that night. Natalie wasn't sure where the rest of the afternoon and early evening went—she slept and ate and prepared for the kids to come.

She answered the door for the first wave, the early ones, and then decided she wanted to accomplish something instead of just waiting for people to knock. She picked up *Crime and Punishment*, which she'd been trying to finish for almost a month now, bit by bit. She didn't like Raskolnikov. But she was intrigued by Sonia, the faith-full prostitute. She was like a biblical character, one of the ones that Jesus was always having meals with.

Knocks on the door kept interrupting her, some timid and some violent, and she was having a hard time concentrating. She took a mixing bowl and dumped candy in it until it was almost full, stirring the foil-wrapped chocolate balls and the little toffee pumpkins with her hand until the mixture was more or less homogeneous. She set it out on the deck on a kitchen chair, with a sign taped to the back of the chair: HELP YOURSELF TO A HANDFUL.

She settled back in her room, sitting in her pillows with her back against the headboard and her blankets over her knees. She could still hear scuffling and voices from the deck now and then, and she imagined little boys wrapped in toilet paper trying to walk without bending their knees, with their arms extended. Once, a cat and a superhero knocked to tell her that the candy was gone, and she emptied the rest of the bags into the bowl.

Rob showed up shortly after. He knocked on the door and when she opened it he stood there with a goofy expression on his face. "Trick or treat," he asked, his teeth dark with chocolate.

"Hi, Rob!" She stepped aside to let him in. "How was work?"

"Oh, the usual." He sat down by the table and started peeling foil from around another sphere of chocolate. "Not much fun."

"If I couldn't find at least one thing enjoyable at work, I'd have to find a new job," she said.

"Yeah. I don't know. I'm kind of more excited about what I do outside of the job, you know? That's just something I do so I don't end up completely broke."

She rubbed her hands together. "It's cold! Do you mind sitting in my room? I'm going to wrap myself in blankets."

She sat back down by the headboard and pulled her blankets around her again. "I lose my heat so quickly," she said.

"I remember that. Why don't you just turn the heat up?"

"I don't think the house itself is that cold. It's just me. I usually wear an extra layer. And it's also partly the fact that it's electric heat and we don't have a lot of money."

"I think everything's electric in this town. Nobody wants to upgrade when the students have to pay the utilities anyway."

He pulled the chair from by the desk and her book fell to the ground, scattering chunks of pages.

"Shit!" He tried to scoop them up before they scattered but it came up more like a deck of cards oriented randomly.

"Don't worry about it, I'll sort it out later. I'm just about done with it anyway."

"No, I'll put it back together." He sat in the chair and spread the pages out on the desk. "What are the highlighted sections for—are you going to write a book review or something?"

"No, I just highlight if something strikes me, in case I want to find it back without re-reading the whole book."

Rob held up a page like an unlearned script, and read with enthusiasm.

"'What are you to do?' she cried, jumping up, and her eyes that had been full of tears suddenly began to shine. 'Stand up!' (She seized him by the shoulder, he got up, looking at her almost bewildered.)

'Go at once, this very minute, stand at the crossroads, bow down, first kiss the earth which you have defiled and then bow down to all the world and say to all men aloud, 'I am a murderer!' Then God will send you life again. Will you go, will you go?'"

She grabbed the page from him. "Yeah, yeah."

He collapsed in the chair, his shoulders hanging.

"What do you want to talk about?"

She considered all the things that they needed to talk through but which she never had the courage to raise: the reasons their relationship hadn't worked the first time around; the short-lived pregnancy. But what if their tentative friendship changed for the worse after she told him? Her friends were becoming fewer and fewer.

"What's this monstrosity?" he asked, nodding at the shrine.

"That? Well, it's kind of grown into something I never really meant at first. It's mostly wax, with a few things embedded in it here and there, like a chicken bone, and those three little boxes we got in Turkey, do you remember them?"

"Yeah! One inside the other. Why'd you put them in there?"

"It just kind of happened. I had a bunch of candles and I was playing with them and started dripping wax on things accidentally. Then I started doing it on purpose, coating things with wax, and it just started growing."

"Besides all that wax down there, it reminds me of those candles in the cathedrals we saw, in a way. All lined up in rows and columns. These are just a little more crooked and odd sizes and colors."

"That's what it's supposed to be, in a way. I like it when it's all lit. It's kind of a meditative thing, all these flickering flames."

They both stared at the unlit candles, saying nothing. She had so much that she knew should be said; the silence was like a vacuum, and she had to steel herself to keep words from being drawn out of her. She didn't just want to just dump it out in front of him.

"What was going on with Tink and Wade?" he asked, turning to her.

"I don't know. Some kind of miscommunication, I guess. Tink didn't say all that much about it. I...she asked me not to tell anyone any details."

"Oh," Rob said, sounding surprised and disappointed, as though he'd just been drawn outside the circle.

If she didn't tell him now, she might never tell him. She practiced in her mind: Rob, I need to tell you, no, you should know something...Remember before you left...Rob, we were pregnant...Nothing sounded right. Come on Nat. Out with it. Vomit it up.

"Rob, there's something…" She trailed off, realizing that she couldn't stop now.

He didn't say anything, looking at her intently.

"Back before you went to Seattle," she started, but her voice was disappearing. She tried to clear her throat. "Just a sec, I need a drink," she said, scrambling off her bed. She drank a glass of water in the kitchen, desperately trying to come up with some way to back out of this. It wasn't right. It wasn't coming out right.

"You okay?" he asked when she came back in.

"Yeah," she nodded, making herself smile. "I was just going to ask you, you know, after you went to Seattle," she paused, "why didn't you ever call?"

"I—" and now he was the one clearing his throat. "I did."

He paused for a second as she started to shake her head, then continued, not looking at her anymore, but through her, into the past. "It was a Friday night, the week after I came to Seattle. I was sitting there in front of the phone for at least ten minutes, trying to work up the courage, asking myself if this was smart or not…Finally I just did it, but you never answered. I got the answering machine, but I hung up without leaving a message."

"And that was it?" she asked. She was remembering something she hadn't thought about for years.

"Yeah, more or less," he said.

"Did you ever try again?" she asked.

"Well…after you didn't answer I was feeling like crap, right? And so I said to myself, 'This is not what love is supposed to be like. You're supposed to feel like you're invincible, not like you've just been tied up with ropes and dragged down the highway.' So I did this thing, I'm a little embarrassed about it because it's complete BS," he said, cracking his knuckles in his lap, "but I said, and I don't even know to who, maybe just to myself, I said, 'If she's not there, it's a sign and I'm going to just forget about her.' And I hit redial, and you still weren't home, so that was that."

Her scalp felt like it was lifting from her head, levitating. "I was there," she said. "It was the first Friday night after you left, and I was alone in our house, and thinking, 'I wish he'd call.' And the phone rang. And I walked up to it, from the living room, and the machine had picked up, so I was waiting for the message to start, screening my calls, because if it was you I wanted to talk, but not if it was anyone else. And then the message ends, and the beep beeps, and there's maybe two seconds of silence and then a click."

Rob's eyes were glistening; she hoped he wouldn't cry.

"And so I let out a breath, and I'm telling myself it probably wasn't you when it rings again. I had my hand on the receiver and then I thought, 'Whoever this is is calling back to leave a message,' so I didn't pick up, and as soon as the message played, I heard the click, and I yanked the phone but it was already disconnected."

Rob's upper lip curled up almost imperceptibly.

"Why didn't you pick up?" he asked.

"Why didn't you leave a message?"

They glared at each other and she was the first to blink.

"I mean, maybe nothing would have changed," she said.

"Maybe. But maybe it would have answered a lot of questions, saved a lot of pain."

"I don't know. Maybe we needed some of the pain. We wouldn't be who we are without it."

"Maybe you needed it," he said. "It's the last thing I needed."

She didn't say anything, and a moment later he continued. "Damn! You were there?"

She nodded.

"Well, hey," he said, "so you didn't pick up the phone, okay. Why didn't you ever call me?"

"The first while I told myself that you'd call, that I didn't have your new number, and after a few weeks I guess I was starting to think maybe you didn't want to. I wrote you a letter, but I didn't have an address."

"You did?"

"Yeah." She pointed at the shrine. "It's folded up in the middle of all that wax somewhere."

"It is?" He turned back to the candles, his hands already reaching out. "Can I get it out?"

"No! It's...listen, it doesn't matter now. I don't want to get stuck in the past."

"I'm not saying I want to get stuck in the past, I just want to read what you wrote."

"Forget about it. It was nothing important," she lied.

"Okay then." He drew back his arm.

"Listen, Rob, I'm sorry, it's just..."

He came and sat beside her. The mattress sunk down underneath his weight and she lost her balance, tilting toward him.

"Hey. Don't worry about it, yeah?" He put his arm around her. She leaned into him slightly.

"So, if we're not going to be stuck in the past, where are we going to be stuck?" he asked.

She smiled. He was cute when he was trying to be smooth. "I don't want to be stuck anywhere," she said.

Rob smiled, considering this. "Fair enough," he said. "But I have a question for you. Two years ago, you said you had to figure things out—did you get them all figured?"

"No," she admitted, tasting something like disappointment. "But I'm starting to wonder if maybe that's okay."

He hung his head momentarily, letting out a breath and then lifted it quickly. "Okay. I'm asking you point blank, here. Where do we stand, you and me?"

"Honestly, I can feel a lot of potential. But for some reason I'm still a little scared. I guess, I haven't had a serious relationship since...you, and it's a little scary. So, if anything happens, it's going to be a very slow process for me, and if you aren't interested in that, I'd understand."

"I wish I wasn't interested in that," he said. "But, what does that mean, exactly?"

"It means I'd like to talk more. It means we'd both have a little better idea of where we're going, even if we're not sure when we'll get there."

"That sounds fine," he said and he kissed her awkwardly, leaning over and twisting to find the angle he needed. He tasted vaguely of chocolate. She wanted to kiss him, to feel his hands in her hair. But the thought was also scary. It had been so long.

"And one more thing. I'm not ready for anything...physical," she said.

"Oh. Was it okay that I—?" He pointed to his mouth, eyes wide, and she laughed.

"It's okay." She kissed his cheek and he tried to kiss her again but she had pulled back and started talking. "But let's not. I mean, I want to be clear that I'm not ready for a romantic relationship with you. I think we have a chance to become good friends again, but I don't want to define it romantically."

He sat back a little bit. "Why?"

"I guess I'm not ready for that pressure. I think it would be better for us to leave it ambiguous for now and just let it become what it becomes without trying to force it into being something it isn't. Does that make sense?"

"It's confusing. I'm not trying to pressure you into anything. If you need more time, that's fine. It really is."

When she was alone again, she lit her candles and turned out the lights. She felt unsettled, like she had just put everything on number thirteen and the ball was circling the roulette wheel.

She stared at the candles and tried to pray as the flames danced with her breath in front of her. She wasn't sure what to pray because she wasn't sure how she felt. Usually she just ended up with the sense that since she didn't know what the hell was going on, she was just going to leave it up to God to work it out. How God can love such a bunch of sniveling, selfish creatures who continually take advantage of him, she couldn't say. It was like she was a bloodsucker or some other kind of parasite that fixed onto God and burrowed in, sucking, using him, feeding on him. *This is my body, this is my blood.*

She blew out the candles and stretched her body upwards, arms raised, fingers splayed, opening herself up, and then leaned forward with her head down. Why was she still so nervous and unsettled about tonight? It felt like she and Rob had put their relationship on life support—it wasn't dead or dying, but it wasn't fully alive, either. There were still too many issues to work through. But if God can raise a man up from the dead, then surely he can resurrect a dead relationship?

Part Two

"Now you ask me how you could help this movement or what you could do, and I have no hesitation in saying, much. Every revolution requires revolutionists..."

–Isabel Meredith, *A Girl Among the Anarchists*

"For what we need to know, of course, is not just that God exists, not just that beyond the steely brightness of the stars there is a cosmic intelligence of some kind that keeps the whole show going, but that there is a God right here in the thick of our day-by-day lives who may not be writing messages about himself in the stars but in one way or another is trying to get messages through our blindness as we move around down here knee-deep in the fragrant muck and misery and marvel of the world. It is not objective proof of God's existence that we want but the experience of God's presence. That is the miracle we are really after, and that is also, I think, the miracle we really get."

–Frederick Buechner, *The Magnificent Defeat*

"Vandalism is a kind of parasitism born from the essence of millennial western civilization. In our current culture we stand fractured, manipulated by technology and commercial interests...We are host organisms and commodity culture is the parasite. We are vandalized objects—bent, warped, covered with markings we can't honestly say we chose by free will."

–Andrew Stillman, in *Adbusters Magazine* (Spring 2000, p.45)

"There is no perfection...this is a broken world and we live with broken hearts and broken lives but still that is no alibi for anything. On the contrary, you have to stand up and say hallelujah under those circumstances."

–Leonard Cohen

Reality is for people with no imagination

He had Cindy's letter on the desk in front of him but he wasn't looking at it anymore. The computer monitor blipped off to conserve electricity every five minutes and every five minutes he moved the mouse a fraction of an inch to make the screen come back to life. It was already dark outside, punctuated occasionally by headlights and voices.

He had been typing out some thoughts, brainstorming for a new project about the media. Somewhere along the way he had started thinking about her letter again, and so he had picked it out of a stack of papers to re-read it. It had come three days before with no warning. If he had known what to look for, he might have been able to pick out the scattered hints that Dave had been dropping for the past few months. But, of course, he hadn't known what to look for.

He hadn't talked to Cindy since December—that was almost four months already. She must have gotten his mailing address from Dave, unless she had taken it that time she came up with Dave and Tad last October. That was when he had told her (after kissing her) that she shouldn't visit anymore. Just before Christmas he had talked to her about Natalie and tried to explain what was going on there. It came out then the same way it was in his head—confused, contradictory, messy.

Someone had told him once that the waves of the ocean are just along the surface of the water—underneath the waves, most of the ocean is calm. That was the part of her that he couldn't get to, the deeper part; he was still getting rolled by the waves. She was keeping everything vague and confusing. Everything. She didn't know what she wanted or when she wanted it, which was unfamiliar and not at all comfortable for him. He was used to having his mind made up until he changed it.

But that still didn't explain why Cindy's letter had unsettled him. She didn't have anything to do with Natalie—not much, anyway. He had known before even thinking about coming back to Bellingham that there was no future for Cindy and him, so why now, six months later, did a letter that she and Dave were hooking up make any difference to him at all? Maybe because Natalie was not working out like he thought she would, he was just taking an inventory of what else was around. Or it could be simply because he hadn't been laid in a long time and that was Cindy. Maybe it was the fact that it was Dave—a close friend who had known them both when they were screwing each other; perhaps he was worried she'd tell Dave things that he had said to her. Maybe it was just the fact that she had found someone else to fill his place. The world goes on without you.

A few months ago Dave had phoned and toward the end of the conversation he had mentioned that he was going to take Cindy out on Valentine's Day to cheer her up. Rob remembered him joking about it, asking Rob if it was okay, as though he needed permission. A number of times since then, when they were talking or when Dave was e-mailing a graphic to Rob for one of his projects, he'd mention briefly something he had done with her, or with Tad and her, but there was nothing unusual about that— they were friends and had always gone out together when Rob was living in Seattle as well.

Cindy's letter didn't come out and say it outright, it was written in a way that indicated she thought he knew already. Maybe Dave was supposed to have told him, or maybe Dave thought he had.

He set the letter on top of the scanner. Tyler wanted the text that Rob was working on e-mailed to him by tonight so that he could put it on the website tomorrow, which meant he had to concentrate and get this done. He moved the mouse again and his notes, in point form, flashed back into existence.

-too much power in the hands of a few corporations
    -power to shape, to influence a nation's (world's) thought patterns, issues.
    -fewer companies = fewer opinions
    -reluctant to investigate, report on their owners
    -mis-use their influence for corporate self-promotion
    -less independent journalism, more syndicates, wire
-issues become soundbites
-disaster as a media event
    -in a few days we forget about it, it's old news
-when did advertising become a media event?

-(is it news when a corporation starts a new campaign? launches a new product?)
-(do we care, or should we, about who got what endorsement?)
-(media attention sells products)
-advertising in general...we are subjected to it everywhere. Ad creep.
-hollywood unreality in movies, actors' and actresses' real lives
   -the cult of the celebrity
   -fame vs. success

The way it generally worked was that he typed an article and then e-mailed it to Tyler, who formatted it and put it onto the website. For the last few days, he had been brainstorming and researching, but he kept finding excuses not to write.

He advertised his site by creating stickers with his website listed on them and slapping them on top of corporate advertisements across town once or twice a month. Tyler kept track of how many hits his page got each month, which gave him a bit of an idea which campaigns drew the most response. The idea was that the stickers would whet their appetite and then once they hit the site, he'd have an article posted that explored the issue more in depth, as well as a link to the previous archive of projects.

He had started making stickers last November, as a joke. It was a few weeks after he had told Natalie that he wanted to photocopy his ass and distribute it to annoying customers. He had been at home trying to come up with something to put on his website and was almost ready to give up on his projects because there hadn't been much response to his first few attempts. It was just after the election, after he had spent days standing on a street corner waving a Nader/LaDuke poster on a stick as though he were a prophet and The End Was Near. Little wonder that he lost his drive after that election.

He decided to make the ass poster one night on a whim. He made sure his door was locked and the blinds were closed and then he dropped his pants and sat on his scanner, wondering whether the intense, slow moving light that was tracing the contours of his flattened cheeks and crack could possibly damage him. When he set the picture up on the page, it looked like a bum pressed up against a window, and he typed a short paragraph to the ungrateful customer underneath it.

Dear sir, I understand you thought that I was rude, that I have an attitude problem. I humbly apologize. Kiss and make up?

He added a lipstick stain on top of the graphic and it was complete. He didn't print t, or give it to anyone, and it actually sat unseen by anyone for almost two months, until after the Georgia Pacific plant announced the temporary shut down. He had written a short web article about the plant and the movement that was building to force them to clean up their act in late October, bobbing along in the wake of a larger local movement that he had nothing to do with. Essentially he rephrased what he had found on their site and took a picture of a bumper sticker that said "GP, proudly polluting Bellingham for over forty years," and then linked back to the page he had taken the info from.

So, even though he had little to do with it, when they announced that they were temporarily shutting down the plant it had given him hope that the people still had some power. And in fact, a few weeks ago, right around the end of March, they had shut most of it down for good. He hadn't really done anything or updated the web page through November and December, but when he heard about the shutdown, he was inspired enough to dig out his old notes and start thinking of a new project to work on.

In January, he had written an article about the power and abuse of power by corporations, and he needed to post it on the website and advertise it. He was going through his files and he came across the scan of his ass again. He transformed it from an apology letter into a sticker and printed up a bunch of them at work. He put four on a page of label stock, and then began to stick them secretly all over town on corporate advertisements and windows.

He called it the "Stick an Ass on Corporate America" campaign. In big print above the graphic, he had written: *Pucker up, Corporate America,* and then in smaller writing underneath: *We've caught on to your whore-style love, your dirty promises. If you want to keep this relationship afloat, the rules have changed. For starters, you'll be planting your kisses here from now on.*

In his first run, he had about twenty stickers in his pocket and he went walking downtown late during the evening, sticking them on every corporate advertisement he could find. He was walking back along Samish and saw a McDonalds ahead, and he pulled out the remaining stickers. He still had six of them left. He wasn't sure if they had the cameras on at night or not, so he pulled on his black mask before walking up to the building. It was closed, so he stuck an ass on the door at eye level so no one who entered could miss it, and then a few more on the promotional posters. He walked around and into the drive-through and stuck one over a column of prices on the menu and was peeling the backing from the last sticker when he heard a voice.

"Excuse me, sir—"

It was coming directly out of the menu and startled him. Somebody was still inside. He slapped the sticker on the menu, half-peeled, and turned and bolted.

He never knew what she was going to say, but with him in a mask and asses all over the building, he didn't want to stay to find out. He wouldn't be surprised if the police were already on their way. He hadn't been ready for that, though, and had taken off down a side street and run halfway back to downtown before stopping to think.

He had learned from that experience. He had a few routes planned now which took him by several prime targets like Starbucks outlets and Coke machines. Once he had driven all the way out to Wal-mart just to stick them. After the first night he had also decided to run extra stickers and leave them out where the free newspapers were distributed by the university so students could pick them up and start sticking them, too. Every time he saw one of his stickers up in a place that he hadn't tagged he got a little rush of energy. His projects were coming to life, snaking themselves in little tendrils into places he didn't know of, by people he'd never met, in ways he couldn't fully control. It was refreshing not to have to pretend to be objective.

He was supposed to go to Natalie's house tonight, but he wasn't sure what they were going to do. He wasn't sure she knew, either. He was waiting to go until after he had finished this story. It sounded like it was going to be a night at home anyway, and it didn't sound like she really needed or wanted him to be there. It was Good Friday, and with all that entailed, it was probably just as well to stay away. He had no problem with her doing her prayers—it was great for her. But it wasn't his thing.

After he had e-mailed his story to Tyler, he stepped out, locked his door and yawned. He wondered how long this relationship could last as it was. A few days ago he had asked her if she wanted to do something over the weekend and she said she was busy Friday night—she was going to have a candle service in her room. She had said he could come if he wanted to, being careful to stress that he didn't have to come if he didn't want to, so he was left to try and guess if she wanted him to come or if she didn't. The thing that he wanted to be sure Natalie knew—and he thought she did know it—was that they weren't going to always be into exactly the same things, and that was okay. He wasn't trying to convert her, and he didn't want to be converted.

He tapped his cane on the ground in time with his left leg, walking slowly. He didn't really need the cane anymore, but he had grown to like it. There weren't too many people his age using canes these days, so it was like a trademark.

The night was crisp and damp, but it wasn't raining. He walked past the university and started down the hill. It seemed like years ago that he had been a student here. It had been years ago. What if he had known back then that he'd be working now in a copy shop and titillating himself by writing stories that nobody read? He wondered briefly again if he was wasting his life.

Natalie's house was at the end of the block. What was she doing in there right now, behind those walls? There was something spooky about the whole thing, the spirituality-and-candles, the type of thing he usually tried to avoid. But it was good to get a window into her world once in a while.

He noticed a faint glow coming from Natalie's window as he walked past, but it looked like all the other lights were out. This house was always dark. He knocked on the glass of the storm door and jammed his hands into the pockets of his pants. Maybe she hadn't heard him. He opened the exterior door and knocked on the wooden door behind it.

The porch light blinked on and Natalie's face appeared in the crack.

"Oh, Rob! I wasn't sure if you were going to come or not." She opened the door and stepped back.

"I said I was, didn't I?"

"You did, but you didn't sound too excited about it. I thought you might have changed your mind." She closed the door. "I told you that you didn't have to come if you didn't want to, right?"

"Yeah, you did. Can you believe I wanted to come tonight?"

Her nostrils flared. She was so beautiful when she smiled and was happy at the same time.

"Well, thanks," she said.

He leaned down to take his shoes off in the carpeted entrance to the hallway, which always smelled of unwashed feet this close to the ground. "So what are we doing tonight, anyway?" he asked, holding his head high as he untied his laces.

She gave him a perplexed grin and a little shoulder shrug, her hands clasped in front of her and knees slightly bent in a way that reminded him vaguely of that picture of Marilyn Monroe with her skirt being blown up while she tries to hold it down. "We could bake some bread," she offered.

He leaned one hand against the wall and stepped on the heels of his shoes one at a time to pull his feet out of them. He kicked them beside all the other shoes and boots that were scattered along the wall. "Oh. That could be fun, I guess. Where's everyone else tonight?"

"I think they were going to go dancing," she said.

He put an arm around her waist and grabbed her right hand in his left, swaying his hips. "But you wanted to bake bread instead?"

He danced her down the hall to the kitchen.

She had already started combining ingredients in a mixing bowl. There was a puddle of water in a crater in the flour, and Natalie pulled a beat-up spoon from the drawer.

"Do you want to mix?"

He took the spoon and cradled the bowl in his left arm. The flour gummed up in the middle but remained a dry powder at the edges, climbing the edge of the bowl and dusting his shirt. He hadn't seen bread made since he was a child. He remembered smooth round loaves, spanked and coated with a beaten egg.

Natalie sprinkled flour on the counter and turned the dial on the oven.

"When did you come up with this idea?" Rob asked.

"What, bread? I don't know. I wasn't sure if you were coming tonight."

"I told you I was."

"I know, but that doesn't always mean you are."

"Well. I didn't know we were going to make bread."

The dough was still sticky, clinging to the edges of the bowl and the spoon. He set the bowl down and pulled the warm dough from the spoon with his fingers. There was still dry flour underneath everything. He started kneading the powder into the middle of the blob. It became soft and saggy, like the flesh on the back of his mother's arms. He lifted it up and it drooped back toward the bowl. He let it drop. Natalie threw a handful of flour into the bowl and when he started to massage it, she flicked his nose. A tiny cloud of flour came off of her finger directly into his eyes.

He drew in a breath, surprised, his eyes already clenched shut as he tried to let go of the dough, blindly shaking his hands but unable to get it off of them.

He rubbed his eyes with the backs of his wrists as Natalie hovered around him, asking him every few seconds if he was okay and tentatively touching his arms as though to pull them away from his face and then releasing them, not wanting to do any more damage.

"Rob! Are you okay?" she asked again.

"Just give me a sec here." He blinked rapidly, his eyes watering. "Can you wipe this stuff out of the corner of my eye?" He was holding his arms open to let her in, tatters of dough clinging to his hands like a disease.

She wiped her hands on her pants and held his face steady with one hand, gently wiping a finger between the bridge of his nose and his eyes, one at a time. She looked like she was going to cry. Most of it was out, now. Not that much had gotten in. But it felt good to have her touching him, feeling concerned about him.

"Is there any more in there?" he asked. "Can you see it?"

"I don't see anything," she said, holding his face in her hands. He looked into her eyes, inches away, and blinked slowly to maintain the illusion that he was still trying to get something out of his eye. He felt himself getting hard, his penis slowly swelling against his pants.

"I'm sorry, Rob."

"It's okay, I'm not blind."

"Are you going to be all right?"

"Yeah." He put his arms around her lightly, holding her with his inner elbows, his gummed up hands feeling like stumps, and kissed her forehead.

They went into Natalie's room while the dough rose. It smelled like she'd been burning incense in here quite heavily. She always used to do that after smoking up, to hide the smell of marijuana. He sprawled out on the bed while she lit the candles. It felt good to lie here after standing all day at work.

"So, now what?" he asked through a yawn.

"I don't know," she said, sitting in the chair by the desk. "I thought about the bread idea, so it's your turn."

"Weren't you planning a 'meditation by candlelight' or something?" He pulled the blankets over himself, snuggling in.

"Yeah. It's Good Friday today."

"I know it is," he said.

"Well, I didn't think you'd be interested in that."

"So you didn't really want me to come tonight."

"It's not that I didn't want you to come, I just didn't think you'd enjoy it."

"So you invited me, hoping I wouldn't come."

"Kind of," she said, and burst out laughing. "I just know that you don't always like that kind of thing."

"You can do some of it now, like, read a little bit of the Bible if you want to. If it's important to you then I'd like to hear some of it."

"Really?"

"Yeah. Just not too much."

"Okay," she answered. She turned to the desk and pulled a book from the drawer. He could only see her silhouette against the flickering candlelight. He yawned again as she flipped pages, a dry rustling in the darkness.

"Then Jesus went with his disciples to a place called Gethsemane, and he said to them, 'Sit here while I go over there and pray.'"

He closed his eyes as she read. It was comfortable lying there, warm, while Natalie's quiet voice sewed words into the air around him with little stitches. "'My soul is overwhelmed with sorrow to the point of death. Stay here and keep watch with me.'"

He followed the story loosely, having heard most of it before and recognizing certain phrases as they were read. "'The spirit is willing, but the body is weak...Are you still sleeping and resting? Look, the hour is near...Friend, do what you came for.'" And then Peter cut off someone's ear, and Jesus put it back on. He wondered what would have happened if Peter had stuck his sword into the guy's heart. Would Jesus have put his hand over the wound to heal it, or stuck his fingers right inside? Why do you cut someone's ear off, anyway? Maybe he was trying to cut his head off but the guy dodged it.

He fell asleep before she read about the trial and crucifixion, and when he woke up briefly, Natalie was crawling into bed beside him. She gave him a quick kiss, her breath smelling like wine, and told him to go back to sleep.

In the morning it was Saturday. There was always something nice about waking up with someone beside you, the heat from the two bodies intermingling in silent conversation. He tried to swallow his morning breath and kissed Natalie's cheek. She gave a little sigh and half a smile without opening her eyes. His eyes felt like they'd been held open all night and dried out his contacts so he forced himself to blink, hoping the contacts didn't pop out or scratch his eyes.

He had to work a half day today. He wondered what time it was, whether or not he was going to be late for work. His eyes felt best when they were closed. He shifted his body and rearranged his pillow under his head.

"Do you have to work today?"

He opened his eyes again. Natalie had turned her head and was looking at him. She slept on her back and snored louder than any girl he'd known.

"Half a day."

"Well, don't be late."

He made a low noise in his throat, then propped himself up on his elbow and looked across the room at the wooden clock on the wall. The gears were installed in the cross sectional disc of a small tree so that the hands circled along the path of the tree's rings. Almost eight o'clock.

"Are we still going to do something tonight?"

"Sounds good," he said.

"We could go to that movie you wanted to see yesterday."

"I didn't really have one in mind. I don't really feel like a movie, though."

"Well, stop by after work and we can decide then."

He didn't have time to walk back home, so he had to go straight to work wearing the clothes he had slept in. There were a few old shirts in the lunch room that were for emergencies such as this—old blue button-ups with stains inside the collars and the Copies On Demand logo stitched on the left breast. "COPIES" in bold capitals and "On Demand" overlapping it slightly in a cheesy script font. His pants were wrinkled and the shirt was a size too small. Luckily he had showered last night before he went to Natalie's.

Work had changed somewhat over the last few months. Ever since he had busted Randall, he'd been more or less the weekend manager, though he had declined the official position when Bobbi had offered it to him six weeks ago. She had convinced him to try it unofficially for a few months before he made his final decision. That meant that he was largely on his own here on Friday nights and Saturday mornings.

He was proud of his part in the discovery that Randall was gaming the antiquated accounting spreadsheet they had used previously to filter small amounts of money into his own pockets every weekend. About three months ago, he had been working with Randall, who had gone into hiding in the office like he usually did, and Rob was left alone to help three customers and complete a job. When Randall sauntered out half an hour later, things had quieted down somewhat, and he had told Rob since things were slow, he could go home early.

Rob hadn't said anything, and that's probably why it worked out like it did. As he was punching out in the break room, he saw the suggestions box beside the time clock and he wrote on a scrap of paper, "Suggestion: teach Randall to stop locking himself in the office and playing games on the computer while I bust my nuts on the weekends."

After he put it in the box, he felt immature, but still angry. The next time he saw Bobbi, she had asked him what exactly Randall did in there, and Rob shrugged. When she found out how long it had been going on, she asked him not to mention anything to Randall. She re-oriented the security camera so it was filming the desk instead of the door, and she watched Randall on tape the next week, adjusting the dollar totals in the spreadsheet they used to keep track of their sales figures and pocketing a few bills.

She didn't know how long he'd been doing it, or how much money he may have taken over the months or years, but for some reason she hadn't prosecuted him. She just fired him and let him walk away. If Rob had been in charge, he would have thrown the bastard in jail. He had never liked him in the first place. But immediately after that, Bobbi had installed another camera above the desk and upgraded the system so that the register sent the sales directly into the computer instead of requiring additional processing.

She had asked him if he wanted to be the weekend manager and his overwhelming reaction was negative, but all he said to her was, "I think...not." It scared him that he was still working here, a job that he had intended to have for a few weeks or a month stretched out into four or five months and now potentially longer and with more responsibilities.

The nice thing was that it was still part-time. He had a few hours a day during the week, with extra hours on the weekends. And he could still print his projects at work.

Bobbi expected it to be slow, so he was the only one working today. He opened a second button on his shirt to reduce the pressure. He felt like he had been shrink-wrapped.

Bobbi had guessed correctly—there wasn't much traffic through the store. He had a few jobs that had been taken Thursday evening and were due at eleven—an hour before the store closed. He could see it already: they were going to be late in picking it up and by then he would be gone, and they would complain and refuse to pay when they came in on Monday because they needed the copies by Sunday. Oh, well—the holiday hours were prominently displayed on the door and the counter, so they couldn't say they hadn't been warned.

At about ten thirty a man came in to copy some bulletins for the Easter service at his church, because the church's copier was broken. Everybody always felt like they had to explain why they came to the shop. My printer's out of ink. My copier's broken. I forgot to print this at home and it's too far to drive back there before my interview. Didn't they realize he didn't care?

By the time it was noon, all but two of the jobs that had been scheduled for that morning had been picked up. He checked what the other two were: business cards and a brochure for a dog training course. Nothing really time sensitive. He locked the front door and struggled out of the tight shirt. He closed down the cash drawer and counted down in the office. Over by a nickel. He signed the envelope and slid it into the safe deposit.

Somebody was banging on the front door. He poked his head out of the office without thinking—if he had stayed hidden they would probably have just gone away in a minute. It was a lady, maybe forty years old, holding a small dog in her left arm and pulling on the door handle with her right.

He sighed and walked over. "We're closed," he mouthed without speaking, pointing at the paper notice that was taped to the door.

She didn't say anything but kept yanking on the door, back and forth, a wild look in her eyes. The little dog looked around, blinking underneath its overhanging eyebrows, seemingly familiar with and unconcerned about the lady's aggression.

He stood there, watching her while she kept pulling, and then he reached over and unbolted the door, half expecting her to burst in and rampage through the place, but she just stood there. He pulled the door open.

"I'm sorry, but we're closed for the day," he said.

"I was told to come in Saturday morning to pick up my brochures," she started, her eyebrows flexing down slightly in the area between her eyes like a storm warning. "I just need to pick them up."

He scratched the base of his head, where it joined to his neck. "The cash register's already been shut down," he said. "You'll have to come back on Monday."

Her face was tight against her skull, her lips thin. "I live in Mount Vernon," she said. "You guys will just have to deliver it, then, because I can't keep coming back and forth."

"We don't deliver that far. We could ship it, but that would be an additional cost."

She let out an angry breath. "Listen, are they finished?"

"I did them myself, this morning."

"Folded, too?"

"Folded, too."

"Why don't you just let me take them now, then, and save us all the hassle."

"The store's closed," he said, ignoring her pointed look at the open door between them. "The register has already been shut down, so you wouldn't get a receipt—"

"I don't need a receipt," she broke in. "I'll just give you the cash, and you can ring it in on Monday."

"Ah, shit," he breathed, turning around.

He pulled the box from under the counter. "Here. Take a look at it; make sure it's like you wanted."

"I'm sure it's fine," she said, pawing roughly through the box. "Thank you so much. It's just such a pain to drive up here when I don't really need to."

She gave him three twenties and a five and told him to keep the dollar plus in change. He watched her back out of the parking area, wondering if he was feeling the way the dogs felt after she had finished training them.

After he had walked home, he settled into his bed and pulled the blankets over his naked body. He could understand the nudists' attraction to living life naked. The feel of cloth moving over bare flesh...but maybe it just felt so good because it was all he had at the moment.

He thought morosely about how Natalie seemed quite content to be celibate. Sure they slept in the same bed every so often—like last night. He was growing used to it and had come to expect nothing more on nights like that. He had pushed her for a while after they had unofficially discussed their relationship a few months ago but after her repeated insistence that she wasn't ready for that, he stopped asking. He didn't want to give the impression that all he was after was sex because that wasn't true. But it was hard. Earlier in the month he had decided he wasn't even going to try to sleep with her or say anything about it until they had two weeks of absolutely no fights, but she kept ruining it. It was like she was doing it on purpose.

Some days he thought she was more trouble than she was worth. He certainly wasn't getting much out of this relationship—at this point, anyway, and the ambiguity was hard to live with sometimes.

"Why do we need to define this relationship?" she had asked him. "Why can't we just let it happen without labeling or identifying everything that occurs?"

The problem with that was that definitions and boundaries were important to give a sense of place, of situatedness. He kept trying to remember how things had been before—before they had traveled and later broken up. If there was a chance for that to happen again, maybe it was worth some discomfort. Then again, maybe not.

He fluffed up his pillow. He could get used to the idea of a siesta every afternoon. He was in a half-sleep when the phone began to ring, and he let the answering machine pick up as he blinked and squinted, looking for the clock. He could tell without even opening the blinds that it was still overcast outside. Summer was almost here; it would be in another month or so.

Natalie's voice came through the machine.

"Hey, Rob, it's Nat. I was just calling because I thought you were off early today and I thought you said you were going to stop by after work. I was wondering whether you wanted to go to Vancouver this afternoon instead of doing something here tonight. Call me when you get back. Bye!"

He pulled the blankets off and felt a rush of cool air on his skin. He walked over to the bathroom and stuck his hand into the shower without pulling the curtain back, using the curtains to protect himself from the cold water as he pulled the handle out.

After a quick shower, he ate the remains of the Chinese food from the night before. He called Natalie just before leaving his place and she said she'd throw something together for a picnic supper and be ready by the time he got there. She wasn't, quite, but she was ready sooner than he expected.

"I hate it when I get lost."

"Don't worry about it, we don't have a schedule to keep or anything."

"Yeah, but this is all wasted time. We could be there by now."

"It's not wasted. Just look around."

"You're not driving."

"Here's a gas station—pull in here and we can ask for directions."

He pulled into the parking lot. "Go ahead," he said, crossing his arms without turning the engine off.

By the time they made it to the park it was late afternoon—past four. Rob had the wipers on low and the blade on his side wasn't getting proper contact with the window, so it left a thin layer of water through most of its arc. The cars in front of them were distorted.

"It's not really picnic weather, is it."

He glanced over, breaking out of the tense posture he found himself in as he tried to stare through the water. "No. Not unless you want to eat in the car. Or get wet."

"At least there aren't many people here. Last time I was here the traffic was awful."

"Do you want to eat in the car?" He was watching the road again, but he could see her turn toward him in his peripheral vision.

"Are you hungry? It's only four thirty."

"I don't care, I'm just saying."

"We can eat now, if you want to, I just thought we'd eat a little later."

"I said I don't give a damn, okay?"

"Okay, let's eat later then."

"Okay."

He pulled the car into a parking spot at Prospect Point. There were a handful of other cars around, people with umbrellas standing by the railing.

"A few drops of water won't hold us back, right?" She opened her door.

He didn't say anything. If they got wet now, they'd be wet the rest of the night and the whole way home. Her door closed behind her and he was alone in the car, watching her run up to the railing through streaks of rain.

As they drove through the rest of the park, she kept running out at every stop while he sat in the car. He wished that she would just stay in the car and they could eat their picnic while they looked out the windows, because he was hungry and he was pretty sure she'd be upset if he just ate the food while she was running around in the rain. Right now she was out looking at the Lumberman's Arch, walking in and out of the stupid doorway of logs like it was a magical thing.

He opened his door.

"Hey Nat, can I start eating?" he called.

She skipped over toward him.

"Boy, you're a poop-suck today."

"I just don't feel like getting wet. And I'm hungry."

She had packed bagels with cheese and lettuce and a tomato that needed to be sliced yet. They sat in the car, looking out as rain landed softly on the roof and ran down the glass in beads. He had tomato guts on his fingers and down in the mechanisms of the tiny pocket knife on his keychain. He took a bite and then set his bagel down on his lap and pulled off a paper towel from the thin roll beside the bag of food.

Natalie paused her chewing and put a finger up over her mouth. "I'm cold," she said, one cheek bulging with food. "Can you turn the heater on?"

"That's because you're wet," he said after swallowing, but he turned the key back and put the heat on anyway.

When they were done eating, the rain had stopped. Natalie wanted to go for a walk, so he parked the car down near Robson Street beside an ice cream store and they got out.

"When we're ready to head back we can get some ice cream, if you want, and eat it in the car on the way home."

She smiled and grabbed his hand. "We'll see how we're feeling then, I guess. I'm a little cold at the moment."

"We can turn the heaters on."

They walked toward Gastown, window shopping and people watching. There were so many stores, so many shopping bags.

"It's disgusting how many unnecessary stores there are in a lot of big cities."

She didn't say anything but she tightened her grip for a moment.

"It would be one thing if they were all little local shops, right? But look at all the corporations—they're exactly the same as everywhere else. You can't even tell we're in another country."

"I think I can. Or maybe it's just that I know we are."

Rain began to sprinkle down, spaced apart wide enough that he was getting hit by only one drop at a time. He saw a sign that pointed with an arrow toward the Skytrain terminal.

"This is not good," he said, looking at the sky.

"I don't care, I'm already wet," she said.

The rain began to come quicker and Rob grabbed her arm, pulling her toward the Skytrain. She followed half-heartedly so he let go and kept running. She came in shortly after him.

"What are we doing?"

"Getting out of the rain, for one thing. Do you want to go for a ride on the train?"

"Where to?"

"Nowhere. Just a ride. We'll go a stop or two that way, then get on the other one and come back here."

"Okay. Why?"

"Why not? It'll be about as fun as everything else we've done tonight," he said.

He was getting cold; the water had soaked through. They stood on the platform as a train pulled in. "Well, this afternoon hasn't turned out exactly like I was hoping," he said as they boarded.

"A lot of things turn out different then I had hoped," she said. "I'm starting to get used to it."

"What do you mean?"

She sat down and he stood leaning against a pole. He ran his hands through his hair; it wasn't wet enough to be dripping, but it was wet.

"Sometimes even though you hoped for something different, what you ended up getting is still good, just in a different way."

"Okay: what's so good about a rainy day, when it could have been a sunny one?"

"What's wrong with it?"

He motioned out the window.

"What's with the pose?" she asked. "You look like you're trying to be a GQ boy or something."

"Me? No. Just bracing myself," he said, but he turned his head to the left and tilted it slightly, clenching his jaw and staring down the station that was rolling away on the other side of the window.

"Isn't this fun?" she asked with mock excitement, twisted in the seat to look out the window.

They were quiet. There was no one else in this section. The whole afternoon felt wasted and here they were on a pointless ride back to where they started. What would cap it off would be a train guard who found out they had no tickets and fined them.

"Do you really think I look like a model?" he asked.

She sat straight again. "I said you looked like you were trying to be one."

He held the railing above him and stretched like a sexy man as the train braked. A woman and two young children walked on, and the youngest, a boy, looked up at him as he walked by, his head rotating on the neck as he walked by. His mother sat down a few seats away from Natalie and the boy kept watching Rob from the safety of his mother's knees.

Rob smiled at him and then looked at Natalie. She was striking her own pose, one arm across her body and the other resting on it as she held her chin between her thumb and a finger.

"I was in a photo shoot once where they kept sprinkling us with water the whole time," she said in a snotty voice. "I was like, 'Get it over with, I get rained on enough out here and I hate it, okay?'"

What the hell? He furrowed his brow without saying anything.

She was looking dreamily out the window. "I hate this city; I hate coming here. I can't wait to get back to New York, or Milan. When are you doing the underwear show?"

The little girl beside Natalie was looking up with wide eyes.

"Oh, I...do the underwear show, next week," he said, trying to look handsome. "Is this our stop?"

"No, the next one. I can't believe they make us ride the train. That's when you know times are tough, when you have to ride the train to a photoshoot."

"Did you ask him why they wanted to do this shoot so late?"

"I think they want a rainy night shot, to use a spotlight on us and catch all those reflections off the water." The kids had stopped looking at them and were on their knees on the seats, looking out the window. They weren't very entertaining actors. Oh, well.

"So we'll be standing out in the cold and wet?"

"Nearly naked. That's why we're getting paid. I just hope I don't get sick. Last time I did a shoot like this I got an awful cold and nearly died."

"I did die," Rob said. He sat down beside her and she leaned against him, smiling slightly.

They sat like that, not moving, until she let out a breath and shifted her weight.

"Why is life so complicated?" she asked quietly, in a voice that wasn't joking anymore. He wasn't sure exactly what she was referring to.

"What do you mean?"

"Oh, I don't know. Just in general. Nothing's perfect."

"I thought you said you were used to that."

"Yeah."

They got off at the next stop and rode back to their starting point mostly in silence. It was still raining when they got there.

"I'm a bit hungry," he said. "Do you want anything?"

"Not really, but if you want to get something, go ahead."

"I'll just get something quick then, otherwise we could get a bite to eat somewhere."

There was a short line of people by the nearest ATM, so they went to the end of the queue. A man dressed in dirty clothes was sitting against the wall, playing badly on a battered guitar and singing to the line of people.

"...and you stick—your—card—in the cash—maa—chine, and out—comes—a—little stack of green."

Nobody was paying attention to him or his open guitar case, and it looked like he'd been rained on pretty badly.

"Poor guy," Natalie said under her breath. The person at the ATM took his cash and walked away and they moved forward.

The man set his guitar down and stood up. "Come on people! You're just going to line up there and get your money and pretend you don't see me, and try to call the cops secretly on your cell phones?"

Nobody said anything or looked directly at him for long.

"Fuck you all!" he yelled, and then went up to the wall beside the ATM. He put his hands against the wall and pumped his hips slowly in and out, against the wall. "And I stick—my—dick—in the cash—maa—chine," he yelled.

Rob laughed as he moved up to the cash machine. He reached in his pocket and pulled out the little bit of change he had, calling the man away from his amorous intentions with the brick wall and dropping the coins in his hand.

"Although, that song makes me a little nervous about touching these buttons," he said, leaning over near Natalie's ear.

He was taking his card out of the machine when he heard the man beside him.

"Thirty-six cents?"

The man was about a foot away from him, holding the coins in an open hand.

"Thank you so much," he said.

He dropped the coins and held his arms in the air like he was waiting for a hug, moving his pelvis back and forth in the air near Rob's leg. Rob brought his left arm up as a block and punched him in the head with his right. The man stumbled back and tripped over his guitar, falling backwards into the brick wall. His head made a solid, wet sound when it hit and Rob heard Natalie gasp. The man didn't get up off the ground.

The machine was beeping, and Rob grabbed the twenty from the cash dispenser.

"Son of a bitch," he said as he walked away, looking over his shoulder at the man's body, still draped over his guitar case. Someone in the line kicked a fallen quarter toward the man.

"We should make sure he's okay," Natalie said from behind him.

He grabbed her arm and started walking again, feeling some resistance. "No we should not. Someone will call the police and they'll take care of him. What we should do is go and kick him a few times, but we won't."

"Rob, don't be an ass."

"I'm not the ass. Did you see that guy?"

"I'm going to see how he is," she said, pulling out of his grip. She walked over and knelt next to the man, who had shifted and was sitting beside his guitar. Her back was to him, but he saw her reach into her pocket.

"Is he okay?" Rob asked when she returned.

"I think he will be." She turned her head to look at him again. "He was crying."

"How much did you give him?"

"Five bucks. Hopefully he can find a place that will convert it for him."

"I'm not going to say anything."

"You already did."

"He was humping my leg, for shit's sake!"

They walked away from the ATM, in the direction that the car was parked.

"Listen, I'm sorry," he said after a moment. "I got a little carried away."

"You should be telling that to him, not me."

"Yeah, well. Next time I see him, I'll let him know."

They stopped at a store along the way and Rob bought two lukewarm pizza slices which he ate as they walked back toward the car. She didn't talk much as he ate, and after he was finished, the conversation didn't want to turn over again. They didn't talk much on the ride home.

He pulled up in front of her house in a no-parking zone. The rain was coming down full force. He put the hazards on and got out to open her door, but she was already getting out herself. They walked slowly to the house despite the rain. He wondered what was going through her mind.

He stood next to her on the porch and watched a drop of rainwater fall from her hair. His clothes were cold, heavy.

"Nat—I'm sorry about tonight."

"Thanks," she said. "I guess it's still possible that it was better than a movie."

"They do make pretty shitty movies these days."

"I'm not even disappointed that we didn't have the wildest, most exciting time ever, you know? I'm trying to appreciate reality more. But it was hard tonight."

"You're trying to love shitty nights?"

"No, I just mean the realness of it, the physicalness. There was a lot of stuff tonight that maybe wasn't as perfect as it could have been, or wasn't quite what we were expecting, but everything's like that. Everything fits into this spectrum—not really of good and bad, but of what we were expecting and what we weren't expecting."

He found himself nodding blankly, not really hearing her, or understanding. She was looking at him but she wasn't really seeing him. It seemed to him that she was looking through him, into her own brain, or somewhere else. That was one thing she had that he wanted: the ability to see past the surface into a dimension of her own, where she could be content with disappointment.

"The challenge is to find the good in the unexpected places, in the stuff we didn't want. In the lukewarm pizza, in the rain on skin, stuff like that. And then once you find something good, to start to love some of the stuff you didn't want, the stuff that reminds us that this is real life," she said.

"The stuff like dirty old alcoholics trying to screw my leg, you mean." He was making a joke to show he had gotten over his initial anger, but instead of smiling, her face became sad.

"No..." She paused, looking over his shoulder into the rain. After a moment she spoke again. "I'm trying to embrace the things that I don't necessarily like at first, but which aren't a part of...our brokenness, you know?"

He didn't understand the distinction, but he didn't say anything.

"It's like this—I love my humanity, my physicality. I recognize that I have limitations. I realize that I'm a creature. But there are things in the world that aren't meant to be like they are; they're broken, and I want to acknowledge that, and hate it, and long for things to be the way they were meant to be, and will be again. Bad breath is one thing, but what about people being forced to live in the streets? Things like violence? Pollution? Injustice?"

"I know, those are different," he said, hoping the conversation would die peacefully. "I was just trying to make a joke."

She was beautiful, her hair matted down by the rain and her arms clasped around herself, staring at her feet. She seemed to have finished her thought. He didn't want to talk about it anymore. He enjoyed hearing her ideas and theories, but sometimes he felt like he couldn't say anything without getting caught on a technicality.

"I guess I should get home," he said.

"You're welcome to stay for a bit, if you want. It's not that late yet. Maybe we could talk for a bit and try to salvage the evening."

It was going well until he tried to take her shirt off.

They were lying parallel beside each other on the bed now, each body following the contours of the other, legs bent at the same angles. She was facing away from him and sleeping. He had his left arm over her waist and his right arm was wedged between them. He wasn't exactly comfortable, but he didn't want to move.

When they had come in, she had raided Shawn's room to borrow some boxers and sweatpants for Rob, and had thrown his wet clothes in the dryer. They sat in the living room with hot chocolate and a blanket over the two of them.

"I think we've redeemed the night already," she said.

"It's nice," he agreed.

"And it wouldn't feel this comfortable right now if we hadn't first been uncomfortable, so there you go."

"Yeah, maybe. But if I had the chance, I think I'd still avoid the discomfort."

"The only thing I'd change would be you hitting that guy."

"I do feel kind of bad about that now, but at the time it seemed like the right thing to do."

The tiny marshmallows in his hot chocolate were soft. He sucked a few of them up while trying to minimize the liquid since it was still too hot.

"Sometimes I still can't believe that you're back in town, or in my living room," Natalie said.

"I know."

"We've got quite a story, don't we?"

"Yeah. We've known each other for a long time, if you add it all up."

"Why do you think we have so many problems?"

"That's a bit of a loaded question. I don't know."

"Well, I've been wondering what are the problems and what are the parts of the relationship that aren't like I imagined or wanted, but are real. Like I was talking about earlier—what parts feel wrong simply because they're not like the relationships Hollywood shows us and which ones feel wrong because they're not healthy?"

"Yeah. I think there's another aspect, too. I'll be honest—I think that the ambiguity around our relationship is unhealthy. I think that I'd be more comfortable knowing one way or the other instead of trying to exist in between."

"I know. I know. I haven't really been fair to you that way."

"I don't want to pressure you, you know that. I'm just being honest."

"Thanks—and I think I know exactly what you mean. Does it help you to know that I think that we're growing despite the ambiguity? I think that maybe not putting a label on us has taken some of the pressure away, for me anyway, and I think that's good. And it's falling away, in various degrees."

"What do you mean?"

"Well, between us, we kind of know that we're floating between 'very good friends' and 'significant others.' But we haven't officially labeled ourselves that way, and I kind of like that. It feels like there's less pressure on us."

"For me, it's...confusing."

"Here. For what it's worth," she said, turning his head and kissing him. He set his mug down and kissed her back, sliding further down the couch. He was sure he was golden when she broke out of the kiss to tell him that he might as well sleep over again. He wasn't sure what he had done wrong after that, but when he had begun to pull her sweatshirt over her head she had tensed up and pulled it back down, making a little noise and then murmuring, "I'm sorry, I'm sorry," and he could feel her tightening up. So it seemed that one brief glimpse of her breasts was all he was getting.

He was either doing something wrong repeatedly or she was playing games with him. He didn't know why he was surprised tonight—this was as far as he'd gotten for months. He had very little hope left until he was touching her, when all the little scraps of hope banded together and charged down into his penis. Every time he'd start thinking this time was the time, and then in the middle of things something inside of her snapped shut like the jaws of a trap and he couldn't get it open again. In January he had been persistent one night and had gotten her down to her panties and bra. Then she started stiffening up and he knew he was losing her, so he started coaxing, kissing her through her protests, and that had frozen all physical relations for more than a month. He hadn't even been allowed to hold her hand and he had just about thrown in the towel on the whole thing.

He wasn't even sure what they were considered. They weren't officially together, though it often felt like they were and her friends all treated them like they were. He had asked her a number of times what their status was, and it was always the same: vague and unknown. She was scared of just coming out and saying it, as though denying it and living in the fog was a solution.

He didn't know what he could do to help if she never talked to him about it. He wondered if maybe she had caught a venereal disease that wouldn't go away and she didn't want him to know about it. That was a scary thought.

Now he was lying here next to her, knowing he couldn't have her, wishing his erection would die. He had read once that Gandhi would test his vow of chastity by lying next to naked young women. But he was definitely not Gandhi, and he wasn't trying to keep a vow.

Lauyn kragt Bakker

Earth First!
We'll destroy the
other planets later

It was still dark out when she woke to the sound of monks chanting. She had been standing in the sky train, and Rob was beside her, but he had his eyes closed and wasn't responding to her voice. The seats were full of people who had their heads down, their bodies bent double. As she looked around, they all slowly unfolded their bodies and sat up, chanting quietly. Everything was slightly transparent, like Jesus in Dali's "Last Supper." She could see through the people to the seat, and through the seat to the wall, and through the wall to the blur of the outside world as they were carried along the track. As their faces came into view, she began to recognize some of them.

Scott was there, still fifteen years old, his face peaceful as he mouthed the words. They were all like that. It didn't look like they were seeing anything, just staring ahead, looking through each other, through Natalie and Rob. She saw her mother on the opposite side from where Scott was sitting and a few people down from him. Her father was there and somehow that hadn't bothered her at the time. The rest of the seats were filled up both with people she knew and those she had never seen before, people who were alive and who had died long ago. Rob wouldn't open his eyes, but she was sure he could hear her.

The chanting continued after she woke up. She hadn't wanted to wake up to the blast of the alarm clock and ruin the whole mood of the morning, so last night as Rob was changing, she had set the timer on her stereo and turned off the alarm clock. It was the perfect CD to use because the voices started quietly and then gradually got louder, so you weren't jolted awake. It was a gentle bridge between sleeping and waking life. She had a nagging headache somewhere in her brain and felt out of sync with reality, as though she were caught half in and half out of time.

Rob was still sleeping beside her, each breath starting quietly and growing in volume until it stopped abruptly, cut off. She wished the chanting would stop, and Rob would be quiet, and she could just go back to sleep, but she slid out of bed anyway. She felt with her hands in the direction of the stereo's power indicator, stepping slowly forward until she found the volume, and turning it down so the chanting was barely audible again. She sat down by her desk and opened the dream journal, jotting down what details she remembered from the dream. Mostly she remembered the facial expressions: Scott's peaceful, Rob's pinched shut. What to make of it? Riding on a train of people who were living and dead, and Rob there with his eyes closed, not wanting to see.

She hadn't planned on Rob staying over last night. It had gotten out of control for a moment again, and just as she started to feel like things were back how they used to be, fear welled up.

Fear that this relationship wouldn't ever break out of the cycle they had been in for months. Fear that the problems really were problems and not just something she was supposed to learn to appreciate or deal with. Fear that he still didn't know her, that he was still in love with the Natalie of two years ago and not the one that had changed so much in the interim. Fear that she didn't know him or how he had changed. Fear that either one of them wouldn't like the truth about the other. Fear that he didn't know yet that she had carried his child for over two months, that he might not forgive her for keeping it secret for so long. Fear that he thought her faith was stupid, or that he was just using her. Fear that she was setting herself up for another big fall, that he was going to leave again.

Their relationship since he had moved back had been unstable, like Jekyll and Hyde. There had been weeks where he had been keeping his distance, pissed off at her while she was wishing he'd come by. Other weeks, she didn't return his calls or visit and she wished he'd go away. And in between there was always a week or two where they were both more or less glad that the other was around, but that never seemed to last.

These fears always peaked when Rob tried to press beyond the indistinct boundaries she had set, like last night. Her problem was that she never reached a conclusion in the meantime and so she had to deal with it at that moment. Last night as he was starting to undress her, she realized again that they weren't ready for what he wanted. The beauty and the trouble with ambiguity was that decisions always needed to be made. Yesterday she had wanted a night without decisions.

It was hard to do, with Rob bemoaning the weather and the people around them. She had to deal not only with her own brain, but with the downer beside her. She wasn't in the mood to discuss anything last night, even though she realized that they did need to talk. She had decided to postpone it until this morning and had asked him to stay over so that she could. It seemed that this morning would be an appropriate time to do it: Easter, new life, new beginnings.

One of the things she felt like she had to tell him about was the pregnancy, but in many ways it also seemed irrelevant. She thought of U2's "One," and hoped it wasn't prophetic: "It's too late, tonight, to drag the past out into the light...We hurt each other, and we're doing it again."

She struck a match and started to light the candles. Sunrise was coming and she still had a headache. Maybe the dream was a message. They had been surrounded by people who were living and who were dead, and Rob didn't want to see them, he didn't want to listen to her. Maybe it wasn't right to tell him about the pregnancy after all these years. Maybe it wouldn't do him any good to know.

She picked up a clay plate and goblet from her desk, both slightly askew. The crumbs on the plate were the remains of her communion from Friday, after Rob fell asleep. She had torn off a chunk from the bread they had baked and poured a glass of wine. *This do in remembrance of me.* She had thought of the idea last year, and decided to do it again this year. The goblet was warped, like it had started to sag before it was fired, and the plate was of slightly uneven thickness.

She had found them in Fairhaven a few years ago as she was walking through some of the studios. All the studios had similar pots and plates for the tourists, with variations in glaze and usually one thing that was unique to the store—little figurines or small indoor ponds. Then she came to a small shop without much in the way of signage, just a small hand-painted sandwich board that said "Pottery. Come in!"

Most of the pots in there were not quite smooth or were leaning a little to one side. One corner of the store was devoted to hanging pieces that were made up of defaulted pots, melded together in clumps as though they had been thrown there as the potter sat at his wheel. The pile of cast-offs was fired and glazed, presented as a hanging art piece instead of as pots. The original shape of the pot was still visible in the squashed and broken forms they had become. They were beautiful.

When she was younger, she had heard a sermon about God being a potter and shaping us like clay on a wheel, using his hand to shape out our lumps and to re-center us. There was something beautiful about the image, especially if you imagined a potter with a perfect piece of clay that responds to his direction. But it didn't seem to apply to the imperfect clay of her own life, which seemed to sag and lean and always be just slightly off-center and full of impurities.

Maybe in our sinful, broken lives, we are expecting God to shape us forcefully into perfect pots, to manhandle us into submission. But the imperfections of our clay keep coming out, ruining the pots that God is working on. And the failed pots are tossed into a pile in the corner, waiting to be glazed and fired and hung on the wall.

She brought the dishes into the dark kitchen, feeling ahead of her with her free hand. She flicked the light on and rinsed the plate off, then swished some water around in the goblet. The remainder of the wine had dried in the bottom, so she left a little water in the bottom to soak.

The candles were still burning but the light from the kitchen ruined the contrast of the darkness to the flame. She closed her bedroom door and sat in the desk chair. There was a hint of light from the outside window. She felt the beginnings of cramps inside her.

"Pssst." She nudged Rob with her foot, leaning her chair back on two legs.

He grunted but didn't wake up. Maybe she should just let him sleep—that way she wouldn't have to tell him anything. It was strange how the longer she kept the secret, the more that length of time became a factor in decision-making. Why tell him now? She found again that she wanted to retain the safety of ambiguity and distance.

She set the chair down and leaned forward to run her hand down his cheek and across his jawbone. His cheeks felt like fine toothed sandpaper. He opened his eyes and stared at her for a moment before trying to kiss her hand and go back to sleep.

"Are you going to get up for the sunrise?"

"Go ahead without me," he murmured.

She watched as he readjusted his position and breathed contentedly. Even if she did wake him, he'd be in no mood to talk. She wasn't even in a mood to talk right now. She tried to watch the growing light in the window but couldn't see much besides street lamps and the houses across the street. She gazed at the candles for two minutes and crawled back into bed.

The room was light when she woke and Rob was sitting on the edge of the bed in his boxers. Her headache was worse. He twisted himself to look back at her.

"Hey. You're awake," he said. "We missed the sunrise."

"Well, sort of. I got up for a little while but you didn't want to."

"I said that?"

"Yeah. But I couldn't see anything anyway."

He yawned, stretching. "I'm going to head over to my place. I'm meeting Tyler for lunch to discuss some of the stuff on the site. Do you want to come?"

"Not today. I don't feel well, and I have a headache. I'm getting my period."

"Well, you could just leave it at the euphemisms, as far as I'm concerned. Why don't you go back to sleep?"

"I think I will. Or I'll lie here at least."

Rob pulled his pants and shirt on while she watched him.

"Hey, Rob. We...need to talk. I was meaning to talk with you this morning—I decided that I would last night, but I'm wiped. I guess I don't feel up to it right now."

"That sounds serious," he said.

"It is and it isn't, I guess, hopefully. Some of it's something I've been meaning to tell you for a long time now, but haven't ever worked up the courage for, I guess, and some of it's just about things in general, like we were talking about last night."

"Well, what is it?"

"I don't know, I can't summarize it without talking about it and I can't do that right now."

"So when do you want to do it?"

"Give me a day, a few days. I just feel like shit right now."

He was standing there, looking at her like he was about to ask something else.

"Sure," he said, and walked out the door.

She spent a length of time falling into and out of sleep, never fully one place or the other. The world was running like the car she'd driven without enough oil in it—things were knocking together out of sync, not well lubricated. She had a vague fear in the back of her mind that everything she knew about anything was false.

Her mother was expecting her—and possibly Rob—for dinner, but she didn't feel like going, and she had forgotten to mention it to Rob. She dialed her mother's number after checking the clock on the microwave to make sure her mother would be gone to church. 10:47.

"Hello, you've reached Harriet Van Poele. Please leave a message and I'll get back to you soon."

"Hi, mom, it's Nat. I'm not feeling well this morning, so can we get together for coffee next week? I know it's Easter; I hope you didn't make anything special. Talk to you later."

She walked toward the bathroom. Everything seemed artificial today. A machine that pretended to be her mother, copying her voice down so it could pretend to be

Natalie later when her mom got home. Her own mom didn't even have the same last name as her anymore. She had changed it back a few years ago, after her dad had moved back to town.

Even the rocks she had gathered on the beach last summer were faded. She had picked them up for their incredible colors, pocketing them and later piling them in a wide glass bowl on the tank behind the toilet. They were supposed to look beautiful, but they looked like plain old rocks. The ocean water that lapped up against them on the beach unlocked their color. She brought them to her home, to a bathroom that was plastic and shiny, pretending to be clean and antiseptic and the colors had died.

She sat down on the toilet and pulled her tampon out. Blood was still real. She stared at the dark stain, trying to forget about digital clocks and answering machines and plastic. When she had opened the bottle of wine on Friday night, she had spilled some on the counter after yanking the cork out. She had soaked it up with a paper towel, folding it in on itself a handful of times, and the wine still soaked through, watery red. Blood and wine were real.

According to the clocks, the world went on slowly laying itself out in a straight line, from the logical beginning to the logical end. But according to the seasons, time was circular or cyclical, like menstruation and tidal patterns. She remembered a poem by Yeats—it was about a falcon on a tether. She couldn't remember it word for word, but it had something to do with history, the "gyre" of history, neither linear nor circular, but both, like a spiral. Like DNA, or a corkscrew. Or a toilet flushing.

She closed the bathroom door behind her when she left, and lay back down on her bed. She was alone for the weekend—Tink was gone home for the break and Shawn was over at Dara's place. Rob wasn't coming back today. She wasn't tired any more but it felt best, or easiest, to just lay there in her cocoon. Was this what caterpillars felt like before hunkering down into their pods to begin their metamorphosis? Just kind of huddling in there, oblivious, their bodies feeling like something was slowly shifting and cramping inside, moving.

She came out of a sort of waking sleep almost an hour later. It felt as though the world had been paused but her life kept going, independent of time, like those scenes in movies where everything is frozen in place except one or two people, who keep walking around.

She didn't feel like showering. She got rained on enough last night to compensate, Shawn would say. She drank a glass of water from the tap and set it, empty, on the counter. The dried up wine had soaked free from the bottom of the goblet, so she swished it around and dumped in the sink.

She went out the back door and locked it behind her. The clouds were thinner than yesterday and it wasn't raining, but the ground was still wet.

She walked the route that she usually biked to work, looking without really seeing, or seeing without really caring. It was wet and drizzly. She wasn't sure what she was going to do there. Maybe work on a painting. Her talk with Rob this morning still sat uncomfortably in her mind. She was always reading into his comments and their disagreements dire prophecies that foretold the doom of their relationship. Why did they argue so much if it wasn't because they weren't compatible?

One of the things that it kept coming down to was that she was scared. At first she had been scared because there were two years in between their lives, and because she had the secret of their pregnancy, and because it hadn't worked the first time. She wondered whether they were a match at all, or whether they were each interested in people who didn't exist. By now she was scared for all of those reasons, but also because she'd been scared for a full six months now. While the machine of this relationship clunked along like an old engine empty of oil, the pressure had built, the expectations were greater, and it just felt like the whole thing was ready to fall apart or seize up completely.

Sometimes, it seemed like he really knew her and understood things about her that no one else did. Other times it felt like he thought she was an idiot.

If she had felt better this morning, she would have definitely told him about the pregnancy. It really wasn't as big of a deal as she kept making it seem in her mind—they had been pregnant, but they weren't any more. And that had been years ago.

Why was death such a part of life? Why did it seem so integral to everything? If nothing died, nothing would live—or not for long. But what had Scott's death brought life to? What had her dead baby made to come alive?

Sometimes death does bring life, but not always. Sometimes death brings death. Or it brings both death and life. Rob had told her once that he believed the earth had a purification cycle—that once any one species got too dominant or started to hurt the earth, the cycle kicked in and destroyed them. He had probably gotten the idea from a movie or something, but he sounded like he really believed it.

"It happened to the dinosaurs," he had said, "and now it's starting to happen to us with all these crazy weather patterns and disasters."

"So the earth is killing us—it's not us that are killing ourselves?"

"Well, I think maybe it's some of each."

"And how did the dinosaurs hurt the planet?"

He had looked sheepish for a moment. "Methane gas?"

There was no doubt that the earth was on track to be destroyed by people, it was just a question of whether they'd figure it out in time and stop the destruction. Someone had told her once that nothing was threatening the existence of life on earth, just certain forms of life—like human life, and the lives of a whole lot of other species. Years ago, when everyone was worried about nuclear war, they said that after the globe was radioactive and everyone was dead, the cockroaches would be the first to crawl back out of the ground and pick up living.

She reached the store and climbed the back steps, fishing in her pockets for the keys. There was no room to move—in the spring her workspace always shrunk dramatically as the students got rid of everything they owned. For a few days last week she and Dorrie had cruised the streets looking for the best cast-offs to load into the truck, but they had to stop because they had no more room to store things. They had to turn away a lot of donations at this time of year.

She snagged her pants on a metal filing cabinet's handle as she squeezed between it and a sofa that was standing on end. Then she was inside her nest. She sat on the stool and looked at the canvas in front of her.

She had tacked a sticker that Rob had created for one of his projects on the wall beside her stool. He had made it in late January or early February, when his "Hit and Run Art" stickers had been a fairly new idea. She didn't really like it because he had taken one of her paintings—the one he had purchased after her coffeehouse show last December—and had put it on the stickers and on his website without asking her. He said he had wanted to surprise her and she knew he meant well, but she had asked him not to use any more of her paintings.

The background pictured a big white mansion with a man and a woman in front of it, reminiscent of American Gothic. The foreground was crowded with garbage cans and bags and trash. There were two things that bothered her most about how Rob had used it. First, the sticker itself was much too small—she couldn't see any of the detail. Second, it was apparent he hadn't done much in-depth study of the image—it was called *Throw Away Society* and he had just taken it at face value, as a modern American Gothic with garbage piled up in front of it.

It was intended in a different vein, and the most important details weren't readily apparent on the sticker. There were people in the trash but on the sticker they looked like cardboard cut-outs, or inflatable dolls. A lady and a young girl wearing fake smiles, jammed into a metal garbage can at an angle.

She probably shouldn't have sold the picture to him in the first place. If he hadn't been so adamant she wouldn't have.

The sticker itself was fairly simple. It had two lines of text above the image:

(it's time to)
THROW AWAY SOCIETY

Underneath the text, all that it listed was his website address and a little logo for "Hit and Run Art." A package of wildflower seeds was impaled on a small nail next to the sticker.

The seeds were another of his campaigns—the one she liked best, probably because he had made it especially for her. Every time he came up with a new one, he would show her to get her opinion, as though doing a field test for a new product.

Near the end of February, they had talked for a while about sin—he didn't think there was such a thing. She asked him, in that case, why he was interested in changing anything, and he said that some things were still wrong but that didn't mean they were sinful. After arguing on the semantics for a few minutes she had let it drop.

A few days later, he had come to show her the stickers from his latest campaign. They were solid black except for the tiny web address at the bottom and in large block letters in the middle, the word SIN with an arrow pointing from the word out the side of the sticker. When he stuck them on posters and signs, he positioned the arrow so that it was pointing to a corporate name or logo or slogan.

"Do you get it?" he asked.

"When did you change your mind about that? I thought you didn't believe in sin."

"Well, I don't, really, at least not in the way you mean it. I still don't like the aura around the word, implying that what we do will bring judgement from the gods or something, but the whole article is a call to rethink the word. The word does still have a lot of emotional power. I'd like to recover the other usage you were talking about—how we're sinning against each other when we exploit or destroy."

"So you're just going to stick these on advertisements?"

"And I'll have the write-up on the web. I was also thinking about making some customized stickers for specific corporations with statistics and specific sins—you know, in case people don't take the time to go to the site, at least they'll get the idea."

She remembered that she had been silent for a moment, trying to figure out what it was about his attitude that didn't sit right.

"Where's the hope in all this?"

"What do you mean?"

"Well, do you have any hope? Or are you just trying to point out all the problems? What are your stickers going to do?"

"They'll start waking people up. There's a lot of crap that people don't know about."

"But what's the point? What are they going to do about it?"

"I don't know. Anything. If you find out who's lying, you know who not to trust."

"Maybe. But it seems…you can either spend your life looking for who's full of shit, or you can spend it looking for what's true."

"Same thing," he said.

"I don't think so."

They hadn't talked much for a few days after that. She was starting to feel like he was milking her for ideas, twisting what she said and using it for a little game he played for his own enjoyment. He was reducing important issues down to one-time campaigns, like they were there for entertainment and could be forgotten after they'd had their moment in the sun. His projects lacked depth—what you saw on the sticker was simplistic and devoid of nuance, and since a conversation with her had inspired it, she felt misrepresented. It reminded her of how he mocked her before he had moved to Seattle, talking about the "the resurrected power of almighty JEEZus."

He was too busy slapping his stickers around town, writing his article, and updating his website with Tyler to realize she was angry. About a week and a half later, he showed up at her door with a huge smile. He handed her the package of wildflower seeds.

"What do you think?" he asked.

He had made a label for the little paper envelope and it looked quite professional. She was surprised. The brand name was HOPE and it had a photograph of a sidewalk with a crack in it. A flower was growing out of the crack.

Instructions: Open package of Hope and sprinkle seeds liberally in sidewalk cracks, on boulevards, on your neighbor's lawn and garden, and anywhere else there is soil. Allow time for Hope to germinate and grow before it blossoms.

One of these days she was going to do that—around her house or maybe the store. In another few weeks or a month, when the weather was officially switched over to summer. Flowers in the cracks of concrete was a good image, if a little clichéd.

If we destroyed the earth, cockroaches would crawl up out of the rubble and wildflowers would sprout from the chinks in our pavement the next day. Death can't stop life. The world would decompose and something else would grow out of it, feeding off of it. When old things die, new things grow or are built in their place.

She remembered going to Seattle as a child and learning about the city underneath the city—the one that was destroyed by fire, the one they built the new city on. Even now, whenever she thought about Seattle as an entity, she found she still had a fragment of the sense of foreboding she had had as a child. Her father had told her that Seattle had been built on top of another city, and in her nine year-old mind, she pictured another city functioning underneath the Seattle she was walking through. He pointed out patches of glass rectangles inlaid along the edge of the sidewalk and explained that you could see light through them from the city down below. She had visions of people living in mostly darkness, etiolated, looking up at occasional geometric patches of stars, predictable rectangular constellations with enormous eyes that had adjusted to a constant lack of light.

That trip to Seattle was the year before Scott died. He had been fourteen then, and he had constantly dreamed out loud about the time when he'd be old enough to drive. And Dad had let him hold the wheel from where he was sitting in the passenger seat while mom sucked in her breath beside Natalie in the back seat and gripped the back of his chair, pinching her fingers into the vinyl.

They had still been living outside of Lynden, between it and Sumas. She and Scott had to bike to town if they wanted to play with anyone during the summers. Every morning during the school year they waited for a school bus to rattle by and pick them up and take them on a round-about path toward the school. Every day they'd loop around the other side of town and turn onto Front Street, passing through the middle of a cemetery.

It was a strange sort of entrance to a town—gravestones on either side of the road as you entered. As soon as the bus passed through the cemetery, a small billboard for the local butcher appeared, facing the other direction. They'd always show the new kids how, if you turned around as you passed it, the butcher's sign advertising "Fresh Meat" stood directly in front of rows and rows of gravestones. Whenever they drove on the road through the cemetery with their dad, he'd say, "Look at this, people are dying to get into this town," which was funny when she was young. By the time she was in high school, she thought it more likely that they were dying to get out.

That wasn't the graveyard that Scott had been buried in. He was buried in a smaller one on the other side of town—the one that her grandparents were buried in.

She wished she'd had a chance to talk to Scott in the dream last night. It had been a long time since she'd seen him. After he had died, he had been in her dreams regularly. She didn't remember most of the dreams anymore—she hadn't had a dream journal then to help her remember, but there was one in particular that she remembered fragments of because she'd had the same dream multiple times.

She and Scott were in a pool, swimming, and the water was gradually getting wilder, with waves and wind, and then the edges of the pool were gone and they were in the middle of an ocean. She tried to swim toward him, but doing so seemed to make Scott get further and further away. She wasn't sure what it meant.

Sometimes she thought that maybe dreams were really a way that her mind ventured into or flirted with another dimension. A dimension that was deeper than time. *God is not the God of the dead, but the living, for to him all are alive.* He fills all of the dimensions we can imagine and all of them that we can't, so time is irrelevant. The past is the future and the present is the past. Scott is still alive and she'd already died and Eve was just about to pluck down an apple as the kingdom of God arrived within us.

But she wasn't outside of time. From here on the inside for the quick and the dead, time was burning down like a coiled fuse.

That she hadn't thought about Scott much lately was normal—by now he'd been dead for more of her life than he'd been alive. She remembered his funeral well, but it was mostly in short segments, stop-motion images.

His pale body in the casket. Her kiss on his cool cheek and her mother worrying that her lips would smear the makeup on his face. People at the funeral home delivering their condolences like tightly wrapped packages. The euphemisms for death—passed away, gone to a better place—that seemed somehow worse for their attempt to make this awful thing palatable.

She also remembered the messy details of death, like the library's overdue notices that started coming nearly a month after he had died. It was almost a year later when Jim Abrams, one of his friends from school who had moved away the year before, was passing through town and stopped by their house asking for Scott. Those types of things were like the fingernails and hair of a corpse in a way. It seems like they're still growing for a while after the body dies, as though there are still little pockets of life remaining. In reality it's just the flesh around them receding.

One thing that disturbed her was that most of the strong memories she had of him were centered around photographs she had in her album. It was as though the photographs were the reinforcement for the memories—that she had to study the photographs to retain the memories and the ones she had no pictures of were subject to fading, forgetting.

A scarier possibility was that the photos, in combination with the stories she'd been told or remembered, had created the memories. Occasionally she found herself "remembering" events that she would have been too young to understand, or events that had occurred when she wasn't there, or before she was born. Things like their trip to the Redwoods in California when she was three, or when Scott pooped in the bathtub. He was one and a half then, which meant she was negative two and a half.

She had a canvas out, an abstract piece that she worked on whenever she felt like painting but didn't feel like painting. On days like this, she would just squeeze out some color and spend time messing around on the canvas, on top of anything that was already painted there. There were at least three layers of paint on it by now, and the existing paint strokes were starting to disrupt what she was painting on top, leaving visible textures and gaps of color from underneath.

The background she was about to work on was a field of color. In varying intensities and levels it was covered with dark earth tones and blues and greens. Last time she had worked on it she had worked in a lot of black in dry-brush layers on top of the color. She smeared an orange arc across everything and it reminded her of the edge of an asteroid or comet, so she started filling it in and mixing colors—the paint was too intense unmixed.

Dali claimed to have a memory from "in utero," of his mother frying eggs. He painted the scene, with himself as a fried egg hanging above the pan, dangling from a string as though it were an umbilical cord. Was it possible that he could have remembered? They say that children are born with an intimate knowledge of the mother's voice, that the strength of her emotions in the months before birth is multiplied in the fetus. That was partly why she felt so guilty about the time while she was pregnant. Did her fetus know it wasn't wanted? Could it feel her sadness and confusion, multiplied in itself?

She continued to work at the edge of the comet and it began to look like a map of somewhere she'd never been. Dorrie had put up a poster of the earth a few weeks ago, with south as up and north as down. All the names of the countries and oceans were flipped 180 degrees from a standard map. She had felt really disoriented the first time she saw it because there was so much water in the top half, and because it felt strange to be on the bottom. There's no up or down in space.

She added darkened areas on her comet in the rough shape of upside-down continents. It looked vaguely like the earth, glowing hot with the continents scorched out, a burning ember. Was it the past or the future? Was it a molten earth being shaped, or an old earth being destroyed by fossil-fuels, or bombs? She opted for creation.

She rinsed her brushes off, finished painting for now. One of the most beautiful things about Genesis was that everything had its conception in a peaceful act of creativity and love. Other creation stories seemed to be random, rooted in violence and meaninglessness.

The hot burning glow she had painted could be a fire that purified rather than consumed. *Touch the ember to your lips and be purified. Kiss the earth.*

Outside the drizzling had finally stopped and there was a slight break in the clouds. She took an alternate route home. The streets were still wet and the sidewalks were littered with soggy worms, some of them fastened to the concrete by shoe treads. A puddle near the gas station was slick with a gasoline rainbow, which was either an irony or a promise.

Thank You For Not Breaking

That she was going to break up with him was certain. What he wasn't sure of was how he felt about it because he felt differently about it at various times. The first emotion had been disappointment. In so many ways they seemed to be a match—they were both interested in the same issues, they laughed at the same things, neither of them fit well in the "real world" of suits and desk jobs. Yet, he had an overwhelming sense of impending failure, like he'd written an important test poorly but hadn't yet received the grade.

He had the impulse to try to gloss this over and convince her to wait, or to quickly try to fix whatever it was that she felt was wrong with them. Either that or break up with her first, like the person who quits preemptively because he's about to be fired. He wouldn't do that, he knew. The point when he should have folded was well past, and now he was just seeing and raising because there was too much money down to back away. He always lost at poker.

Now that he was starting to get used to the idea, he felt a weight lifting, a sense of relief about the whole thing. The pressure to pretend that they could make this work was being released. It was a little disconcerting to him that she was going to break up with him again—but was there any shame in that? Something indicative about the fact that he had been rejected twice by the same person? It's better for the self-esteem to do the initiating than to have someone else do it to you, better to give than to receive.

But somehow he couldn't envy Natalie her position. She obviously felt badly about it and was having a hard time doing it. Who knew how many months she'd dragged her feet on this? No wonder things had seemed strained between them.

If she was going to break up with him the next time they talked, he decided that he was going to make it easy on her. Whatever she said, he would nod and say he understood and agreed, and that he, too, hoped that they could still be friends. All the usual comments, and no fuss or misunderstanding or hurt feelings. Make it clean and antiseptic, straight edges, like a surgery with a sharp scalpel.

He stretched his body out in his boyhood bed, which still seemed out of place in a room other than the one he grew up in. His feet hung over the end of the mattress when he elongated himself like this. He had been lying here awake for some time already.

He wondered what time it was. It was light out but his mother hadn't come in to wake him. He had to work this afternoon, so he planned on driving back up to Bellingham this morning.

After he had been at Natalie's place on Sunday, he found himself home alone with no weekend plans and almost two days left of his long weekend. Bobbi had asked him to take Monday off because he had worked Saturday and she didn't expect things to be too busy on Easter Monday.

So he had come home for a few days. He was starting to wonder how much longer he'd have the chance to come down and see his dad. He hadn't really enjoyed his time here, but felt compelled to come. Mom was holding up remarkably well—now she had someone to care for, something to keep her busy. It was watching Dad that was hard. He still showed effects of the stroke and Rob wondered if he'd ever fully recover. He had to sit so often, and he walked slowly, as though he was unsure that he was walking in the right direction. Sometimes he'd be drooling without realizing it, a trail of slime leaking over his lip or out of the corner of his mouth on the left side.

It was a good thing that they weren't on the farm anymore—though it could be argued that not being on the farm had accelerated his illness. He didn't know how to keep living when he was off of the farm. Rob wasn't sure if it was wrong to feel glad for his mother. She still had Dad around the house, but now he wasn't always pacing around or overseeing everything she did.

He found his watch in the pocket of his jeans. It was already ten o'clock. He pulled his pants on and found a t-shirt. He walked across the hall to the bathroom. He could hear someone moving around in the kitchen—probably his mother making his breakfast. He pissed into the toilet water, directing the stream of urine away from the tiny bubbles that formed and into the smooth areas of water. It was an eternal game, trying to cover the surface of the water with a layer of bubbles. There was always that little area that couldn't be filled. He flushed the toilet, then splashed his face at the sink and rinsed his mouth out with tap water.

His father was in the kitchen, standing slump-shouldered beside the counter, weeping silently. The cabinet in front of him was open, and the counter and floor around him were covered in cereal. He saw Rob as he came around the corner and tried to wipe his big, beefy face with the back of his right hand. He didn't have complete control of his left side anymore. He walked with a noticeable limp, and sometimes items that he was holding would just slip from his hands.

Rob walked in and averted his eyes, not wanting to draw attention to the fallen cereal. He faced the stove and got out a frying pan, turning a burner to medium. He opened the fridge and took out the bacon and eggs and butter while his father swept the Cheerios beside the garbage can and brushed the ones that were on the counter into a bowl. He felt something under his foot crunch and turn into powder.

"Morning, Dad," he said, watching the butter melt in the pan.

"Morning."

After the eggs and bacon had filled the bottom of the pan and cooked together into a circular conglomerate, spattering and popping, he slid them out onto a plate and sat down next to his father by the table. He felt another Cheerio disintegrate under his foot but pretended not to have noticed.

"How are you doing?"

"Shouldn't complain."

"Where's Mom?"

"She went to Mrs. Belkin for coffee this morning."

Rob noticed as he ate that his father kept looking at his plate and he wished that he had remembered that his dad couldn't eat this kind of a breakfast anymore. The entire kitchen smelled gloriously of bacon and eggs while there he sat eating bland cereal with skim milk.

"So you're enjoying your work?" his dad asked for the third time in two days.

"Well, it's kind of boring. I'm still doing my own writing on the side."

"Are you getting paid well?" he asked, taking the conversation in a new direction.

"Enough to live on."

"You should have stayed home and farmed."

"Too late now."

Rob finished his breakfast without talking and told his father he had to go to make it back in time for work. He left a note for his mother on the table.

He was back an hour and a half before he had to work, so he showered and made an attempt to clean his apartment. Work was slow and he spent the first few hours finishing some small jobs and then began to browse his website. It was a fairly decent site—clean, uncluttered, and it had some good graphics. Bobbi called him and he closed the browser casually—a move he'd perfected. Do it too quickly and it'll look suspicious.

"I'm about to head out," she said. "There was one thing I wanted to ask you, though."

"What's that?"

"Are you interested in being the weekend supervisor?"

"Oh, yeah, I forgot. I was going to tell you, I've thought about it and I'm not sure I'm really interested in it at this point."

She closed her desk drawer and didn't say anything for a moment. "Listen, I'll be honest with you. I don't really want to waste time advertising and hiring and training someone new if I've got someone here already who can do it. If you don't want to, fine. You've basically been doing it already for a few months but you just haven't had the official title and you aren't making quite as much as you would—it'd be about a quarter or thirty-five cents an hour more. If we get someone else, your schedule will probably be adjusted to fit them in."

She raised her eyebrows and held out a clenched hand with the thumb up, then rotated the hand so the thumb was pointing down. "Yes? No?"

He wasn't sure what to do. His gut feeling was to say no, but there was a question in his mind. "You said I've already been doing it for a while?"

"Basically. It's just a weekend thing. During the week it'll be exactly like it is now, but on weekends you'll be the supervisor."

"Which means exactly what?"

"Well, you'll be in charge. You'll be responsible for bank drops, for the way things are running, and so on."

He scratched his head. "What the hell. Why not."

"Good. I know it's not the most glamorous thing in the world, but if you're already doing it, you might as well get the extra money."

After she had left, he spent some time leaning on the counter, staring at the front door, the copier whirring behind him. He didn't feel very good about that decision. When he took stock of where he was, it wasn't comforting—he was about to be dumped by Natalie and he was getting further and further entrenched in a worthless job. The one redeeming factor was the time spent at Freedom Collective, a loose group of anarchists and "culture jammers" he had begun to meet with a number of months ago. It was always good to meet with people who thought along the same lines, who supported what you were doing. By the sounds of it that group was about to disband, too, when most of them left to live in a communal house in Seattle.

Dave and Tad and Cindy were all coming up next weekend for a hike; he would talk to them about it. He hoped there wouldn't be any awkwardness between himself and Cindy or Dave. And Natalie wanted to talk yet, too. Hopefully by now she'd worked up the courage, or scripted her lines; he didn't feel like going over tonight anymore, tomorrow would be soon enough. He felt lethargic as he closed the store. Everything took more energy than usual.

His car was noisy. The muffler or the exhaust pipe had a hole in it somewhere, rusted out, but he hadn't gotten around to bringing it in during the last few weeks. He was starting to tune it out in his mind but now when he drove past people they would turn their heads.

There were four messages on his answering machine. He hit the button on the computer and as it beeped and started waking up, he pressed 'Play.' Buttons everywhere. He started to unbutton his shirt.

"Rob, Tyler. I've been looking at the stats for the site and…they're not great. Not a lot of hits. I don't know what to say. Maybe we need a new method of marketing, maybe the stickers aren't working. Anyway, I'll see you tomorrow."

BEEP.

"Hi, Rob? It's Nat on…Monday night. I hope you're having a good visit with your parents. Give me a call when you get back, or stop in."

BEEP.

"Robbie, this is Dave. You're probably out screwing Natalie, huh? I'm going to be out of the house tonight but call and leave a message or just e-mail me with the information. I'll have a lot of time before the weekend to work on the project, and then hopefully I can bring it up with me when we come. By the way, we want to go for a hike."

BEEP.

"Rob, this is Hope, from Freedom. I know you've already had the option and declined, but Trev's backed out of the house so there's an extra opening again, in case you want to come with. If I don't hear from you tonight, James is going to offer it to someone else. Let me know."

He played the messages again, deleting the first three and sprawling out on the futon when Hope's came on. She was in charge of filling the house in Seattle. Almost a month ago, they had finalized the list of names. He had declined to go without telling Natalie that he was even considering it. He told her that a bunch of the anarchist group was leaving in a few months and her first response was to say that maybe Philosophy Night could be resurrected again after they were gone.

It had died about four months ago, shortly after he had started attending meetings at the Freedom House. But he wasn't what had killed Philosophy. That wasn't long after Wade and Tink had broken up again, this time for good, and so Wade was out, and then Tink didn't want to go anymore. Shawn and Dara didn't come regularly after they got engaged. Eventually, after a month of people sometimes coming and sometimes not coming, everyone got the idea and stopped showing up.

"Let me know," Hope said again on his answering machine.

This was an interesting turn of events. He wasn't physically attracted to Hope, but there was something there, something pulling him. It might have simply been the fact that he knew she was attainable, and that it had been a while. She almost slept with him one night a month ago when he had crashed on a couch at Freedom, but he had surprised himself by declining gracefully. He had thought that things with Natalie were about to improve and had managed to remember that as Hope came and crawled on top of him in the middle of the night, kissing his face and waking him from his sleep. He remembered being confused, unsure of where he was, or of who was on top of him, kissing him, kneading him with her hands.

He had fallen off the couch and Hope went rolling into the legs of the coffee table, silent for a moment, maybe catching her breath, and then laughing. In that moment where he realized who she was, where he was, and what was going on, he regained his wits enough to overcome his physical appetite for a willing body. Things might have ended differently had he known Natalie was just waiting for the right moment to break up with him. Things could still end differently.

But it wasn't just Hope. He was feeling the pull of Seattle again, a new option, something ready to be injected into his life like a drug, a high. This whole thing could work out nicely. He wouldn't have to tell Natalie about it until a few days or a week after she broke up with him, which would be appropriate timing. He could give his two weeks to Bobbi next month, which hopefully wouldn't feel as stupid as he felt after just telling her he'd be the weekend supervisor. Most of his anarchist friends would be moving with him, and Dave and Tad would be down there already.

He was trying not to feel badly about the fact that Natalie was staying behind. Dave had told him once that when a relationship was breaking up, it was important to think about the problems, the things that had been annoying.

He gave it a try, but there were a lot of characteristics that had two sides—a bad side that also had a good side. She was hard to understand some days, hard to get along with. But she was trying to figure the world out instead of accepting the status quo. She was too religious sometimes (though she'd hate to be described that way). But it was those same beliefs that guided the way she felt about a lot of issues, and which caused her to end up on the same side as him on a lot of them. She wouldn't have sex with him. He wasn't exactly sure why—probably because she knew she was going to break up with him eventually and didn't want the emotional attachment.

He knew it wasn't true, but he tried to believe that she was just toying with him, building up her ego by leading him on for all these months, never intending it to go anywhere. If he could believe that, it would be easier to let her go. It was hard to manufacture an emotion. He was going to miss her for a while again. The space between her front teeth. Her smile, her snort, her laughter. Her independent spirit, her search for truth. Her breasts.

This wasn't helping. The other part of Dave's advice was to visualize the girl when she was most ugly, maybe right after she got up in the morning with a swollen face and bad breath, or while she sat on the toilet and squeezed shit out her ass. Something to turn you off.

The phone rang and he debated whether to answer or not. He picked it up.

"Hello?"

"Rob, this is Hope. How are you doing?"

"Great."

"Listen, did you get my message?"

"Yeah, actually I just heard it now and was thinking about it."

"I know you already said you weren't interested, but I thought I'd throw it out there, just in case. No pressure."

"None taken. Actually, I've been thinking about it and I'm starting to think I really want to do it."

"Seriously?"

"Seriously."

"That's perfect! We could really use someone who knows how to write."

"Oh, so that's all I am: a person who knows how to write?"

"Of course not. I'm starting to get really excited about this move."

"I think I am, too."

"So can I call James and let him know you're in?"

Rob paused for a moment. "Yeah. That would be great."

After he hung up, he sat in front of the computer screen and wondered why he had turned it on. He was opening up his e-mail when he remembered Dave's message. Dave had agreed to do some illustrations for the projects Rob was working on. He gathered up various scraps of paper and notes he had jotted to put them together to send to Dave so that he could go through them and produce something from them. It could be his last independent campaign—at least in Bellingham.

He untacked a page of *Crime and Punishment* which was stuck to the wall behind his computer. Natalie had thrown the book out when it fell to pieces, and he had rescued it, intending to read it at some point. He never had, but before he had thrown it out again all these months later, a loose page from near the end of the book had caught his eye—another passage she had highlighted. He began typing.

dave,
here's the passage I'm going to put on the website, from crime and
punishment:

\ 'I am going to foreign parts, brother.'
'To foreign parts?'
'To America.'
'America?'
Svidrigailov took out the revolver and cocked it. Achilles raised his eyebrows.
'I say, this is not the place for such jokes!'
'Why shouldn't it be the place?'
'Because it isn't.'
'Well, brother, I don't mind that. It's a good place. When you are asked, you just say he was going, he said, to America.'
He put the revolver to his right temple.
'You can't do it here, it's not the place,' cried Achilles, rousing himself, his eyes growing bigger and bigger.
Svidrigailov pulled the trigger.

I've got two possible taglines:
WE'VE COMMITTED THE CRIME; IT'S TIME FOR THE
PUNISHMENT

or

THE WORLD IS GOING TO AMERICA (IN A HANDBASKET)

I think it's going to be mainly about the westernization of the world, based on the above ideas. Something along the lines of: the world is getting westernized. If every country in the world was as gluttonous as us, the world would be destroyed in about 3 seconds. So 'going to america' (ie. westernization) is like shooting yourself in the head with a gun. And of course the second references the cliché "going to hell in a handbasket" which I have no idea what the handbasket means in the original, but for our purposes refers to commercialization, globalization, materialism. buy buy buy. Can you go with this much info? The article's not written yet.

By the way—it looks like I'll be moving back to seattle in a month or so. Party?

Robbie rob rob

He sent the e-mail and turned off the computer. Apparently there weren't many people who would end up reading the articles, anyway, if Tyler was right. But instead of getting upset about that, maybe he just needed to view it as another finger pointing toward the house in Seattle. If he wasn't making a difference here, he might as well join up with a group of others and see if they could do something together.

He didn't feel like talking to Natalie tonight. He started playing a videogame he bought a few months ago—a secret agent type game, a James Bond knock-off. He liked to play in sniper mode and crawl around close to the ground or dodge around corners and pick people off. At the end it gave a report that tallied up your score based on how many shots you took, how many people you killed, and how many artifacts you recovered. It was a challenge to try to take the people in the head, because otherwise it usually took two shots to kill them. But beyond the extra points, there was something inherently pleasing about a head-shot and the way the body fell immediately like a sack of flour. Bulls-eye.

The phone rang once but he didn't answer in case it was Natalie. Whoever it was didn't leave a message. He didn't have to work the next day so he played for a few hours before going to bed. He slept until past eleven, leaving barely enough time to run through the shower and drive over to campus, where he was meeting Tyler for lunch.

He met with him briefly once or twice a month, usually when a new campaign was ready to be uploaded to the site, so he could go over it with him and they could discuss how it was going to be presented. Tyler was usually the one who made an introductory graphic or animation for each new article he posted, so when people came to the site they had a little teaser right away, something tied in with the graphic on the stickers.

Tyler was waiting for him in the cafeteria, a book open in front of him.

"Hey, Tyler. Do you want anything to eat?"

He looked up. "Naw. Maybe just some apple juice or something."

Rob ordered an egg and toast and two juices and came back to the table.

"How's it going? I got your message last night."

"Yeah, I was looking at the stats, and we're not generating a lot of interest. I think last month we served something like 650 pages. I mean total hits, not unique ones, and that includes all the hits you and I gave when we put up the new page."

"Well, that's not too good. It's not as good as I'd hoped."

"I think you need to start finding new ways to advertise—in addition to the stickers, you know? Maybe put inserts into those free newspapers, or put a classified ad in one of them with the address. Swap banner ads with another small site."

"I guess so," he said, leaning back as the greasy haired guy from behind the counter brought out his egg and toast with their juice. "I don't have the graphic for the next story yet, and I'm not completely done the article, either. I'll e-mail that to you when I get it. It might be the last one."

He scooped one of the eggs onto a piece of toast and cut a corner off with the edge of his fork. Yolk oozed down onto the plate and he tried to sop it up with the bottom of the toast that was speared on his fork.

"You're going to throw in the towel?"

Rob shook his head as he finished chewing. "I'm going to be moving down to Seattle again and working with a group of people down there."

"How does Natalie feel about that?"

"She doesn't know yet, but I don't think she'll care too much. We're going through some rough times, I guess would be a polite way to say it."

Tyler laughed. "Have things ever been any other way with you two?"

"Shut up. Are you still e-mailing that Canadian chick you met at the club in Vancouver?"

"Every few days."

"That sounds pretty serious."

"Nothing's serious on e-mail. It's all still stupid and little smileys and it's starting to feel too mechanical. I haven't seen her since that night at the club and that's almost three months. She doesn't even know how to scan a picture."

"Ask her to send one in a letter."

"See, that would be more of a serious thing, and that might scare her."

"Uh huh, somebody's in love."

Tyler just shook his head.

"So, how many guys like you does she have hanging on around the country? Three, four?"

"Maybe three."

"Listen, don't tell Natalie about Seattle when you see her. I want to wait a bit yet."

"Sure."

When he got home, he called Natalie's number and left her a message telling her that he was planning to come over after she was back from work so they could finish their conversation from Sunday. Three days had to have been enough time for her to organize her thoughts. He was going to try to follow any hints she tried to give and to lead himself in the direction she wanted. If she balked and didn't say it, he would probably break up with her instead. Maybe that's what she'd been waiting for all this time so she wouldn't feel as guilty about yanking his chain for so long.

He tried to work on his article for the website, but found himself distracted, Seattle on the brain. It would be something like college except without the classes. They'd probably have their own sorts of Philosophy Nights or planning sessions for parties and things to do. They'd been doing that already here, to a degree. Last week when they met they started plans for a party in town with everyone—those who were staying in Bellingham and those who were leaving to the house in Seattle, and anyone else they could convince to come. They were going to stage it in an abandoned lot downtown, the basement of a burned out building that had since been demolished.

It was surrounded with chain-link fence and had been empty forever. There were a handful of the Bellingham'ers (the ones who were staying) who were working on a campaign to reclaim the plot as public space, a plaza or a park. They claimed that the city council wasn't working with them or acknowledging the ideas they submitted. The city was trying to fast-track some sort of a sweetheart deal with a company for about a tenth of what they paid for it. They were going to build retail shops there. Revitalize the downtown economy and all that b.s. They'd probably sell a spot or two in the new building to Starbucks so they could choke out the local coffeehouses and start cannibalizing each other. There were already plenty of abandoned buildings they could make retail in. It was a conspiracy. But everything's a conspiracy, we just don't always know how or why. So they were trying to find a way to take it back on their own.

He drove over to Natalie's when it began to get dark. The house lights were on. He knocked three times and stared down at the rough wood of the front porch. He heard the sound of someone at the door but he waited until the door was opening before he looked up. It was Tinker.

"Rob! I haven't seen you in a while." She stepped back to let him in.

"I know—it's been busy. Did you go home for the weekend?"

"Yeah, I came back Sunday night. Natalie said you went to Vancouver."

"On Saturday. Sunday I drove down to my parents place and stayed there until yesterday morning."

Natalie came around the corner from her room and waved at him, wearing what seemed to him a frightened little smile and limping slightly.

"Hi Nat."

"Hi. How are you?"

"Good."

Tink backed into the doorway of her room, waving. "We should hang out again soon."

"Sure," he said.

"You went home?" Natalie asked.

"Got back yesterday. Then I had to work yet yesterday evening."

"How is he?"

"Still pretty rough, but Mom's taking good care of him. How are you?"

"Good, I guess. Besides the fact that I sprained my ankle today."

"What happened?"

"I just slipped off the bottom step and turned my ankle. It's really swollen."

"You've had some time to...think?"

She nodded.

"I guess you don't really want to go for a walk, though."

"Let's go to my room," she said.

She sat on the chair in front of the desk and he sat on the edge of the bed, leaning back on his elbows.

"You've probably been wondering what that was all about on Sunday."

She paused and he nodded without saying anything, not wanting her to know that he already knew what she was trying to figure out how to say.

"Well, there's something I've been meaning to tell you...something I should have told you a long time ago," she said slowly. "But something always comes up, or I lose my nerve, or I tell myself it doesn't matter anymore but then I find out it does for some reason."

She was quiet and they sat watching each other. Her chest rose and fell as she looked at him, unblinking.

"Nat, you can just spill it out, you don't have to try and make it sound nice or anything."

"It's just that it'll sound so...blunt, and I don't want it to," she said.

"Listen, I think I've got a pretty good idea of what's coming," he said, intending it to be gentle but worrying that it came out too harshly. "I mean, there's only so many things it could be, and I think we can be pretty sure that it's not that you're pregnant or something."

She blinked rapidly a few times and he was afraid she was going to cry. He sighed and got up to hug her. So much for a little humor to lighten the atmosphere. She sniffled on his shoulder once as he was starting to feel awkward, leaning down to hug her while she sat on the chair. He stood there, bent at the waist while she hugged him, waiting for her to let go so that he could.

He was looking over her shoulder at the desk—it was covered in various places with an uneven layer of wax and little shavings scattered loosely across the surface. He wondered what had happened to the shrine. She let him go and sat there looking at him but saying nothing. She turned and started rummaging in a grocery bag beside the desk.

She pulled a wrinkled envelope from the bag, stained and oily with candle wax clinging to it in places.

"This is for you," she said, handing it to him.

He sat down on the edge of her bed, feeling the waxed envelope with his thumb and examining the front. It had his name on the front, but instead of an address all it said was "Seattle." There was a stamp, cancelled in Bellingham on February 11, 1997, and another near his name that said "Return to sender: undeliverable." Natalie's name was in the upper left corner, above the address of the house which they had lived in together. He was suddenly unsure of what was happening. This letter was like a museum artifact, something from another time.

"What is it?" he asked.

"Open it."

He had a hard time peeling it open. He slid the single sheet of paper out of the envelope and unfolded it.

February 9, 1997

Dear Rob,

You've been gone for a few weeks now and I'll be honest: I miss you. Sometimes I wonder if I should have gone with you. Sometimes I wonder if I should head down there now. But sometimes I realize that there's a lot of stuff I am figuring out—I told you this already—and I am planning to do that. I don't know what will happen after I do this figuring, and you do whatever figuring of your own. Maybe our paths will cross again, or maybe that's just something I tell myself that makes me feel better about now. But there's something I found out shortly before you left that I should have told you and I didn't. The timing just never seemed right and then you were leaving and I told myself you'd prefer not to know, and now I am wondering whether that was the right decision. I'm going to mail this tomorrow and if somehow the post office finds you and your new address, I hope you do want to know this. If they don't, I'll assume that this is something that you don't want or need to know.

Remember how toward the end of the trip I was feeling sick and we thought it was the tap water that I drank in Nicaragua—well, the doctor didn't give me any pills to take care of that like I told you he did. He told me I was pregnant. Based on his estimate, it must have happened in Thailand. I don't know if I forgot to take a pill or what. When the morning sickness stopped, I hadn't told you yet, and then we had that fight and it wasn't long before we were talking about splitting up. I decided if you really left I wouldn't tell you.

I'm not trying to compel you to come back or anything. I tend to think that that would be a bad idea, to be honest. But if you get this, I'd really like to know what you think I should do. I don't know, I'm just kind of scared, I guess. Anyway, I hope you get this.

Love, Nat.

He didn't look up for a moment, pretending instead that he hadn't finished reading. When he did, he saw Natalie watching him.

"Did you have the baby?" he asked, and she moved from the chair to the edge of the bed beside him.

"No." Her voice was quiet, almost a whisper.

He turned the letter over, as though there might be another message on the back, or the words JUST KIDDING in big magic marker. "Why are you showing me this now?"

"I don't know. I wasn't planning to tell you at all after the letter came back, and I hadn't thought about it much for years."

She wasn't looking at him as she talked, focusing instead on the letter he was holding in his lap.

"But then when you came back, when I saw you in the restaurant, it was like...It was the only thing I could think of for a little while—how you didn't know yet, and it was two years later already. I couldn't figure out how to bring it up at an appropriate time, so during that first month or so, I convinced myself that it was something you didn't need to know, or didn't want to know, and that it would go away again after a few months. You know, that I'd stop thinking about it so often, that I'd stop feeling guilty again."

He sighed. Trust Natalie to keep feeling guilty for things for years and years.

"But you didn't stop thinking about it?"

"Well, mostly I did, but then it would still be there sometimes—like Saturday night it happened again."

He was starting to get an unsettled feeling in his stomach. This conversation wasn't going as he had expected.

"So, this has been bothering you all along? You keep remembering this, feeling guilty—"

"No, not really. Well, partly. It's a combination of all this—partly also that you didn't know this and I hadn't ever told you, and partly that I'm scared, I guess."

"Of getting pregnant again?"

"Not necessarily—I think I'm scared because we've got so many glitches in our relationship and I'm scared sometimes that it's not going to work out, and then I'll end up being hurt again if I let myself go."

He didn't say anything for a moment, then folded the letter up and slipped it back into the envelope.

"What does that mean, 'let yourself go?'"

"Give myself permission to just go with this whole thing, with us. I don't know, enjoy the relationship I guess. And part of it is physically. It's not that I haven't wanted it or don't want it now. I don't know. I still haven't figured out how to put this feeling into words."

"I've noticed that."

There was a long silence again. He had the feeling that all of this talking hadn't shed much light on anything besides the fact that she had once been pregnant, which didn't really clarify anything.

"I guess I don't know what else to say right now. Do you have anything you want to ask me? I'll try to answer."

"I'm sure I do," he said. He was looking at the photos on the wall beside her desk. Philosophy Night, before it died, everyone in their chairs with the table between them. A picture of him in a transparent red garbage bag at the Halloween party—a blood fluke. A picture he took at the stroke of twelve on New Year's Day, holding the camera out as he and Natalie kissed. Her eyes were shut like she was praying, he was looking out the corner of his eyes into the camera.

"I guess I might come up with some questions after I've thought about it some more," he said. He lifted up the envelope. "How long after you got this sent back did you get the abortion?"

"I...never got that far," she said. "It miscarried. They said it happens more often than people think."

"Then what did you feel guilty about?"

"I feel guilty about a lot of things. I feel guilty about not telling you."

"Don't worry about it."

"I feel guilty about setting the appointment for the abortion. I feel guilty about not loving her when she was still alive—I feel like it was a girl. They couldn't tell, or they never told me anyway."

"Why the hell would you feel guilty about that?" he growled.

"I heard once that if the mother gets startled the baby can feel the effects of it for hours. Sometimes I think she let herself die because of what I was thinking and what I was feeling about her. I had already decided to go in and get it taken care of."

She wasn't looking at him, as though it were easier to talk at the wall instead of to him.

"Come on, Nat," he said. "Don't be stupid. You've got an overactive imagination. It just happened."

She was nodding almost imperceptibly, over and over in profile. "I know that in my head."

"Stop feeling guilty about things you didn't do."

"Sometimes I can't control how I feel. Sometimes I start feeling guilty for feeling guilty."

"You know what I think? I think all this guilt you suffer from is just part of your parents' religion that you never got over after you grew up. And now you're fucking us up again because you can't get past it."

She was silent for a moment and when she spoke it was barely audible.

"I guess I'm finding out that there are a lot of things that I haven't gotten past," she said as she let her body fall backwards onto the bed.

He felt like he needed some time—to figure out how he felt, what he was going to do, to cool down. He leaned over and kissed Natalie's forehead quickly as she lay there and then told her that he was going to go home. She didn't say anything but rolled her head to the side to watch him leave.

He drove home slowly. They had been pregnant. How would his life be different, if at all, if he had known it at the time? It was strange to imagine a mixture of himself and Natalie, entwined, combined. Something that was part of each of them but yet distinct. Why didn't it take? Was there something incompatible between his and Natalie's genes that caused it to die? Not that he wanted a baby at this point, but he wondered.

He had heard someone say once that a fetus was a parasite, feeding off of the mother's body, stealing her energy to live. And then there were the real parasites, like the one that tricked the crabs into thinking it was pregnant. Whatever parasite Natalie was growing was still feeding on her, guilting her for things she had no control over, years after they had happened. He didn't know if she could be cured.

Laryn kragt Bakker

Jesus, save me from your followers

This was the first weekend she'd been able to spend time with Tink in a long time. Friday night they'd stayed home and watched a movie: Tink had picked it so it was a romantic comedy, which was unfortunate. It was a British film—*The Very Thought Of You*—about these people who'd met in an airport accidentally and known from first sight that they were supposed to be in love, but they lost each other and each one didn't know the other's name. They spent the movie searching for each other and in the meantime, by chance, both of the man's best friends have met the woman and fallen in love with her. By the end, of course, the original couple is back together and has overcome all of the earlier misunderstandings and they are having sex in their airplane seats on their way to Iceland. Can't keep true love down.

Probably that was what she hated most about those types of movies: the warm, fuzzy idea of love that they're based on. She had never seen someone in an airport and been ready to go anywhere or do anything for him. And she could never solve all the problems she had in a two hour time span, that was obvious. She had gone over to Rob's place a few weeks ago and he was watching one of those dating game shows, where they take people who are together and have them tell the world all the problems with their relationship. Then they send them off on dates with other people and when they come back they have to choose who they like better. As though the problems in a relationship can be worked through in a half-hour TV show, or by going out with someone else, and all the decisions are made in a split second. That's not how she worked—she might slog through her problems slowly, but at least it was genuine.

Regardless of that, Tink had enjoyed the movie. When they had talked afterwards, it had made Nat a little uncomfortable because Tink sounded wistful, like she wanted to believe that romantic love was like fate: uncontrolled and uncontrollable, and you just had to bet your life on it, going all in one guy at a time.

She hadn't seen Shawn for almost two weeks—ever since he and Dara had become engaged, he'd been spending most of his time over at her place. She'd hear him sometimes in the morning, coming home to get new clothes or to shower before work, or she'd find his dishes in the sink, evidence that he had recently eaten here. If he was home, Dara was usually here, too, but they were in his room with the door shut, mostly. As long as he kept paying his part of the rent, she shouldn't complain, but she missed him around the house. The community was disintegrating.

Saturday night, she and Tink had gone out dancing with a handful of girls. She spent part of the night trying not to think about Rob. It had been two days before that she'd told him about the pregnancy, a secret that had seemed like a big thing until now.

It felt like a hard lump had been surgically removed from her lungs. Or maybe like something alive that had been imprisoned behind her ribs was free. What had been inside was out, but she still had the feeling of having been stretched.

She hadn't talked much to Rob since then. It was Sunday morning now, and she hadn't talked to him since Thursday. She had called him at home and they talked briefly, referencing it only once.

"Did I make the right decision yesterday, to tell you?"

"Of course, yeah. I guess, maybe you should have told me sooner. It's just weird to think about, it's so long ago. I don't really know what to do with it."

Then it was small talk about a copier that had blown up, her boring day alone behind the counter. He said that he was going to be gone for most of the weekend—to a planning meeting with his anarchists on Friday and Saturday nights and hiking with his Seattle friends today. He'd invited her to come on the hike, but she had twisted her ankle after work on Friday and it felt too sore to hike on, so she'd stayed home. This way she'd get to do coffee with her mom, anyway, and she wouldn't have to back out two weeks in a row.

She was looking forward to talking with her mother, for the most part. The only part she didn't like was the pitch at the end. Usually, just before the visit was over, her mom would throw a plug in for church, trying to get Natalie to come with her, just once. Nat usually just said, "Mom," in a whiny-and-slightly-annoyed sort of voice and that was that, but last time her mom had been persistent, because it was going to be Easter, and Natalie had said she'd think about it. Hopefully that didn't set a precedent.

The truth was, there was nothing appealing about going back to church. The last time she had been inside a church was when she and Rob were traveling—when they had walked through cathedrals in various cities they visited, if that counted. But they were nothing like the church she'd grown up in. The last time she'd been there had been in high school, when she lived at home and was forced to go periodically, prior to her move to Bellingham and the university.

It had been a long time, but she still remembered the looks she got when she was a senior in high school and happened to show up, the whispers. When you sit in the back you have a pretty good view of everyone else, especially when they slowly turn around in their pew to look at you and then slowly turn around again. It felt like they had an alarm at the door that went off when sinners entered; a warning system for the saints. Or a moral measuring equivalent to the plywood clown by the fun park rides, holding his hand up. *You must be this righteous to worship here.* And it felt like they were keeping score, making a mark in your column every time they thought you might have sinned, adding it up.

When she broke the shrine open to get the letter out for Rob, she had rediscovered a small photocopied passage from Flannery O'Connor's short story, "Revelation." The main character is a judgmental, racist old lady who reminded her of some of the people in the church she grew up in.

She opened the back cover of her Bible, where she had deposited it with a handful of other scraps of paper, some copied and some handwritten.

...a vast horde of souls were rumbling toward heaven. There were whole companies of white-trash, clean for the first time in their lives, and bands of black niggers in white robes, and battalions of freaks and lunatics shouting and clapping and leaping like frogs. And bringing up the end of the procession was a tribe of people whom she recognized at once as those who, like herself and Claud, had always had a little of everything and the God-given wit to use it right. She leaned forward to observe them closer. They were marching behind the others with great dignity, accountable as they had always been for good order and common sense and respectable behavior. They alone were on key. Yet she could see by their shocked and altered faces that even their virtues were being burned away.

She remembered putting that scrap of paper in the shrine. Dorrie had given her a copy of O'Connor's *Complete Stories* that first Christmas that she had been at the store.

For birthdays and Christmas, they wrapped up items from the store and gave them to each other. She had taken it home to read and then photocopied the last page of the story. She had sliced out the passage with an X-Acto knife and fastened it face up in a puddle of liquid wax on top of the shrine. It had been visible until a few weeks or a month later, when enough time had passed for a new layer of wax to obscure it.

She had it scraped clean of wax now, though the toner had flaked off in places and the words were harder to read.

Behind it was a piece that she had added to the shrine more recently, spoken by Marmeladov in *Crime and Punishment*:

> 'You too come forth,' He will say, 'Come forth ye drunkards, come forth, ye weak ones, come forth, ye children of shame!' And we shall all come forth, without shame and shall stand before him. And he will say unto us, 'Ye are swine, made in the Image of the Beast and with his mark; but come ye also!' And the wise ones and those of understanding will say, 'Oh Lord, why dost Thou receive these men?' And He will say, 'This is why I receive them, oh ye wise, this is why I receive them, oh ye of understanding, that not one of them believed himself to be worthy of this.' And He will hold out His hands to us and we shall fall down before him...and we shall weep...and we shall understand all things! Then we shall understand all!

The next one was from Jesus:

> Do not judge, and you will not be judged. Do not condemn, and you will not be condemned. Forgive, and you will be forgiven. Give, and it will be given to you...For with the measure you use, it will be measured to you.

She had written that one out as a reminder to herself not to judge people for judging people, which was hard. People judging each other was like mirrors reflecting each other—it went to infinity. It seemed, though, that everything she hated about most of the Christians she'd known were the exact things that Jesus hated about a lot of the people he knew. They took grace, but they didn't know how to give it. If mercy and love was shown to a child who had squandered her inheritance, they were the older brother, hanging around outside the house, refusing to go in, sullen and angry.

Sometimes she wondered how it was that the Jesus whom all these church-goers claimed to believe in had come to the ungodly, the outcasts, the sinners, exactly the people who feel least comfortable in church. What did it mean that there was such a division between the Christians and the people Jesus loved? Were they afraid of being contaminated? She wondered how they'd respond if Jesus came into their church—one from whom men hide their faces.

Sometimes she pictured Jesus as sickly and deformed. If kids then were anything like kids now, he would have been soundly mocked. Even if he looked normal, he was poor and illegimate. Maybe that's why he seemed to identify so well with the outcasts. Our past is within us, and we can't escape it.

She sometimes wished that God would communicate audibly again, maybe come to the front of the churches in a pillar of fire and say to the minister, "I'll be giving the sermon today." It would cut down on the glut of people ready to claim that they're speaking for God.

Once, maybe two years ago, she had responded to a classified ad that she had seen in the newspaper. It was two lines long, in the Miscellaneous category:

God is love.
To learn more, send a postcard to THE PROPHET.

She had been curious to see what The Prophet was all about, and since the mail system was relatively anonymous—no faces, no voices—she had sent a postcard to his box. Not much more than a week later, she had received a letter back from him, with no name in the return address, just THE PROPHET and his post office box number, written in sloppy uppercase script.

Inside was a single sheet of paper with a few lines written in the same handwriting:

NATALIE, THANK YOU FOR YOUR POSTCARD. IF YOU ARE INTERESTED IN WHAT I HAVE TO SAY, PLEASE CALL ME, IT WON'T TAKE LONG, I PROMISE. SINCERELY, THE PROPHET.

Then, underneath his phone number, he had written:

PS. IF THOU BELIEVEST IN THINE HEART AND CONFESSEST WITH THY TONGUE THAT JESUS IS LORD, THOU SHALT BE SAVED, BUT THE WRATH OF GOD ABIDETH ON THE SINNER.

She hadn't called him—the postcard had answered all her questions. There was a subculture among the Christians whose lexicon reverted to the King James Version whenever they talked about "religious" things, as though those things were separate and distinct from the rest of their lives.

Christians had a tendency to make themselves into easy targets. She had seen a man at the gas station once, wearing black jeans, a black t-shirt, sunglasses and bare feet, filling up his old boat of a car with the windows wide open and his radio blaring a Christian radio station in all directions. When he went to pay, he walked tenderly, wincing like his feet were hurting. She wasn't sure if the radio blasting was supposed to be a form of outreach to the lost or if it was meant as a form of penance for the man himself, condemned to listen to poor quality programming and walk barefoot wherever he traveled.

She had waited behind a different man in a grocery store line once, who wore a t-shirt with slogans inscribed in magic marker. The front said GOD'S LAST NAME IS NOT DAMN, and on the back was inscribed IT'S ALL FUN AND GAMES UNTIL YOU BURN IN HELL. She had heard fragments of the conversation he was having with the man he was standing with.

" ...and then I said to him, 'Can you redeem mankind by the shedding of your blood?'" he said, and they both laughed, as though he had said something witty. It was people like that that made her hesitate to identify herself as a Christian. Guilt by association.

She took her loaf of bread out of the freezer and pulled two slices off. She was running a little behind schedule, but her mom would wait at the restaurant. While the toaster was toasting, she found the jam in the fridge. She wasn't used to late nights anymore—not like college days, where she'd be up until two regularly and often go out on weekday nights. Last night had been fun, for the most part, except for the last hour and a half, when Tink, Angela and Ruth started a competition to see who could get taken home by a better looking guy. Natalie wasn't playing, and so she sat most of the time while the game was running. Ruth ended up winning by default, even though the guy she left with wasn't that hot, because the other two didn't go home with anyone.

She stuck the jammed sides of the toast together and wrapped them in a paper towel. She went into her room to put out the candles that were burning on top of the shrine. She had tried to piece it back together, fitting pieces into each other and melting the fault lines with a lighter. There had been a big pile of wax that was in small pieces and shavings which she had broken and peeled off of the envelope before giving it to Rob, and she had piled them up on top and spent an hour dripping new candle wax on top of the mound. It looked broken and disfigured, with strange lumps in places that they shouldn't be, but it was whole again. She blew out the candles.

It was almost afternoon already, but the sun wasn't at full strength, filtered by an overcast sky. She made sure that her small handbag had some money in and locked the back door behind her, clutching the toast and the bag in her left hand.

"Nat!" A woman's voice came from behind her. She didn't recognize the voice, and when she turned she could see no one. There weren't even any cars in the street.

She started down the steps and opened the package of toast, peeling the top one off of the bottom. As she was biting into the corner, the voice came again.

"Hey, Nat!"

She chewed slowly as she turned around. The voice had been close, but there was no one where it had come from. She thought of the story of Samuel, when God called him and he didn't know who it was. Goose bumps were developing on her heart and lungs. If it was God, what was she supposed to say? She swallowed.

"Speak, Lord..." she said in a voice barely audible to herself.

"What's the matter? You can't hear me?" God said, annoyed.

"Shut up," a man yelled. "I told you, I'll be right back. Just wait there like I said."

"Matthew, I am leaving now!" A car door slammed and the sound of an engine accelerating came from beside the house. She saw the car go by in her peripheral vision but didn't look at it. She found she was still breathing a little faster, her heart pumping a bit harder.

She was on the bus, halfway to Bellis Fair and completely finished with her toast when she thought that maybe it had been a joke, God's sense of humor, like a wink and a smile. Making the voice bounce off the buildings just right so it seemed to be coming from beside her, distracting her just enough so that she'd hear the voice say "Nat" instead of "Matt."

She stepped off the bus opposite the Bellis Fair Mall and walked down to Archie's, a little local dive somehow surviving in the middle of the strip malls and chain stores. She walked in and instead of waiting to be seated like the sign instructed she went around the left to the corner table she and her mother usually occupied. Her mother was already there, tipping back the last of her coffee.

"Hi, mom."

"Natalie!"

They hugged and she endured a prolonged stare as her mother looked into her eyes for a few seconds. The wrinkles beside her mother's eyes were becoming more pronounced.

"How are you doing, baby?"

"Really well. I think God talked to me this morning."

She told the story of the voice, motioning to the waitress as she went by to bring more coffee.

"You always did have an active imagination."

"Yeah, I guess so. Are you feeling better?"

"I'm recovered from last weekend, but now I've sprained my ankle. It's getting better. How was church today?"

"Oh, it was good," she said after a moment. "Nothing like last week, when they had those kids sing, like I told you about."

"I was thinking about that after you mentioned it. Do you remember that one night when we were little and we had to sing in front of church? Scott kept scratching himself and pinching his crotch in the front row," she said, smiling.

"And you weren't singing, either."

"Yeah, but Scott was pinching himself!"

The waitress came back with a new mug and filled both it and the empty one. Her mother squeezed a little canteen of non-dairy creamer into hers and mixed it around.

"Didn't dad spank him for that when we got home?"

Her mother didn't answer. They were both holding their coffee cups the same way. The handles pointed away from themselves and their hands wrapped around each side of their mugs, the fingertips of each hand overlapping underneath the handle. It was a way to soak up the most heat from the coffee; she had inherited her mother's poor circulation and her hands lost heat quickly.

"I saw your father today," her mother said.

Natalie's eyes snapped to her mother's face, but her mother was staring into the surface of her coffee like it was a tool being used for divination, the milky brown liquid still gently swirling.

"What did he have to say?"

"Oh, I didn't talk to him," she said, glancing up with a tight attempt at a smile. "I just saw him. Well, I guess I heard his voice, too. He...no, they, came to our church." She still thought of it as Natalie's church, too.

"What was the occasion?"

"Well, her family all goes there, you know? At least they had the decency to start going to a different church when they came back. But today one of her sisters had her baby baptized, so they came to see. She's pregnant, she looks pretty big."

At first she just shook her head. Everything that her father did was cut off, unrelated to her life. Her mother kept looking at her without saying anything, and Natalie stared at her and processed the information. She was pregnant. Who was pregnant?

"Shit," she breathed. That meant she was going to have a half-sister, or a half-brother, someone who shared a lot of her genes. That bastard! At first it had been just him and Naomi, and Natalie and her mom had to deal with it. Now he was introducing a third party, an innocent person to the mix.

"He sat behind me, I don't know if it was on purpose or not. I could just feel the eyes of everyone on me, even the ones who weren't looking. I kept hearing his voice during the songs, behind me, I could pick it out of all the rest. It still sounds the same. Maybe it was my imagination, but...I thought when we were saying the Lord's Prayer, that he said 'forgive us our debts' a little louder than he said the rest of it. I don't know."

She swallowed nothing and lifted her eyes, smiling slightly, hopefully.

Natalie reached across the table and placed her hands around her mother's so the coffee cup was buried beneath two layers of hands which were folded around it and each other like a prayer. Natalie stroked her thumb on her mother's hand, silent, until her mother quietly cleared her throat.

"I had to leave right away after the service, I wanted to leave before it was over, but I didn't want to make a scene in front of everyone, marching down the middle of the aisle." She pulled one of her hands out and pinched the bridge of her nose, rubbing the corners of both eyes with her finger and thumb.

She was always so worried about what they would think, what they would say.

"Why do you keep going back there?" Natalie blurted. "You're always complaining about the people." She wished it hadn't come out like that, placing the blame on her mother.

"I'm sorry, Mom," she said. "It's just, they're all fakes, they're all just as fucked up as the rest of us."

Her mother breathed in, a ragged breath. "Why do I keep going back?" She looked at Natalie and exhaled slowly. Her eyes were glazed with something liquid, their blue deepened in intensity like the coastal stones that depend on ocean water to unlock their color. "I keep going back because when I see them, I...because maybe...maybe, God has enough grace...maybe God can love even...fucked up people, like them, like me." She faltered with the word, obviously unaccustomed to using it in conversation. "I keep going back because that's the only hope I've got."

"Sorry," Natalie whispered.

She wanted to walk home when they were finished with their coffees, but her ankle was sore so she accepted the ride her mother offered. She wondered why this car was still around, still being used. If it had been hers, she would have sold it and bought something different, something that didn't keep reminding her of other times she'd ridden in the car with other people. This had been her mother's car ever since they had purchased it new in Natalie's last year of high school, and this had been her seat every morning.

It was a reminder of a time in her life she would rather forget. No one really enjoys high school. She remembered it as a time when she didn't like anything or want to be anywhere—not home, not at school, not even at parties, completely. There was always the feeling that something in her or around her was wrong and was out of her control.

Growing up, she'd been a model child. She did well at school, participated in theatre productions, went to church with her parents every Sunday. But what they saw on the outside didn't always match how she felt inside. She had friends, but she was lonely. She did well at school, but she didn't enjoy it. She went to church, but didn't believe it.

She wondered how much of her mood during that time related to Scott's death. After he died, they spent a few months adjusting to the hole in their lives. They all had seemed to recover quickly and completely, but she had a view from behind the stage curtains of the drama that was their home. She saw the tears, the silent dinners, the irritated comments; she also saw the smiles for the public, the cursory pecks on the cheeks when they thought anyone they knew might be watching.

She also had her first period a few months after he died, in a seventh grade geography class. She had biked to school that day, and as fate would have it, she had worn a pair of tan shorts. She remembered feeling sick, having to put her head down on her desk, and the unfamiliarity of the cramping. She looked down and saw blood soaking through, a small bright oval growing slowly larger as she watched. She had untucked her shirt and hoped it would cover her as she walked quickly to the back of the room and out into the hallway, ignoring the teacher's voice as he called her name after her and imagining all the heads turning and watching her. She wasn't sure what was happening. By the time she reached the privacy of a bathroom stall, the stain was too large to hide and a small trickle of blood had begun to run down her leg.

She had wiped as best as she could and then filled her panties with bunched up toilet paper, stuffing her pockets for backup, and biked home to curl up on her bed and die. The school called her mother at work that afternoon, explaining how she had left in the middle of class, leaving her books open on her desk and hadn't been seen since, so she had to explain what had happened. Her mother had tried to give her a talk, explaining womanhood to her, but she had sighed, exasperated, and changed the topic, claiming she knew everything already.

By the time she was in high school, she really did think she knew everything about everything, and her parents were the ones who were getting exasperated. Her grades continued to plummet, and the only extracurricular activities she participated in were drinking and smoking up at parties. She stopped going to church whenever possible, though her father tried to make her go every week. Eventually, her mother mediated and they agreed that she'd go to church half time. The idea was that maybe instead of dragging her in every week, she'd walk in on her own every second week, and maybe something magical would happen and she would start to like it there.

But these were the days when she'd sit in the back row, sullen and stone-faced, yawning at the organ and waiting for the benediction so she could dart out before the minister. She would sit in the car and listen to the radio, waiting for her parents to stop talking so they could go home.

It was her senior year in high school when her parents bought this car, new, and she had driven to school with her mother five mornings a week for a year without saying much. Her father had joined them for the second half of the year, because the car he had been driving—an Omni, an ugly white hatchback that farted out dirty, black smoke whenever he put it in second gear—farted its last one day, halfway through the year. Then place shifting had occurred: dad went behind the wheel, mom went into the passenger seat, and Natalie went into the back.

It had marked a departure from tradition for them—up until then, they had always had cars that were at least fifteen years old and they drove them until they died. They were bottom-feeders, in that way: the last people on the chain of car ownership. She remembered the embarrassment of trying to take her driver's test in the Omni, because the clutch had been acting funny and the gears ground every time she shifted. She had failed and had to take the test again, borrowing Aunt Dorothy's car, which was in working condition and had an automatic transmission.

Somehow, even though she had grown up resenting the old cars she was forced to drive around in, when they bought this Taurus brand-new, she resented that, too. It seemed to her that it was like a shiny exterior to her dirty, unhappy life. People on the outside could look at the family's stuff: their new car, their well-kept yard, and they could do the calculations and determine that things were just fine.

So she sat in the car every morning and resented it. She remembered sitting there, not saying anything, in the front seat for the first months and then later in the back seat, scratching her fingernails into the rubbery plastic of the armrest on the door. This had driven her parents wild in their desire to treat the new car with the proper respect and care it deserved. She remembered her father threatening once to have her "declawed."

Her mother was still making small talk, and she realized that she was responding with nods and little noises of affirmation. I'm listening, her body said without consulting her mind. She ran her hands over the scratch marks, which were still visible on the door's armrest. They'd been polished by time but were still visible.

The car pulled into the alley behind Nat's house.

"...I haven't seen Rob since Christmas, I don't think," her mother said, putting the car into Park and turning to face Natalie.

"No, I know. We've been meaning to come up. We'll have to see when works."

"I could come down here, too, if it's a trouble to get up to my place. I'm just interested in the people my baby's spending her time with. I'd like to see more of you, too."

"I'll let you know," she said.

"Okay."

She had just swung the door shut when her mother called out again.

"What was that?" she asked, pulling the door partly open and leaning against the side of the car, looking in.

"I saw Susan—Mrs. Fisher—as I was leaving church and I mentioned I was going to see you. She said to say hello."

"Oh, well, thanks. Hi back."

She watched the car back out of the alley and walked up the steps to her back door. So her father and the new wife were pregnant. He had called her shortly after he had come back, inviting her to dinner with him and Naomi. She had declined then, and he had called every few months to see if she'd changed her mind, until finally she told him to stop calling. That was over two years ago now.

She wondered if he ever felt guilty about what he had done. Rob told her that guilt was something she hadn't "gotten over," as though it were a defect, and maybe sometimes it was. But sometimes it seemed appropriate.

"Forgive us our debts," her mother thought he had said. And then what, he's off the hook? And everyone can go and buy a new car and drive around in a shiny smile because the world's okay again. Except the Christians will still be whispering to each other, remembering. And her mom would still be sitting among them, hoping that maybe, just maybe, even the Christians could be saved.

Not all who wander are lost

Sometimes it's easier to remember how much you've missed someone if they're with you, because you're forced to think about them. His car was running rough, so Dave had offered to drive his tiny Geo Metro, and they were sputtering up the side of the mountain testing the limits of his cheap speakers with Phish from back in the day: *Junta*. They were laughing at everything, telling stories that started off with "Remember when...", like the questions asked on the *Chris Farley Show* on *Saturday Night Live*, back when it was still funny.

"Remember when we played Risk drunk that one time?" Dave was driving with one hand on the wheel, one hand scratching an armpit.

"Yeah, and then you launched a massive attack on Rob because he said something stupid."

Dave had a proud little smile on his face. Rob turned the music down slightly. "I don't remember saying anything stupid."

"I'm pretty sure you did."

"Boys, we've got to get drunk again sometime."

"Remember last time we got drunk together, when Rob was a maniac and got thrown out of the club?"

He remembered. That was the same night he had accidentally slept with Cindy, the night before he left to come up here. There was a disconnect between the smile on his face and the thoughts in his head. Cindy was sitting in the back seat, looking out the window, not saying anything. She had just giggled, briefly and possibly insincerely. Was she remembering the same things he was? He was trying to adjust to being around her now that she was with Dave. Their interaction before had almost always been peppered with sexual innuendo and physicality. He probably wasn't supposed to do that anymore.

"Okay, okay, enough picking on me," Rob said. "Remember when Tad got distracted by that hooker and hit that parked car?"

"Hey, I didn't hit it. I just grazed the side of it."

"And knocked the mirror off."

"And knocked the mirror off," he verified. "And she wasn't a hooker. Just a scantily clad female."

Dave turned down the music all the way and the yelling and laughter petered out.

"What's up?" Tad asked.

Dave turned his head to Rob, in the passenger seat, and said, "I just wanted to remind everyone that Rob's moving back to Seattle!" Then he started bouncing up and down in his seat, clutching the steering wheel. Tad grabbed Rob from behind and tried to squeeze him with the seat in between them.

After Tad leaned back, Cindy spoke. "When are you moving back?"

"Well, I'm not sure, exactly. There are some details to work out."

"Can we all agree that on the first night back, we'll all go get drunk together?" Tad asked.

Dave and Tad started whooping and Rob turned the music back up.

Conditions weren't going to be the best today. Already on the way up, he could tell. Toward the bottom, it was beautiful; trees were draped in lush hanging moss in greens and browns and yellows. There was a slight mist further up the mountain, which obscured some of the higher trees. As they climbed, snow appeared along the edges of the road, but it had already started to melt. The top was crusted with the dirt that had remained as the snow disappeared, a sinful multitude that had missed the rapture. The bamboo wands that they stuck in the snow to mark the edge of the road when the snow was high had started sagging, and some had fallen over completely.

When he had come up here a few months ago, in February, with Shawn, the wands were all in place. They had just had some fresh snow the previous night and it had still been snowing slightly as they drove up. The lane on the other side of the road—the one going down—was still covered in a thin layer of white powder; the lane going up had twin bands carved out down to the pavement. No tracks going down generally meant the conditions would be good up there. People went up and stayed up.

Shawn hadn't been very talkative that day and Rob had dozed in the front seat. The morning sun was chopped into segments by the trees as they drove by, delivered to them in staccato bursts like a strobe light, or machine gun fire. Shawn took his snowshoes, and Rob had rented a pair at the store where Shawn worked. He was still a little leery of snapping his leg into skis, but snowshoeing had sounded safe and he had never done it before. He had never talked much with Shawn—and he didn't talk much to him that day, either, but it was more than usual.

They had taken their snowshoes out at the parking lot and put them on. Rob felt stupid walking in the plowed parking lot with snowshoes, but Shawn didn't seem to notice. The trees were bare limbed but covered white with snow and frost, and they looked like plaster casts. Even when they started walking in the snow, it felt like the shoes were unnecessary; he thought he could have gotten by with a good pair of boots. But as he followed the shuffle of Shawn's snowshoes, the powder got deeper, looser.

The snow was virtually untouched out here, slightly off into the back country. The peaks out ahead were smooth white lumps with an occasional wavy track left by a skier or boarder carved into the even surface like the path of a wood beetle on a stump after the bark is peeled away.

They had climbed up a small hill, his body starting to sweat already, and Shawn had turned around and told Rob to run back down. He went first, kicking up snow behind him. It was like walking on the moon. He sank down slowly into the powder on each step and bounded up again, and the slope made it seem like he was jumping higher than he really was, because the ground fell away in front of him.

He wasn't expecting anything like that today. They might not stay up here too long. They had brought plastic garbage bags with them so they could slide down on their butts every now and then, and who knew how long that would keep them interested.

They rounded a hairpin turn near the top and the mountain dropped off beside the car, giving a view down over the trees. It was worth it just to come up here and look. They all started to move again, shifting in their seats, reaching into their bags for mitts, pulling on their jackets as the car struggled to make the last stretch. They parked in the upper lot and piled out. Rob wore the backpack with the water bottles in it and they hiked out to the edge of the groomed slopes. Dave and Cindy were walking in front, holding hands.

Rob's eyes kept finding a path back to their clasped hands, then bouncing away again. The snow was wet. They hiked up about a hundred feet and he unshouldered the pack. He pulled out four large, translucent red garbage bags, big enough to step into and be covered up to the waist.

It worked well, except that there was no good way to regulate your speed since your feet were inside the plastic. After a few runs Dave was going down, gathering momentum, and he sprawled off to the side in an attempt to slow down. When he stood up, he was covered with wet snow and his pants were dark with moisture. Tad jumped into his bag and tried to aim himself at Dave as he was brushing himself off. He wasn't close enough to hit him, but when he came near, Dave tackled him and started rubbing snow into his face.

While Dave and Tad were wrestling down below, tumbling a little further every so often, Cindy stayed back. She was standing beside Rob, and they watched the guys, laughing without saying anything. Tad's garbage bag, hastily and incompletely worn, had come away and began drifting down the slope.

Rob felt like he should say something to Cindy while he had the chance.

"So, things are going well with you and Dave?"

She looked over at him, into his eyes. "Yeah," she said. "He's great." She paused, looking back down at Dave and Tad. "Natalie didn't stay away because I was here, did she?"

"What? Of course not!" He had said it too loud, with too much expression. It must have sounded fake. He wondered how he suddenly felt like he was trying to cover something up or tell a lie, when he really was telling the truth. "To be honest, she doesn't even know about you. About you and I, I mean. At least, I don't think so."

"You've never told her anything about us?"

"Just that we're good friends—which is, I guess, all that we are now, right?"

She opened her mouth, her brow suddenly furrowed, but didn't speak. She turned back to the guys and started walking down the slope, her feet slipping underneath her.

"Hey! Cindy!"

"Forget it," she said without looking back, her garbage bag clutched to her side.

They walked back to the lodge after about an hour of playing in the snow and ordered hot soup. Rob's pants were soaked.

"This is good," he said after swallowing the first spoonful.

Tad was breathing in and out quickly to cool his mouth off. "Hot, though."

"It's been a long time since I've played in snow," Cindy said.

"This snow's not the best. We should have done this earlier in the year."

When he was finished eating, Rob slouched down on the bench.

"Do you want to go back out there?" Dave asked.

"Not really. I'm ready to go back home any time."

Dave turned to Cindy and said something to her quietly. She nodded with a little smile.

"We're going to go for a little walk, then," he said.

"I'll be here. Don't go too far and make us come and rescue you."

"I guess I'll stay here, too," Tad said.

Dave and Cindy went out and Rob slouched down in the bench beside the heater, his jacket balled up behind him for lumbar support. He had another moment of discomfort as he watched them. He didn't even want Cindy, but for some reason he didn't want Dave to have her, either.

When he had come up here with Shawn in February, they had spent some time as they hiked, talking about women in general and Natalie in particular.

"I don't know what it is, exactly," Rob had said, "but some days I feel good about things, some days I think it sucks, but the next day I'm still here, still going over to her place, still calling her on the telephone."

Shawn wiped his mouth off and recapped the water bottle.

"She's your thirty degree slope."

"I don't know what that means."

Shawn pointed to one of the areas further out, a flat plane of snow, an opening in the trees. "Thirty degrees, more or less, is the magic number. On a day like today, thirty-degree slopes are the most dangerous. If it were a little steeper, the snow wouldn't pile up as much because it would just slide down right away, and if it were a little less steep, the snow wouldn't slide as easily and would just pile up. So you get this pile of snow on a fairly steep slope, and that's where avalanches come from. For you, things don't suck enough for you to just take off now, and they're not so great that you never wonder why you stay. Right in that middle place is the extreme avalanche danger."

Extreme avalanche danger. He stood up and stretched. Tad was lying a little further down the bench. He arched his back with his hands made into fists, pressing into the small of his back to try and crack it.

"I'm ready to go home and change into something dry," he said to Tad's horizontal form.

Tad slowly pushed himself up. "They come back yet?" he asked, blinking.

"No, but we can probably find them."

"Come on. Imagine it was you and Natalie having a little romantic walk on the mountain. Would you want someone interrupting to say he wanted to go home?"

"The way things are between us lately, I'd probably be grateful," he said.

"You've got problems?"

"Have we ever not had problems?"

"That sounds bad."

Rob sat down on the bench. "I don't know. I'm just a little sick of it at the moment. I go through phases."

"Hence the move back to Seattle. How does she feel about that?"

"Well, she doesn't really know about it yet."

"But you're...going to tell her, right?"

"No, I'm just going to slip out one day and let her figure it out, what do you think?"

"I don't know. You told us, what, the day before you left?"

"Yeah, but that was different. I didn't know myself until the day before."

When Dave and Cindy came back, they drove back down the mountain and ate Mexican food in Bellingham, near Rob's place. Just before they left, Dave handed him a CD and Cindy hugged him. He thought she was going to kiss him on the cheek, but she didn't.

After they had driven off, he plugged his kettle in to boil water for a cup of tea, or hot chocolate, and then sprawled on the futon. Maybe he should have made his remarks about moving to Seattle a little less unconditional. Now he was getting into a tighter and tighter place, with more and more people expecting him to go, and Natalie not knowing anything about it.

He flipped the switch for his computer and slumped back in his chair to wait while it booted up. It was not a comfort to think that Natalie had secrets or parts of herself or thoughts that were buried where he couldn't access, things she wanted to share but didn't, keeping them inside for way too long. Generally he liked to leave things until they came up on their own. In this case, he could either wait for them to come out or he could start digging. He didn't have the time to wait.

He dropped a tea bag into a mug and waited briefly while the little bit of water in the kettle came to a boil, then poured it in. He left it on the counter to steep and went back to the computer.

He slipped the CD into the drive and loaded up the image that Dave had saved on it. It was a digitally altered photograph—a man holding a gun to his own head with a look of bliss on his face. He thought he recognized the man—one of Dave's friends. The man's finger held the trigger down, and a motion blur emerging from the barrel of the gun traveled straight through the man's head. The spray was made up of particles that were in the shapes of distorted corporate logos, stars, and stripes and were mixed with blood, which spattered on the wall beside him and dripped down. The surface of the bloodstain reflected dollar bills, and tens, and twenties—dead presidents looking out, stony-faced.

This was a lot better than he had expected. Dave had e-mailed him back and told him to use the second of the two taglines he had come up with; he was right, it was better.

The world is going to America (in a handbasket).

He loaded the sticker template and replaced the old image with the new one. The unfortunate thing was that the stickers were so small, and some of the details—the logos, the reflections, the stars and stripes—would not be immediately visible, you'd need to examine the image to see them.

It was already past nine o'clock. He didn't want to talk to Natalie tonight, but he knew he should probably call her. He hadn't talked to her much since Wednesday. He had spent Friday and Saturday evenings at Freedom House, eating chips and salsa, playing cards, and brainstorming. They had thrown out ideas and organized tasks for both the party that was going to be held in the vacant lot downtown in a few weeks and for the house that was being put together in Seattle in little more than a month from now.

James hadn't been there either night because he had flown out to Quebec City for the Summit of the Americas. Rob wished he had gone. He always missed the big events, and spent his time working on the little ones, the ones that no one read and that made no difference. It was hard to listen to the reports coming back from Quebec—the riots, the demonstrations—and realize he was thousands of miles away from the action.

He hadn't given much input to the house discussions and hadn't taken any planning functions, in case he decided to back out in the next few weeks and stay in Bellingham, though he didn't tell them that. When they were dividing up tasks for the Pit Party, he had signed up instead to make posters and distribute them. Trevor was going to do the food with his girlfriend, Hope was going to bring some gardening and art supplies. Rob was going to get a list of media contacts together and give them to James. James was going to be in charge of informing the media about the event once it started as well as putting together a system to make sure the cops couldn't just haul them all out of the Pit. One of his plans was to suspend someone from a big metal tripod, so they couldn't take it down without endangering the person up top.

After the official part of the meeting was over he had talked with Hope for a long while. She was actually quite an interesting girl. She had no strings attached—no family (at least none that she knew about), not many friends besides those in her anarchist circle, and really, no job. She was an activist full-time, working part-time cutting hair to pay the rent. She had been to an activist training camp in California where she had learned all kinds of techniques for resistance and civil disobedience.

She said that almost all of the important direct action that happened was tied somehow to anarchists and anarchy. Her definition of anarchy was quite loose and included anyone who resisted oppression and she included them in her comments without any qualifiers: people like the disciples of Jesus, Tolstoy, and Thomas Jefferson.

They had talked late, and he slept in. He was late for work the next morning, but only slightly. He had stopped in at Natalie's place briefly afterwards, but she had a list of things she needed to do and wanted to go grocery shopping. She asked if he'd come with her, since she needed to do it and they hadn't talked or spent time together for days. He said he needed to prepare some information and mock-ups for the Freedom meeting that night, which was a lie. And he told her the Seattlites were coming up today, and invited her and Tink and Shawn to come, but they had all declined for various reasons. Natalie's ankle was sore so she said she couldn't hike. Those two worlds had never really meshed well—his friends were still distinctly separate entities from her and her friends, two clusters of friends orbiting around him like moons, never meeting.

So he hadn't talked to her since yesterday afternoon. He dialed her number, wondering what excuse he could give to avoid going over there tonight. Her answering machine picked up and he felt relief, like quickly looking down at his dashboard after passing a police car and realizing that he wasn't speeding after all.

"Hey, Nat. Sorry I missed you, it's Sunday night. We had fun on the mountain this afternoon. I've got a few things I'm going to work on and then I think I'll go to bed a little early today. I'll stop by your place after work tomorrow. Maybe we could make something to eat, or go find a place to eat. See you then."

He wasn't in the mood to continue working on the stickers and didn't want to start the posters for the Pit Party. He turned on the TV and flipped channels until it was late, watching commercials and imagining them doing this scene over and over and over until it was perfect.

When he woke up he pulled on a pair of shorts and opened his fridge to hunt for food. He found his tea, well steeped but cold. He did that more often—making something he craved and finding it later uneaten, as though the act of making it had fulfilled the need in his mind. He took a carton of eggs and a loaf of bread with him and wandered out into the kitchen to fry some breakfast.

One of the other tenants had used his frying pan and left it crusted with something burnt. The carpet had stains all over it, and little particles of food in all the cracks and beside the walls. Who ever heard of a carpeted kitchen, anyway? Everyone shared this kitchen and it was always disgusting—the tragedy of the commons. He thought about living in Seattle with a bunch of people in a big house. They'd be better than this there. He hoped. The difference being they had all decided to live together in Seattle whereas in this place, they were just together by default and didn't know each other.

He was almost ten minutes late for work, so he was hoping he could sneak in without being seen. He parked behind the store, in front of the dumpster because they usually picked up the trash in the morning and he didn't want to waste any time looking for parking. He went in the back door. His nametag wasn't in his box; sometimes he forgot it in the office after counting down his drawer. He looked out the window of the break room and saw a cluster of people around the front counter. An unhappy customer with boxes of folded papers on the counter in front of her. She must be complaining about something, probably demanding a reprint. He looked at her, hair in a butch cut, hard eyes, the beginnings of wrinkles around them. He recognized her as a customer but not much beyond that.

He stepped out and made his way to the office.

"That's him! He'll remember."

She was pointing at him, and her eyes, fixed on him, reminded him of where he'd seen them before—staring at him this same way, from on the other side of a locked glass door on a Saturday afternoon. Bobbi was up there in the cluster of people trying to resolve the problem. She beckoned him come with her index finger and he had a sinking feeling.

"I'll be right over," he said cheerfully, "I've just got to get my nametag and clock in."

He went in the office and swung the door partly shut.

"Shit," he muttered. What did he remember of her? He had let her in after hours to get her job, but he had made her check it over, he distinctly remembered that. He found his nametag on top of the safe and punched his code into the computer.

He came out, pinning his nametag to his Hawaiian shirt as he walked so he could look down at it for a little while longer instead of looking up at her.

"What's up?"

Bobbi and the lady started talking at the same time. Bobbi held up her hand.

"Just a moment. I'll have you explain what's wrong in a moment." She turned to Rob again. "Okay, here's the deal. Mrs. Hoechstetter had these printed here a little over a week ago. Unfortunately there's a problem. Why don't you show him what's wrong."

The lady thrust the pamphlet that was between them toward him.

"Okay. When you made me rush to check these over I didn't even notice it, but I gave one of my customers one of these and he noticed it immediately. The text on the inside is all pushed over and about four lines are cut off completely. I can't give these out to anybody."

He looked at the paper and saw that it was true. The formatting had shifted around and broken the lines in the wrong spots.

"Did we print this from your disk?"

She nodded. "You said it would give better quality. It's in one of these boxes," she said, pulling the tops off of a few more of the boxes.

"Well, the photos—the mid-tones—come out better when they are printed from disk," he said, "but whatever program it was done in was probably a different version than the one we have here, or maybe you used a font that we don't have, and in the conversion things may have shifted a bit."

"Well, these are useless for me. I'm going to need to have them redone, and I don't think I should have to pay for it."

"Did you sign off on a proof?" He started to finger through the drawer that held all the signed proofs from the last few weeks.

Bobbi pushed it gently shut, giving him time to pull his fingers out. "I checked already and didn't find one. We'll redo this one. Doug, can you take a new order, and run a new sample? Make sure to get a signature on the proof."

Mrs. Hoechstetter stood on the other side of the counter, looking grimly righteous, as though she were sad that this had to happen but was also well aware that she was standing on the moral high ground.

"I don't need these," she said, pushing one of the boxes closer to their side of the counter. "You can keep them."

Rob almost said something smart, but Bobbi gave him a little push.

"Let's talk in the office a second," she said.

He let her hand guide him, leaving Doug to clean up the mess with his cheerful thank-you-ma'am-may-i-have-another demeanor. He sat down on a swivel chair in the office.

"This is a bad start to a day. I guess that was my bad—I didn't notice the text had shifted."

"It's also a bad end to a day. The screw-up isn't that big of a deal. It's rare that your jobs need re-do's. Once in a while they happen."

"You know what pisses me off? When they offer the trash back to us, like they're doing us a favor." He tried to mimic her voice: "Here, I can't use these. You guys can keep these."

"That's when you're supposed to smile and get them out of the store as quickly as possible. There's something else we need to talk about, but I didn't think we needed to discuss it in front of her. The biggest issue was that she didn't have a receipt. I wasn't sure if we had even done that job, or if she had gotten it at another shop and was trying to get a free re-do from us."

"Yeah, we definitely did it. I remember when she picked it up."

"That's what I wanted to talk to you about. She said that the reason she didn't have a receipt was that you never gave her one."

Rob had a sinking feeling as he remembered the registers being shut off, and him taking her money and putting it in his own pocket. He didn't remember where it had gone after that.

"We both know how things will look to the other employees if it turns out one of the cashiers has been selling jobs and not giving receipts, maybe not even ringing it through the register. We're still under Randall's shadow and we can't afford to have even the appearance of anything under the table going on. What happened that day?"

Rob had a half dozen half-truths floating in his mind. He didn't want to sit silently for too long or it would be obvious that he was trying to iron his story out. The truth of it wasn't actually bad—he didn't do anything intentionally that was wrong, he was trying to do what was right.

"Well, let's see. It was a week ago Saturday, the one that we closed early on. I think I had just finished counting down my drawer and was getting ready to leave, and when I walked out of the office I heard this banging from the front door. I went over and told her we were closed and she was getting furious. I told her she wouldn't get a receipt because the register was down, but she said she didn't care. I think she said she lived a long ways out of town, so I decided—for customer service—to let her take the order. I pulled it out and had her check it over, and I didn't rush her at all, by the way."

Bobbi sighed and slumped her shoulders. "I was afraid it would be something like this. And what did you do with the money?"

This was the part that could get him into trouble. He thought that his face had probably already given him away. "I don't remember," he admitted, trying to look confused. "I think I rang it in on Monday."

Bobbi didn't say anything for a few moments, looking down at the surface of her desk. "I'm not sure what I'm going to do with this. I believe you. But after Randall, we need zero-tolerance for anything like this. And unfortunately, everyone on the floor got dragged into this before I got there, so it's not something we can just keep between ourselves. I'll keep your pay rate at the current level, but I'm going to have to suspend you from being weekend supervisor until I figure out what I'm going to do." She got up with a sigh and began walking towards the door.

He wasn't sure why he suddenly felt anger building inside him. It was more than fair. But he felt attacked and he didn't like it. He thought about Mrs. Hoechstetter standing there, righteous behind the counter and behind her, rows upon rows of other customers, angry and dissatisfied, always right.

"You know, don't even worry about it. I quit."

Bobbi stopped, halfway to the door, and turned around. "Rob, take some time before you say that. You're just a little upset right now."

"No, I'm serious. This is it."

"Come on. You're one of the best guys I've got."

"Well, I'm sorry for you, then."

"Listen, give me two weeks. If you change your mind at any time, you're free to stay. If you still want to go at the end of the two weeks, then you can go."

He wanted to leave now and never come back, but there was something else to think about. If he stayed, he could still print his next batch of stickers and all the posters for the Pit Party. If he quit now, he'd have to pay for them.

"Okay. I'll work today through Friday and then next week Monday through Friday. You can find a new weekend supervisor."

He worked the rest of his shift with a strange lightness, looking at everything around him and knowing that it was now a temporary thing. It was like the machines and this place had become part of him, entwined somehow in his life, and this was the beginning of the extrication process. One week from Friday, he'd run out the front door and be free to go anywhere, do anything. He should have quit a long time ago.

If he cut all his strings he'd be like a nomad again, ready to pack up and leave following something or wandering in search of it. If he did decide to go to Seattle, he wondered for how long his thoughts about Natalie would have to go through a simila extrication process—like he was uprooting something that had begun to grow around him, pulling her out like a weed, finding out where she had been inside him without him knowing until he felt the spots where she had left a void.

Question everything

According to the placemat, she was a Tiger—sensitive, generous, emotional. And she tended to be stubborn and unpredictable. Goats and Oxen are trouble. Dogs and Horses are fine. Rob was a Rabbit, outgoing and friendly, artistic. At times superficial and opportunistic. These same placemats—red and yellow ink printed on thin white paper—were in every Chinese restaurant she'd been in; they must be standard issue.

Rob came back from the restroom and settled into the bench across from her, sighing with pleasure.

"Bad news, Rob."

"What is it?"

"Well, apparently you're supposed to marry a pig."

"What the hell?"

"Or a dog." She tapped her finger on the placemat.

"Oh, that," he said, looking down to read his own. "I'm a Rabbit. Hey, look, I'm friendly and artistic."

"I'm stubborn and unpredictable."

"These are strangely accurate."

The waitress came by and set her tray on the empty table next to them and picked up the plates, one in each hand.

"Eggplant Delight?" she asked, sliding it in front of Natalie before she could respond. She set an empty plate down in front of Rob. "Moo Shoo Pork." She had four thin pancakes on her tray yet and she plucked some of the filling up from a bowl and dropped in onto the pancake, folding it and wrapping it with chopsticks into a sort of Chinese version of a burrito. The sight of the chopsticks manipulating the pancake, folding it in on itself, reminded Natalie of a spider wrapping up a fly or a little beetle, turning it around with its thin arms.

"We forgot to order soup," Rob said to Natalie after the waitress had gone.

"Too late." She used her chopstick to poke at a little piece of eggplant, coated light green. "You know what's interesting?"

"What."

"You're supposed to marry a pig and you ordered pork."

"Or a dog. But I didn't see any dog on the menu."

This was going to be a pleasant night just spending casual time with each other. A week ago last Wednesday she had told him about the pregnancy, a couple of years too late, and she hadn't been sure how it had gone over because he hadn't really talked to her for the first three or four days afterwards. Monday night after work—after he had given his notice at work—he came over and they had talked for a while. All this week, he'd been over for a little while after work each day. He seemed different, though.

He was going through some changes within himself and without. It was good that he had quit his job. He hadn't really taken to it and it didn't seem to bring him any life or pleasure. Now the trick would be finding something that would. She hoped he wasn't going to find it with his anarchist friends. He'd been spending a lot of time with them lately, and that worried her. Maybe because their own relationship seemed to be changing, too.

He'd been somewhat harsher lately, more verbally aggressive. At first she hadn't been sure how to take it but she had decided to take it in the best way possible—to appreciate the interest he was showing in her, in her thoughts. And now they were finally breaching some of the areas that they'd been avoiding for a long time now, probably in an attempt to avoid conflict. It had just dragged the conflict out in longer lasting, less overt forms. She felt like the important issues were getting turned over, and the fresh air felt good.

A few days ago, Rob started asking her strong questions out of the blue, like he had been loading and aiming in his mind and then suddenly opened fire on her.

"I don't believe in God. Am I going to hell?"

"What are you talking about?"

"I just want to know if you think I'm going to go to hell."

"Why?"

"I want to know."

"I don't know, I'm not going to be the judge. Thank God."

"Well, what about Jews, or Muslims?"

"I'm not God—why don't you ask him?"

"Do you think anyone will go to hell?"

"Maybe, maybe not. I'm hopeful not, but I'm not confident enough to bank on it."

"Well, how do you stay out of it?"

"Jesus," she said in a high voice, trying to imitate a child answering a question in Sunday school. She laughed because she thought it was funny and because she knew it would be lost on him.

"I'm serious."

"Me, too. I really think Jesus is the only path that allows us to move toward God, however slowly."

"So what about me, or a Muslim?"

"Well, Jesus is the only path to God, but is Christianity the only path to Jesus? I'm not sure of that."

"It's hard to discuss when you keep saying you don't know anything."

"Sorry, but I'm not going to pretend. I know it's fashionable to say that anything's as good as anything else, but it breaks down. I've tried it. There are things that everyone agrees are not good, or right."

"How can you know that what you believe is right and good? How can you base your life on it?"

"Do you even know what I believe? I can understand your concern—nobody's interested in committing to anything anymore. We've got to have 24 types of cereal on the shelf. Then we have to stand paralyzed with indecision in the aisle."

"Yeah, but you don't have to base your life on cereal."

"No. But I think 'I can't base my life on this,' is often code for 'I can't be bothered to commit myself to anything because I want to do what I want to do when I want to do it.'"

"But my point is, to make that choice carries with it the distinct possibility that you've chosen wrongly."

"I understand your point. It's not new. I struggle with it all the time, and that's hard sometimes, but it's preferable to not dealing with the issue."

"You're a great one to be talking about commitment," he muttered.

"What?" she asked, and he looked off to the side, out the front window, before turning back.

"What about the girl who's born over in Saudi Arabia? Her decisions are going to be lot different just because she popped out over there. How can you say that she's got o believe what you do?"

"Are you talking with me or are you talking at me? I never said that. I said I'm perfectly happy to leave that one to God."

She thought he was going to drop it before the conversation looped around again and started over. Instead, he regrouped and came at her from another angle.

"Either way, how can you believe in a God that would torture people for an eternity? Why not just obliterate all the ones who didn't make the cut? That would be more merciful, wouldn't it?"

"You're just full of them tonight, aren't you? I think the language of fire is symbolic of either punishment or purification. Maybe hell will be a time where people are purified. But maybe not. Maybe it is going to be a time of punishment. I don't know. It's going to be an absence of God and things that are good, you know? It'll involve loneliness, depression, fear. Headaches and hunger. Remember that Nordic hell, where they kept eating and that just made them hungrier?"

"Yeah."

"You know what I think the trouble is? Too many people think Christianity is about hell and about getting yourself saved from hell. And then they sit at home and pray 'I'm ready! Come quickly, Lord,' and wonder why he's waiting, without thinking of all the people who aren't ready yet or all of the good they could be doing here and now. I don't think you can become a real Christian if you're just doing it to try to keep yourself out of hell. It's something that happens in your heart, not a decision made out of fear. It's about love, that's all. Love God and love others."

Rob hadn't said anything but looked like he was thinking, or reloading.

She didn't want to deal with answering aggressive questions tonight; she just wanted to relax a bit and spend some time with him. He was cutting the end off of his second pancake with the edge of his fork.

"Can you lay off a little?" she said.

He chewed slowly. "What are we going to do tonight, anyway?"

"I thought maybe we could go over to your place and play a game."

"I don't have to work tomorrow," he said.

"Oh, yeah! Do you want to do something?"

"I can't. We're having a get-together with some of the Seattle crew. It's an anarchy thing."

"You're really getting into this anarchy stuff, aren't you?"

"I guess so."

"You're not going to go crazy with it, are you?"

"What does that mean?"

"Like, you won't go out at dark and spray paint trains or anything."

He lowered his fork from his mouth without eating the food on it and smiled.

"We should do that again."

"No. I still can't believe you painted the anarchy symbol on that train."

"Why not? Do you know what that symbol means? I didn't know it at the time, but the A is for Anarchy and the circle is the O for Order. Anarchy is Order."

"That seems a little counter-intuitive."

"Why?"

"Because when you spray paint it on other people's property, you're trying to claim that anarchy is order through social disorder."

"Maybe that's the point."

"It's the same sort of thing as the media campaigns you do against big media, or a 'No More Pavement' sticker on a car. Or the guy in the newspaper, wearing Nikes as he smashes the windows at Niketown. At what point does it become hypocrisy?"

"I don't think any of those are really the same thing. The media campaigns are just fighting fire with fire. The pavement sticker is saying we've got enough pavement already, we don't need more. The guy with the Nikes that everyone talks about—I don't know. I'd be willing to bet he thought he was doing something very symbolic by destroying Nike while wearing Nikes. A house divided against itself, you know? Here's a good example. The people that run the Billboard Liberation Front aren't just defacing billboards to destroy an advertisement; they're turning the billboard against itself, against its makers. It's called a detournement."

"Well, maybe that works for the media stuff, but not for anarchy."

"Why not? Do you know what anarchy is?"

"Order?"

"Okay," he said. "I mean, do you know what the philosophy behind anarchy is."

"No rules, every man for himself. Survival of the fittest. Things like that—it seems very adolescently male."

"See—that's the image the media portrays but it's just a half-truth. Or not even. Maybe a quarter-truth. At its root, anarchy is just rebellion against oppression. You're an anarchist in a lot of ways."

"Well, I did spray paint a train, after all. Not that the train was oppressing me."

"You have to remember that anarchy always gets misrepresented by people. Not every anarchist spends every night out spray painting the neighborhood—they're working for social justice, campaigning, volunteering. It's a complete movement, you know: social, political, economic. This isn't something random from the last few decades—this is a philosophy that's hundreds of years old, or more. There are a lot of famous people that had anarchist streaks in them. Jesus' disciples, Tolstoy—he was a pacifist anarchist, J.R.R. Tolkien leaned toward it, Thomas Jefferson was an anarchist of sorts. The hermit-monks in the 4th century were anarchists."

"I doubt it. If your definition is true, then I think you'd be hard-pressed to find someone who wasn't an anarchist to some degree."

"That's exactly right."

"What about the full-blown anarchists? What do they believe?"

"Well, there's a bunch of different strains of thought, and some of them are pretty wild, but you can't judge the entire philosophy because of a few extremists. The fact is that most of the important direct action that is getting done has anarchists involved in it."

She didn't say anything because she didn't want to say the wrong thing. It was discomforting how close his defense of anarchy and her defense of the ideals of Christianity were. Both Christians and anarchists were imperfect people with imperfect morals, incomplete knowledge, and inaccurate interpretations of the cause, but can you fault the ideal for the people who profess it and don't follow it, or those who are following a distorted version of it?

"I still don't understand how anarchy can be order if it's by definition a struggle against an oppressing force. What is anarchy when the oppressor is removed? How is the order realized?"

"Well, that's where there are differences of opinion among anarchists. How does it look in the final analysis, and how do we get there? I guess my view is that if nobody is oppressing anybody, then there will be order by definition. People will be getting along."

"You're more idealistic than I am. Do you really think people are just going to get along?"

"I think there's a better chance of it if nobody's oppressing them. There's certain principles that we all agree on: freedom, equality, free association, and solidarity or cooperation. But in the meantime there's a lot of work figuring out how to get there."

She didn't want to fight, so she dropped it and they prepared to leave. The waiter put the remainder of her meal into an origami-style take home box. Rob's car still wasn't working normally; it stalled twice on the way back to his place, but it started immediately again both times. She didn't come over to his place very often, because she didn't have a car and because it was so tiny and dirty. She wasn't sure how he lived in this place, with one room besides your bathroom to call your own, and sharing one small, filthy kitchen with three strangers.

Rob took the chair from in front of his desk and put it beside the small, round table, which was near the glass sliding door. Beyond the door was a deck not much larger than a child's playpen, with overgrown grass penetrating the flimsy crosshatched wood barrier. An unfinished piece of 2x4 was wedged between the sliding door and the wall as a primitive lock.

She turned back to the room. Rob was walking away from her.

"You can grab the games if you want," he said. "I've got to go to the bathroom. Oh, new message."

He hit the play button on the answering machine as he walked by and started peeing with the bathroom door open so he could listen to the messages.

"This is Hope, from Freedom. I know you've already had the option and declined, but Trev's backed out of the house so there's an extra opening again, in case you want to come with. If I don't hear from you tonight—"

There was a beep as he reached out from the bathroom and pressed a button on the machine—skip or delete, she wasn't sure—and it went to the next message.

"Old message," he said and then flushed the toilet.

"Hey, Rob. Tyler. I'll have the new page up on the site by tomorrow afternoon. Nice graphic."

Rob emerged from the bathroom and held a button down.

"Delete all messages?" the computerized voice asked, and then beeped a moment later.

"That means I'm just about ready to start the stickering for my last campaign," he said as he turned toward her.

"Your last campaign? Really?"

"Well, the last one in the current setup. Things aren't really working—there's not too many people reading it."

"What's next, then?"

"I don't know. Maybe I'll see what some other people have going. Definitely the internet's going to be a key part in it, because it's accessible to so many people from all over the world. The problems and the corporations are worldwide, so we have to be, too. Maybe the trick is that it's got to be tied more directly to the action. Right now

I'm mostly editorial, informational. I've learned a lot by joining Freedom—I think I should do something with them."

"Are they still trying to get you to join their house in Seattle?"

"What?"

"The first message."

"Oh, that. I hadn't gotten around to erasing that message yet, but it was an old message. I guess somebody dropped out and they had an extra room, so they were calling around."

"Did they find someone?"

"I'm pretty sure they have. I didn't call her back that night, but I'm sure they won't have trouble getting someone."

He was looking down, dumping the Scrabble pieces onto the table.

"Are you ever sorry you turned down the chance to go?"

He spread the pieces around on the table and they both started to turn them upside-down, one by one.

"Yeah, I guess so. Lately I've been wondering, if another opening came available, what I'd do."

She stopped turning squares over and looked up at him. "Really?"

"Sort of. Especially lately, you know—with my site not generating much interest here, with me out of work now, and with most of Freedom moving down there. It's like you're the only thing in this town that I'm interested in."

"That's all, huh?"

"Yeah, but I was thinking the other day, I wonder if you'd have any interest in going to Seattle?"

"Yeah right! Not this again."

"Why not? I'm just asking."

"I think I'm having déjà vu."

"Come on. Can't you just play along? I'm not asking for a commitment, I just asked a hypothetical question."

"Okay, where would I live?"

"You could live in my room in the house, with me. They won't mind. I'm serious."

"I don't think I'm ready for that," she said.

"That's fine, because I could sleep on the couch downstairs, I'm pretty sure."

"Why are you pressing this? I'm not sure I'd fit in with a bunch of anarchists, anyway."

"I just think it's an interesting idea. And in the off-chance a room opens up again, it'd be good to have discussed it already."

"You're serious about this."

"I just think it's fun to imagine possibilities."

"Well, don't sign us up for anything without asking."

"Don't worry. How many pieces do we start with?"

"I don't remember. Let's say seven."

They each took seven pieces and turned them over.

"On your mark, get set, go."

They each turned over their seven tiles and began to arrange them, muttering to themselves and moving them back and forth on the table. They took turns leading; one of them fit the two new pieces in for a number of turns in a row while the other tried to keep up, frantically trying to arrange the influx of letters into words.

"Go."

"Go."

"Go."

"Slow down, woman. I'm scrabbling as fast as I can but I can't keep up."

She smiled slightly, but didn't respond. It was funny—once while they were playing he had looked in the dictionary and discovered that "scrabble" was a real word and ever since he always found one or two times to use it in conversation while they played this game.

"Go."

"Damn it!"

"Oh, your lucky day. I just got the Q and I have no U and no blank."

"It's about bloody time. Now I can take it slow and get this in order."

She watched him organize and reorganize the letters.

"Do you have anything to drink?"

"Yeah. How about a Rum and Coke?"

"That sounds good. I'll make them while you straighten out your words."

"Great."

"But you can't pick up the next two until I'm back."

"Fair enough."

She took a tray of ice cubes from the freezer and opened the fridge to find the Coke.

"I've got the squiggly N so I get extra points."

"We're not counting points."

"I still get them."

He kept his liquor bottles on top of the fridge. She poured his strong and set the glasses down on the edge of the table.

"I'm going to go to the bathroom while I've got the chance."

"Okay. I've almost got it here."

"I'll be right back."

Rob had peed all over the seat, so she had to wipe it down with toilet paper. His bathroom was always scary—that was one thing she didn't miss about living with him. If this house typified what the anarchy house was going to be like, she already knew her answer. Bathrooms that were disgusting, space shared with complete strangers, crumbs and stains and dirty dishes in the kitchen, cramped conditions. Nothing very appealing there.

She flushed and rinsed her hands. Rob was leaning back in his seat when she came out. She sat down and took a sip of her drink.

"I think you took my drink," she said, swapping the drinks. "Did you get all your tiles placed?"

"Yep. By the way, I added some extra rum to that one because it was a little weak. Go."

"Wow. This drink is stronger than the other. How much rum did you put in?"

"I slipped a little while pouring."

"Take this back." She passed the drink back to him and took the first glass back. "Still no U."

"I've got one."

"I'll trade you for it."

"No way. Go."

They each pulled two more letters from the middle. She was always a step behind him in completing her board.

"Go."

"There's my U."

They played, trading control back and forth and not talking except to say "Go." She wanted to go to the fridge and get the Coke, so she could add some more of it to her drink, but she couldn't leave the game when it was this close.

"Go. Take one tile only."

"Wait—"

"Done!"

"I had only two tiles left, and I think I have a place for them."

"Too late."

"Wait a sec—I've got to check yours and make sure they're all real words."

"You don't trust me?"

"No." She came around and looked at his creation. "I wonder if you can do a psychological analysis on someone based on the words they come up with in this game?"

"What do you mean?"

"You know, if you look at a person's words, does that give you some kind of insight into the way their mind works or what they're thinking about at the moment? Does the fact that, given certain letters, a person comes up with certain words before other possible words mean anything?"

"I doubt it, but I'm not taking any chances" he said, making a swipe at the collection of tiles that made up the words he had created. He knocked a corner out of the construction.

"Hey! I'm not done checking the words yet."

"That was the point."

"Did you even have any two syllable words at all?"

"Shut up."

"Do you want to play again?"

"Not really. Do you want to play something else?"

She stretched and yawned. "Sure—your pick."

"You know what it's going to be."

"All I know is it better not be War."

"Yep."

She sighed. "Only one game or less."

Rob got up to get a deck of cards while she pulled the tiles off of the edge of the table and into the box. She brought the box over to the mesh shelving system beside the fridge and set it on top of the old Genus Edition of Trivial Pursuit. He had hung the painting he had bought from her on the wall above the shelf.

It was strange to see her work hanging in his house—and more so because it depicted her own body jammed into a trash can. Why had he wanted this picture?

"You ready?" he asked.

She turned back toward him. "I guess. Let's get it over with."

Rob started shuffling. "Do you believe in miracles?"

"Why?"

"Well, because I'm curious."

"Sure, why not? Crazy shit happens."

"Okay, explain. There's got to be rational explanations for things. Think about it—you can't walk on water. Unless it's frozen."

"What if that rational explanation is that God changes things in our world from time to time, and works in it, and suspends some of the other laws?"

"That's not rational."

"Why not?"

"It's just not."

"Who says rationality is all it's cracked up to be, anyway?"

He dealt the last card and they each made their cards into neat stacks.

"You know what I think?" she asked. "I think it's irrational to think that there's nothing deeper than science, that there's nothing that science can't quantify or measure."

"But how can we know anything that we can't see?"

"We can keep looking and seeing what we see, but we have to be humble. I love some of the old science, the naïve theories. The simplicity, the mystery; it's beautiful."

"Like what? The flat earth?"

They were playing their cards quickly, sweeping them onto their own piles if they won the hand. It was her way to try to get the game over with as soon as possible and Rob seemed to like it that way, anyway. She wasn't sure why he liked this game so much.

"Yeah, like the flat earth, and things like spontaneous generation. Maggots come from meat, because if you leave meat out and watch it, then maggots start coming out of the meat. Or ideas like levity—if gravity is pulling things down, then there must be an opposite force that pulls things up, so grass can grow upwards."

"They're simple, but they're wrong. We've discovered a lot of stuff since then."

"But what I'm saying is that there's something beautiful about these old theories, their attempt to understand the world based on what they knew at the time. But there's something beautiful about a lot of theories, about how things seem to fit, we seem to understand, but we also have to remember that we might seem just as silly to scientists a little further along. We can't be so arrogant to assume we've figured everything out. In five hundred years, people might look back on us and think our theories are so quaint, so simple."

"Well, that doesn't mean we have to assume everything we know is wrong."

"No, but—I guess I'm talking about miracles again—science classifies everything, and tries to explain it—I think it's important to recapture the mystery, to see God in daily life."

"I understand what you want to do, but spiritualizing everything makes me nervous—it's like superstition, or voluntary stupidity. If you know an explanation for something, why would you want to pretend that it's something more mysterious and unknown?"

"I wonder, what do you think gives meaning to our lives?"

"We do."

"See, I think you're missing out on a big part of our humanity. Do you remember Jean, from school? She was in my class."

"I think so."

"Doesn't matter. She gave me this quote once, I think it was from the Kabbalah; it was something like this: 'We hold in one hand a morsel of dust, and in the other a cluster of stars.' It's like, we're not only physical, rational beings, and we're not only spiritual, either—we're both at the same time, there's a tension."

"Well, sure, but how can you know anything about the spiritual part—you can't see it or touch it or anything, so it's like making stuff up out of thin air."

"Well, that's only true if you try and use physical measures for spirituality. There are other ways to know about the spiritual."

"What, like feelings, or emotions?"

"Partly."

"Maybe some people have tools that I don't have."

"Or tools you have but don't know how to use."

"Okay, already. Let's drop it."

"Why are you getting pissed? You're the one who started this conversation."

"Well, here's a question for you, then," he said. "If we decided we'd like to go to Seattle and then a room suddenly opened up for us in the house, would that be a miracle?"

"I thought that this was a conversation we had agreed to drop."

"That's perfect, because now that means we've got a conversation neither of us wants to be having. Would it be a miracle?"

"The greater miracle would be us deciding we want to go there. You're clenching our jaw like you do when you're getting pissed off. What do you have to get pissed off bout?"

They continued the war in silence for a number of hands. What a stupid game. It was completely random chance. At first she had been winning a lot, but now she seemed to be losing them again. The cards just had to find their equilibrium and eventually they'd stop sloshing back and forth from one hand to the other. It was kind of pointless.

"Can we stop the war? I surrender."

"Come on," he said.

She pushed her cards toward him. "You win."

"You don't like this game, do you."

"Have I ever?"

He stood up. "Do you want another Rum and Coke?"

"No, thanks. I think I had about three already in this one. A glass of water would be great, though."

She was feeling the rum. She went over to his desk and picked up a sheet of paper from a stack, then leaned against the desk to steady herself. It was a full-sheet label with a picture of someone shooting himself in the head. THE WORLD IS GOING TO AMERICA (IN A HANDBASKET).

"Is this the campaign?" she asked.

"Yeah." The ice cubes clinked as he handed her the glass.

"Wow. These are big stickers."

"I know. I think they look so much better. I probably should have been doing full-sized stickers all along, but I thought they'd for sure notice it at work if that many sheets of label stock were gone every time I did one."

"Or you could have just bought some labels."

"Or I could have done that."

"What's the article about? Can you summarize it?"

He shuffled through some papers on the desk and gave her a small piece of paper.

"This is what started the idea—it's from *Crime and Punishment*. I'm not sure how well it fits with the theme anymore, but I'm going to put it on the site anyway."

Rob made the futon while she read the passage and he struggled for a few moments, trying to convert it into the sofa. He sat down on it, leaning on the armrest.

"This is why I never put this thing up."

She sat down beside him. "Don't worry about it."

She set the sticker on the table.

"I don't think you should stop making the stickers or writing the articles yet."

"Why not?"

"I think they're important. It's good for people to hear about it."

"But the point is, not many people are hearing about it, at least not through my site. Maybe I need to concentrate my energy somewhere where it'll be more effective."

"Maybe. As long as you have somewhere to put it, I guess. Are you sad?"

"Kind of. But I guess it helps to think of it, like, Gandhi called his efforts 'experiments in truth,' you know, and it helps to think like that. What I do is all trial and error, and sometimes it'll work, sometimes it won't, and sometimes I'll be right and sometimes I'll be wrong. As long as I learn from my mistakes, right?"

She was leaning back on her arms, bracing herself in the absence of a backrest. He ran one of his hands up and down the arm that was closest to him.

"Listen," he said. "I hope I haven't been too much of a dick this last week. I guess I've had a lot on my mind. A lot of things are happening and it's kind of like I'm not sure how things are going to all fit together yet."

"Thanks," she said.

"Have I been pretty bad?"

"Well, there were a few times when I felt a little like I was under attack or something, like this was turning into an inquisition instead of a relationship. But once we're talking about something it's usually okay."

"Yeah. The last little while I've been thinking about it and I realized we should talk about some of these things."

"I think so, too. I guess I usually thought you didn't want to."

"I usually didn't want to."

"So why the change?"

"I'm not sure. Lately I've been wondering how much of you I know, and how much is kind of hidden inside."

She didn't say anything.

"I just want you to know that I don't mean to be as harsh as I sometimes feel, after the fact. I don't know if I've ever said it, but I think it's great that you believe in everything you believe in. It really is. And I want to know more about it. I've been doing some thinking about it and I think I get defensive about it sometimes—not because I think you shouldn't believe it, but because I don't think I can. I think we just need to be able to accept that what works for you doesn't always work for me, and vice versa. But keep talking about it with me, okay? Even if I'm an ass sometimes?"

He slipped his arm around her and pulled her into a loose hug. Despite the aggressive questions, it had been a relief to be able to share some of the things that she hadn't often shared with him.

"Thanks for being interested," she said.

He kissed her, and the kiss gradually transmuted into something else as they fell back on the futon and shifted positions. She ran her hands underneath his shirt, dragging her fingernails lightly across his shoulders and back and chest as they kissed. He pulled away and yanked his shirt up over his head, extracting his arms one at a time, and took her face in his hands, kissing her softly.

Her shirt came off, and Rob struggled with the clasp on her bra. She wasn't sure if it had taken him a long time or no time at all—she seemed to be hanging outside of time, while the world kept spinning around her, Rob kept kissing her, undressing her. They were underneath the blanket now, together in the semi-darkness, and she let her hand travel down his back until it reached one of his buttocks. It had become exposed somewhere along the way, like the rest of his body. She squeezed it gently, as though testing its firmness. Her breasts rubbed against the texture of his chest, and she remembered the pleasure of skin on skin. He was licking her neck. The question of whether she was choosing this or whether she was just letting it happen rose briefly but she ignored it.

My God is too big to fit inside one religion

He hoped he wasn't getting himself into something he was going to regret later. He got along well with most of the people from Freedom, some better than others, but there were a few people that he hadn't met before who were going to be in the house as well. One of them wasn't here this morning, but the two that were gave cause for worry. Kathleen was showing them around the house now, talking in a nasal but eager voice. He wasn't sure what it was about her that grated on his nerves, but he didn't like her. Alice wasn't as bad—she just hovered in the background, watching and following.

Kathleen had greeted them at the door this morning wearing what looked like a medieval pirate's outfit, silky and billowy. Maybe it was her excitement that he didn't like. It seemed counterfeit and excessive. As she took them through the house, she was going over every detail. The kitchen has a fridge, a stove, an oven, a dishwasher, a sink and garbage disposal, all these cupboards and drawers, this much counter space. All things he could see with his own eyes.

She threw the end of her silk sash back over her shoulder as she made her way for the stairs and it fluttered behind her like something half dead. He followed behind her, alternately watching her ass cheeks flex against her skirt and then following the backs of her feet as they climbed from step to step. The stairs were wooden, each one visibly worn in the middle.

Hope's voice came from behind him.

"What do you think, Rob?"

"Seems like a nice big house, so far."

"When we came down a couple of weeks ago we picked rooms. Trevor had the one right at the top of the stairs, to the right, so that's where you'd be. And Natalie."

While they were driving down, he had thrown the idea of Natalie staying in the room with him out for discussion. They hadn't seen any problem with it, but thought that he should ask the entire group. It had just been James, Hope and himself in the car. He was just coming to take a look at the house, and his room in particular. They were already bringing some of their stuff down because they were moving in earlier than everyone else. They'd be in within the next few weeks and everyone else was going to be coming after next month.

That meant Natalie had about a month to make her arrangements for getting out of her current house and quitting her job and preparing to move. He was glad, because one thing that he knew would not go over well was to ask her if she wanted to come when the move date was about four days away. Now he just had to convince her that it was a good idea. That was going to be hard, but he thought he could pull it off. She seemed to be softening. He just had to make sure not to do or say anything too stupid in the next weeks.

His room was tiny, which didn't really bother him—he had lived in a tight spot for a long time now—but he wasn't quite sure how Natalie would feel about it. He had to find a way to make this room and this house seem more desirable than perhaps they really were. It did have a nice big window; that was good. Natalie would like it here once she adjusted to the new place and the people. He didn't think he'd say too much about the piratess, though. Except for the fact that she wanted to paint a mural on all of the living room walls, floor to ceiling and wall to wall, and that she was excited about the fact that Natalie was an artist.

Kathleen took them on a walk-through of the other three rooms on the floor and turned around with her hands on her hips.

"That's it! Isn't this going to be great?"

Rob nodded. "It's a nice place."

One of the other things that was bothersome about Kathleen was that she hovered in the area between being attractive and not, which made him want to keep staring at her, to figure out whether she was beautiful or not. Her hair was tied in a straight black ponytail, slightly greasy, and it hung down in the middle of her back. Her face was symmetrical but maybe a bit too thin. He found his gaze being drawn to her upper lip, where a thin, barely visible moustache had sprouted. Maybe that was part of why he kept thinking of her as a pirate.

He imagined her body underneath the costume: would one of these legs be a peg? Did she have an anchor tattooed on her skin? Maybe on one of her breasts. In his mind he kissed the anchor and she wrapped her peg leg around him and they made love and as the boat squeaked underneath them she began to groan, "Aaaarrrrrr."

"What's so funny?" Hope asked, and he tried to stop smiling.

"Nothing. This looks good, but I'm going to have to try to convince Natalie that this tiny room is a good idea."

"It wouldn't be the worst thing in the world if she didn't come, would it?"

"No, I guess it wouldn't be the worst thing, but I'd really like her to come."

"I think you'd forget about her in no time once you were down here, anyway."

He helped them move their boxes from the trunk and back seat of the car and up into their rooms. These rooms were both larger than his; he noticed that every time he entered them with a new box. They had gotten a late start; it was already early evening by the time they had finished moving the boxes up. They decided to stay there for the night and head back Sunday morning. If he hadn't spent time last weekend with Dave and Tad, he would have found a way out to their place now, but he knew if he did, they'd make tonight the night they all got drunk together, and tomorrow he'd be riding in a car with a hangover. Besides, Dave probably had plans with Cindy already.

They sat around the table with beers and Rob sketched out some rough drafts of the posters he was going to print up for the Pit Party next weekend. James suggested that he make handouts instead of posters, so that they could be distributed on the day of the event instead of posted all week. He didn't want the police to be waiting at the gate. Once they were in, they could send people all over town with handouts and invite others to join them. They'd already been in planning with a few other local groups so there was going to be a significant number of people there without any public advertising.

They moved to the living room and turned the TV on, not giving it their full attention. The pirate kept flipping channels as they talked. They brainstormed about how they could use the space in this house. James wanted to have a weekly meeting where the public was invited to discuss local issues and plans of action, and he wanted to set goals of a certain number of actions per year. They didn't decide anything because most of the people weren't there and they couldn't vote.

Alice gave him a blanket to use and he spread it out on the floor in his room. James and Hope had the couches downstairs and Kathleen and Alice already had their beds in their rooms. He brushed his teeth with a little toothpaste on the end of his finger and then wrapped himself in the blanket. At least it was carpeted.

James and Hope were probably screwing each other down there. He remembered again when Hope had tried to have sex with him on the couch at the Freedom House, and was proud of himself again for resisting. That was before he had mentioned Natalie to her; it wasn't her fault.

Last night had been the first time he'd slept with Natalie since he'd moved back to Bellingham. It had been so long since he'd had sex that he was like a virgin again, probably. He kept expecting her to stop him, to whisper "Not tonight," or something like that, so when she didn't he had this extra rush of adrenaline along with everything else. It was definitely a positive sign.

Now he just had to convince her that she wanted to move to Seattle, to this room. The floor was hard, despite the carpet. He turned over and curled slightly to help balance himself on his side, resting his head on a small pillow from one of the chairs in the living room. He couldn't fall asleep immediately but that probably had more to do with the fact that he was on the floor than with the unfamiliar surroundings.

He woke up cold and remembered pulling his blanket tighter during the night, trying to get more coverage, more warmth. His neck was stiff and it hurt whenever he turned it to the left. They ate homemade granola with soymilk when they woke up. He was awake before James and Hope so he showered first and used one of the two spare towels. Someone was going to have to double up and reuse a wet towel, which was unpleasant but at least it wasn't him.

They left the house midway through the morning and drove in mostly silence until they were in the outskirts of Seattle. They say that often friends who room together end up enemies. What about when you room with mere acquaintances, people you barely know?

"You're coming down next month, right?" James asked Rob.

"Yeah."

"I think maybe I'll leave my bed up there until you're coming down and then we can use the same truck to haul it. Hope could do that, too, and save some money."

"And then what? We'd have to sleep on the couches for a month?"

"Yeah, or the floor, or camping foam or something."

"That's fine with me," Rob said.

When they dropped him off at his place, he pushed the front door open—none of the four who shared the kitchen locked the door, despite Gordon Nerburn's stern warnings—and then fished out the key to his door and went in, bolting the door behind him out of habit. He thought about making a sandwich or boiling some macaroni, bu he didn't have the impetus. Inertia took him to his futon and he flopped down on his fresh sheets and sighed. He must not have gotten very deep into sleep last night.

When he woke up the sun was bright behind the blinds of the sliding door. It felt wrong to be lying in bed, but he couldn't make himself get out. It felt good to have the blankets over him, to bask in the heat he had managed to generate and imagine Natalie's body underneath here with him.

He lay there for a while without looking at the time and then found when he finally did that it was almost three o'clock already. He pulled himself out from under the covers and called Natalie on the telephone. It rang for a while.

"Hello?" The voice sounded sleepy.

"Nat?"

"Hi Rob, this is Tink. Just a sec, I'll get her."

He heard the phone clatter as she dropped it or set it on the counter.

"Hello?" She sounded tired, too.

"Hi, Nat. I hope she didn't wake you up."

"No, we both woke up for the ringing and were trying to remember where the phone was."

"Well, do you want to have supper together tonight?"

"Sure. Do you want to come over here and we can make it?"

"Okay. I'll come over about five thirty. Go back to sleep."

"I will. How was Seattle?"

"It was good. I'll tell you about it tonight."

He almost crawled back into bed—everybody else was doing it. But he turned the computer on instead and began to design the handouts for next weekend. He'd print them tomorrow and be done with it.

> *You are invited to a community celebration on public space. Join us at the corner of Railroad and Holly this afternoon and evening. Free food and community. All are welcome.*

He inserted a cheesy clip-art picture of a jester on a unicycle, so the words arced over the top of him like he was juggling them. He spent close to twenty minutes changing the font, trying to find a playful style. This was always a time waster, choosing fonts. He decided to find the font at work tomorrow before printing it, so he saved it and closed it.

Natalie was awake when he arrived, almost ten minutes early. She was sitting on the little wooden bench on the front porch with a glass of orange juice.

"Hey." Rob came over and sank into the tattered old recliner beside her.

"That's disgusting. Don't sit in that thing."

"Why not?" he asked, as he felt water seep through the back legs of his pants. He sprang up.

"It's growing moldy and it's probably infested with mice."

"Why do you guys keep it here?"

"It's Shawn's. He had it in college and doesn't want to get rid of it yet."

Rob sat down beside her and put a hand on her neck, massaging slightly.

"Something on your mind?"

"Not really. I'm just enjoying the air."

"How was your day?"

"Not bad. I painted for a while this morning and then met Mom at Archie's."

"That's the second week in a row, isn't it?"

"Yeah, but I had missed about three weeks before that. She asked me to ask you if you would come over for coffee next week."

"Oh. I guess so. Did you have a good talk with her?"

"It was good. It's just that...I don't know, I always enjoy it, but the last few times she keeps asking me if I'm going to come to church with her one of these days."

"And?"

"And I always say no. And it always makes me uncomfortable. And I wish she'd stop asking."

"Why don't you just go once?"

"You're supposed to be on my side."

"I'm not saying to go, I'm just wondering why you don't want to."

"I grew up in that church. I just don't feel comfortable around church people."

"Do you see any of them during the week?"

"No."

"Do you care what they think?"

"No, but..."

"Would you be going to church for their approval?"

"No!"

"Then why do you care?"

"I don't know." She breathed in and then let it out all at once. It seemed like she was going to say something, so he sat there silently, rubbing her back.

"If I do go next week, as a surprise for Mom, would you come with me?"

He stopped rubbing. "Me?"

"Yeah."

"Why?"

"I don't know. I don't want to go alone."

"Why do you have to go?"

"I don't have to go! But you've just been telling me that I don't have a good reason not to go!"

"I wasn't saying you should go," he said. He paused and she looked at him as though she were waiting for something.

"I'll think about it," he said.

She was shaking her head as she stood up. "I don't understand you sometimes," she said. "Are you ready for supper?"

"Yes." He stood up and grabbed her around the waist, pulling her toward himself, and she knocked over the empty glass that had had her orange juice in it. He kissed her.

"All I've got is rice and beans tonight. We can put them in a tortilla and put some salsa and cheese on them."

"That sounds good."

"You've changed, you know?"

"What do you mean?"

"Even six months ago, you would have said something about the distinct lack of dead meat on the menu."

"Yeah, I guess you're right. Are you taking the farm out of me?"

They set up plates and glasses on the table and Natalie checked the pots that were on the stovetop.

"Still a few minutes to go," she said. "So tell me about Seattle. What did you do?"

"Well, I was helping James and Hope move some of their stuff down there."

"How did their new place look?"

"It looked good. There are a couple of big rooms that are shared by everyone: a big kitchen, living room. They're on the main floor, and then there's also a bedroom down here, which is going to be for someone who is already living there; we don't know her."

"The rest of the bedrooms are upstairs?"

"Yep. There's four upstairs. And maybe you should sit down for this; oh, you are sitting. Well, it turns out that there's a room that they hadn't filled yet, and I said we might be interested in taking it."

"What?"

"You and I."

"What?"

"What do you think?"

"I think you should have asked me first."

"That's what I'm doing—I told them I'd have to ask you, but said that we might be interested in it."

Natalie was taking the pots off of the stove, her back toward Rob. She put them on the table and slid a stack of tortillas into the microwave, wrapped in paper towels.

"I don't think we need to tell them tonight, or anything," he said.

"Well, that's a big relief."

She didn't seem to think it was a miracle.

"Can I get anything?" he asked.

"I think there's a block of cheese in the fridge, in with the dairy stuff. The salsa's on the shelf."

He retrieved the salsa and the cheese and put them on the table.

"How did the painting go this morning?"

"Not the greatest. Most of what I painted is going to be painted over, so it kind of feels like a waste at the moment."

"Why are you painting over it?" he asked, preparing a burrito.

"It's not right. It didn't come together today. Sometimes I think I'm in that building too much during the week and I should try to find another place to paint. The thing is, it's free space, and I don't have room here to set up."

"One of the girls who's going to be living in that house in Seattle is a painter, too. Maybe she knows of a place down there where you can have space."

"Is there a lot of space in that room?"

"I don't know if I'd say a lot. It has a nice window, though."

"Would there be enough room to have an easel set up?"

"I don't know. Did I tell you that the one girl wants to paint a huge mural on all of the living room walls? She was excited that you were a painter, too."

"No, you didn't mention it."

"Well."

"Can we lay off the house for a little while?"

"Yeah, sure."

He watched as she began to run the cheese back and forth across the grater. He couldn't think of a better way to present it to her. His track record of pitching Seattle wasn't encouraging, though. They both watched the cheese as it was ripped into shreds without saying anything. Why was she being so difficult about this?

"Hey, Rob, I think it would mean a lot to Mom if we went to church once with her."

"Now we're talking about your damn church again?" he said, knowing he shouldn't have but enjoying the pleasure of release.

"Are you trying to piss me off?"

"I'm not trying to piss you off. I just...the thing is, it just didn't feel like our other conversation was finished yet, and then you come out with church again. Sometimes I wish you wouldn't lay it on so thick. I don't know, it feels like you're always trying to convert me or something."

She looked at him without saying anything, as though waiting for him to continue. "I can't believe you said that."

"Why not? It feels that way sometimes. I'm just being honest."

"I thought that sharing ourselves with each other was part of what we were interested in—not just talking about the things we always agree on."

He felt her watching him and made sure not to make eye contact. She didn't say anything, but started to pack another burrito skin with rice and beans.

"Listen, I don't want to fight about it."

"I'm not fighting."

He didn't respond immediately and she looked at her plate, using her thumb as a stop to force a mound of rice onto her fork and slowly lifting it to her mouth.

"You know, sometimes I wish I could believe," he said.

"Sometimes I wish I couldn't," she said through the rice.

"What?"

She swallowed and took a drink of water, then set her cup down. "Eat your food before it gets cold."

He smeared sour cream on his burrito and cut a corner off of it with the edge of his fork. His chewing was loud, or maybe it was just that everything else was quiet. What was something they wouldn't argue about?

"How does your week look?"

She rubbed her temples with the fingers of her left hand.

"The usual, I guess. Well, we're having this dinner for Shawn and Dara on Wednesday evening, which you're welcome to if you're not working. Other than that, it's just working and painting and eating and sleeping and anything that we do in between."

"I'll probably be working. Bobbi scheduled me to work all evenings this week since she found out I'm still planning to leave after Friday. She's got to work on training somebody else for the evenings and weekends, during the day. Except I told her I wasn't going to work Friday evening, so I'm working during the day then."

"That was thoughtful of you. What do you want to do?"

He thought about how to phrase his response diplomatically.

"Well, I've got that meeting at night for final preparations for the party on Saturday. I thought maybe we could go out to eat a little early and then I could make it to the meeting a little late."

"Oh."

He started gathering up the dishes, stacking the plates with utensils and cups.

"We can fill up the space in the dishwasher with these," she said, taking the bowls with the rice and beans.

He rinsed while she loaded.

"Will we see each other tomorrow?"

"Yeah," he said. "I've got to work in the evening, but I'll stop by after work for a little while. I think I'm going to print the handouts for the party at work tomorrow and I'll show you tomorrow night."

"Okay. I'll see you then—I told Tink I'd spend this evening with her. We haven't really talked for a long time because our schedules keep crossing."

"Are you kicking me out?" he asked as he slid his wet hands down the back of her pants to wipe them off on her underwear.

"Yes. And thanks for that," she said.

"It'll dry off." He squeezed a cheek in each hand. "Especially if you take the pants off."

"Nice try." She began to shuffle toward the door, pushing against him as he ran his hands along her contours, moving backwards.

As he kissed her, a particle of rice moved against the interior of his cheek, dislodged from between his teeth, and he swallowed it. He massaged one of her breasts gently as they stood by the door.

"Rob," she said, grasping his hand and pulling it away.

"What?"

"No, you know, we can talk about it later."

"Just tell me."

"I just—I don't know how I feel about the other night."

"What do you mean?"

"I mean sleeping together."

He didn't say anything, and tried not to let what he was feeling register on his face. After a few moments, the silence seemed to be communicating his disappointment, so he spoke.

"I don't understand," he said.

"I don't either."

"Maybe you just need to adjust to things yet, or something."

"Maybe."

"I should go," Rob said.

"I'll see you tomorrow."

"Good night."

He turned around and listened to the door closing behind him and he felt like slamming it. She was hard to understand—always second guessing herself, their relationship, him. One step forward, two steps back. That's how it always went. He spent his time trying to avoid arguments instead of just talking with her. He had thought they were making progress, but were they any further ahead now than they were three months ago? Six months ago?

Lauyu kragt Bakker

Jesus Loves You (Everybody Else Thinks You're An Asshole)

A green Ford Explorer with shiny chrome trimmings pulled up behind a small car at the red light in front of her as she neared Garden Street. A matching silver outline of a fish with "Jesus" crammed inside it was mounted on the back door. It seemed to her to be ironic. When had Jesus traded in his sandals and donkey for an SUV? The light turned green and Jesus laid on the horn immediately. He had good reaction time but little patience. He gunned the engine and tore out around the corner with a throaty roar.

Rob was already at her house when she got home, sitting in the living room watching the news.

"Hi."

"Hi, Nat. How are you?"

He was slouched in the chair as though all his strength had left him and his body was draped over it, unable to pick himself up.

"Good. You're ready to eat already?"

He pushed himself up into more of a sitting position.

"Yeah, I've got that meeting tonight..."

"I know."

He started to push himself up out of the chair.

"You can stay there for a bit yet. I'm going to change into some other clothes."

She knocked on Tink's door.

"What?"

"It's me."

She poked her head in and found Tink lying in bed, her neck straining to keep her head raised off of the pillow.

"Sorry."

"It's okay. I wasn't asleep yet—Rob knocked just after I laid down the first time."

"I just wanted to see what you're doing tonight."

"I'm going to get recharged here a bit because some of us are going to go dancing. You're welcome, if you want."

"Thanks. I think I need a night to relax and unwind, though. I was going to see if you wanted to watch a movie or go out for coffee or something."

"Sorry."

"No, it's okay. I'm going out to eat with Rob first. Shawn and Dara aren't around, are they?"

"Uh uh. I think they're going to a movie. But you probably don't want to join them there."

"Hmm. Oh, well. I'll figure something out. Have fun tonight."

Tink motioned her closer, and she walked toward her. Tink put her hand to her mouth as though she was going to whisper a secret, so Natalie leaned in.

"Remember what we talked about. You belong here."

One of the corners of her mouth pulled out a little bit in a half-smile. "Thanks," she whispered, and hugged Tink. "At the moment I don't feel like it's going to happen, but I told him I'd give it a few days."

She felt like she was stealing a lot of heat from Tink's body; her hands and body must have been cold.

"We should do something later this weekend."

"That'd be good."

She was glad that they'd had the chance to talk yesterday. On Sunday they'd spent the evening talking, just the two of them, and she'd told Tink about Rob's plan to go to Seattle, and take her with him. Tink hadn't said much then, but Natalie could tell that she was trying to come up with something. Then, early in the week, they'd made plans to go for coffee together and Nat knew what they were going to talk about. So, yesterday they'd gone out for coffee after supper. They went to the café adjoining the Co-op where Tink worked, about two blocks from the house, and talked over fairly-traded coffees.

"So, why do you want to go to Seattle?"

"I don't think I do."

"But he wants to."

"Yeah."

"And he wants you to come with him."

"Yeah."

"That's bullshit."

Natalie laughed. "What do you mean?"

"Why does the girl always have to follow the guy? Why don't you say you're moving to Alaska, or something, and see if he follows."

"I don't have to do anything. He asked me."

"Why's he going? He found a house or something?"

"Well, he's been with this anarchist group in town and I guess a bunch of them are moving down to Seattle and living together in this house."

"That's cool, I guess, but you're not an anarchist."

"How do you know?"

"I don't know, you don't seem like one."

"I know."

"Don't go there just to be with him. It wouldn't work."

"Why not?"

"You told me yourself on a number of occasions, that it isn't even working here, so why would it work there?"

"I think things are starting to change, though. There's a dynamic between us that I haven't felt for a long time. A good one."

"Don't lie. I think you should tell him he's got to make a choice."

"'Rob, I can't take it any more!'" She held her wrist limp in front of her forehead. "'It's either me, or anarchy.'"

"I didn't say you had to be a drama queen about it. Why do you want this to work out so badly?"

"What do you mean?"

"You guys don't get along. You fight all the time. What is it about him that makes you care?"

Natalie didn't answer immediately so Tink continued.

"You know what I think? I think that he's just this part of your past that you don't want to throw away just because it's part of your past. So you're trying to hang on to it and pretend that it's working."

"No," she said. "Not really."

"What then?"

"It's not always fighting, sometimes we just disagree. And that's supposed to be healthy. We don't try and make each other believe what the other believes, it gives us freedom to have different opinions about things."

"Freedom to be mad at each other."

"Come on, two people don't have to agree on everything to be compatible."

"No, but they've got to agree on a certain percentage of things. I don't know what that percentage is."

"We agree on a lot of stuff!"

"You'd know better than me."

"And it's always been, like, neither of us really fits into real life with real jobs, real communities. We always seem to find a few people for our inner circles and we're tight with them, instead of having huge numbers of friends that we know so-so. We're the same that way."

"Except now he's got the anarchists."

Natalie realized she was right. The unsettled feeling she'd had for weeks had nothing to do with anarchy, or not as much as she thought. She was jealous. And worried in some way that Rob was losing interest in her.

"I guess so," she said. "But it's also... I guess, you know, in our society we've got this idea that if anything breaks or if we just don't like it anymore, we can just throw it away and get a new one. It's like that with everything: your belongings, and your faith, and your relationships."

"Yeah, but you have to throw some stuff away."

"Maybe the analogy breaks down."

"You can't tell me that this is a relationship that you're casually discarding. You've been trying to make it work for way longer than anyone else would have."

"We'll see," she said.

"For what it's worth, I don't want you to go."

She felt like taking a shower, but since Rob was waiting, she just put a little perfume on her wrists and rubbed it on her neck. It was true that there was a new dynamic between them, and it was partly true that it felt like a good dynamic. It also felt dangerous, and awkward, and it had for about the past week or so—ever since she slept with him again. She wasn't sure what exactly it was. Probably to some degree the fact that all this week they'd only seen each other briefly in the evenings after Rob got off work and before she went to bed. She'd been unlocking in the mornings this week, which meant she had to be to work on time, which meant getting to bed before midnight.

But it was more than that. It was also that Rob seemed to be obsessed with this party he was getting ready for. He had tried to explain the excitement to her one night—this seemed to him to be a chance to finally do something physical, something tangible, something that his writing and research weren't accomplishing. She wasn't sure exactly what they expected to accomplish by having a party in a vacant lot.

The sex seemed to have deepened the stakes, too, or at least added a different dimension. It had been kind of underwhelming, but yet it felt like it meant more than that. It felt like it was a last-ditch Hail Mary and as it fell to the ground it beame clear that there had never been a chance of a completion after all.

That night she had convinced herself that some of the big problems had somehow gone away, that they had reached a certain understanding. And maybe they had, but the problems hadn't disappeared at all. In some ways they seemed larger than before. Now it seemed that he was taking for granted that she was going to come, and she felt an increase in the pressure to go, the pressure to make this relationship work. More and more things seemed to be depending on it.

The worst part was that she had these decisions to make, and they kept commanding her attention, refusing to allow her to just sit and think about the relationship in general and forcing her to think about the relationship in particular as it related to these questions. If you don't go, the relationship will go off the rails. If you do go, there's the chance it will straighten out and be just fine. There's also the chance that it won't, and then you'll be screwed.

Then she'd end up thinking about all the things she liked about Rob and then all the things she didn't like, and she'd try to balance the two. And she'd weigh all the things she liked about Bellingham and her life here against all the things she didn't like. And finally she'd imagine what might be good about being in a community in a house in Seattle and what might be bad about being among committed anarchists when she didn't know much about it and wasn't a true believer.

She walked out toward the living room. Rob pinched the remote and the TV blinked off when she came around the corner.

"Where are we going?"

"The Tavern. Are you ready?"

"Yeah, I will be in a second. I've just got to get my shoes."

"I'll go start the car," he said.

When she settled into the car seat, she felt herself shiver. It was colder out than she had expected. She pushed the lever toward the red.

They found a parking spot just around the corner from the restaurant. A man was walking toward his car and Rob staked it out, his blinker on, ignoring a honk from behind.

The Old Fairhaven Tavern was one of Rob's favorites. It was in the historic district of Fairhaven, which was kind of touristy but still fun to go to sometimes. There were a bunch of art shops that had things like furniture, made out of branches that were bent and twisted into shape, and lamps that consisted of stacked rocks with a hole bored through the middle as a route for the electrical wires. The tattoo parlor was in an old train car. The shop where she had found her slumped goblet and plate was further down.

There was a small alley beside the restaurant, and the entire wall facing it was always covered in graffiti. She wasn't sure who they commissioned to do it, or whether they just allowed people to paint on it, or what, but it was constantly changing, evolving. There were a lot of layers of paint on the wall. The inside had a strange mixture of a kind of simulated seediness and faux high fashion that seemed to go in and out of style with the college students but was always more or less constant. One of the walls inside seemed to be made of plaster and was painted blue. At some point, before they had been in school, the tradition of scratching things on the paint had begun, etching words down into the plaster so they showed through, white on blue, an interior graffiti.

Not everyone who ate there scratched on the walls, of course, but over the years the wall had been covered from one end to the other and top to bottom. The markings were more and more sparse the higher they were, but a few people had managed to reach all the way to the ceiling.

It was busy inside, and the lobby was full of people waiting for a table.

"You're looking at about a twenty minute wait," said a black haired woman holding a menu by the front door.

"What do you think?" Natalie asked. "I know you're in a bit of a rush to get to your meeting."

"It'll be fine," he said, looking at his watch. "Let's walk around a bit and come back for the table in twenty minutes."

"That sounds good."

They put their names on the list and walked down the slope toward the water.

"You've been kind of quiet lately," he said. "Is everything okay?"

"I don't know. I think there's just too much going on at once. I need some time to just sit and not have any outside pressure on me."

"Well, if you need anyone to talk at, I'm always willing," he said.

"Thanks. I kind of feel like I just need some time alone, though. Maybe I'll go and paint tonight."

"Sure," he said.

They walked down and looked at the metal plaques embedded in the boulevard, like headlines from an ancient newspaper, taking turns reading each one:

CLEOPATRA'S BARGE: Lions and camels paraded here 1891

HUGE FREIGHT WAGON DISAPPEARED BENEATH QUICKSAND HERE: 1890

CITY GARBAGE DUMP SITE: "Smells like the breath of an elephant" 1890

PICNIC BEACH OF 1870: Fiddle music provided for dancing

SITE OF CITY DROWNING POOL DOGS ONLY: 1891

HERE IS WHERE MATHEW WAS CUT IN TWO BY A STREET CAR: 1891

Then they walked along slowly, not talking. It was nice to walk with him and not feel like she needed to make conversation. She didn't feel like talking about anarchy, a house in Seattle, or the event he was planning for tomorrow, and those were what had been on his mind lately.

"Do you mind if we walk back up?" she asked.

"No. We're up soon anyway."

They were directed immediately to a table in an adjacent room. The tables at the Tavern were heavy and wooden and they were filled with scratches, like the walls. They must have been easier targets because at some point management had put down a heavy layer of glass with rounded edges, cut to fit.

A spilled drink had managed to find its way underneath the glass that was set up over the tabletop and the liquid spread as far as it could, surrounding one of the rubber o-slip grips that held the pane in place. Something that might have been mold or a collection of dust resided along one edge of the spill like a barrier set up to prevent the liquid from traveling any further.

"Do you want the usual?" Rob asked.

"I guess."

Rob walked back to the front and placed their order with the waiter, catching him as he was headed toward another table. She sighed. It wasn't worth going out to eat when he was like this. They might as well have ordered in or made something themselves. She felt like she'd been penciled into his schedule in a slot that wasn't very big and instead of time with him, it was only time near him.

"I told him we're in a bit of a rush," he said when he came back.

"That's great."

"Do you realize," he asked, "that I am now an unemployed and unrestricted free agent? Well, mostly."

"Thanks a lot."

"I meant job-wise," he said.

"How did it go today?"

"It was good, but I was ready to leave before I arrived. I did manage to get a few things printed for tomorrow, so that was good."

"Did Bobbi cry?"

"Yeah, right. I think she kind of hardened on me when she realized I wasn't going to stay. Isn't love fickle?"

The waiter came by with a beer for Rob and a margarita for Natalie.

"Thanks."

"What did she do?"

"Bobbi? Nothing, really, but she just seemed kind of resentful or something."

"Is she going to mail you your last check?"

"Yeah."

"So what's next?"

"Well, this thing tomorrow."

"I mean, how are you going to fill your time next week, or the week after?"

"I guess it depends what we decide about the house in Seattle. If we're going, I'll probably just start preparing for that. If we don't go, I don't know yet."

She tried to let the conversation die so that she didn't have to discuss it again.

When the food came, Rob dug in immediately. She cut a piece off the quesadilla and chewed it slowly, watching Rob devour his burger. A mushroom squeezed out and something liquid was running down the side of his mouth and he set the burger down on his plate to wipe it off.

"Of course it's going to fall apart now," he said. "Once you pick it up, you're not supposed to set it down again."

They ate and talked mostly about the food. Rob finished first and wiped his mouth and hands with another napkin. He crumpled it into a ball and rolled it onto his plate, grabbing one last crispy fry and then his beer. He internalized a belch.

"That was good."

"It is good."

"I don't know about the spinach."

"Here, try some."

"No."

She shrugged.

"You're coming tomorrow, right?" he asked.

"I'm planning to."

"Good. It'll start in the afternoon, but you can come in the mid or late afternoon and it should be set up and rolling."

"That'll give me the morning to sleep in. Should I bring anything?"

"No, it'll all be there. Well, maybe some old paint brushes. Do you have some?"

"Yeah. What are we painting?"

"We've got to plan it a bit further yet tonight, but we're thinking of getting a public mural started. Some of the girls are working on a big banner already."

"That sounds fun."

He smiled at her as she put the last bite in her mouth.

"I should go," he said. "I'm already late for the meeting."

"I'll be happy when this party's finished tomorrow. You've been quite preoccupied with it all week."

"I'll be happy when this party's started. You will, too. You'll like it."

"Good," she said.

Rob motioned to a waitress as she walked by with a tray of iced tea, the ice cubes rattling in the glass.

"We're ready for our bill."

He started reaching in his pocket and she put her hand on his arm to stop him.

"I've got it," she said, because it was her turn to pay.

"You sure?"

He got up and went over to the corner of the wall.

"Yep, still here," he said, running his fingers over a spot that he checked every time they came here, where he had carved his name. "But it's getting encroached on by all this new stuff. That was over two years ago."

"I'm going to go to the bathroom a second," he said. "Why don't you carve something into the wall?" He threw his keys to her. "There's a little knife on there."

She sat with his keys in her hands, shaking them slowly like dice, until their waiter came back with the receipt. He took the empty plates.

Rob still hadn't come back. She slid a twenty under the receipt and unfolded the knife. She scraped the edge of her thumb with the tiny blade. It was fairly sharp. The walls around the tables were full of scratchings. There were too many of them, almost; some of them overlapped and obliterated each other. If she could get high enough, she could write something in the empty space, but she wasn't going to stand on the table.

On an impulse, she stuck her head under the table and looked at the wall. It was not bare, but there was more empty space than the wall above the table. She pushed her chair away from the table and took the candle from on top, setting it on the floor as she crouched. She didn't know what she was going to carve.

She felt something like the cave dwellers in France, perhaps, as they stared at the empty rock walls of their cave before spitting their dyes onto them, making handprints and horses.

She began to carve, up near the bottom of the tabletop. She used a butter knife to split the key ring and slide the little jackknife off of it so that the keys wouldn't jangle every time she made a mark. The lines were barely visible so she had to do it twice and dig out some of the plaster. She was just finishing up when she felt the table moving above her. The legs scraped on the floor; the one nearest to her pushed against her slightly.

"What are you doing down there?"

She squinted up at Rob for a second, through the crack he had made by moving the table away from the wall. "Making a mark on the wall."

He had his face near the table and was trying to look down and see what she had made.

"A stick man? From an artist?"

"It's a petroglyph." She noticed something on the wall that she hadn't seen before "What's this thing?"

"What?"

She crawled out from under the table and set the candle on top of it. "Help me pull this a little further away."

They pulled the table a few feet further away from the wall. The edge of the table had hidden a small inscription, right above where she had carved her little stick man. It was a short phrase, carved in tiny, bold letters.

    GUSTAVO IS FREE

The asterisk was above the head and slightly to the right, as though the words were a thought, as though the star were a light bulb that had just lit up.

"Is everything all right?"

She looked over at the waiter who had stopped. "Fine. We're just looking," she said. "We found a secret message. It's kind of exciting."

"I don't think I'd go so far as to say 'exciting.'"

"Well, you should. Because it is. What do you think he is free from?"

"I don't know, sounds like prison, maybe," Rob said as he pushed the table back into place.

They walked out to Rob's car.

"You want to go to paint, right?"

"Please."

He unlocked her door and went around to his side. She opened the door and sat down as he fell into place beside her. He started the car and gunned it once before they lurched forward. He had picked it up from the shop yesterday and they had fixed the engine stutter, but the clicking sound coming from the back hadn't gone away. Rob said that he had told them not to fix it because he was going to try to take care of it himself. She didn't think it was going to get fixed.

Rob was looking straight ahead and one of his knees was bouncing up and down slightly.

"What are you thinking about?"

"What? Oh. I was thinking about the Pit Party tomorrow."

"I'm not even out of the car yet and it's like I'm not even here."

He took his right hand off of the shift stick and rubbed the back of her neck. His hands were cold.

"We're going to hike up the arboretum tomorrow night and watch the sunset, right?" she asked.

"Yeah. Well, let's try to do that. I'm not sure how long this party's going to go. Worst case we can hike up in the darkness and look at the city by night."

"And Sunday?"

"I know. I already said I'd go. I just hope she appreciates it."

"She will. And I will. I don't want to go alone. I'll call her tonight and let her know we're coming."

"I thought you wanted to surprise her."

"I'm just going to tell her we're coming for lunch."

Rob pulled into the alley behind the store.

"Thanks for the ride," she said, stepping out.

He yanked the parking brake and opened his own door. He hugged her for a few moments and then slowly ran his hands down her back and sides, clasping them behind the small of her back.

"Nat, there's one more thing..."

"What is it?"

"I told James and Hope that I was going to take the empty room in the house."

"What?"

"In Seattle."

"When did you decide that?"

"Not long ago."

"And what am I supposed to do now?"

"You're supposed to come with me."

"You shithead! I thought we were going to discuss it with each other."

"I just needed to secure the room so they didn't give it to someone else. I really want to do this and I want you to go with me."

"And what if I say I can't do it?"

"I've been trying not to think about it."

"Well, maybe you should think about it."

"Maybe I'll stay, too. I might have to pay a month or two of rent in both places, or something like that, but it wouldn't be the end of the world."

He started to kiss her goodnight. It felt like he was trying to wedge his tongue into the space that was between her front teeth and it started to just seem silly, so she broke it off and said good night. He was sitting in his car, waiting to make sure she got in as she unlocked the door. She pulled the door open and he honked twice, short and staccato, as he crept out to the road in reverse.

She didn't feel much like painting when she sat down inside. This felt like a re-run of a bad TV show.

She had talked about it with Dorrie earlier today. She mentioned it first in mid-morning, and Dorrie hadn't said much; she wasn't expecting it. Then throughout the day, she'd make a comment or open up a discussion about it, to see how Natalie felt about moving, or what she thought about living with Rob again with no other friends nearby. It was helpful to put things in a perspective set back from Rob and herself.

"Do you want to go?" Dorrie asked.

"No. I don't know. That's the problem."

"Well, how about this: if Rob were out of the picture completely, would there be any draw to go to Seattle?"

"Not really, but that's not a fair question, because he's not."

"How far in the picture is he?"

"Some days I think more than others."

"So the real question isn't as much whether you want to go to Seattle as whether you want to keep in touch with Rob."

"Kind of, but not only that. It feels like I've got to make all these decisions that are just out of sync with each other, like I can't get them all into focus at the same time. Thinking about one of them makes all the others shift slightly, like they're all hinged together on independent hinges so one bends that way and another bends the other way and I can't get them all to fold correctly at the same time."

"So you feel like you can't control things even by making your decisions."

"Yeah, it's like nothing's dependable anymore. I can choose to stay, but what if Rob goes anyway? Or if I choose to go, what if our relationship isn't strong enough to survive and implodes anyway? Do I want to sacrifice the friendships I've got here on that chance? But what if I go and things really work out? Would it be worth it?"

"What's the worst-case scenario?" she asked.

"I'm not sure. I guess it could be either I stay and he goes and things would have worked out but now they don't, or I go and things don't work."

"Are things working out with you two now?"

"Not perfectly."

"I didn't think so."

"I mean we fight and we don't see eye to eye on a lot of things, but there's something holding us together. And we do agree on a lot of things and we get along well most of the time."

"Let's think about those two scenarios for a second."

"Okay."

"One. You go to Seattle with him and it doesn't work out."

She wrinkled her nose.

"Then what? You'd have to come back home, I guess, right?"

"I guess. I guess it wouldn't be the worst thing in the world."

"Well, no, I guess it wouldn't be the worst. But, two. You stay here while he goes, and things would have worked out."

"That's probably worse."

"Well, not so quick. Why would things not work out?"

"He'd be there, and I'd be here."

"What about things like telephones, and letters?"

"Oh." Somehow she hadn't even thought about that. Maybe because last time he left they hadn't had any communication after he shut the car door and drove off.

"And how far away is Seattle?"

"A few hours."

"Not the furthest thing in the world from here."

"No."

"And who's to say that he'll go if you say you're going to stay?"

Dorrie picked up her lunch box and held it up to show that she was going to go in the back room and eat.

"So, you think I should stay?"

She raised her shoulders and smiled.

"I don't know how we'd do with the long distance thing. I don't know if it would work."

"I don't know either."

Natalie looked at the canvas again. She stripped to her underwear and pulled on her painting clothes. The room was chilly, so she plugged in the little space heater and directed it toward her work area. It began to blow warm air obediently and she sat hunched in front of it for a moment.

She stared at the painting. It had been an upside down map of earth a week ago and she should have stopped then. Now it was just a mess of paint without any real cohesion holding the image together. This is what the wall at the Tavern would look like if instead of allowing people to scratch things into it, they left paints and brushes out—a collection of random strokes that didn't really relate to each other.

She liked the carvings, though. The graffiti of etched words and images on the wall worked together despite, or maybe because of, their random application. *Gustavo is free.* It was rough and unpolished, lacking the gleam of a chrome plastic fish or the easy statement of a slick bumper sticker, and it seemed to mean something.

She sat facing the canvas, still pretending that she was about to start painting, and then she squirted some dark paint directly onto the canvas, smearing it around with a rag. She pulled the package of seeds off the wall and tore a tiny hole in the corner. A small pile of seeds formed in her palm as she tilted the package, and she slapped it into the middle of the fresh paint, smearing it around with her hand.

She folded the corner over and shook the package of seeds like a maraca. This was the loneliest place to be on a Friday, especially if she wasn't really painting. She felt like carving on a wall again, or whittling a little stick—she still had Rob's little knife, or at least she didn't remember giving it back.

It was in the front pocket of her jeans, along with a red and white swirly mint from the restaurant. She unwrapped the mint and put it in her mouth, then unfolded the knife and ran a hand along the wall. Faux wood paneling. The lines would show up well. The only problem was she had no idea what to carve again. And she wasn't sure what she'd say to Dorrie.

On an impulse, she swiveled on the stool and gently slashed at the canvas. The small blade carved a groove through the wet paint and into the hardened paint underneath. She bit the candy in her mouth, crunching it. The knife hadn't gone through the canvas. She started to etch her petroglyph onto the top of the paint cautiously, sometimes going over a section three or four times to peel out little strips of dried acrylic.

She had completed a thin outline of the petroglyph's torso, but when she was tracing the outline of the head, she pressed too hard and the blade pushed through the canvas, cutting down through the paint and making a solid puncture mark.

The scissor-shears she used to cut canvas were in a little tackle box near the easel. She opened the box and got them out, debating in her mind how to do this. It worked best to take the canvas off of the easel and hold it in her lap. She slid one blade of the shears into the hole she had made with the knife, sliding it in as far as it would go and then cutting gently. She cut slowly around the outline of the petroglyph and a little man jumped out of the canvas, hanging by his legs, waiting to drop. She caught him on her lap when he fell and he left a small mark in wet paint. She set the canvas back on the easel and picked him up. He stood in her hands, his feet set, his arms raised like he was flexing his muscles.

"Gustavo is free," she whispered to herself.

She wrapped him around the package of seeds and slid them into the front pocket of her backpack. She'd tack him on her wall at home and maybe plant the remaining seeds in sidewalk cracks around her house sometime this spring.

The canvas was drooping in several places where the man had been cut out—the space between the arms and the legs, between one leg and the other, between arms and head. She wondered if there was a way that she could make the floppy parts stand straight again, so that there would be a sharp outline of a man missing with the canvas remaining more or less smooth, as though a cartoon had just walked through a wall and left a perfect outline of his body in the brick. Maybe if she could find some thin strips of wood she could glue them on the back for support.

She untwisted the top from the black paint and squeezed a little bit out. She went around the outline, holding the limp canvas with one hand and applying paint to the edge and border, so the outline was framed in black, fading back roughly to the mess of color on the rest of the canvas. In the top left she painted an asterisk and the words, trying to mimic the style of the letters as they were on the wall of the restaurant: short, thick letters, bold.

It was ugly, but she liked it. After she got the wood strips in the back for support, she could mount Gustavo near the painting so the positive and negative space were connected in the same visual area.

She collected her paintbrush and the cover of a broken CD case that she used as a palette. The bathroom was connected to the main area, so she walked back into the store to rinse them. Walking through the empty store in the darkness, with the only light spilling through the backdoor from her one lamp and the glowing of the streetlights through the windows was like walking through the setting of a dream. Everything was recognizable but slightly off; something in the atmosphere was abnormal.

She changed back out of her painting clothes and picked up her backpack. When the light was out, she had to feel ahead of her with her hands, finding the narrow pathway to the door.

She stepped out into the alley, lit starkly here at the end by a street lamp. She turned the key in the lock and started down the stairs. Two men were sitting on the sidewalk against the outer wall of the coffeehouse when she walked by. They were having a conversation, or play fighting. She recognized Dennis, a homeless man who came into the store once in a while. She gave him free clothes sometimes and had short conversations with him.

"Hi, Dennis!"

Their conversation had paused and he nodded at her.

"How's it going tonight?"

"Well, we're not completely back to life yet, but we're getting more animated every day," Dennis said.

"Okay," the other man said, watching her approach. "You're going to scare the lady."

Dennis' face was darkly stubbled and his hair greasy. They both had a paper coffee cup beside them, with plastic lids on and the little flap turned up so they could drink out here while the music played inside. A cup of tea would be good right now.

She went in and stood in line at the counter, listening to the music. She recognized the girl who was taking orders. She had usually been here when they had Philosophy Nights last year.

"Hi."

"Hey! Haven't seen you in a while."

"No, things started to fall apart with that."

"Too bad. What can I get you?"

"Oh, how about a chai tea?"

"Sure. For here?"

She nodded.

She found a seat at a table in the balcony floor, sitting across from an old man who was reading a book. There was a fragment of a community newspaper on the table and she began to flip through it. This coffeehouse was one of the first places she'd ever seen Rob, maybe the very first. Things had changed a lot since then.

At the time, she had been more interested in low-commitment partying: alcohol, marijuana, loose relationships that usually didn't last more than a few weeks. He had been sitting at the table two or three down from where she was sitting right now—he had tried to be smooth and she had pretended that he was, figuring that he'd be worth a fling even though he wasn't the most handsome guy in the world.

He asked her if she wanted to go out for a smoke, and she agreed because it was almost time for her break. Later she found out that he'd been watching her for a few nights so that he could time his invitation appropriately. As they had stood out there, smoking and talking, she remembered being intrigued by him. He told stories about growing up on a farm, about swimming in a lake filled with old tree stumps, and chasing Canadian geese around the field.

The things that most interested her about him was that he was funny and he spoke of his childhood like it was something he remembered fondly. Most of her friends were like her—if they ever talked about their families or their lives before school, it was derisively. When Nate, the shift manager at the time, had come out to tell her that her break was long over, Rob said he'd like to wait around until her shift was finished. She spent the next few hours finding excuses to go and wipe the tables up in the balcony and she'd watch him as he studied his papers and jotted notes, and she'd imagine whether he was good in bed or not, and wonder whether she'd find out that night.

He drove her back to campus and they spent a number of hours walking around, as though to look at the outdoor sculptures. He lived off campus and she had asked him—she was still embarrassed when she remembered this—if she could see his place. By this point it was past two in the morning, so it was a fairly obvious request to spend the night there, and he had said, "It's getting late. I'll take you there another day."

She remembered feeling rejected because she was offering him sex and he had turned it down. He walked her up to the door of her hall and they stood there for a moment without saying anything. She wondered what it was that he didn't like about her. She waited for him to talk.

"Natalie, you're beautiful and you're a lot of fun. I'd like to spend more time with you."

"I'd like that, too," she said, surprised.

And he'd kissed her on the cheek, fooling her as she opened her mouth to kiss him and was left kissing the air. Then he pinched her ass as he dropped his arms from the hug, turned and walked away. She was left wondering if he had really grabbed her, or if it was an accident. She hadn't heard from him for a week. The next weekend, he'd been back at the coffeehouse and apologized to her profusely. He had forgotten to get her telephone number or her last name the weekend before, so he'd been coming in here every evening, hoping that she'd be working, but she hadn't been scheduled for any evenings this week, except for Saturday.

Her chai was already getting lukewarm. She wondered whether it was smart to reminisce about the past instead of concentrating on the present. He had been so.. gentlemanly. Almost innocent. For months after that, or years, because they pulled it out every now and then, the joke had been that Rob had tamed her wildness and she had corrupted his innocence.

The performers tonight were kind of middle ground: not bad, but not good, either. It was a man and a woman, both middle-aged and sort of depressing. She assumed that they had sad lives, that they had been trying to make it big for years and they still wound up in little coffeeshops. The man had lank hair, greasy and thinning, and his face was starting to sag as well. Something about it reminded her of a rodent. The long thin nose, maybe, and the small eyes. She couldn't see the lady very well, because she was playing the piano, but she was filling out and her hair was limp, with the bottoms curled out slightly.

The man was singing and playing guitar, and his forehead was glistening. He reached up to wipe between his eyes and pulled his fingers down his long nose. As he pulled on the end of his nose, the saggy skin from his cheeks went taut, and it slackened again when he let go. He wiped his hand on his shirt and started playing again, smiling at someone down on the main floor in one of the recliners.

It occurred to her that they might perform here because they enjoyed it. Maybe they weren't trying to make it big, and get out of this hole, because they liked it here, because they knew all the regulars and had relationships here.

She dropped a dollar in the jar on her way out and walked the handful of blocks home. Her path took her past the abandoned lot where Rob and his friends were planning to have their party tomorrow. It was a void surrounded by chain link, a gouge out of the concrete like an empty eye socket. Maybe in new light it would look more inviting. Maybe it would be fun.

When she got home, it was already past eleven. She dialed her mother on the phone.

"Hello?"

"Hi, mom. I hope I didn't wake you up."

"No, of course not. I'm just watching a movie with Susan."

"Well, I won't keep you long. I just wanted to let you know that Rob and I are planning to come over for lunch on Sunday. What time should we come by?"

"Oh, wonderful! Well, I usually get back from church a little before noon, so you can come around that time or anytime after."

"Great, mom. See you then—enjoy your movie."

"I love you, baby."

"You, too."

She hung up the phone, smiling at the image of two middle-aged (were they considered old by now?) ladies watching a movie together. She didn't know what movie they were watching or what their mood was, but in her image they were giggling

like schoolgirls. She was glad that her mom hadn't asked her to come to church again
because she wanted to surprise her, maybe by walking in and sitting in front of her s
that she'd have to wait the whole service with them in front of her. Except that sh
might not—she might get up and hug them and make a big scene. It would probabl
be better to go early and meet her outside before the service began.

It was going to make for interesting dinner conversation—Rob was going to go t
Seattle again, with or without her. The foreboding Seattle had held for her as a chil
seemed now to be justified. The city was going to swallow him again, just like it ha
swallowed him last time, just like it had swallowed itself, before the new city was buil
on top of the ruins.

She blew out the candles on the misshapen shrine and sat there in the dark, smellin
the smoke and incense and she prayed. What was she asking for? She wouldn't hav
refused a direct revelation, a verbal instruction, or some sort of audible guidance o
what to do, which choice to make. She was starting to wonder if maybe the silence wa
the only answer she was going to get. She wanted to believe that this didn't necessaril
mean that God didn't hear, or even that he just wasn't answering. That he was broodin
over the surface of the chaos in her mind and helping her make sense of things, slowl
Slowly.

If you can't change your mind, are you sure you still have one?

Part of him was hoping that the cops would come down into this pit and start clubbing people. He wouldn't mind having some kind of battle scar. Besides, he'd probably get a lot of money out of it. There were a few handheld video cameras floating around down here, recording the evidence. Unfortunately, the cops had already indicated they weren't going to arrest anybody if they stayed peaceful.

He was inside the vacant lot, sunk below street level. It was hollow underneath the sidewalks, around the perimeter. This pit had been empty since a fire destroyed the old Mason building in 1994—while he and Natalie were still in school. He remembered hanging around the building the morning after it burned, taking pictures, in the hope of doing a story on it for the paper. They hadn't needed it because they already had people there.

It had been empty and ugly ever since, and the city had purchased it a number of years ago to try to make the space into a parking garage. That hadn't worked, and now they were trying to suddenly turn it into retail and residential space. James and Hope had organized this event to build pressure on the city to keep it public, maybe to build a park here, or a town square.

This afternoon, more than thirty of them had climbed the fence and lowered their bodies into the pit with ropes, or hung from the edge and then dropped. Once the first few were in, they had set up a large metal tripod and suspended a small swing from it. Hope was sitting in the swing so that it would be nearly impossible to remove her without endangering her. A couple of other guys whom Rob didn't know very well had lowered ropes from the roof of the parking garage next door and were sitting on swings up there against the wall. They had unfurled a large banner between them—it had been painted during the evenings this past week and showed the Pit converted into a park, with greenery and benches and happy people. While they were up on the roof, they had secured a cable and someone else had tightened the other end down on the far side of the Pit. James was hanging in some kind of a basket or hammock that was fastened to the cable, suspended about fifteen to twenty feet above the ground.

The police had come while those four were setting up, and the rest of them were painting on the walls and planting flowers in the flower beds they had made. Rob had left the Pit and started passing out his invitations to people in the streets and taping them to store windows and putting them under the wipers on cars. By the time he returned the police were making sure nobody else descended into the Pit. He had waited up top, shouting his support down and wishing he could sneak over until an hour or two later, when the police had disappeared.

He was going to climb over and lower himself down, but James called out from his hammock and told them to open it up to the public. Somebody hammered the lock off of the small gate in the corner near the parking garage and set up a bunch of old metal barrels and crates to form a rickety staircase down into the Pit, and a thin line of people made their way slowly down like ants.

They were working on a wooden stairway system now, measuring and cutting wood, drilling screws in to hold it together. Once that was up, the number of people down here would increase dramatically. Right now a lot of them were up on the sidewalks that looked down into the pit, leaning on the chain link or milling around up there.

Natalie had shown up half an hour ago and was standing down here beside him now, still a little uncomfortable with the whole thing, it seemed. She had brought a handful of old paintbrushes like he had asked her to, but she was just holding them, not using them. The plain concrete walls had been transformed into brightly colored pictures and slogans—yellows and reds and blues and greens.

A group of people beside them was taking turns with a big sledgehammer and a few pick-axes, smashing and digging up concrete. Others hauled it away in an old shopping cart and dumped it in a pile near the wall. After them came the people who were hauling dirt in to replace it, building flowerbeds in the excavated areas and planting them with flowers, herbs and strawberries.

"Come on, Nat—let's do something!"

"What do you want to do?"

"I don't know, paint a picture on the wall or something."

"It feels strange to be in here with the police standing around like this." She motioned to the cops who had returned and now lined the Pit on the other side of the chain link, and the silhouette of the police officers on the roof of the parking garage that the guys were hanging from.

"They already said they're not going to arrest us. And they're letting people come down here now; look."

"Okay."

They took two small cans of paint and found a spot on the wall that wasn't painted yet.

"Everything's got to have a slogan, doesn't it," she said, looking at the murals and the words that accompanied them.

"Something short and catchy isn't forgotten as easily as an essay," Rob said, looking around. "And it gets read more often. The trick is coming up with a good one."

Do something (de)constructive.

Stay free.

Existence precedes government.

People before profits.

This is the revolution of everyday life.

Buy less, work less, live more fully.

End racial profiling.

Imagine!

The one next to her was above one of the new flowerbeds.

Resistance is Fertile

"How about I paint some flowers?" she asked.

"Great. I'll paint over here."

He took the widest paintbrush she had and began to paint, one letter at a time:

Make spaces for people, not corporations.

When he finished, he looked over at Natalie. She had a bunch of flowers outlined on the wall and was looking for another color so they wouldn't all be the same.

"Here's blue," he offered.

"Thanks."

She began to paint, and he watched her profile, concentrating on the wall in front of her.

"Have you thought about the house in Seattle at all?"

She stopped painting and sighed. "Of course I've thought about it. Have I come to any conclusions about it? No."

"The only thing is that we don't have that much time to decide."

"You know I hate being pressured into things."

"I'm not trying to pressure you, I'm just saying."

She dipped her brush again and painted a few more strokes.

"Why are you concerned about this space, anyway, if you're so set on moving out of town?"

"Well, I'm in this town at the moment. And there's a lot of people staying here. Besides, we might even stay here, right?"

"I don't know. You've been putting enough pressure on to make me fairly certain you're going."

A couple of people began to hula-hoop near them, so Rob put his hand on Natalie's arm and led her away. They walked past a handful of guys who were shooting a rubber basketball into an old five-gallon bucket that was tied onto the chain link at street level. He led her to a spot underneath the sidewalk. The shelter gave shade from the setting sun and anonymity from most of the crowd looking down from the sidewalk, behind the chain link.

"Nat, I'm not trying to pressure you. But sometimes situations come with a lot of pressure, whether you want it or not. You can't stop the world to make a decision. Sometimes you just have to make a decision and run with it."

"I know," she said. "But I'm not ready to do that yet. Give me some more time to think about it—they aren't moving for a month, right?"

"It's less than a month now. It's not really fair to keep them hanging like this, either, and then pull out at the last minute."

"I thought you said you were definitely going to go."

"I told them I'd take it."

"So why does it matter if I figure it out now or in a week from now? Either way, the room's going to be filled, right?"

"Come on, Natalie. It matters because I'd like to know what's going to happen more than a few days before we go. And I told you, if you really, absolutely don't want to go, I could stay here and find someone else for the room."

"How about this: tomorrow we'll go visit my mom. We'll go to church and eat lunch with her afterwards, and then I'll spend some time alone in the afternoon, and by tomorrow night I'll make a decision."

"Okay. I want to do this, Nat."

"I know."

They stepped out from underneath the overhang and looked around. People were painting on the concrete of the floor that hadn't been broken and hauled away; someone had fashioned a mound of dirt that looked like a grave, spelling out the word "CAPITALISM" on top of it in small fragments of shattered concrete and lining the edges with larger chunks.

He looked up at the fence that lined the Pit. There was a TV camera filming up there, for the evening news. He had seen a guy he recognized from the newspaper taking pictures earlier as well.

"Is this really going to help?" she asked, nodding toward the grave.

"The only way to find out is to try, right? Can't change the system by not doing anything."

"If you want to change the system, you've got to change the people first. When they change, the system will change. You'd probably get more accomplished by holding a debate, or going door to door and talking to people."

"That would take too long. Maybe we should get some TV commercials or something, beam it out to hundreds of thousands of people at once."

"I don't think it would do what you think it would."

"Why not?"

"It would look like a carnival, a bunch of crazy people. Something to watch and not participate in. Besides, I tend to think that most of the important stuff that happens in the world is largely unnoticed, silent, like the way the earth works. Like erosion, slowly and patiently sculpting rock, or a tree growing, being shaped."

"What about mountains? Isn't that the tectonic plates colliding?"

"Yeah, but I think it's still a slow process, humanly speaking."

"How about earthquakes. That makes a big change in a hurry."

"That's true. But they kill people and destroy, and then people build on top of them again. Earthquakes don't make Grand Canyons."

"Sometimes things need to be destroyed."

"I guess. Sometimes it seems like you're being influenced by the culture of big. Big business, big government, big media, big farming, big protest, big everything. Super-size it."

"You've got to fight fire with fire, right?"

A few people were up on the sidewalk, attaching plastic clips from bread bags to the chain link in a geometric pattern, a tedious job but one that did wonders for the fence.

"I think I'm going to go help them," Natalie said.

"Okay, I'll be down here."

An old Willie Nelson double who had been playing his guitar in the opposite corner had stopped and a group of dreadlocked hippies with shakers and djembes began to produce sound. It felt good to be a part of this. The wooden stairs they had built were helping—there must have been one or two hundred people down here, and maybe that many again watching from the sidewalk above.

He picked up a watering can that someone had left and dribbled out the tiny bit of water that was left inside it onto a strawberry plant. The guys with the sledgehammer were slowing down. Some of the concrete just wasn't breaking and they were getting tired and sweaty.

"Can I take a whack?" he asked.

"Go for it." He was a skinny boy with no shirt on, wiping his face with his arm.

Rob took the sledgehammer and hefted it. The handle was made of old weathered wood, not smooth. He brought it down and was a surprised to find no damage to the concrete, as though it should have suddenly exploded into crumbs and powder.

He worked at it until his hands were too sore. A long, narrow blister had formed on his palm. Trevor and his girlfriend had set up their little table in the meantime, near the bottom of the stairs, and they were giving out the free food he'd been waiting for.

There was a small crowd of people dancing hard enough to get sweaty and Rob joined them for a few minutes. Hope was looking down from her perch on the tripod, calling him.

"Rob! I know I'm not supposed to come down from here, but will you switch spots with me for a second? I want to do some painting and dancing and eating before getting back up here."

He helped her lower herself down on the makeshift pulley system and then sat on the wooden swing and began to hoist himself up. Hope scampered off and he watched from his perch as the carnival continued below. Natalie and the rest of street level were still slightly higher than him, but not much. He watched Natalie as she snapped colored bread clips onto the chain link one by one, concentrating.

She was beautiful. He liked to watch her when she didn't know she was being watched. The breeze was making the bread clips flutter and the fence looked like it was shivering. Someone had hung a banner from the fence a little further down, but it was facing the opposite direction, toward the street, and he couldn't read it.

Natalie stood up and looked down into the Pit. He waved one of his arms but she was looking for him on the ground. He called her name and she turned her head in his direction. She couldn't find him for a few seconds, but when she did she smiled broadly and he tried to wave at her again.

He still hadn't completely found his balance up there and had been holding onto the tripod with his hands. Taking his right hand off to wave at Natalie had made the swing start turning slightly and he had grabbed the tripod again, reflexively. He felt very vulnerable, as though he had just dramatically saved himself from a plunge to his death, and his heart was pumping fast.

He couldn't have been too close to actually falling because Natalie was still standing there smiling at him, the gap between her teeth visible even from thirty feet away. Still he was ready to get off of the tripod.

"Come down again," he called to Natalie.

"Are you coming off of there?"

"In a minute or two. You can get some food down here, though. Lentil stew or rice and beans."

She made her way down the stairs, which had a constant exchange of people going up and coming down, and went to the food table to get a plastic spoon and a paper bowl filled with stew. She came and stood underneath him.

"What are you doing up there?"

"Just filling in for a few minutes while Hope runs around and stretches her legs. She's coming back up here right away." He looked for her in the crowd but didn't see her immediately. It was getting darker; he hadn't really noticed until now.

Someone was working on getting a generator down here to set up some lights. He saw Hope by the wall, plugging one ear and talking on someone's cell phone. He saw a paper in her hands—probably the list of media contacts he had put together last night, with names and numbers for people who worked in newspapers, TV and radio. He pointed her out to Natalie.

"When she gets off the phone, can you tell her I'm ready to come down?"

She nodded, her mouth full, and wove her way toward Hope, between some people who were just standing there and watching everything, around a group of guys with sweaty, bare torsos and thick hemp necklaces, doing what looked like interpretive dancing. He began to loosen the rope from where he had tightened it around the top of the tripod to keep himself suspended.

He saw Natalie and Hope coming back and began to lower himself down. They were there by the time he reached the ground, but something was wrong. Hope seemed fine, but Natalie seemed upset about something.

"Thanks, Rob. Could you get me some lentils to eat while I'm up there? I didn't get a chance to eat yet."

"Sure."

He took Natalie's hand and led her away while Hope saddled herself on the seat.

"Is something wrong?"

"Get her the food. I'll be over by the wall I painted."

The food table was about to be dismantled and taken away, but he scraped the bottom of the pot and managed to find two medium bowls of stew and he put a scoop of rice on top for good measure. Hope hadn't raised herself up yet, so he gave her the bowl and helped steady her while she balanced it on her lap. She looked like there was a smile about to break on her face, but it never did.

"I hope I didn't say anything wrong," she said, "but Natalie didn't seem too happy."

"About what?"

"Well, we were just talking about all this and I pointed out what I had painted over there on the wall. It was like those seeds you gave me, so I told her about that. She seemed a little disturbed by that. And I apologized for kissing you that night; I assumed that you had told her about that."

Rob grimaced.

"Sorry." She shrugged her shoulders.

"No, it'll be fine. She'll get over it."

He helped her up and made sure she had fastened the rope.

"Were you just calling media?"

"Yeah. The newspaper already has someone here taking pictures and one of the TV stations already had some cameras here earlier; they aren't going to send them back again. I might keep calling others from up here."

He made his way over to Natalie. She watched him walk the whole way over.

"Hey," he said.

She pointed at the wall beside her without saying anything. Someone else had completed the partially painted flowers that she had left on the wall and painted the word HOPE underneath them.

"Isn't that a coincidence?" she asked.

"What's wrong?" he asked.

"You said you made those seeds for me! You never told me you gave them to other women, or that you made out with them afterwards." He was trying to look at her face, but the light wasn't great; they hadn't managed to hook up the generator yet.

"I did make it for you, Nat, you know that. I made two in case one got messed up, but they both worked out. I don't know, her name is Hope, so I just thought—"

"I know her name is Hope!"

"And I didn't make out with her. She was trying to kiss me one night when I slept at Freedom House, but when I woke up, I knocked her off."

"She was on top of you?"

"Come on, you're making this a bigger deal than it should be."

"How come you never told me about it? How come I had no idea?"

"I thought you'd prefer not to know," he said.

"Oh, well, thank you for your concern," she said. "And now you want to go and move into the same house as her?"

"There are separate rooms," he said, and was angry with himself for getting defensive.

"Great," she said.

"Is this really how much you trust me? What, do you think I can't control myself? That any girl that comes on to me can get me in bed?"

Natalie didn't say anything and they stood there. The noise of the festival filled in the silence. Rob sighed and went over to try to hug her.

"Can we talk about this later?" he asked. "We're in the middle of something here."

"I can't believe you gave my seeds to her."

"Natalie." He exhaled. "I know you're upset, and I know we need to talk about this. But right here and now is the wrong place and time."

"I guess we missed the sunset," she said after a moment.

"Yeah. But maybe we can still walk up there later tonight to talk a bit."

"How long are you planning to stay here?"

"I don't know. Until the party ends, I guess."

"You're still planning to come with me tomorrow, right?"

"If you want me to, I'll come, definitely."

"Good," she said.

"Are you leaving?"

"I think I'm going to go home for a bit. Maybe I'll come back in a few hours and see if things have calmed down here, and we can head over to the arboretum. If it's over before then, stop by my place."

"You're not going to stay until the end?"

"No. I'm not in the mood anymore. And I guess I don't know enough about the issue."

"What do you mean by that?"

"I don't know anything about the process behind this lot or anything. And I guess I don't see what would be so bad about putting apartment units in here—people could walk to work and keep some cars off the road."

"Well, that's great, but we need more public space, more places you can go without having to pay to be there, or buy something to sit there."

"Maritime Park's only five or six blocks away, isn't it?"

"Yeah, but I'm talking about the heart of downtown. There should be a public space, a square or a plaza or something. Maybe a place for public discussions and meetings."

"I'm not saying it's a bad idea—I just don't know all the details."

"Well, that's the point—the public should be involved in the details of what happens to this space. We're not saying it has to be a park, but we are saying that the people should be able to decide."

"I'm not sure this is the way to make that point."

"What do you mean?"

"Well, when I was up there by the fence, putting the bread clips on, the sidewalk was covered in chalk slogans—things like *Stop capitalism NOW* and *End sanctions against Iraq*. Or the slogans they're painting on the walls—*End racial profiling*? What's with all the anarchy symbols? Is this about anarchy, or public space? Do they really think this little protest is going to end capitalism or institute anarchy? It seems like this is more about protesting everything than it is about starting a serious debate on the issue of what's going to happen with this plot of land."

A boo started somewhere in the Pit and grew louder.

"They're taking down the clips," an anonymous voice called out.

He looked up and saw two cops meticulously removing the bread clips from the fence and putting them in empty grocery bags.

"Off the pig!" someone yelled above the booing.

"Let it be; it's not hurting anyone," Rob called to the police officers, but they continued without changing expression or slowing their pace.

Trevor tried to direct one of the generator's lights so it was trained on the officers like a spotlight, and it lit them up slightly.

Natalie shook her head.

"See you in a few hours," she said.

He hugged her again, but her arms remained by her side. As she walked away, someone next to him said, "They're going to start arresting people."

He watched her climb the stairs, in the middle inching her way past a group of three that had started down at the same time she had started up. There were two police officers at the top and she talked with them as people streamed past her, out of the Pit.

"They're not going to arrest anyone. They already said that if we're peaceful we can stay here as long as we like," he told the people beside him, who were getting in line to go up the stairs.

Natalie was making her way back down the stairs.

"That was quick," he said.

People all around were talking and whispering loudly, motioning to the police by the gate.

"Rob, they're going to start arresting people."

"I don't think they will. I think it's just a way to start clearing people out."

"Do you want to come over to my place for a while?"

"No, I've got to stay here for a bit yet."

"Why?"

"We're not done. We have to show them that this is public space and they can't just command us around when it belongs to us."

"Come on, Rob. You're going to get arrested for this?"

"Maybe."

"Well, I'm not."

When she was gone, he stood there beside the flowers that were painted on the wall and watched the people milling around in the shadows, far below the streetlights. There were people climbing the stairs and people descending, but more of them were leaving then were coming in.

He knew he was in the doghouse with Natalie, and that pissed him off because he didn't feel like he had done anything wrong. He hated how much work this relationship took sometimes. When did they reach a point of diminishing returns? It was like trying to decide when to stop dumping money into an old car—the line was never well defined. On the other hand, any relationship was going to take work. But he was at the point where he was looking forward to her decision about Seattle, and was starting to care less about what her answer would be.

Either answer would help him out of the love and hate cycle he found himself in. If she came, great. Hopefully it would be a positive step and their issues would diminish. If she didn't, that would end all the hassle. It would be hard for a while, and disappointing, but there would be a sense of relief at the same time.

Trevor was on the opposite side of the Pit, standing on an old crate with a megaphone, warning everyone inside that the police might start to arrest people and thanking them for coming. "You can stay in here with us—we hope you do—but there's no shame in leaving if you need to."

He walked over to where Hope was suspended above the ground.

"How's it going up there?"

"I'm fine. I didn't screw your relationship up, did I?"

"No, it's okay. She's just a little sensitive sometimes."

"Are you ready for the main event?"

"Do you think they'll do anything?"

"Definitely."

"I thought they said we could stay here as long as we wanted if we were peaceful."

"They did. But the media's all gone, the presses are running, the news has already aired..."

"I kind of think they're just bluffing."

"They're not. Do you know the plan?"

"Yeah, I think I'm linking arms."

"Be ready. You're doing solidarity if you get arrested, right?"

"I guess so."

Somehow this didn't feel exactly like he had expected it to. Regret from missing protests like Seattle and D.C., combined with the stories that James told him from the Summit of the Americas made it all seem so glamorous and exciting. Was this worth getting arrested for? Maybe Natalie was rubbing off on him. But he couldn't leave here and show his face at Freedom House again.

A police officer on the sidewalk spoke into a bullhorn. "Attention everyone in the Pit. You must leave the area or you will risk arrest. Those that remain in the Pit will be trespassing. You have two minutes."

A number of people were dragging old mattresses out from under the sidewalk overhang, positioning them around the tripod. These were part of the inner circle. They had lockboxes to chain themselves together around the tripod, arm to arm so that they couldn't be pulled apart without being inflicted with a lot of pain. He was in the outer circle—the extras that were going to link their arms around the hard-core circle.

The policeman by the gate began to swing it shut and a group of young girls who were standing on the stairs settled their indecision, running up the stairs and pushing at the gate; the policeman dutifully swung it open again. When people stopped coming out, he swung it shut again and waited there with his partner until three more cops joined him.

The inner circles were locked together around the tripod already, three around one of the tripod's legs and four around another. Most of the remaining people—more than twenty, it looked like—were standing in a circle outside of them. Rob stepped over the lockbox between Trevor and his girlfriend.

"What are you protesting?" someone called down from the crowd up above.

"We're not protesting—we're just speaking our minds," James called back from his hammock. "We think people should be able to have a say in their own affairs."

One of the policemen opened the gate and started down the steps, his partner close behind him. The crowd on the sidewalks began to boo again and the outer circle sat down and linked arms. Rob linked up with Trevor on one side and a big-headed man he'd never met before on the other. The man was in a new, matching sweatsuit and incandescent sneakers. Probably all made in sweatshops.

"I just moved here two weeks ago," he whispered. "I don't know anyone."

"Nice to meet you," Rob said.

The police walked up to the circle and seemed to confer for a second, walking slowly around the circle as though playing Duck, Duck, Goose. They began to pull on a small girl who broke free from the circle quickly. They carried her by the armpits so her feet were dragging behind her and the crowd began to taunt the police officers for choosing a tiny person first. The circle healed itself behind her.

A drunk man began to swear at the police officers, daring them to try to arrest him, threatening them, and the crowd began to yell as two more police officers entered the pit.

"Hey! Don't put me in a position that makes me feel like I've got to defend the cops!" Hope yelled at the crowd. "It's not them, it's their job."

The cops pulled people from the circle one by one and hauled them away, up the stairs that these same people had made to get down into the Pit. Rob heard Trevor muttering that they should have destroyed the stairs to make the job of removing people much harder.

"Solidarity! Solidarity!" They were chanting to keep their spirits up as their numbers dwindled.

When they got to the man next to Rob, with the big head and bright shoes, he let go almost immediately and Rob was hanging on, playing tug-of-war against the cops with this man's body. He let go when he started to worry about hurting him, and the man walked out on his own two feet with the police barely even touching him, just touching a hand on his shoulder, as though he might make a break for it in his shiny new shoes.

The circle was getting smaller, and they reorganized around the remaining leg of the tripod, beside the other two links. A pizza deliveryman came with a pizza and tried to walk down the stairs into the Pit; Rob didn't know who had ordered it, but it was a touch of genius. The police blocked the gate and the pizza man walked away from them and flung the box into the Pit like a Frisbee.

The police hadn't come back into the Pit yet, so Rob unlinked himself and grabbed the box, opening it in the middle of the circle. A big cheer went up from the spectators. The remaining members of the outer circle fed the ones that were locked together so that they didn't have to loosen their hands, and someone threw a piece up to Hope, and one up to James in his hammock. The police waited for a few minutes, allowing them time to eat, and then came down again.

They came for him next, and he held on as tightly as he could, squirming and trying not to let them get a grip on him. When they had finally twisted his arm loose, he went limp and they tried to haul his bulk, but it was slow going. Hope yelled something about solidarity and a third cop came down to help the other two, and they slowly brought him up the stairs. As they brought him through the gate at the top of the stairs, he saw Natalie standing about ten feet away, watching.

Free Tibet

She was hiking up the Sehome Arboretum trail with a backpack on, heading up to the lookout tower. It was dark out, so she could imagine that her thoughts were not restricted to her head—they floated around her and she heard them in the trees. The arboretum was supposed to be closed at dusk, but there were no gates, and she had gotten the idea in her head to sleep up on the tower. Besides, the cops were probably more interested in the Pit Protest at the moment.

It had seemed like a great idea at the time. She and Rob had planned to watch the sunset from the tower at the top of the hill; that he was in jail now and the sun was already down had changed the plans. She had gone home after Rob was dragged into a police car and driven away, and she had decided that she was going to climb to the tower anyway, by herself. No one was going to get out of jail until tomorrow afternoon at the earliest.

She had packed up her sleeping bag, the shrine, and a few books in the hopes of camping at the top and seeing the sunrise instead of the sunset that she had already missed. She had brushed her teeth before she left and was ready for a night looking down on Bellingham.

That was her plan—to be here now, walking alone in the darkness was something different. She felt as if she was on a pilgrimage to someplace holy, or at least unknown. It was dark and she could almost imagine that no one had been there before her. The sky was hoarding its light and she was shuffling through complete darkness, after every handful of steps holding a lighter out in front of her, with one hand cupped to block the light from her face and try to reflect it in front of her. It didn't light anything up except when she was too close to the edge of the path, when it illuminated leaves and branches and gave her a chance to correct her direction.

She couldn't get used to the unexpected sound of birds' wings in the darkness nearby. Some animals could see in the dark. She felt like she was trespassing and imagined them all lined up in the darkness, watching her. She began to see things in the shadows and hear them in every little noise: wild animals or thieves.

"Hello," she said, her voice breaking the silence unnaturally. It sounded sacrilegious, the sound of talking during a wedding or a funeral. People have been conditioned by movies and suspense to be scared of the dark; she tried to imagine the darkness as a friend, but it didn't work. Maybe later, when she was in her own room, she could convince herself of it, but not here, not now. She shifted her backpack and started walking again.

She was a container for a strange mix of feeling lately. Every little thing seemed to affect her powerfully, so her emotions were all over the map. When Rob had told her Friday night at dinner that he was definitely going to go to Seattle, she had felt something blow out inside her, some little hope or spark that flashed and was gone, like light from a dying bulb. Or earlier that night, the opposite feeling, when she had been scanning the graffiti at the restaurant and found the single line that was gouged out in rough block letters: GUSTAVO IS FREE. We're not completely back to life, but we're getting more animated every day.

Why did it seem like life was an old LP with a deep scratch, so events kept looping and she never made much progress? How was she supposed to pick up the needle and move it in a little? Maybe history really does cycle until you make peace with it—until you've wrestled with it all night and the daylight is appearing. You're hanging on, and it wants to get away, but you've got it in a headlock, refusing to loosen your grip until it blesses you.

There had to be a point at which the past was the past and the future began. Instead of always looking back, beating herself up for things that she'd done or not done, she had to learn to push for what was ahead. Leave the past in the past—you're not the salt of the earth just because you've turned into a pillar of it.

She came off of the trail and walked up a stretch of paved road until she reached the upper parking lot and beside it, a small hut and a radio tower. There were no cars. A metal box on the side of the hut buzzed with intensity underneath the pale street lamp. Every time she came up here, she found it strange to find this in the middle of a forest. If the people were too lazy to hike from the bottom, they shouldn't get to see the view; it was no good making roads up to the tops of mountains so that people could just drive up. She walked past, away from the parking lot and into a tunnel that was blasted through rock. She lit her lighter in the middle of it and even though it was a short tunnel. She couldn't see beyond the entrance on the other side. The walls were rough and cast dark shadows; the night outside hid everything.

At the far end, outside of the tunnel, she stopped and squinted to read a plaque by the flickering glow of her lighter. The tunnel had been blasted in 1923 for Model T's to get through, but had been closed to cars since the sixties, when this area became the arboretum. It was neat to imagine Model T's sputtering through the physical space that she was occupying. Or when she was in the middle of the tunnel, to imagine that the rock that had been blown out was still there, and she was encased in rock. Even the air that she was breathing—if she followed it back far enough, it had probably cycled through dinosaurs.

Things that happened in the past or in our memories die and as they decompose they find their way back into the present in a new form. We can't see deep enough or back far enough to trace them through to the beginnings, but everything in the present feeds on and is made up of everything in the past. Alas, poor Yorick.

She was approaching the tower—she was coming to a clearing and could see the silhouette even one shade darker than the sky. She swallowed loudly, listening for any sound, worried that there would be someone on the tower. There was no help near if anything happened and she was alone. She started up the steps with a cold dread in her throat and chest, but she couldn't go back now.

She stomped her feet as she went up the steps and cleared her throat once she reached the second level. She didn't want to surprise anyone in the darkness. The top level was empty, but she walked to each corner to be sure she hadn't missed someone in the dark. She had come up here during the evening last year without looking around and had found a homeless man folding his clothes in the corner behind her after she had already been there for a few minutes. His sleeping bag had been unrolled on the ground, which is probably what had given her the idea to sleep up here.

If anyone came up the stairs, she'd feel it—the vibration of footsteps traveled all the way up the structure and if the person was heavy enough, the tower even seemed to sway slightly. She unshouldered her backpack and leaned on the railing looking out over Bellingham. Behind the tops of the trees of the arboretum there was a glowing mist hanging over the city as the night fog mixed with the light pollution. The subdued sound of traffic was constant in the background, like internal gears on a machine. She couldn't see the Pit.

She watched for perhaps a few minutes and began to feel the chill of the air. Hiking up had been fine, but now that she was stopped, the sweat and the breeze magnified the heat loss. She opened up her backpack and pulled out the sleeping bag, which was on top. Once it was unrolled she was tempted to climb in and start trying to sleep. That was why she had come up here, after all.

But she had hauled up more than just a sleeping bag, and she wasn't about to just haul everything back down tomorrow without having used it. She reached in and gripped the mass of wax from the bottom of her pack, but the pack held on. She tried to shake it off of her arms, and eventually it did fall, leaving her holding the shrine. She had started peeling it off her desk after she had decided to sleep up here, sliding a knife underneath it slowly and lifting it gently from one side. Once she had started, she pulled out all kinds of tools to operate on it: knives, spatulas, and even a hammer. There was a stress mark where it had nearly cracked and a handful of wax that she had scraped off the desk later, but it was mostly intact. She had the scrapings along in a plastic bag to add to the top again.

The shrine was deformed and lumpy like cancer from when she had broken the top off to find the letter. She turned it over, nesting it in her crossed legs. There was Rob's photo, smiling out of the bottom of the shrine like it had been doing for years. It was the picture from just before they had left for their travels. He was sitting on the side of the road with a hand-lettered sign that said, "Everywhere Or Bust." A scratch from the knife had just missed his chin, etching a line across his collar.

It was strange, and funny in a way, how looking at this picture brought back memories of looking at this picture. When Rob had first moved to Seattle, she sat at her desk during the evening and looked at the picture by candlelight. While her emotions flip-flopped, Rob just sat there smiling, permanently happy, but never talking, never calling.

One night after looking at him, maybe a week or two after the miscarriage, she had turned him over so she didn't have to see him laughing at her. As she had blown out the candles that were beside the photo, she had bumped one and it had tipped over, spilling its pool of hot wax onto the back edge of the photo, fastening it upside-down to the surface of the desk. She had just about yanked it up before the wax had hardened completely, and she probably would have if she hadn't gotten some wax on her own hand. Once that was peeled off, she had calmed down and the wax spill on the desk didn't look as bad.

She had relit one of the candles and sealed up all the edges of the picture, dripping wax methodically until Rob's face was completely sealed off from the outside. It had felt good at the time, as though she had sealed him out of her life, but he was alway there. He didn't suffocate in his tomb and fade from her life forever, he just festered underneath the surface and eventually made his way back out, like a shard of glass.

She set the shrine down on the floor at the head of her sleeping bag and lit the candles, blocking the slight breeze with one hand and using the lighter with the other. They wavered but weren't blown out. The shrine cast a small radius of light, like the first star. If the tower didn't have a roof on it, she'd have been able to lie here on her back and watch the stars. She looked past it and could see nothing in the darkness past the shadowy presence of the railing. Was it darkness, or just an absence of light?

She crawled into her sleeping bag and lay on her stomach, facing the shrine. She took the scrapings of wax that she had removed from her desktop and began to meld them back onto the shrine, holding them near a flame until they dripped back into it. It was strange how things were happening again, like a déjà vu that was real—Rob wanting to move to Seattle, her not wanting to.

The more things were the same, the more they had changed. But at some point in the spiral, the center wouldn't hold, things would fall apart. Maybe by wrestling with it, a person could move their history down the spiral, away from the center. As history cycles and repeats itself, there is always the potential for change, the potential to move forward.

Her sketchbook and a pen were in the front pocket of her backpack. She pulled them out and shimmied away from the shrine so that she had enough room between it and her for the book to lay. She opened it to a blank sheet and folded the pages back on each other, around the spiral of the bind. She tried to draw a spiral like the spiral of history but it came out like a scribble.

She began to sketch one of the candles. So there Rob had been, buried under a mountain of wax, and after more than two years, just when she thought she was getting over him and everything related to him, he resurrects himself. He had come to Bellingham directionless, without any goals or plans, and he had started sucking energy from her, using her for ideas, drinking her life like a parasite. And then when he had taken his fill, after he had used her, he was willing to just pick up and leave again. Maybe that's all life was, was letting people feed on you, or feeding on them. All the same, she wished the whole thing hadn't happened.

It was hard to understand him. Why would he wait around for six months of a rocky relationship, and then when things were just possibly beginning to turn around, throw down an ultimatum that couldn't do anything to help? She sleeps with him and he starts packing his bags. All her months of holding herself back, protecting herself, were out the window. And now a piece of her, some internal organ or a soul, was already aching again.

She rubbed her face. She was getting upset and she shouldn't. Maybe he had done her a favor after all. A compost pile needs to be turned in order for all the organics to decompose best. And once it was decomposed completely, it could be used to grow new flowers, new plants. The old supports the new. The new city is built on top of the remains of the old.

There was that thought again. A thought that came twice was important. She wrote it in a few different ways in the corner of the page, searching for the best way to phrase it.

-The past decomposes and nourishes the present.

-The present is made up of the past.

-The present grows into a living future on the strength of what has died in the past.

She tore the corner from her sketchbook and held it on the top of the wax in front of her. She used a candle that wasn't attached to tack the scrap to the top, dripping wax onto each corner and then filling in all the edges to hold it in place. It glared out of the shrine like a mantra, endlessly repeating itself.

Now the question was what to do about tomorrow. This was just one more time that plans to get Rob and her mother together had fallen through. Except that this time it was because he was in jail. Things were never clear, except sometimes in retrospect.

She didn't need to arrange her life around him. She could still go. If she woke up early enough with the morning light she could hike down and shower and catch a bus up. She let the candles burn for a few minutes longer and then blew them out and curled up in the sleeping bag to try to sleep.

When she woke, the birds would not shut up. They were calling out in a cacophony of voices: chirps, caws, and warbles. She crawled out of her sleeping bag, comfortably stiff. It felt good to move. She was cool, but not cold. The sun wasn't fully up yet—the morning was being born.

Fragments of dreams flitted about in her head like the wings of birds. She remembered a garden floating on a pond whose bottom was littered with trinkets from foreign places: coins, pictures, small models of cathedrals and houses. There were people swimming in the water; it was some kind of wishing pond. There was also a grassy ridge with hundreds of slides gouged out of the earth, which all met up together at the bottom, like a natural waterslide.

The biggest and most clear of all of the dream fragments took place in an airport. She could fly, which was not new: she had flown in dreams before. It was always the same way, too. She would fly, but then would concentrate so hard on flying—thinking about it too much—that she would glide roughly back down to the ground like an airplane that had lost its engines. Last night had started off that way, too, and there had been a group of people who were trying to pull her down out of the sky.

She had gone off by herself for a time, flying clumsily and flailing her arms and legs, as though her controls had an electrical short and worked only part of the time. She was ready to give up and let herself crash to the ground in a spectacular heap, when she accidentally did a back flip in the air. When she stopped thinking about it and stopped trying so hard, she could fly by thought alone. She began to play and became bolder, doing the backstroke through the air or landing and then jumping off the ground and jetting away.

People started to chase her, asking her to touch them, which frightened her and she flew away from them. A small boy was staring at her in wonder, and she called out to him without thinking. He lifted his hands to her and she reached down to him as she flew over, yanking him into the sky. He drifted off like a boulder through space, squealing in delight.

Near the end of the dream, she was floating down the airspace above a stairwell, and there was an eclectic group of people coming up toward her: a dwarf, two people hobbling, a fat lady. She launched them all, dodging a few protestors who were still trying to drag her back down. She saw Rob's face among them, intense and pleading, willing her to come down to him. Even at the end, she bobbled and sputtered and felt like she might tumble down until she remembered that it wasn't really anything she was doing that kept her in the sky. Even in her dreams, it was hard to go on faith.

She leaned on the railing of the tower, contemplating for a moment a leap from the edge to see if she still had the gift of flight, but her faith was too small. She rubbed the sleep from her eyes and resisted the urge to pack everything up and start the hike down. She was too efficient sometimes. I'm at the top? I guess it's time to sleep. I just woke up? I guess I'll start hiking back. It was a sad state to be in. She had to learn to take more time out to think, to meditate, to try to pray. She looked down on the city like an explorer on a mountaintop, surveying everything around her.

The railing was pockmarked with various scratchings, which told a history of their own: etchings and the censorship of putty painted brown. There were the usual we were here's, names and initials, but also little symbols, and a phrase in gibberish of some kind: caca, oabznk, naka, maka, aabka.

She sat cross-legged on her sleeping bag with her eyes closed and listened to the birds as they gave their morning sermon. She wondered how Rob had fared in his jail cell. Hopefully it was cold and uncomfortable—he deserved at least that.

She had determined that this whole Rob fiasco could be traced back to one day at the end of last September. She had replayed that first day in her mind a number of times and there was a whole string of interconnected events that worked together, played off each other. If that light bulb hadn't burned out, she wouldn't have had to steal the bulb from the bathroom, so she wouldn't have had to put candles in there. If there were no candles, she wouldn't have had an atmosphere conducive to meditation, and so she would have come out of the bathroom sooner and might not have burned her spaghetti. If she could have eaten her spaghetti, she wouldn't have had to eat at the Casa Grande before Philosophy Night, so she wouldn't have bumped into Rob. If she hadn't seen Rob, he might not have decided to move to Bellingham so rashly.

She remembered a conversation she had had with Rob at one point. What are the odds that events will string themselves together like that? What did it matter what the odds were? Despite the odds, things keep on happening. Someone who burned the supper hundreds or thousands of years ago could be responsible for a nation's rise or fall without knowing anything about it. The little things we do every day don't seem to make much difference until they're extrapolated out over years and lifetimes. A little Chaos Theory goes a long way. She glanced down at the broken shrine, which was still reciting its mantra to the sky and an idea occurred to her.

She wrestled it into her backpack again and started walking down the steps, leaving her sleeping bag and pillow up top. With nothing else in the pack, she could feel the density of the shrine—the emptiness of the pack was amplified by the weight of such a small volume in the bottom. It could have been a tiny body instead of a mass of wax. She set the pack beside the trunk of a tree.

If she had thought about doing this beforehand, she would have taken proper tools along. She used a broken branch to scrape away a layer of leaves and then dug into the soil. When she had a shallow grave ready, she reached into her backpack and removed the shrine, setting it into place and packing the dirt back around it. *The past decomposes and nourishes the present.*

She looked at the dirt on her hands and brushed them off over the shallow grave. She took her prayer book from the bottom of her bag and let it fall open in the middle where the spine was cracked.

Agnus Dei, qui tollis peccáta mundi, miserére nobis.

Agnus Dei, qui tollis peccáta mundi, miserére nobis.

Agnus Dei, qui tollis peccáta mundi, dona nobis pacem.

She closed the book with hands still muddy but not impure. Sometimes the distinction is important when you're caught in the middle of things, clutching mud in one hand and grasping at the stars with the other. Behind the prayer book was a little package of seeds. She unfolded the torn corner and scattered the remaining seeds over the mound of soil. On top of everything she set a tiny cut-out of a man, painted on one side and rough canvas on the other.

Acknowledgements

This book has been work in progress for many years and is by now a work of historical fiction. When I began it was set in the present, or very recent past, of late 2000 and early 2001. Thank you to everyone who encouraged me along the way, nagged me about it, or read early drafts of one chapter or another. I'd also like to thank my friends on the West Coast who were an inspiration at various early points and who may recognize fictionalized versions of certain events. A special thanks goes to Janel, who has read multiple drafts of the novel and has given detailed comments and helpful suggestions. The Kabbalah quote came second-hand from a book I picked up a used book sale as I was writing, and which had certain other themes that meshed with concepts in some of the chapters—so thanks to Alan McGlashan and his book "Gravity and Levity." I should also thank my mom, who encouraged my creativity as I grew, even if she didn't always like what I produced, and my brother Patrick, who traveled Europe with me for a handful of months, scribbling in our journals and daydreaming about our individual writing projects. Finally, here's to Kirstin and Rob at *cino, who were willing to take this manuscript on top of their busy schedules and think creatively about how we could partner together on the publication.

About the Author

Laryn Kragt Bakker was born and raised in Winnipeg, Manitoba. He has a degree in graphic design and computer science from Dordt College and is currently living in the Washington, D.C. area with his wife and daughter. He painted the original cover art used for the novel. In addition to writing and art, he is a graphic designer and web developer for non-profit organizations. This is his debut novel.

About *culture is not optional*

culture is not optional has been publishing online since 2002 when *catapult magazine* went live with bi-weekly, themed issues that weave together faith and everyday life with communal storytelling. The spirit of *catapult* has been embodied in print through the quarterly *road journal* and *The Road Map Series*, and in person through camping, conferences, workshops and, most recently, the purchase of an historic school building in Three Rivers, Michigan. With an off-campus program for college students and services for at-risk youth, the building will be a hub for imaginative, integrated personal and community development.